WHAT FALLS BETWEEN THE CRACKS

By Robert Scragg

What Falls Between the Cracks

WHAT FALLS BETWEEN THE CRACKS

ROBERT SCRAGG

Allison & Busby Limited
12 Fitzroy Mews
London W1T 6DW
allisonandbusby.com

First published in Great Britain by Allison & Busby in 2018.

A CIP catalogue record for this book is available from
the British Library.

First Edition

HB ISBN 978-0-7490-2279-2
TPB ISBN 978-0-7490-2284-6

Typeset in 11/16 pt Adobe Garamond Pro by
Allison & Busby Ltd

The paper used for this Allison & Busby publication
has been produced from trees that have been legally sourced
from well-managed and credibly certified forests.

Printed and bound by
CPI Group (UK) Ltd, Croydon, CR0 4YY

For my wife Nicola, my children Lucy and Jacob, brothers David and Gary, and my parents Margaret and Bob. My past, present, and future, wrapped up in one amazing bunch of people

PROLOGUE

May God forgive me.

He folds the single sheet of paper, places it carefully inside the envelope. He looks around the room, at everything he has built, crashing down around him.

I tried, Natasha. God knows I tried.

He moves on autopilot, shrugging his jacket off, pinching the collar to fold down the middle, letting it drape down over his arm to quarter it. He lies it by the wall, brushing away imaginary specks of dust from the spot next to it before sitting down, back flat against the cool plaster. He closes his eyes, picturing her again, smiling. Happier times before it all went to shit.

Focus on her. This is for her.

The gun feels surprisingly heavy as he cradles it in his lap. He sits like that for what feels like several lifetimes, listening to the drone of conversation from beyond the door. They will come running in when they hear the shot, but for now he is glad to be alone.

Now. Do it now. Be a man.

He clamps the barrel between his teeth, eyes scrunched shut as if in pain, thumb resting on the trigger. The tip touches the back of his tongue, and he pulls it back out with an involuntary retch. His breathing picks up pace. He has to do this now, or the coward lurking deep in his brain will make a play for life. Her face flashes in his mind again, reminding him why he doesn't deserve to live.

It's the only way. For her.

He blinks, tears blurring the edges of his world. He owes her this. *Deep breath. On three. Inhale. Exhale.*

One.

One swift movement. The end of the barrel kisses his temple this time.

Two.

He closes his eyes. He doesn't want the last thing he sees to be a storeroom full of boxes. It should be her. He pictures her face again, sees her smile, hears her laugh. No false starts this time. He takes another lungful of air. His last. Holds it. Feels the trigger move.

Three.

There is no blinding light, only darkness, and peace.

CHAPTER ONE

The maintenance man knocked again as he pushed the door to flat 10 halfway open. It was dark inside, the flat still shrouded from the early morning sunlight by the curtains. A musty smell filled his nostrils.

'Hello?' he called into the silence. 'Building maintenance; we've had a leak reported. Anyone home?'

No reply. He hit the light switch by the door but nothing happened.

Click, click.

He tried two more times, frowning. Still nothing. He pulled a small torch from his pocket and pointed the narrow beam inside. There was a rustling sound as he opened the door the rest of the way, a pile of papers and leaflets that had been sat behind it shuffled out of the way like a messy deck of cards. Glancing down at them, he saw a mixture of residents' newsletters and flyers mingled in with the post, that some enterprising souls must have gotten past the secure entrance to deliver.

He walked down a short hallway, sweeping the torchlight left and right, calling out as he went. The hallway led to an open-plan space incorporating the kitchen, dining and living areas. He was no interior decor expert, but the place definitely had something of a retro feel to it.

A faint hint of an odour hit his nostrils and he stopped to look around. He wrinkled his nose in disgust as he bent over a coffee cup on the nearby bench and sniffed. Spots of brownish green mould clung to it and he stepped back out of range of the smell, noticing the thick cloak of dust on the bench as he replaced the cup in the spot that it had been protecting. He made no effort to mask his footsteps as he looked around, calling out to minimise the surprise to any occupants, but nobody responded.

He went back to the open area that accounted for most of the floor space and looked around, mentally calculating where the leak would be located from what he'd seen of the layout downstairs. As it turned out, the answer was glaringly obvious when he saw the pool of water on the kitchen floor over by two white appliances – a fridge and a freezer, he presumed. They were short stocky units, a little above waist height, pale cream in colour with matching chrome handles, doors closed on both, but the water pooled on the floor was a giveaway as to which one was the culprit. Maybe a power failure had caused it to thaw? The contents could have leaked through a gap in the door seal. The model looked like one he'd had in his first flat years ago.

He set his toolbox on the bench and lay his torch on the floor so it illuminated the area by the base of the freezer. Expecting some form of leakage, he had brought an old towel from downstairs, and laid it out now over the puddle. It'd also come in handy to soak up most of what would no doubt spill out when he opened the door. There was a token resistance when he tugged at the handle, but it opened with somewhere between a cracking and a sucking noise as the seal gave up its grip. He watched the miniature waterfall trickle over the interior edge and soak into the towel. Not as much as he'd feared, but then again most of it was downstairs now. He was less prepared for the cloying stench that made him screw his eyes closed, flinching away as surely as if he'd been slapped across the face.

He pulled the neck of his sweater over his nose and mouth, bandit style, and looked back, still wincing, at the four identical compartments inside.

Eenie, meenie, miney . . .

He started at the top and worked his way down, a cursory scanning of soggy bricks of cardboard packaging, looking for the source of the smell. The drawers rattled open and closed in quick succession, until he reached the fourth one. Instead of closing it, he just stared, open-mouthed, as his brain caught up with his eyes, and finally told him what he was looking at.

The act of opening the drawer had caused the severed hand inside to rock gently. Its fingers were outstretched, ready to shake on a deal. Ragged shreds of grey skin clung around the edges of the severed wrist like dirty wet cloth.

He jerked upright and away in the same motion, stumbling back into the opposite kitchen bench.

'What the fuck?'

The words slipped out before he could stop them. He quickly put a hand to his mouth, looking around. It occurred to him that although he'd called out when he came in, he hadn't actually looked in any of the other rooms. What if he wasn't alone in here? What if the owner of the hand was in here somewhere? More to the point, what if the person who removed it was, too?

He stumbled out of the kitchen and down the corridor, looking over his shoulder as he did, not stopping until he reached the safety of the hallway. He jogged to the lift and jabbed the button with one hand, pulling his phone out of his pocket with the other, and dialled 999. His eyes never left the doorway. He'd not even closed up behind himself. Had no intention of going back to do so. Whatever had happened here, it hadn't ended well for someone.

Detective Inspector Jake Porter spotted his partner waiting patiently for him by the main entrance to the apartment complex as he pulled into the last available parking space this side of the police cordon. It never ceased to amaze him how many people were content to loiter by the edge of the tape without a clue of what was going on, hoping to catch a glimpse of something worthy of gossip. On one level it was almost ghoulish, but he dealt on a regular basis with people who had far worse traits than that.

He rubbed a fist in each eye. They felt gritty and raw. He had dreamt about Holly last night. She didn't visit him every time he slept. Probably once or twice a week, but when she did, it was like losing her all over again. That five or ten seconds of no man's land between dreams and the real world, lines blurred between the two. The empty pillow next to him a reminder of where he was; of where she wasn't. He almost welcomed those mornings in a masochistic kind of way. It was worth the pain to see her again, to feel for the briefest of moments that she was still alive. Almost two years without her now. After Holly's funeral, his mum had put an arm around him, fed him the cliché of time being a great healer, but Porter was leaning more towards a term like *quack*. The face staring back at him in the rear-view mirror was a tired doppelgänger of the man in his wedding photos only three years back. He had spotted the first of the grey hairs amongst the dark brown a few months ago, but didn't care enough to do anything about them. He sighed, grabbed his jacket from the back seat and headed over to join Nick Styles inside the cordon. London had almost shrugged off its winter coat, but the contrast between the heated car and the fresh February morning gave Porter goosebumps.

Styles stood with his back to the outer wall of the building, like a suspect in a police line-up. His six-four frame meant he towered above the officers who stood guard at the door. He was focused on tapping a message out on his phone and didn't sense Porter's approach over the ambient noise of the scene until they were practically side by side.

'Morning,' said Porter, tilting his head to compensate for the difference in height.

'And there was me thinking you must have had a better offer, guv,' Styles replied, both thumbs still pecking away at his phone.

'Well, you know me with my packed social calendar.'

'I may have got bored and poked my nose inside already while I waited.'

'Come on, then.' Porter patted him on the shoulder as he walked past him towards the door. 'You can give me the plot summary on the way upstairs.'

Styles peeled away from the wall and followed Porter inside. Their reflections in the polished glass elevator doors made for an incongruous pairing. Styles had his weakness for all things Hugo Boss, his image neat and orderly, close cropped hair, number two all over. He had been christened office pretty-boy by a few of the older crowd, part jealousy, part banter, but he took it all in his stride. A few had referred to him as the Met's answer to Thierry Henry, until they saw him try and play five-a-side. Porter was from Irish stock, his wardrobe more high-street fashion, and his appearance, while not unkempt, had a more lived-in feel to it; hair so dark it bordered on black, refusing to be fully tamed by gel, but with a sense of messy style to it. Styles started to bring Porter up to speed as they waited for the lift.

'It's one of the stranger ones I've seen,' he said as he tucked his phone into his jacket. 'Call came in from the maintenance guy. He went in to turn the water off after it started leaking into the flat below, except it wasn't a leaky pipe.' He paused as the lift doors opened and they stood aside to let a crime scene tech out first. The camera in their hand left no doubt as to what they'd just been up to.

'Come on then, don't keep me in suspense,' Porter said as Styles hit the button for the fourth floor.

'First guess was that the freezer had packed in, probably a while back cos those things are usually pretty robust, but the door seals do give way eventually. Turns out that there's just no power. Not sure why yet. The freezer thawed, water ran down the front, through the cracks in the floor tiles and ended up waking the downstairs neighbour during the night.'

'I'm assuming you'll get to the juicy part soon?'

'Yep. The maintenance guy figured out where the water was coming from and was about to start patching it up when he got spooked and called us.'

'Spooked by what? What's got him rattled? A domestic? A burglary? A spotty teenager fresh out of training could handle that. Quit stalling and tell me why we're here.'

'There're no flies on you, guv,' said Styles in mock acquiescence.

'Yeah, yeah, I know, just the marks of where they've been.' Porter finished the tired old joke for him and looked at him expectantly.

'Sorry, I'll quit playing. Turns out it wasn't just food going off in the freezer. There's a hand in there.'

That got Porter's attention. 'Just a hand?'

'As if that's not enough?'

'You know what I mean.'

Styles nodded. 'Yep, just a hand; female by the looks of it, and missing the little finger.'

'Do we know whose place it is yet?' Porter asked just as the doors opened to reveal the fourth-floor hallway.

'The flat is registered to a Natasha Barclay and has been since 1981. You need to see this place to believe it,' said Styles, nodding to the officer guarding the door as they each slipped into a white Tyvek crime scene suit and entered the flat.

The first thing Porter noticed was the smell. The unmistakable perfume of decay hung in the air. Without the update from Styles, he'd have put that solely down to the rotting food, but he knew better than that now. Layered over the top of that was a general sense of mustiness. He stopped in his tracks and looked around. A small wooden table six feet into the hallway had a phone handset that looked like the one his mum used to have. A visible fuzzy blanket of dust coated it and the table surface. He looked at the walls. The wallpaper too looked like a relic from a bygone era. Styles had walked on ahead of him, presumably headed for the kitchen, and Porter hurried after him.

He caught up with him in what he assumed was the main space of the flat. A dining table, clear except for an empty vase, sat over by the far wall. The relatively narrow kitchen area was bordered on two sides by worktops, with the remaining space housing two sofas and a TV that looked almost as old as Porter himself. *Never mind retro*, he thought, *this place looks like it's stuck in a time warp*.

Styles waited patiently by the open freezer door while Porter peered inside. Each of the drawers had been pulled out to varying extents to allow for inspection of the contents. The resulting image reminded Porter of a mini staircase, with the bottom drawer practically hanging out and each of the three above it revealing less and less. The bottom drawer housed the main attraction. The hand sat in the centre of the plastic compartment. It was palm up, its fingers outstretched and curled in ever so slightly at the last joint, as if begging for loose change. The little finger had been severed at the first joint above the knuckle. It looked like a clean cut, and a small circle of bone stared up at him, a white pupil in an iris of grey flesh.

'Ah, Detective Porter. I see you've found exhibit A.'

Porter looked back over his shoulder, recognised one of the senior scene-of-crime officers, Will Leonard, approaching from the hallway. It was hard not to, even with the protective mask over his face, Leonard's eyebrows like black caterpillars marking him out at any crime scene. He had a mop of greying hair underneath the hood of his Tyvek crime scene suit, though, and Porter was convinced he dyed the brows. Why the brows and not the rest of his hair, though? One of life's great mysteries.

'Oh, hi, Will. Looks like a fun one here. What you thinking?'

'Hard to say yet.' Leonard shrugged. 'It's fairly well thawed now, but impossible to say how long it's been in there until we run the usual tests, maybe not even then. I'd say a fair while, though, judging from the freezer burn on the skin.' He pointed at the blotchy pattern across the back of the hand. 'My guess is twelve months, maybe more.'

'What about the rest of whoever this is? No sign of any other body parts?'

Leonard shook his head. 'Just this for now.'

Porter turned to Styles. 'What have we got apart from this?'

'It's a strange one.' Styles shook his head gently. 'There's some opened mail here addressed to a Miss Natasha Barclay. Whether she lives here alone we don't know yet, but we're trying to track her down to ask.'

'What about the neighbours?'

'We've been knocking on doors but only been able to speak to three so far and they've been no help, but this is where it all gets a bit weird. Nobody's seen her, or anyone else, coming or going.'

'What's weird about that? People can live in a building like this and not see each other for weeks.' Porter walked around the living area, soaking in the details.

'Try ever.'

That stopped Porter in his tracks. He turned back to Styles. 'Ever?'

'Nasty echo in here,' said Styles playfully. 'Yep, ever. We spoke to three other residents, one of whom has lived here since the early nineties, and not one of them can remember ever seeing or hearing so much as a mouse squeak in here. Same goes for the maintenance guy, although he's only been here for five years.'

'OK, that is a little strange, I'll give you that. I'm assuming you've got more than just that, though?'

'That opened mail I mentioned: there's a bank statement, a dental appointment letter and one from a friend in Edinburgh. The thing is that they're all dated 1983. Make of that what you will.'

Porter frowned. '1983?'

'There's that echo again.'

'Where's the mail? Show me.'

Styles pointed at a few sheets of paper that lay neatly stacked on the kitchen bench. Porter picked them up one at a time and scanned the contents. Sure enough there was a dental check-up arranged at a local surgery. The statement for her current account confirmed her as a Barclays customer. Porter speculated as to whether there was a connection with the surname but dismissed it as coincidence for now. He looked up again, first at Styles, and then around the room, but more closely now as if seeing everything for the first time. The TV was a big bulky thing that belonged in a museum, with knobs on the front to change channel and volume. From the pattern on the curtains and the fabric on the furniture, to the same layer of dust everywhere he looked, the flat seemed like a snapshot from the land that time forgot; a TV or film set that had just been taken out of storage to air it.

'What do you think, then?' Styles said from behind him.

'I'd say we need to speak to Miss Barclay about the standard of her housework, but I have a feeling she's not been in here for some time.' Styles nodded and Porter went on. 'The way the dust has built up on the surfaces, I'd say it's been months since anyone set foot in here, at least, maybe a lot longer. Let's just hope that wherever she is, she's got nothing more serious than a few chores around the house to worry about.'

It took another half hour for the crime scene techs to finish up. Everything was painstakingly catalogued. Styles had joked in the past that the process was like a macabre fashion shoot, and Porter could see why. By the time the pictures were taken, the techs had dusted surfaces with fine powder like a make-up artist applying foundation. Fibres were snipped from the carpet like a hurried pre-catwalk haircut. They chose their camera angles carefully to capture every detail, like David Bailey immortalising the perfect profile.

Porter decided Styles had understated in the extreme when he had called it a strange one. Everything looked to be from that same era, from the peach, pale blue and soft green curtains to the light brown furry-looking sofa that screamed 1980s. Add that to the correspondence that hailed from the same period, and it was as if they'd travelled back thirty years when they crossed the threshold.

The bedroom did nothing to alter that perception. Porter could almost feel the dust lining his nasal passages as he breathed in. Styles moved across to the curtains and opened them with both hands simultaneously, sending wispy plumes of dust up into the air like ash from a volcano. Two of the curtain hooks on the left-hand side relinquished their grip on fabric made weak by time, and tore free of their fastenings.

Porter moved over to the wardrobe, one door slightly ajar with gauzy strands of cobweb laced across the gap like the back of a corset. He opened it slowly, watching to see if the web's architect was at home, but there was no sign of life. Porter was no fashionista but the suits that hung in the wardrobe reminded him of some of his mum's outfits from family pictures before he was even born, let alone a toddler. It was starting to feel like an eighties version of *Great Expectations*, and he'd walked into Satis House with Miss Havisham lurking somewhere inside.

Satisfied that there was nothing of immediate interest in the bedroom, they made their way back out to the kitchen area in time to see Will Leonard placing the hand carefully into an evidence bag. Porter turned and scanned the living room. It reminded him of a party he'd been at last year where a fight had broken out. An armchair lay on its side like a wounded animal. A small coffee table that had presumably been next to it was upturned, one of the legs snapped off at the halfway point. A magazine lay face down, pages sprawled open and spine pointing upwards.

He saw dark smudges on the far wall, and moved in for a closer look. The cream paint was flecked with dark spots, a night sky in reverse. A handful of evidence markers, little yellow tents, had set up camp on the carpet around a series of brown stains. All in all, the room looked like a jigsaw smashed by an angry child, none of the pieces seeming to go together just yet. He wandered over to where Styles waited at the door.

'Let's head back to the station then and see if we can track down Miss Barclay, or at least rustle up some family and friends to speak to.'

'After you,' said Styles, gesturing towards the door. Porter had just walked past him when he added, 'Do you think the techs can manage to carry everything, or should we offer to give them a hand?'

CHAPTER TWO

Natasha Barclay was a ghost, figuratively speaking, at least. Between them they couldn't find a single mention of her dated past 1983. Her flat was one of fifteen in a five-storey late Victorian building near Walthamstow, in North East London, built originally as an orphanage. The airy high ceilings and ornate cornices had reminded Porter a little of his own place, although he guessed his flat could fit inside these twice over.

They left three uniformed officers at the building to go door to door with the remaining eleven residents to see if anyone knew Natasha Barclay. It wasn't out of the question that she was just a private person, and didn't make small talk with the neighbours. The interviews with the first three residents, particularly the one who'd lived there for over twenty years, didn't sit well with him. Sure, people led busy lives, but for those lives to have never intersected with as much as a neighbourly nod while leaving or entering the building in over two decades seemed highly unlikely. Then there was the eerie air of dormancy that hung over the place. The dated decor and coat of dust that cloaked every surface had given him the feeling that the apartment had been slumbering for some time before the leaking freezer had rudely interrupted.

They headed back to the station at Paddington Green, along Edgware Road, lined with a cultural melting pot of takeaways, competing amongst themselves to ruin your waistline. Porter's window was halfway down, spices and fried chicken wafting in on the breeze, making his stomach growl in protest. Compressed storefronts jostled for space, offering everything from Persian carpets to a bet on the three o'clock at Newmarket. Blocks of flats had been built up behind them over the years, peering over the tops of the two- and three-storey buildings on the main road like nosy neighbours. Typical mid-twentieth-century fare, blocky and functional. The station itself wasn't any prettier. The jutting window ledges around each floor made Porter think of the Stickle Bricks he had as a child.

As soon as they got inside, Styles disappeared into the small kitchen area, returning armed with two mugs of steaming black coffee. Porter realised he'd been staring at a smudge of dirt on the window and blinked his eyes quickly to snap himself out of it.

'I've told you before, you're wasting your time batting your eyelashes at me. I'm a happily married man,' said Styles. After a few years working together it was impossible not to be aware of his partner's little quirks. He jokingly referred to this one sometimes as Porter's 'Spidey sense' after the Marvel comic-book hero's preternatural ability to read situations and intuit danger. He'd seen it happen on more than one occasion where Porter had progressed a seemingly dead-end case by zoning out like that and joining dots that no one else had spotted.

'You can't blame a guy for trying.' Porter took a cautious sip of the coffee before putting the cup on the desk.

'Any flashes of inspiration, then?' asked Styles as he settled into the seat at his desk that adjoined his partner's.

Porter shook his head. 'No, no, ladies first this time. You got a theory?'

'Kind of, actually,' said Styles. 'Well, more of a question really,' he corrected himself. 'The food in the freezer – that make sense to you?'

'I was a little preoccupied with the hand to have much of an appetite.'

'I wasn't fixing to make myself a snack,' said Styles. 'I'm talking about the packaging. I'm assuming you missed that part?'

'Afraid so. Go on then, enlighten me.'

'The whole scene was just odd,' Styles began. 'The clothes and decor you could put down to individual taste. The dust and cobwebs might just mean she's been living somewhere else for a while, maybe with a boyfriend. The boxes in the freezer make no sense, though.'

'How do you mean?' asked Porter.

'The packaging,' said Styles. 'It was as dated as the rest of the place. Not that I'm an expert in the field of graphic design by any stretch, but it looked ancient compared to what you see in shops today. None of it had the nutritional info on either, and that's been stamped all over everything for years now.'

Porter raised his eyebrows as he realised what Styles was getting at. 'So you're saying you think no one's been in for years rather than months?'

Styles shrugged. 'I know stuff keeps for longer in there, but who keeps food for that long?'

'So we're saying nobody's been in there since she last opened her mail?'

'Maybe, maybe not,' said Styles. 'I'm pretty certain nobody's lived there for a long time. Whether anyone has had a reason to be there or not is another matter.' Porter opened his mouth to reply, but was stopped in his tracks when his phone started to ring.

'Hold that thought,' he said, holding up a finger at Styles as he took the call. 'This is Porter.'

'Porter? It's Will Leonard. You asked me to call as soon as we had something.'

'Hey, Will. What have you got?'

'It's only a preliminary overview, but hopefully it'll help get you started. The prints from the hand are consistent with the few clear ones we managed to find at the flat. I wasn't sure what we'd find with it being like a museum in there, but we got lucky. We pulled some fairly clear ones from fatty deposits around the oven, and on and around the make-up products in the bathroom, so it's reasonable to assume that both they and the hand they come from belong to somebody who lived there. I'm going to run them now and see if we get a match.'

'OK, thanks, Will. Anything else?'

'We'll be doing DNA tests on hair from the hairbrush and a swab of the toothbrush to check against tissue from the hand and the blood from the living room. Results should be back in a day or so. There's nothing so far to suggest more than one person living there. There were a few smudges that look like they used to be prints in the other rooms, but not as well preserved as the ones in the kitchen.'

'Good stuff. Let me know when you get the DNA tests back.' Porter was about to sign off but as an afterthought he mentioned Styles's theory about the food. Leonard promised to look into it and ended the call. Porter gave Styles the highlights of the conversation.

'What you said, about the food. I hadn't twigged to that. You're right, it does seem weird.'

'Oh, I'm not just a pretty face,' said Styles. 'What's the plan, then, boss?'

'First things first, we need to find out what family she has. My gut tells me that it's most likely her hand we found. I checked with one of the lads working the scene, though, and the amount of blood and distribution on the carpet isn't consistent with it being removed there, so it begs the questions of where and why.'

'Speaking of the flat, it would have been a fairly pricey area to live in even back in the eighties. How does a young woman living alone afford somewhere like that?' asked Styles.

'Good question,' said Porter, reaching for his coffee again. 'You look into the property and check out her finances. See if anything shows up apart from the account with Barclays. I'll see if I can track down her parents.'

They agreed to meet up again as soon as the officers responsible for interviewing the neighbours returned, and Styles slid his own chair sideways on its casters to park himself at his desk. Porter drained the lukewarm dregs of his coffee and got to work. He hoped tracing the parents wouldn't prove too tricky, although these conversations were the ones he hated the most. Being the bearer of potentially bad tidings was something he'd had to do more times than he cared to remember, but he'd never get used to it. He remembered it from the other side of the scenario; seeing the blurred shape visible through his front door. Not realising that all that separated him from the blow they were about to deal to his world was an inch-thick rectangle of wood and glass. The struggle to remember what life had been like before he opened the door to see the police officers outside. The bad news they carried carved into every crease on their forehead.

Best case, Natasha Barclay had been the victim of an assault, and worst case her injuries may have been fatal. Without immediate medical attention, she could easily have bled out after her hand was removed. The fact that at least part of the attack looked to have taken place inside her home meant there was a good chance she may have known her assailant. What Porter couldn't quite reconcile, though, was that if she was alive and well, why nobody, including her parents, had bothered helping to look after her flat. On the flip side, if something more sinister had happened, why had nobody reported her missing? The last thought that struck him as he leant forward to start the task of locating her parents was a little less palatable, but one that would need careful consideration nonetheless. What if those closest to her knew she was missing but had a vested interest in hiding that fact?

CHAPTER THREE

The canvassing of the remaining neighbours took up most of the morning, but proved fruitless. As far as they were concerned, the flat may as well have stood empty all these years, and none of them had heard of Natasha Barclay, let alone laid eyes on her. The search of her flat had yielded a few interesting snippets of information, though. The three constables returned from their door-knocking and set to work sifting through the boxes of letters, photos, and everyday detritus that had been packed up and brought back to the station. One of these included the unopened mail that had been piled like a snowdrift behind the front door. Buried in there was a series of bills from various utility companies: British Gas for power, British Telecom for the phone line, shortening to BT around the early nineties. The water bills told a tale in their own right. There was a mixture of both Thames Water Authority and Thames Water. The latter had only been founded in 1989, which lent further credence to Porter's suspicion that the flat had indeed stood empty since before that. The bills covered the period from 1983 right through to 2012, whereupon they were accompanied by demands for payment citing a failed direct debit, and finally notices to disconnect services, and the other utilities followed suit around the same time.

Porter listened while one of the PCs, a young man by the name of Edwards, summarised what they'd found. They'd also catalogued a series of bank statements that showed the same current account as before, dated 1983. The funds, healthy at first, slipped steadily away like sand through an hourglass, without a single deposit to stem the tide, until they were depleted around the time the demanding letters started to arrive. The power had been cut, alright, but not through any fault or error of the provider.

There had been over nine thousand pounds in the account back in 1983. That would have stood out to Porter as a healthier than average balance even today. The birth certificate they had tracked down said she would have been twenty-one back then. Set against the context of her age, plus the fact the balance was from over thirty years ago, that was a staggering amount for her to have just lying around in a current account.

He was trying to figure out how to work out the modern day equivalent, taking inflation into consideration, when he heard Styles end the call he'd been making. Styles had specialised in financial crime before he'd made the move across to the Homicide and Serious Crime squad. Porter was sure that his partner was the man to ask, and swivelled around to face him.

'Anything from the door to door?' asked Styles before Porter could open his mouth.

'More of the same,' said Porter, shaking his head. 'No one's laid eyes on her full stop. I've got something you can help me with, though,' he said, picking up the bank statement, and explaining what he was trying to do.

'Yep, that's easily done,' said Styles. He turned to face his monitor and one quick Google search later, had a site up that promised to do the calculation for them. 'How much did you say she had?' he asked.

'A little over nine grand.'

'What I'd give for that now, never mind thirty years ago,' said Styles. He tapped the figure into a box, used a drop-down menu to select the year in question, and clicked the button to calculate. He looked at the result, then sat back and whistled through his teeth.

'That look right to you?' asked Porter.

''Bout three times that in today's money – yep, looks around what I was expecting.'

'Where the hell does a twenty-one-year-old get that kind of cash from?'

Porter rubbed his hand over his chin, feeling tiny pricks of Braille-like stubble that he'd missed with his razor.

'Have we found anyone we can ask the question to yet?'

Porter shook his head. 'Not quite, but I found out a few interesting things before I got distracted with the update on the neighbours.'

He filled Styles in on the progress he had made. Starting with her parents' details on her birth certificate, he had found Nathan Barclay first. Natasha's father had committed suicide back in 1983, although Porter had yet to find out the exact details of where, when and how. Her mother, Anne Barclay, had died giving birth to Natasha, ending the parental line of enquiry almost as soon as it had begun. Nathan had, it transpired, remarried when Natasha was ten years old, to Mary Atkins, who took on his name and bore him a son, Gavin. The marriage had not lasted, though, and they had divorced in 1981. Porter had run a background check on Mary Barclay, and found that she now went by the name of Mary Locke, and lived at an address in Edgware.

'I would have preferred an actual family member,' said Porter, 'but she's the only person I've found worth talking to so far. I say we have a drive up there this afternoon. I haven't looked for the son yet. I figure she can point us in his direction to save me a job. We should be able to get a DNA swab from him as well to see if there's a familial match against the sample we took from the hand.'

Styles grunted his agreement before he spoke. 'My turn now?'

Porter nodded, settling back into his chair. Styles shuffled through a small stack of paper fresh from the printer. He had confirmed with the bank that the only activity on the current account had been the direct debits that had paid the bills, and that she had no other accounts with them. Styles was always a keen advocate of following the money trail, so he'd taken a step back and looked at the flat. With no sign of a mortgage either, he, like Porter, had been curious as to how she'd financed the purchase. Lucky for him, Natasha Barclay had been organised as far as her personal affairs went, and had bank statements filed away in a cardboard box at the back of a large storage closet. There had been four deposits, adding up to a little over the purchase price of twenty-five thousand pounds. They'd all come from the same account with a payment reference starting *AH* and followed by a sequence of six numbers, each string of digits different from the last.

The Land Registry showed that the flat, previously owned by Atlas Holdings, had been sold to Miss Barclay in 1980 shortly after her eighteenth birthday. A quick check at Companies House showed Atlas Holdings to be a wholly owned subsidiary of Locke & Winwood, who had a head office registered to an address near Gravesend.

'That can't just be a coincidence,' said Porter. 'Same name as her stepmum.'

'Yeah, I'll be surprised if there's no link there.'

Neither man had heard of either company before, but a link between Atlas and Natasha Barclay soon became a lot clearer. The list of former directors included a Nathan Andrew Barclay. The deposits in his daughter's account had, in all probability, come from her father's company.

'So Daddy paid for the flat, and kept her account topped up?' said Porter. 'That explains that, then.'

'Mm hmm,' said Styles, dropping the pages casually on his desk. 'You couldn't even buy a garage in parts of London for that price nowadays.'

Porter shook his head, not in disagreement but disbelief. He knew it to be true and was thankful, not for the first time, for the sanctuary of his own small flat. It had belonged to his wife since long before they had first met, left to her in her grandmother's will, mortgage free. It was a compact two-bedroom flat, but without her to share it, the space sometimes felt disproportionately bigger than it actually was. He forced his thoughts back to the present situation.

'Why you'd want to live in a garage is beyond me, but your tastes have always left a lot to be desired. Shall we head off and see if Mrs Locke is around for a chat?' he said.

Styles nodded in agreement, springing to his feet and grabbing his coat from the back of his chair. Porter did the same, although with a little less enthusiasm, and slipped the envelope of photos into his jacket pocket as he headed for the exit. His brief flirtation with Holly's memory had left him, as it often did, with the surreal sense that it had all happened to someone else. His recollection of her was still so fresh, as if he had kissed her goodbye on the way out to work this morning. Many people were haunted by ghosts from their past, but Porter classed his as more of a bittersweet relationship. As much as the flashbacks were a mixture of happy memories tinged with sadness, he cherished those he had, unable or perhaps unwilling to let go just yet.

The moment had passed by the time he made it outside, and he slid into the driver's seat of the car, closing his door at the precise time Styles pulled his shut to give one synchronised *thunk*. Porter started it up and pulled away without a word. Time to speak to Mary Locke, and discover whether any more ghosts would be created today once they had done so. His subconscious kicked in with the afterthought:

What if Mary Locke has been living with ghosts of her own for some time already?

CHAPTER FOUR

If the house they pulled up outside on Nan Clark's Lane was any indication of status, Mary Locke had managed to shelter from the storm of the recession in relative comfort. They had only left the M1 a few minutes ago, but the impressive detached residence a short hop from Edgware had a secluded, exclusive feel to it. The dark wooden gates covering the driveway were closed, but the roof of a pristine white Range Rover poked over the top of them. The house itself looked perfectly symmetrical; a pair of sandstone effect columns flanked the doorway on either side, like soldiers standing to attention, with the lintel made from the same material. The matching sets of windows, three up and three down, on either side of the front doorway, acted like mirrors rather than portals into the interior, although Porter wagered that Mary Locke herself had never had to stoop to polishing them to get that shine.

He had toyed with calling ahead to check somebody was in, but that would open up a line of questioning he would rather pursue face-to-face. Porter pulled up on the opposite side of the narrow private road they'd driven up to get there, and motioned for Styles to stay in the car while he went to push the intercom button on the gate; no sense them both getting out unless they knew they'd be staying a while.

He pushed the button and held it for a three count, then took a step back. There was no immediate sign of life from inside. A double garage sat off to the left with both doors closed, no doubt harbouring an equally expensive vehicle to rival the Range Rover. There was a split second of static from the intercom, followed by a woman's voice.

'Yes, who's there, please?'

'Mrs Locke?' said Porter.

'Yes, speaking. Who is this, please?' she repeated her question politely.

'Mrs Locke, my name is Detective Inspector Jake Porter with the Met Police. I'm here with my partner, Detective Sergeant Nick Styles. We'd like to ask you a few questions about a matter we're investigating, if you can spare us a couple of minutes, please?'

There couldn't have been more than two or three seconds of silence before the burst of static again, but the time oozed past like treacle, making it seem like double figures. Was she thinking of an excuse not to let them in, or just a little flustered to have police on the doorstep? Whatever would the neighbours say? Porter reminded himself they were in an unmarked car, and he hadn't been in uniform for many years now, so the secret of their visit was safe from prying eyes for now.

'Can I ask what it's about, Detective?'

'It would really be a lot easier to explain if we came in, Mrs Locke,' said Porter.

Another brief pause. 'Do you have any identification with you, please, Detective?'

Porter fumbled in his jacket pocket and pulled out his warrant card. As he held it up to the glass eye of the intercom camera, he looked over his shoulder and gestured to Styles with his free hand that he should join him at the gate. There was a soft *click* followed by a low buzzing noise. Porter placed one hand on the gate and gave a tentative shove. It gave before him and swung open.

The short driveway looped around in a tight semicircle, passing the front door and curving back round past the garage doors, and exiting out through a second wooden gate. Porter and Styles walked almost shoulder to shoulder towards the door. It opened before they were halfway there, just six inches at first, then swung slowly until it was halfway open. Porter assumed the face that peered out was Mrs Locke herself, although if she could afford a house like this she may well have a maid.

From what he had read at the station, she was seventy years old, but she could have passed for a decade less. She reminded him a little of a younger version of Mary Berry, her short sandy hair cut just above shoulder length and tucked back behind her ears. Her eyes were a startling blue that demanded attention, but her body language screamed timidity, not the confidence and poise that often radiated from someone of her relative affluence.

'Mrs Locke?' asked Porter, just to be certain.

'Yes, I'm Mrs Locke,' she answered hesitantly. 'Can I ask what this is about? Has something happened to Alexander?' She spoke softly, with an accent that would cost a small fortune at elocution lessons.

'Alexander?' said Porter, looking to Styles and back to her.

'My husband.'

'No, Mrs Locke. This has nothing to do with him. I'm sure he's fine. Could we come in for a few minutes?' said Porter, looking past her into the house.

'Of course, please, come in.'

She stepped aside to let them in, closed the door and turned to face them. Porter noticed that she seemed uneasy despite being on home turf, but then again the majority of people went through life without ever having the police turn up on their doorstep, and he put the vibe down to a simple case of nervous anticipation.

'We can go through to the living room,' she said, gesturing through a doorway set in the wall to their left. She led the way and they followed close behind. The room was like something from a show home. Porter wondered if the sofas had ever been sat on. The cream leather looked smooth, buttery and unblemished, free from any telltale creases or wrinkles. A pair of matching two-seaters faced each other over a glass coffee table, with a single armchair from the same range at the head of the table. Mary Locke shepherded them towards the nearest sofa and took up residence on the other, keeping a safe distance, with the no man's land of the coffee table between them.

Porter perched on the edge of the seat, loath to lean back lest he disturb the artfully arranged cushions that looked plumper than a Christmas turkey.

Styles had no such qualms, settling back into a large mocha-coloured cushion and crossing his legs as he took out a small black notepad from his jacket. Mary Locke sat upright in the centre of her sofa, back straight and hands clasped in front of her on her knees.

'I'd offer you a drink, Detectives, but I was just on my way out so can't talk for too long. What's this about, please?'

'I'll not waste any time, then,' said Porter, with a polite smile. 'We're trying to locate your stepdaughter, Natasha. There appears to have been an incident at her flat and we'd like to speak to her about it. We're hoping you can help us reach her.'

Porter studied her face as she absorbed his words. Her already stiff posture held firm; her tongue stole out a fraction and nervously wet her lower lip.

'An incident? What kind of incident?'

'A possible break-in and some kind of altercation is as much as we can say right now, Mrs Locke, but we really do need to speak to Natasha. Do you know where we can find her?'

She fidgeted slightly, smoothing away an imaginary crease on her trouser leg before clasping her hands back together.

'I've . . . not seen Natasha for a long time, I'm afraid, not since . . .' Her voice tailed off.

'Not since when, Mrs Locke?' prompted Porter.

She looked down at the floor for a second before she met his gaze again.

'Not since just before her father died.'

'So that would be April 1983?' asked Styles.

She nodded slowly. 'Nathan died less than a week after Tash's birthday.' Her voice tailed off as she spoke, her thoughts clearly drifting back to a memory she would rather not revisit.

'And you saw her when, exactly?' Porter asked.

'Sorry,' she said, aware she had been starting to drift. 'Um, let me see. I think it was the day before her twenty-first birthday. I'd gone around to drop off her birthday card.'

'So you've not seen your stepdaughter in over thirty years?' Porter asked, his tone low and even.

Mary Locke shook her head. 'Tash and I were never what I'd describe as close. She was a proper daddy's girl when I came along and I think she saw me as just someone who was stealing his undivided attention away from her.' She smiled wistfully. 'Of course, I tried to show her I wasn't a threat, but I never quite got through to her. Nathan had always been a workaholic before I met him, and she used to get the lion's share of what free time he had.' She shrugged. 'I think perhaps she found it hard to share him at times.'

'I can understand that must have been hard, Mrs Locke,' said Styles, 'but if we can focus more on where she might be now. Where does she work? Is there anyone else she's close to who can tell us how to contact her?'

'She had a hard time dealing with Nathan's death. The last I heard she was teaching children to speak English in a school over in Poland. She'd travelled around Europe for a while after she finished school and ended up teaching somewhere near Kraków for about six months, so I guess it was easier to go back there again instead of sticking around here without her father.'

'Do you have an address or phone number for the school?' asked Styles.

She shook her head quickly. 'Sorry, it was so long ago. I don't know that she even gave me one.'

Porter pulled the envelope from his jacket, reversing the pictures they had taken from Natasha's flat so they faced Mary Locke, and slid them across the glass tabletop towards her.

'These are copies of pictures we found in Natasha's flat, Mrs Locke. Could you point out Natasha for us, please?'

Mary Locke stared at them, only her eyes moving as she flicked between them. She made no move to pick them up. Porter waited patiently, and was on the verge of prompting her when she spoke.

'That's her in the denim jacket. Her and Nathan,' she said, her gaze still fixed on the picture. 'Nathan took her to see The Rolling Stones up in Aberdeen for her birthday, the year before he . . .' She left the sentence unfinished.

Porter reached across and spun the picture back round. That would make Natasha nineteen or twenty when it was taken. She had an arm wrapped around the waist of the man Porter now knew to be Nathan Barclay. They wore matching black T-shirts with the iconic tongue and ruby red lips that had long since been synonymous with The Stones. There was no mistaking them for anything but father and daughter. Her hair, so dark it was practically black, matched his, and two sets of identical blue eyes, creased at the corners at the promise of the evening to follow, stared back at Porter. He nodded a silent hello to Natasha, glad for a face to focus on. It made her finally feel real.

Porter decided to change tack. 'You and her father were divorced when he died, is that right?'

'Yes, we'd been apart for a few years by the time he passed away.'

'And do you think she blamed you for the break-up?' asked Porter.

Mary Locke paused for a moment before replying. 'I'm not perfect, Detective. We all make mistakes. Mine was that I fell in love with someone other than my husband.'

It might just have been a trick of the light, but Porter thought it looked as if her eyes were glistening a touch more, a precursor to tears.

'Nathan was a good man, but not always easy to live with. He'd worked hard to build up his business and by the time he . . . well . . . you know . . . It had been losing money long before we split up, and he'd had to sell up to pay off his debts. Things like that take their toll on any man.'

'If you don't mind, Mrs Locke, we don't have much information on what happened to Nathan other than that he took his own life. Can you fill in the blanks for us?'

'What does that have to do with Natasha?' she asked, looking puzzled.

'Maybe nothing' – Porter shrugged – 'but if nobody has seen her since around that time, it might help us understand her frame of mind, where she might have gone, that kind of thing.'

She swallowed hard. These were the types of memory that people kept locked up as tightly as possible, and stored in the darkest of recesses. Her eyes danced from side to side in short staccato movements.

'Nathan . . . he, um . . . he shot himself. It happened in one of his warehouses.' The glistening in her eyes finally gathered enough momentum and turned into matching menisci of tears, balancing on her lower eyelid. 'Sorry,' she said, forcing a nervous smile. 'Even though we were apart by then, it was still hard, you know?'

Porter and Styles both nodded. Neither had lost a loved one this way, but they'd both seen enough people grieve over lives lost to be able to empathise. *Too many*, thought Porter. Still not enough to have prepared him to deal with Holly, though. No amount of consoling others could prepare you when the time came to swap places with them, to be told the news by an apologetic stranger.

There was a brief lull in the questioning while they gave her a few seconds to regain her composure. She blinked and the dam broke, solitary tears from each eye racing its rival down her cheek. She tugged at a paper handkerchief that had been hiding up her left sleeve and used it to dab at the damp tracks. Porter half expected to see a trail of coloured ones flowing out behind it, like those of a magician at kids' parties. It reminded him of his grandmother, who always had a hankie stashed like that in case of emergencies. He waited till she'd stuffed it back into its hiding place before asking his next question.

'Did he leave a note?'

She nodded.

'I know it's a long time ago, but do you remember what it said?'

'Not word for word; it's been so long. All I remember is something about being sorry for the hurt he'd caused his family, and that this was the only way to make things right.'

'What did he mean by that?' asked Styles.

She took a deep breath in and shook her head. 'I assumed he meant that he'd lost everything – his money, the business, their financial future. I knew he'd not been himself, but if I'd only known how far he'd been pushed . . .' Her words tailed off again, eyes unfocused and looking back across the years.

'Pushed?' asked Styles. 'What do you mean by pushed?'

She snapped back to the present and blinked three times in rapid succession.

'I mean just by the sheer weight of everything he had bearing down on him.' Her words faltered a little at first but soon gained strength. 'Anyway, I don't mean to be rude, Detectives, but that was a long time ago and you were asking about Natasha. I really don't have anything else to share that would help you. Now, if you'll excuse me, I have to head out and meet my husband. He doesn't like to be kept waiting.'

She stood up, the clear message being that she expected them to do the same.

'Of course,' said Porter. 'We don't mean to keep you. One last thing, though,' he said with a genial smile. 'Your son, Gavin? Is he still in contact with his sister, and are there any other siblings?'

He could have sworn she flinched when he asked the question. 'Alexander and I couldn't have any more children. Not since I, uh . . . we lost a child. A few years before all of this happened. A son. A few weeks before he was due to be born. There were complications, and I, uh . . . No. No other brothers or sisters. As for Gavin, he's not mentioned it to me if she has been in touch, but you'd have to ask him.'

'What about friends from school or other family members? Is there anyone that she was close to who might help us get in touch with her?'

'Not that I know of, but like I said, we weren't exactly close.'

She was edging closer to the door leading to the hallway as she spoke. They took the hint and thanked her for her time. Styles asked her for the best way to reach her son, and jotted down the address and phone number she gave him for Gavin. They retraced their steps to the front door and Porter pulled a business card from his wallet.

'Just in case you think of anything else after we leave,' he said, handing it to her.

Porter and Styles didn't speak again until they were back in their car.

'What did you make of that, then?' Styles asked his partner.

'I've seen a few people brick it when a copper turns up on their doorstep, but she looked like she was expecting us to slap the cuffs on her.'

'Crimes against fashion?' asked Styles, arching one eyebrow.

'Her outfit probably cost the same as a full term at private school.'

'Doesn't mean it looks good.'

Porter tilted his head in agreement. 'Let's see if the brother is around to speak to, and I want to take a look at the file on the father's suicide as well. You thinking what I'm thinking?'

'Do you mean could the hurt he caused his family be actual harm, and he topped himself out of remorse?'

Porter nodded grimly. 'Wouldn't be the strangest thing ever, and for his suicide to happen in the same week that she was last sighted, that's a fair sized coincidence, don't you think?'

Styles nodded. 'You think she knows more than she's saying?' he said, nodding towards the house.

'I think there's more she could have said but didn't,' said Porter. 'Whether whatever she's keeping back is relevant to wherever Natasha is or whether it's just cos it's events she'd rather forget, I don't know. Did you see her when she said the part about him being a "good man"?'

'No, I must have been writing something down then. Why?'

'Just a little thing, but when she said it, she was shaking her head. It's one of those gestures that tend to show a person doesn't actually believe what they're saying. Maybe he wasn't quite the nice guy she's making him out to be?'

'Worth a look,' said Styles. 'Actually, speaking of things that are worth a look, do me a favour and pull over just around the corner.'

'Why, what's up?'

'I'm curious to see if she actually comes out of the house any time soon. She said she was running late to meet her hubby, but we've been out a full two or three minutes and she's not exactly flying out of the house to meet him.'

Porter nodded his head in approval as he started the engine and pulled away.

'Looks like some of my detective know-how might be rubbing off on you after all.'

'Don't flatter yourself,' said Styles. 'I picked that one up from an episode of *Scooby-Doo*.'

Porter shook his head but said nothing and conceded that one. He pulled the car around the corner and switched off the ignition. Five minutes passed and there was still no sign of the gate to the Locke house reopening.

'Guess she's had a change of heart about meeting the hubby after all,' said Styles. 'Fancy a bite to eat on the way back?'

'Yep, but I'm choosing this time,' said Porter. 'That grotty little cafe you picked last time served me a gastro-bomb with a time delay fuse. I had half a mind to call Environmental Health.'

He had one last glance in the rear-view mirror before pulling away. The conversation with Mary Locke had left him with an uneasy feeling. Most people's reaction to hearing that there'd been an incident involving a loved one, and he used the term loosely here after the family history he'd learnt, was to ask if they were OK. The fact that he wouldn't have been able to answer that either way was immaterial. Asking that question would be an unavoidable reflex for the majority of people. The reason that the minority, like Mary Locke, didn't ask after their welfare tended to be because they already knew the answer, and that rarely worked out well for all concerned.

CHAPTER FIVE

Styles called Gavin Barclay while Porter drove. Locke picked up on the first ring, as if he'd been expecting the call. Had Mary Locke called ahead to let him know they'd be in touch? Styles quickly gave him the same line Porter had spoken into Mary Locke's intercom, and he said he could meet them for a coffee near his office, and gave a brief description of his appearance so they'd know him.

The cafe he had chosen was in Farringdon, and they took a shortcut through the deserted Smithfield Market to get there. It always reminded Porter of an upturned ship's hull, blue and white girders curving overhead. It was deserted at this time of day apart from a few others cutting through. Turn up after 8 a.m. and you'd missed the party. Ironic that meat was still sliced and diced today, on the same spot that saw the likes of William Wallace executed centuries ago. Porter wondered what Wallace would make of the tourists taking selfies outside, angling their cameras upwards to catch the sculptures of the dragons that guarded the entrance.

When they arrived, Gavin Locke was already there. It wasn't hard to spot him; he was hunched over a large coffee cup, both hands encircling it and his index fingers tapping out a nervous beat either side of the handle. His hair looked like it had been combed with a branch, and his waxy pale face made him look ten years too old. He wore a dark grey suit with the faintest of pinstripes running through it, and a conservative dark blue tie with no pattern. The combination of average urban office-wear and clean-shaven face was the uniform of countless city jobs. He stood up when they approached.

'Mr Locke?'

'Yes, that's me.' Locke gave a nervous smile, his eyes flitting between the two of them.

Porter took the hand that Locke held out, and noted the clammy palm that met his. They introduced themselves and pulled out a chair each.

'Can I get you a drink?' he asked.

'No, thank you, Mr Locke,' said Porter.

Locke resumed the cradling of his cup. 'So you want to talk about Natasha,' he said. It was a statement, not a question.

Porter nodded. 'We need to speak to her, Mr Locke, and we're hoping you can point us in the right direction. It doesn't appear that she's been home to her flat in some time. When was the last time you spoke to her?'

'My mum didn't tell you?' he asked.

Porter and Styles looked at each other, both noting the significance of the question. When Styles had called him there had been no mention of the fact they'd spoken to Mary Locke, or that she was the one who had given them his number. That meant she had indeed called him, and in all likelihood the call had been made as soon as they had left her house.

'She didn't think you'd had any recent contact with her but said we should ask you the question.'

'I've not seen her since her twenty-first birthday.' His eyes fixed on the dregs of coffee that lurked in the bottom of his cup as he spoke. 'I was only six years old. It was that long ago I can't even remember what the last thing she said to me was.'

Porter waited and let a few seconds of silence settle over the table in case Locke planned to elaborate, but when nothing else was forthcoming he stepped back into the gap in conversation.

'What about any other form of contact? Have you spoken to her on the phone since then? Swapped emails?'

Locke gave a wry smile. 'There was no such thing as email the last time I saw her, but no, in answer to your question, I've had no contact with her since then.' He paused, then added, 'Or should I say she's had no contact with me.'

'What do you mean by that?' asked Styles.

'I mean she's the one that disappeared off into the sunset. I know there was no Facebook or Twitter when she left, but I'm sure it wouldn't be too hard for her to find me if she wanted. I've searched for her online a few times over the years but never found any mention.' He shook his head softly. 'I know it must have been hard for her when Dad . . . did what he did. I was too young to really understand at the time. I guess she needed some space to work things out her way. I just didn't realise it would last this long.'

'Were Natasha and your dad close?' Porter asked.

Gavin shrugged. 'Memories from that far back are fuzzy, but yeah, from what I remember.'

'Any arguments, fallings out, that kind of thing?'

Gavin frowned, silent for a moment. 'Why would you ask that? What are you saying? That Dad had something to do with her disappearing?'

'Just a routine question,' said Porter, shaking his head. 'We need to understand what was going on in her life back then. Whether she was happy, anything that might affect her so much that she felt the need to take off.' As much as he had his suspicions about Nathan Barclay, sharing them with Gavin Locke wasn't going to help him coax the answers he wanted. Not without anything to back them up, at least.

'How about her relationship with your mum?' asked Styles, changing direction.

'Like I said, I was only six. What little I remember was OK, I guess. I don't remember them not getting on for what that's worth.' He shrugged. 'I know Mum had her good and bad days back then, and she spent a bit of time in hospital. I don't know if she told you about Simon?' Porter and Styles both looked blank, so he continued. 'Simon would have been my little brother, but he died before he was born.'

'Ah yes,' said Styles. 'She did tell us, but hadn't used a name. Sorry.'

'I wasn't allowed to visit her for a while afterwards. They kept her in for weeks. She's had counselling for it off and on for years now. I can't remember a hell of a lot else about it,' he said with a sad smile. 'My family isn't great at talking about their feelings, Detective. My mum's the best person to ask about how well they got on, but she'll probably just tell you it was fine either way.'

'What about other family, or friends?' asked Porter, bringing it back to the present. 'Is there anyone else she might have kept in touch with?'

'Anyone that meant more to her than her own brother, you mean?' he said with a trace of bitterness, stopping himself before any more of it spilt out. 'Sorry. I just have a hard time understanding why she doesn't want anything to do with me or my family. She has a nephew she's never even met.'

Porter steered him back on track and away from more introspection. 'So is there anyone else who might know where she is, then, Mr Locke?'

Gavin Locke shook his head. 'No, not that I can think of. She was fifteen years older than me, so we didn't exactly hang out together. I was the annoying little brother. All her friends from school went off to university, and she was long gone before any of them came home.'

Was fifteen years older. Porter let Locke's use of the past tense slide without comment. 'What about her flat? Have you ever gone there to see if she's returned home?'

This brought a slight frown to Locke's face. 'That's the thing, you see – until you called me and said something had happened at her flat, I didn't even know she still had one round here.'

'So you've never been to her place on Rainton Avenue?' said Styles.

'Why would I have been there if I've only just found out she lives there?'

'We're just trying to piece things together, Mr Locke,' said Porter in a conciliatory tone. 'I'm sure you can understand we need to be thorough, especially when nobody seems to have seen her for so long.'

Gavin Locke sat back in his seat and let out a deep sigh.

'Sorry,' he apologised again. 'I think about her all the time; wonder where she is, if she's OK, if she's happy – that kind of thing. It's been a while since I've actually spoken about her with anyone, though. I know you're just doing your job, and if there's any way I can help, I will.'

'There is one thing,' Porter ventured. 'The incident that's taken place at her flat; our guys have taken a number of samples, fingerprints and hair from a hairbrush, to run some DNA tests. It'd be really useful if we could work out which samples belong to Natasha. That way we can tell if anyone else has been inside her flat.'

He was being economical with the truth, but it served no one's best interests for him to disclose the contents of the freezer just yet, at least not until they knew for sure.

Locke looked confused. 'How can I help with that?'

'As her brother, you'll have a certain amount of DNA in common. If we can take a sample from you, we can match that against any that belongs to Natasha.'

'Are you saying she's in trouble? Could she be hurt?'

'We really don't know at this stage,' said Porter. 'But things like this will help us try to find her and work out what's going on. If you're OK to do that I'll arrange for somebody to come either to your office or your house to do a cheek swab.'

'Of course,' said Locke, his voice softer now as his thoughts drifted away to where his big sister might be and what kind of trouble she might be in.

He promised to come down to the station for the swab, preferring the anonymity it would give him as opposed to officers turning up at his home or office. They all left together and shook hands outside before heading off in different directions. Porter looked over his shoulder as they walked towards their car, making sure Locke was definitely out of earshot.

'Stop me if you think otherwise,' he began, 'but I think we're both fairly confident the cheek swab will match up to the sample from the hand.'

'I'd lay money on it,' agreed Styles.

'So the question, then, is whether Ms Barclay bled out once she parted company with her hand, or whether whatever led to that sent her into hiding somewhere. We're fairly sure it didn't happen at the flat, so it's pointless checking old records at local A & Es just yet.'

Styles jumped in before Porter could continue. 'Agreed. Realistically, without medical attention, we're looking for a body rather than a scared woman in hiding. I say we find out more about the dad, and how he met his maker. If he had something to do with whatever happened to her, that could be what tipped him over the edge.'

Porter nodded in agreement. 'I'd like to read his note if it's on file anywhere. I'd also like to know where he got his hands on the gun he used to kill himself.'

As they wound their way back through traffic, Porter tried to make sense of what he knew so far. It was distasteful, but sadly all too common in his line of work, to come across parents that harmed their children, either physically or emotionally. If Nathan Barclay had indeed been responsible for severing his daughter's hand, why would he place it in the freezer to preserve it before taking his own life? Was it as clichéd as him not being able to live with something he had done, but equally wanting to take responsibility for it, albeit making sure he wasn't around to face the consequences of his actions? Porter always tried to see things from the perspective of those who perpetrated the crimes he investigated. It reminded him of a quote he'd once read from the Chinese general and author of *The Art of War*, Sun Tzu, who counselled people to '*know thyself, know thy enemy*'. The idea of spending too much time trying to inhabit the same dark places as a man who would harm his own child, however, was far from Porter's idea of fun. It was necessary sometimes, though, to let a case steer you towards that fine line that separated dark thought and darker deed from those of us who abide by the rules.

He'd seen evil take on many faces, here on the streets of London, and on his tours of duty overseas with the army. In the here and now, his gut told him that face was taking the form of Nathan Barclay. Whether Mary or Gavin Locke had already known that to be the case remained to be seen.

They went for the divide and conquer approach back at the station, Styles calling the coroner to get a copy of the report on Nathan Barclay, while Porter dug through the archives to unearth any information from the original investigation into Barclay's death. Styles completed his task first and left the copy with Porter on his way out to meet his wife for dinner. He'd offered to stay and help review the file, but Porter waved him away.

The coroner's report held no surprises. Nathan Barclay had died from a single gunshot wound to the head. The bullet had come from an old Walther P38 that was found at the scene three feet from Barclay's outstretched hand, with his prints on the grip. The body had been discovered in an office at a warehouse owned by Atlas Holdings when a security guard doing his rounds stumbled across it. There had been no other injuries and no evidence to suggest it had been anything other than the last act of a deeply troubled man. He had left a note at the scene, a handwritten sheet of lined A4 paper. Porter put the rest of the file down on his desk and studied the copy of the note.

I've lost almost everything I hold dear and caused so much pain to those I love. It has to stop here, and I hope you understand this is the only way to make sure it does. I'm sorry I couldn't be the father and husband that you all deserved. I tried, Natasha, God knows I tried. I'd give anything for a second chance but I know it's too late.

May God forgive me.
N.B.

He grabbed a pad of paper from his desk and read the note a second time, jotting down a few thoughts as he went. Once he'd finished, he placed it back in the file and reached for the collection of photographs. There were six of them, all A4 size glossy prints, the sharpness of the colour slightly faded. The first few were taken from around ten feet away, and showed the body in situ. Nathan Barclay had sat down against the wall before he pulled the trigger. Porter found that curious. It wasn't as if he would feel any pain by the time his head hit the floor had he stood, but it was hard to say what thoughts were going through someone's mind when they'd got to that stage in the decision-making process. He'd also taken off his suit jacket, and folded it neatly by his side, positioning the note on top of it. Other pictures showed the scene from several angles, two of them showing close-ups of the entry and exit wounds.

Barclay had a key ring with him that included a master key to this and several other warehouses nearby. He'd used this to let himself in, and there was no suggestion that anyone else had been there at the time. The investigating officers at the time had also included in their report a cursory line of enquiry into Barclay's business and finances as a possible motive for his actions. According to their notes, Atlas Holdings was a haulage firm operating nationally through the UK. It had been started by Barclay's father back in the forties, just after the end of World War Two. It had run into financial difficulties at the start of the eighties and had been bought by Locke & Winwood in April 1983.

Porter stopped when he read about the sale. It didn't say anything else about Locke & Winwood or what they did. He realised he'd forgotten to ask Mary Locke about whether her husband was involved in the business, and made a mental note to follow it up. Either way, it was intriguing that Natasha's father sold his business the same month he committed suicide, and also around the same time she was last seen. A grouping of key events like that could be a coincidence, but there was a long way to go before he'd settle for that explanation.

There was nothing at all in what he read that made him doubt the verdict of suicide, but the note was ambiguous enough to leave him with a list of questions. Was he referring to actual pain caused, or emotional distress?

It has to stop here.

What had to stop, and what had he actually done in the first place? Why had he singled out Natasha for a mention and not his son or ex-wife?

God knows I tried.

What had he tried? Did he mean he tried to stop himself doing whatever had happened to her, or was there something or someone else in play here? She had last been seen in the week leading up to his suicide, so if he was responsible for Natasha's disappearance, why would he not give her stepmother and brother the peace they deserved and spell out her fate as part of his last words? If nothing else, Porter thought they were owed at least that.

Gavin Locke kept his promise the following day, and the results that came back twenty-four hours later proved beyond any doubt that the hand did indeed belong to Natasha Barclay. Styles made a wisecrack about it only being a familial match and that there could be other siblings out there who had disappeared as well. Porter just shook his head and grimaced in mock disgust. He looked around and caught the eye of one of the junior officers across the room, beckoning him over. He gave him a hastily scribbled note with Natasha Barclay's name and date of birth on, and sent him to check local hospitals to see how far back their records went.

'I've been busy digging up some useful facts as well, though,' said Styles. 'You were right; there is a connection between Locke and Barclay. The company that bought Atlas Holdings lock, stock and barrel was owned by Alexander Locke, currently married to Mary Locke.'

'What about Winwood?' asked Porter. 'Who's he?'

'He died back in the seventies, cancer of some sort. The company has been around for a while. Winwood set it up with Locke's father and had no family, so Locke Senior ended up owning the whole thing. Locke Junior took over in the mid-seventies. Guess he kept Winwood's name in out of respect or branding. They're essentially an import-export business but do the whole lot themselves – the shipping, storage and distribution; they're into everything from food and drink to electrical goods and clothes.'

Porter nodded. Now he thought of it, the name was familiar for another reason aside from the connection to the case. Lorries bearing the Locke & Winwood logo could usually be spotted on motorways up and down the country.

'Atlas ran up a tonne of debt and Locke stepped in and purchased it for the princely sum of a pound.'

Porter's eyes widened. 'A pound?'

'I see you've still not had the echo fixed yet. Yes, a pound. Don't forget, though, he took on all the debt that came with the company for that pound. You're looking at just over a million quid. You can multiply that by three for today's equivalent.'

'Sounds like a pretty shitty deal to me,' said Porter. 'Why the hell would you do a thing like that?'

'Depends on the reason for the debts, I suppose, but buying a haulage firm like that gave Locke a national reach. Don't forget that the assets would be worth something as well, the warehouses and lorries Atlas owned.'

'Fair point,' agreed Porter. 'Interesting coincidence. Saves asking Mary Locke about the connection. We'll still need to talk to both of them again now we know it's Natasha, though.'

'There's someone else we should speak to first,' said Styles.

'You found someone else who knows Natasha Barclay?'

'Nope, but we need to speak to Simmons.'

'What's she got to do with the case?' asked Porter, looking confused.

'It's not just about *our* case. It's about how ours has overlapped with hers.'

Eve Simmons was a bright young thing who had joined fresh from university. Porter had used her as a dogsbody on a few cases in the past, but she had recently been promoted and moved across to the drugs squad within the Criminal Investigation Department. She was partnered up with Mike Gibson, a twenty-year veteran, who Porter knew by reputation. She was in safe hands, and would learn a lot from Gibson if she paid attention.

'I'm all ears,' said Porter, sounding mildly confused.

'Turns out Mr Locke is allegedly quite an interesting man, and I'm talking about the husband here, not the son.'

'Only allegedly?'

'Hedging my bets there. It turns out that Simmons and the rest of her merry band of men have been working their way up the food chain tackling our nation's drug problem. They haven't made any major arrests yet, but they've got a source on the inside of a major operation right here in our fair nation's capital. They can't prove it just yet, but Simmons believes Locke & Winwood, with their fleet of trucks and minor empire of warehouses, is responsible for a healthy slice of the heroin and cocaine supply in the UK.'

'How close are they to making a case?'

'The guy they have on the inside is one they busted for dealing. They offered him a deal to switch sides. It turns out he's a warehouse manager for a company called Claremont Storage. They've got a load of warehouses down by the river. Containers come off the ships and sit in one of those places till they get picked up and dropped off wherever they're destined for. They've got all sorts in there – TVs, washing machines, clothes – you name it.'

'So how does that tie in with Locke?' said Porter, getting impatient.

'Claremont Storage is owned by Locke & Winwood. The goods they store come off Locke & Winwood boats, and when they leave the warehouses, they're in Atlas Holdings trucks; Atlas Holdings of course being owned by—'

'Locke & Winwood,' said Porter, finishing the sentence for him.

Styles nodded and flashed him a grin. 'Knew you'd get there eventually. There's more to it than just that, though. She's upstairs now if you want the gory details?'

'Lead the way,' said Porter, feeling the slight but unmistakable stirring in the pit of his stomach that the day was about to get a lot more interesting.

Porter felt a twinge of satisfaction listening to Simmons rattling off the details of her case. Six months before she moved over to the drugs squad, she had once confided in him about the pressure she felt of trying to succeed in a male-dominated profession, but none of that showed now. Her update was short and to the point, not garnishing the facts with anything irrelevant or extraneous. Styles had long since made occasional wisecracks about her hero-worship of Porter bordering on a crush, and that a lesser man would have taken advantage of it long before now. It wasn't that Porter found her unattractive; she had a look of Audrey Hepburn about her. Even allowing for the fact that on the job she was all business, favouring dark trouser suits, white blouses, with dark brown hair scraped back from her face into a tight ponytail, she turned more than a few heads when she walked into a room. His stock response was the old locker-room cliché of 'you don't shit where you eat'; inwardly, the thought of being with someone again, letting someone behind the barriers that had held those kinds of emotion in check since Holly, was still alien to him. He forced his mind not to wander and focused on her words.

'So the guy we've flipped to work for us has done time already for possession. The problem he had this time was that he was greedy, and cut the coke with all sorts of weird and wonderful extras. Unfortunately for him, not all of his customers reacted too well to his new product. A twenty-year-old student from UCL ended up in the emergency ward and never woke up.'

Porter shook his head softly as he listened and felt his cheeks flush with anger. It was bad enough that men like that peddled the stuff in the first place, but to put their customers' lives in even more jeopardy than they already were was a level of selfishness that never failed to get a rise from him.

'I take it we can prove he sold to the student?' asked Styles.

'Luckily for us, neither of them had spotted the CCTV camera in the club they were in, so yep, we've got him bang to rights,' said Simmons, nodding. 'He's got a healthy fear of his employers, but the only option we gave, other than locking him up for manslaughter, was to work for us.' She saw the look in Porter's eyes at the idea of the student's death going unpunished.

'He'll still go away for what he did,' she said quickly. 'We need to cut the head off the snake, though. Dealers like him are ten a penny. He's given us some names and we're going to wire him up when he goes to pick up his next delivery.'

'So he's giving us Locke?' asked Porter.

'No,' she said. 'Locke owns the lot, but Owen Carter – that's our inside man – has only met him once and doesn't deal with him direct.'

'But we know Locke is involved?'

'Jury's out. We don't know for sure, but we strongly suspect.'

Porter had been perched on the edge of his seat, leaning forward, but sighed and sat back at her last comment. She sensed she was losing his interest.

'We've got good grounds for the suspicion,' she added. 'Locke and his old man both have a chequered past. Locke did eighteen months for GBH when he was twenty, and his old man has form for smuggling goods into the country. Admittedly, his vice was cigarettes and alcohol back in the sixties, rather than Class A drugs, but still, they're far from being whiter than white, and they know how to shift products below the radar.'

Porter and Styles glanced at each other, their interests once again piqued. Simmons grabbed a sheet of paper from the printer by her desk and scribbled a name in the middle.

'Carter picks up his monthly quota from a guy called Andrew Patchett.

Patchett works for Claremont as well and runs the teams of security guards that patrol all their sites.' She jabbed at his name on the page as she spoke.

'There're a dozen sites in total and Carter says Patchett controls distribution to a man in each of them – coke and heroin,' she said, drawing twelve lines downwards from Patchett, with little boxes at the end of each. 'And Patchett answers to James Bolton, who just happens to be head of security for Locke & Winwood.'

'And let me guess,' said Porter as she added Bolton's name above Patchett's, 'Bolton answers to Locke.'

'Got it in one,' she said, flashing a triumphant smile at both of them, although Porter felt her gaze linger on him a split second longer than it seemed to on Styles.

You're imagining things, he thought. *This is all just down to Styles and his constant piss-take.*

'Have we got anything linking Locke directly to either the product or those selling it, apart from the fact he owns the company, obviously?' asked Porter. He suddenly felt warm and hoped to God he hadn't betrayed his thoughts by blushing or popping out a stray bead of perspiration on his forehead.

'Not directly,' said Simmons. 'He's insulated himself with these layers.' She pointed at the sequence of names and scribbles that now resembled a pyramid. 'But Carter overheard Patchett and Bolton talking one time. He only caught the last part of the conversation, but Bolton was telling Patchett that Locke just wanted the problem fixing, and that the last thing Patchett would want is to have to explain himself to Locke personally. We don't know what the problem was, but they both clammed up when they saw Carter, so we don't see Locke being an innocent bystander here.'

'So what's your next move?' asked Styles.

'We've got eyes on all four but the plan is to work our way up one step at a time. Carter has agreed to wear a wire next time he collects from Patchett and will try to get close enough if he sees him and Bolton getting cosy again. Hopefully that gives us one or both of them, then we move on to Locke.'

'Do we think Locke is definitely the top dog?' asked Porter. 'What if he's just another link in a bigger chain?'

'If we're lucky and we get him, he'll give up his overseas suppliers and we can pass that on to locals, whatever country there're in, but as far as the UK goes, we're pretty sure there's nobody above him in the food chain. He owns the lot, and it's a privately held company so he answers to no one.'

'How much product do we think he's shifting?' asked Styles.

'Our best guess is street value anywhere between eighty and a hundred million a year,' said Simmons.

'He keeps a hell of a low profile for a man heading up a national operation with numbers like that,' said Styles, unable to hide the surprise in his voice.

Simmons shrugged. 'That's why we'd never heard of him until recently. He's very careful. He doesn't live beyond his means as a successful businessman and trusts very few people. Bolton is one.' She tapped his name on the page and scribbled another down next to it. 'Oliver Davies was another. He was head of operations for Locke & Winwood, whatever that meant. As far as we can tell he's the only other man who ever had that kind of access to Locke.'

'Had?' asked Porter.

'Carter told us he heard that Bolton and Davies grew up together, and threw in with Locke around the same time. Bolton's around the same age your missing girl would have been now. Fifty-four, we think.'

Past tense again, thought Porter. Was he the only one willing to maintain even the slimmest of hopes that she might still be alive?

'They both did minor spells inside for assault when they were younger,' Simmons continued, 'but cleaned up their acts after that. With Bolton, it sounds horrible to say it but if it hadn't been for the student dying we might never have had enough to start building a case. If even half the stories about him are true, then he's not the kind of guy you want to get on the wrong side of. Trouble is that people who end up there tend to have a run of bad luck. Falling down stairs, tripping into traffic, that kind of thing.'

'If he's that bad a man, it could be him that's in charge. He could just be using Locke's premises to store the goods. As head of security he'll have access to all areas. What's to say he's not doing all this right under Locke's nose?'

Simmons nodded. 'We haven't ruled that out yet, but after what Carter overheard, we're still leaning towards Locke.'

'What about Davies?' Styles asked.

'Davies died back in 1983. He was found in his car, length of wire wrapped round his neck. No arrest made. Best guess is a run-in with a rival operation.'

There was that year cropping up again, but Porter dismissed it for now. He was struggling to make the connection. Simmons had a solid case, at least for Carter and Patchett, but even if Locke was the shadowy figure they suspected, and it was a big *if*, Porter couldn't join up the dots to link him to Natasha Barclay. No matter how bad a man he was, it didn't change the fact that her father had killed himself, or that he'd left a note that was vague enough to make Porter wonder if he had a hand in his daughter's disappearance.

'So I bet you're wondering what this has to do with us?' said Styles. Porter found it a bit disconcerting how he did that sometimes, pre-empting his thoughts.

'You took the words right out of my mouth,' said Porter, smiling.

'So, that mountain of debt Locke took on when he bought Barclay out? It turns out that Locke could well have been the cause of it in the first place.'

'How do you mean?'

Styles handed Porter a folder. 'It's all in here but I'll give you the highlights. The debt was racked up in 1981. Atlas borrowed big when they were getting ready to expand. They bought new trucks, new warehouses, hired new staff, all to handle a new contract they had won. Turns out one of Barclay's guys, a guy called Arnold Bembenek, had paid a few people off to make sure they won it, and the contract was declared void. Bembenek denied it and said he'd been set up, but they had a paper trail to prove it so they were left with the bill for all the new equipment and infrastructure but no contract.'

Styles paused to take a sip from his coffee and Simmons jumped in to fill the gap in his flow.

'The contract they'd won was with a Chinese firm called GFD who were trying to break into the UK market. No prizes for guessing who currently handles all UK import and distribution for GFD.'

'Locke & Winwood,' said Porter.

'You're good at this game,' said Styles.

'So they walked away, then came back to give all their business to essentially the parent company of the people who had just caused them public embarrassment?'

'It gets better.' Styles turned and winked at Simmons. 'Tell him the rest about Bembenek.'

Simmons picked up the prompt and continued. 'Arnold Bembenek was a second generation Polish immigrant. He'd worked at Atlas for twelve years and never had so much as a parking ticket since he came to the UK. Claims that two men tried to bribe him to sabotage the deal. He said no and told Barclay, but never reported it to the police. The next thing he knows the bribe story explodes with him at the centre, and proof that money changed hands is found in his office. This mystery man was part of his defence, but he was never located, and Bembenek went down for five years. I pulled the file from his case.' She grabbed a single sheet of paper from the table behind her and handed it to Porter. 'The two guys that approached him, one was big, around six-six, dark hair and a scar across his chin, and didn't say much. The other one did most of the talking, and on the way out said he might send the big fella, Jimmy, round to have a private word if he didn't reconsider.'

Porter quickly scanned the copy of Bembenek's statement, and then looked at the picture held in the top corner by a paperclip. The black-and-white shot of the man was from a distance, but didn't disguise the fact that he was a giant. Porter noticed the sloping shoulder muscles that rose to his neck in a triangular fashion, and arms that bulged against the fabric of his suit; a gymaholic if ever he'd seen one. The scar started along the lower part of his jaw and ended up like a second chin dimple, just off centre by the real thing.

'Who've we got here, then? This the guy from the statement?'

'Say hello to James Bolton,' said Styles. 'I'd say he's a more than reasonable match against Bembenek's description, wouldn't you?'

'So Locke sent his man to sabotage the deal so he could get Barclay's business on the cheap, I get that,' said Porter. 'You've convinced me he's not a nice guy. What I'm still not convinced of is that it has even a remote connection to what happened to Natasha Barclay.'

'Locke is far from being a nice guy; same goes for Bolton, and bad things have happened to anyone who doesn't give them what they want, but the connection is there. We're just not sure how all the pieces fit together yet,' said Simmons.

Styles picked up a grey folder from the desk and handed it to Porter. It was a copy of the crime scene report that Will Leonard had promised but Porter had yet to read. He started scanning from the top of the front page, but Styles reached across and lifted the sheet up and over to reveal the one beneath it. He pointed at a section in the middle and Porter quickly took in the paragraph. He was only halfway through when he saw it and stopped, his eyes fixed on one word, a name. When he looked up, Styles and Simmons were both watching him, waiting expectantly for a reaction.

'Him?' said Porter. 'He was there? In her apartment?'

Styles nodded. 'Yep, fingerprints are only partials but it's a definite match. That a solid enough connection for you?'

'Where were they?'

'They were in the kitchen. It's not often prints would last that long, but we got lucky. The bench next to the oven had some trace fatty deposits, most likely from somebody's cooking, and we picked them up from that.'

Porter stood up and dropped the file back onto the table. He felt his pulse quicken as he spoke. 'Ladies and gentlemen, we have ourselves a suspect. Let's go round James Bolton up and ask what the hell he was doing at a crime scene.'

He started to walk around Styles and Simmons but she put a hand on his shoulder to stop him.

'You can't do that, sir, at least not yet.'

Porter stopped, his face a mask of incredulity. 'You're telling me I can't speak to a man suspected of assault at best, and worst case, murder? Who's going to stop me?' he snapped as he pushed past her, and headed for the door.

'Sir!' she called after him. 'There's much more at stake here.'

Porter stopped and turned to face her. 'More than bringing a murderer to justice?'

'You said yourself murder is worst case. You don't even have a body.'

He scowled and looked away, but she pressed on, lowering her tone to take the heat out of the situation. 'If we go in there now, they'll know we're looking at them, or him at the very least. How much more careful do you think he'll be then?'

He couldn't decide what pissed him off the most: the fact that he'd lost his cool and let the case get to him, or the fact that she was right. Either way, Bolton would have to wait, but it didn't stop him from feeling like he was becoming the latest in a long line of people who had let Natasha down.

CHAPTER SIX

Porter drove in silence and mulled things over in his head as Styles chatted to his wife on his mobile. He knew everything Simmons had said made sense, but that did little to gloss over his irritation at having to leave Bolton alone for the time being. The identification of the prints in Leonard's report was a step forward, though; the first real moment of clarity in an otherwise confusing haze of facts fogging up his mind. It had come as a surprise; his first instinct told him to expect the prints to come from Natasha's father. Simmons and her series of revelations had made him think she was about to reveal evidence that confirmed Alexander Locke as a suspect as well, but knowing that James Bolton had been inside the flat gave rise to a new spur off from his main theory.

Bolton was Locke's man, so could as easily have been there carrying out his master's bidding as being on his own business. Either way, his prints in the flat suggested he had been part of whatever had happened there. His print was the one true connection, stretching back across three decades, that placed anybody in Natasha Barclay's flat apart from her. That was enough to bring him in for questioning, but they would need more than that to press charges. They would need Natasha, alive or dead, or a confession that he had harmed her, and he didn't think the latter would exactly be served up on a plate for them.

Porter pulled up outside the Locke house in exactly the same spot they had parked in on their first visit. He waited patiently while Styles finished the call to Emma.

'Sorry,' said Styles with a bashful shrug. 'Em's having a feud with her big sister and needed someone to vent to.'

Porter waved away the apology, and they walked across to the intercom by the gate. Mary Locke sounded surprised to hear Porter's voice again, but second time around did not hesitate to open the gates. When she opened the door, her face looked strained. She tried a smile, but the rest of her face didn't follow suit. Porter wondered if she'd gone down the Botox route, or if she'd been under the knife. Either way, it made for a slightly unnatural look.

'Detectives, Gavin said he'd spoken to you. I didn't expect you to be back so soon. Have you found Natasha?'

'Not exactly, Mrs Locke. May we come in?'

She stepped back and they went inside, heading into the living room via the same route as the previous visit without waiting to be asked. Mary Locke followed behind, and they each assumed their same seats from the day before.

'You said "not exactly", Detective. What did you mean by that?'

'There was evidence in her flat that leads us to believe that Natasha was the victim of some form of attack, Mrs Locke, and that she may have sustained serious injuries.'

'What sort of injuries?' she asked, her eyes fixed on his.

Something in the way that she was speaking bothered Porter. Was it what she said, or how she said it? It had dogged him since his first visit: an unreachable itch right at the back of his subconscious, nagging and undefined, but just too far to scratch.

'We've compared the DNA sample we took from your son to evidence found in Natasha's flat. There was blood found in the living area that has been identified as hers.' He paused to let that sink in before dropping the real bombshell. Her mouth dropped open a fraction and her eyes flitted about the room, everywhere but on either police officer.

'We also found a hand in her freezer that matches the same sample; it belongs to Natasha.'

Mary Locke's eyelids fluttered and she raised one hand sharply to her mouth, the other pressed flat against her chest. This time there was no protracted build-up of emotion, and the tears sprang forward unchecked. She closed her eyes and kept them that way for a three count, as if that could stem the tide. Porter hesitated, feeling like an intruder on the most private of moments.

'Mrs Locke?' The sound of his voice brought her back, and she opened her eyes. 'I know this must be hard for you to process, but we're coming into this whole thing late on. Whatever happened in that flat looks like it happened a long time ago, so we need you to cast your mind back and tell us absolutely anything you can remember about Natasha. Who were her friends, what hobbies did she have, did she have a boyfriend?'

'She was such a good girl.' Mary Locke had a faraway look in her eye, her mind stretching back over thirty years, and her voice was quiet when she spoke. 'We had our differences but she would never have hurt anyone.'

'Mrs Locke, I need you to focus for us. Who did she hang around with? Is there anyone you can think of that we can speak to who might have seen her the week you last saw her?'

Mary Locke shook her head. 'Excuse me for just a minute. I need to get a tissue.' She stood up and walked quickly through the door and back out into the hall. Porter and Styles turned and looked at each other. Styles raised his eyebrows, and leant in close to whisper.

'You know she didn't need to get a tissue, right?'

Porter nodded. He had spotted the tell-tale lump of the handkerchief just beneath the hem of her sleeve as well. They sat patiently until she returned several minutes later, dabbing at her eyes with a scrunched-up paper hankie. Porter gave her a sympathetic smile as she took her seat again opposite them.

'I do apologise, Detectives. It's just come as a bit of a shock that something might have happened to her. I really can't think of anything that might help, though. I hardly knew any of her friends to speak to back in the day, let alone where they are now.'

'What school did she go to?' asked Styles.

'St Agnes' Catholic School. It's near where we used to live, when I was still with her father, that is.' She pulled at the tissue as she spoke, tearing it in several places and winding the strands around her fingers. Styles jotted the name down. They could speak to the school and get details of who else was in her year.

'If only she had . . .' Her voice trailed off as the crunching of gravel outside was accompanied by the low growl of an engine.

'If only she had what, Mrs Locke?' asked Porter.

She craned her neck to look out of the window as a sleek black car swung round towards the double garage. The car's windows were tinted, but Porter thought he saw only one occupant. He looked back at Mary Locke, who seemed not to have heard his question. He repeated it a second time, but she was already on her feet and moving towards the door.

'Excuse me a second, that's my husband coming home,' she said without turning around, and then she was gone.

Porter and Styles looked at each other, and then back to the window. The engine noise became briefly muted, and then stopped altogether. They heard a soft whirring, presumably the garage door motor, followed by soft footsteps on the gravel, and the click of the front door opening as Mary Locke prepared to greet her husband. He walked past the window too quickly for them to get a good look, other than to see he was wearing a suit. Porter heard strains of a conversation, and leant forward, tilting his head to the side, as if the extra few inches would improve the sound quality, but he couldn't make anything out.

Less than a minute later, Alexander Locke strode into the living room. He reminded Porter of the actor George Hamilton, silver hair but minus the permanent mahogany tan that Hamilton sported. The information Simmons had given on him put him at seventy-four, but with a relative lack of the years' wear and tear on his face, he could easily be mistaken for ten years younger. He sized them both up as he approached and made his pick as to the alpha between them, extending his hand to Porter first, who rose from his seat to take it.

'Good afternoon, gentlemen, I'm Alexander Locke. You must be Detective Inspector Porter?' said Locke, shaking Porter's hand with a firm grip.

Porter nodded in acknowledgement. 'Hello, Mr Locke, and this is . . .'

'Detective Inspector Styles?' asked Locke, switching his hand and smile away from Porter.

'Just Detective Sergeant for now,' said Styles, smiling at the correction, 'but who knows, one day?'

Locke gestured for them both to sit back down. He took the seat opposite that his wife had previously occupied, while she, after following him meekly back into the room, sat timidly to his right. She had been a nervy thing to start with, but Porter noted that the arrival of her husband had taken this to a new level. She looked from her lap, where one hand sat protectively covering the other, up to her husband, and back again, but not at Porter or Styles.

Locke unbuttoned his jacket, leant back against the sofa and crossed his legs. 'So my wife tells me you think something has happened to her stepdaughter?' There was just the faintest hint of North London in his voice. Porter wondered if it came and went depending on the company.

'That's right, Mr Locke,' said Porter. He quickly summarised the case so far while Locke listened impassively.

'And you're sure the hand belongs to Natasha?' he asked when Porter had finished.

Porter nodded. 'We have a DNA match to Gavin, so yes, we're sure. We've got people checking local hospital records and I'm sure you'll understand we're concerned about her welfare after an injury like that. How well did you know Natasha yourself?' He wasn't sure how to refer to her relationship with Locke. She wasn't his stepdaughter; Porter wasn't even sure she was anything in terms of a formal link, so he opted for the safe option of using her name.

Locke cleared his throat. 'She was my wife's stepdaughter. I knew her, of course' – he shrugged – 'but we'd only been together a few years the last time either of us saw her, and she took it quite hard when my wife' – he placed a hand over hers – 'and her father got divorced. She and I were never that close.'

'When was the last time you saw her, Mr Locke?'

'Let me see, that would have been around the time her father died. I wish I could be more specific, but I'm sure you can appreciate that was some time ago,' said Locke, loosening his tie and top button.

'Is there anything either of you can think of that might help us find her?' said Styles, deliberately using the plural to try to tempt Mary Locke back into the conversation.

'We wouldn't even know where to start after all this time,' said Locke, giving his wife's hand a gentle squeeze. 'But if we think of anything we'll be sure to give you a call. Now if you'll excuse us, we have an event to attend this evening in the city and need to get ready.'

Porter nodded. 'Of course, Mr Locke.' He had more questions for both of them, to get a sense of what kind of girl Natasha had been, and he had the feeling that Mary Locke, at least, had more to share. Alexander's arrival had most definitely brought down the shutters for now, though. Porter and Styles both stood.

'We'll see ourselves out,' said Porter. 'Thank you both again for your time, and we'll be in touch when we have anything to share.'

They all shook hands, and Porter and Styles left the Lockes in their living room. Styles waited until they were beyond the gate and practically back at the car before he spoke.

'One way or the other, I have a feeling that won't be the last trip out here we do. There's something they're not telling us.'

'Yep,' said Porter. 'I get the feeling more so from her than him. I think she was just about to open up, at least a little bit, before he turned up.'

Styles nodded. 'Her body language as well; she was nervous enough to begin with, but when he walked in it was off the charts.'

'Mm, it wasn't exactly hard to miss,' said Porter. 'He's not your usual poster boy for the drug trade, but I get the feeling he doesn't suffer fools. He may be the man who has everything, but it doesn't exactly strike me as a house filled with love and happiness.'

'That's my mum's favourite cliché – money can't buy happiness. I keep telling her that she might well be right, but if I had the cash at least I could buy plenty of stuff to keep me amused until happiness comes along,' said Styles.

Porter chuckled and pulled away, occasionally glancing at the gate of the Locke house in his rear-view mirror until it was out of sight.

'You going to Anderson's leaving do later?' Styles asked.

'Yeah, I'll show my face for a few,' said Porter with a sigh. 'Are we sure he's actually going to leave this time?'

'He bloody well better. This is the second time I've chipped in for his leaving present. He's not getting a penny more out of me if he changes his mind again.'

Porter dropped Styles off outside a new Italian bistro where he was meeting Emma, near Angel Tube Station. He almost gave in to Styles's prodding to join them for dinner, but wriggled out of it by saying he was popping by to see his mum on the way home and didn't want to turn up at hers too late.

Once he had the car to himself, Porter cast his mind back to what he'd witnessed at Locke's house. He had seen countless different relationships from all walks of life in his time on the force. Tragedy could bring people together, reforge bonds that had been broken and give people the stage on which to showcase the strength of the human spirit. On the flip side, it shone a bright light into the dark corners, and stripped away the veneer to show some people for what they truly were.

What he had seen in the living room had not fitted neatly into any of those usual boxes. Mary Locke's reactions had seemed somewhat muted for a person who had just been told that their long-lost family member was at best seriously injured, with the inference being that in the worst case she had died from her injuries. He supposed that the passing of time and the far from strong relationship she'd described with Natasha could account for that, but he decided to shelve that train of thought for now and move on to Alexander Locke.

His presence had all but gagged his wife, and his own reaction was bordering on apathy. The gentle squeeze of her hand could just as easily be interpreted as a silencing gesture as being one of comfort. He had closed down the questioning with an almost carbon copy of his wife's previous exit strategy of an engagement to attend. The typical reaction of a person when faced with the sort of news they'd delivered is to ask a flood of questions, most of which Porter wouldn't have been able to answer anyway, due to lack of information. The Lockes, though, had made Porter feel like his visit was more of an inconvenience.

In amongst all these fresh questions, he knew one thing with unshakeable certainty. For whatever reason, Mary Locke was afraid of her husband. She had flinched when he took her hand, an almost imperceptible movement, but Porter had seen it. She had been timid enough when she had been alone, but with him in the room she was practically subservient. Domestic abuse takes many forms, physical and emotional, and he had seen no signs of the former, but would wager a hefty sum that she had experienced the latter. Wherever and whenever in the past it had happened, Mary Locke had learnt that life was easier if she played second fiddle to her husband. Porter hoped for her sake she hadn't suffered too much in finding that out.

Alexander Locke watched through the gap between curtain and wall as the two detectives got into their car and pulled away.

'Mary?'

No answer. Hiding upstairs, no doubt. No matter. She'd keep for now. He tapped a number from the list of saved favourites on his phone and counted the rings. Never more than three. Two rings later a low voice answered.

'Boss.' Short and sweet, unlike the man the voice belonged to.

'James, I'm going to need you to meet me at the office.'

'When?' A man of few words, as ever.

'Now.'

'On my way. What's up?'

'Let's talk when I see you. It can wait till then.'

He ended the call, eyes still fixed on the space the car had occupied. It could wait half an hour. It had waited a damn sight longer than that already.

Styles followed the waiter through a narrow slalom of tables to where Emma waited. She hadn't seen him yet, and sat staring at the specials on the chalkboard, rolling the slender stem of her wine glass between finger and thumb. He hadn't realised how hungry he was until he walked past the open kitchen and headfirst into a virtual wall of garlic mingled with fresh-baked pizza dough. Shouts of *prego* and *grazie* from the waiters rang out above the general hum of conversation as they glided through the gaps between chairs, plates perched precariously from wrist to elbow. Italian was more Emma's thing. Food-wise for him, most things came a distant second to his mum's cooking. Her Cou-Cou with fried fish, and the dozens of other recipes she plied him with whenever he went round, reminded him of summers visiting family back in Barbados when he was younger. His mum even had the original recipe book her own mother had insisted she took with her when she came to London, years before he was even born.

He glanced at his watch. Five minutes early, and still she made him feel like he'd kept her waiting. She turned to face him as the waiter reached their table ahead of him, smile starting at her lips and spreading outwards, lighting up every inch of her face.

Porter liked to remind him every so often that he was punching above his weight, and he had to agree. She hadn't aged in the ten years they'd been together, not in his eyes at least, her dad's Mediterranean blood showing through in the faintest tint of olive skin, and a laugh that bounced off every surface in the room. He smiled back, leaning down to kiss her, before folding himself into the seat opposite, legs knocking the underside of the table.

'I'm bloody starving,' he said, grabbing a piece of crusty bread, still warm to the touch. He tore a piece from the middle, rolling it into a loose ball and popping it in his mouth. She lifted the bottle of Chianti and poured him a healthy glassful.

'How's my favourite crime fighter?' she asked, with only the barest hint of her Irish lilt left.

'He's good. Couldn't tempt him to join us for dinner, though. Something about heading to his mam's for tea.'

'Ha ha, very funny,' Emma said, eyes rolling.

'I'm fine, thank you, darling,' he said, putting his best *Made in Chelsea* voice on. 'And you? How's your day been?'

'Long. I've been craving this since lunchtime,' she said, waggling the half-empty glass towards him.

Emma was an assistant manager at a branch of Zara in Watford. He knew she liked the job, but didn't love it. She had often joked of giving it up to be a teacher, but had yet to pluck up the courage to do anything about it. When you stripped life down to its bare bones, Emma was all that mattered. Even if it meant tightening their belts for a while, he would push himself to breaking point and beyond if it meant she was happy.

The waiter took their food order and topped up the carafe of water. Styles listened while she worked her way through a rambling tale about one of the girls who had called in sick so she could go and see Beyoncé at the O2, only to be rumbled after somebody tagged her in a picture on Facebook at the venue. He could happily let her witter away all evening without interrupting, just comfortably quiet in her company. He couldn't imagine what it must have been like for Porter when he lost Holly. He had been partners with Porter for almost a year when it happened. Styles had met her half a dozen times by then. Had seen how different Porter was when she was around. Visibly more relaxed. More at ease.

As far as he was aware, Porter hadn't talked about what happened, to him or anyone he knew of. He hadn't even gone down the clichéd route of drowning his sorrows. Once the funeral was over, it was as if Porter had tucked it away in a box, along with the version of himself that Holly brought out, and filed it away. The man left behind looked similar, but not quite the same. Extra lines crept in around the edges that had nothing to do with laughter. He still joined in with general office banter, but his smile struggled to find its way to his eyes the way it used to.

'How about you, my love?' Emma asked once she'd finished the O2 saga. 'Any luck tracking down your missing girl?'

Styles shook his head. 'Nope. No joy yet. We went to see her folks today. Well, her stepfolks, anyway. They're an odd couple. Money to burn. Enough so that they make you feel like you should be grateful they're even bothering to speak to you. Probably wallpaper their bedroom with spare fifty-pound notes. I'd love to be a fly on the wall, mind. She's scared stiff of him. Clammed up when he came home.'

'What did they say, then?'

'Not a lot. Haven't seen her for over thirty years. They don't seem too bothered about that, though.'

'What does Jake have to say about it?' she asked, sitting back as the waiter appeared at her shoulder, producing matching plates of spaghetti carbonara.

'*Godere!* Enjoy!'

They both smiled their thanks, and Emma took a mouthful as Styles spoke. 'He's pretty sure the wife had more to say before her husband turned up.'

'How's he doing?' she asked, face softening into a concerned frown.

'Same old Porter. Intense as ever. Wanted to charge after a suspect today and lost his rag a bit when he got reined back in.' He twirled a bird's nest of spaghetti around his fork and paused with it in mid-air. 'On a positive note, he had Simmons from the drugs squad batting her eyelashes at him again today.'

'Oh, Nick, just leave him be. He'll be ready when he's ready.'

Styles grinned. 'I know, I know. But a small nudge never hurt anyone.'

'Unless they're stood at the edge of a cliff,' said Emma.

Styles held a hand up. 'Whoa, whoa, whoa. I do the jokes in this relationship. Don't mix up our roles. You're the pretty one, and I'm the funny one.'

She fluttered her eyelashes at him, giving an exaggerated pout. He smiled again as they each loaded up a forkful of pasta, coated in creamy carbonara sauce. He knew she was right. Porter would find his own way back to normality, or something resembling it, when he was good and ready. Today's flare-up of temper wasn't the first time Styles had seen his partner let a case get to him more than it should. He wondered if it was the Lockes' apparent lack of concern for Natasha that had set him on edge. It could just as easily be the thought of a young woman's murder going unsolved. Just like Holly's had.

He had tried to get Porter to talk about it in the past, but the shutters came down, and his partner either clammed up or changed the subject. Maybe it was worth asking if he'd given any more thought to talking to one of the psychologists they had access to on the force. No, he should probably just do as Emma suggested and leave it for now. He looked across the table at her, feeling relief that he didn't have to cope with what Porter had gone through. Was going through. He prayed he'd never have to find out for himself.

CHAPTER SEVEN

Porter's parents had lived in the same four-bed detached house in Pinner since before he was born. The sort of neighbourhood where hedges were trimmed to within an inch of their life on a weekly basis, and lawns looked like they'd been clipped with scissors and edged with a ruler. His mum was standing on the doorstep as he arrived, waving as the reverse lights on his sister's pale blue Citroën people carrier lit up. *Shit!* With all that had happened earlier, he had forgotten that he'd promised to try and make it an hour earlier to see her and the kids. He flashed his lights as he pulled up alongside her in the driveway, winding down his window as he came level.

'Hey, sis,' he said, pulling what he hoped was a sufficiently sheepish grin.

'Gotta go, Jake.' She shrugged. 'These two need feeding.' She jerked her head towards the back seat. He climbed out and saw two pairs of excited eyes peering from the passenger side window, small hands rapping out an excited beat.

'Hey, trouble one and trouble two,' said Porter, tapping the window with his knuckles, making them flinch backwards. 'Sorry, Kat. Got stuck with—'

'A work thing,' she finished for him. 'I know, I know. It's fine,' she said with a roll of the eyes. She stabbed a finger out the window at him, her tone and eyes warning in equal measure. 'But don't you dare forget about tomorrow.'

'Tomorrow? What's happening tomorrow?' he said, feigning ignorance. She narrowed her eyes, and tried to swat him with the back of her hand, but he stepped back. 'Joking. Of course I won't forget,' he said, making a mental note to get cards and presents for the twins on his way home tonight in case he forgot between now and their party.

Truth be told, he'd rather be forced to spend an hour naked in Trafalgar Square while tourists snapped his picture than sit through an hour-long party at the leisure centre. Sixty minutes of exquisite torturous small talk with the parents of the other kids, dodging the plastic balls hurled like missiles by five-year-old hooligans. Plan B was to turn up at Kat's house in the morning and wish Tom and James happy birthday then, instead, and fall back on the clichéd excuse of work to cry off for the afternoon.

'I'll drop you a text in the morning to remind you just in case,' she said as she started to reverse.

The twins waved frantically at him, and he stood waving back at them until Kat finished backing all the way down the drive and disappeared behind the hedge. He wandered over to where his mum stood, arms folded. She and Kat were practically carbon copies of one another, separated by thirty years or so. The same high cheekbones and practically pointy nose. Thirty years. It struck him as he approached her that his mum was around the same age as Natasha would be now. He gave a slight shudder as he leant in to hug her.

'Ooh, someone walk over your grave?' she asked him.

'Something like that. You alright, Mum? Sorry I'm a bit late.'

'Well, you were born late, so I suppose I should be used to it by now.'

He smiled, just like the first hundred times she'd cracked the joke, and followed her into the hallway, lined with a *This Is Your Life* array of photos. Everything from him in just a nappy, sat on the same doorstep he had just crossed over, to him in full uniform, fresh onto the force. He lingered for a fraction of a second as he passed his own wedding photo, and took off his jacket, hooking it over the newel post at the bottom of the staircase. The colour on the walls had changed a few times since he was a kid, but the smell of constant cooking was a given. Harriet Porter always had something on the go: bread in the oven, boiling fruit to make jam. Today smelt suspiciously of cauliflower, and Porter opted to breathe through his mouth.

'What you got on the boil, Mum?'

'Cauliflower soup. There's plenty if you're hungry?'

'I ate at the office, thanks.' He felt bad for lying, but he'd have felt worse with a belly full of pureed cauliflower.

'The twins were disappointed not to see you.'

Reading between the lines, she was the one disappointed that he hadn't been there to spend any time with them. He shrugged apologetically, flicking the switch on the kettle.

'You know how work can be, Mum. I'll definitely be there for the party. Cuppa?'

'You know they worship you, what with you being the exciting policeman uncle. It wouldn't kill you to spend a bit more time with them. And with your sister,' she added.

She was right, of course. It wouldn't kill him. It wasn't easy, either. Not like it used to be. Not since Holly. They had been trying to start a family when she died. Only for three months, but trying all the same. She wanted two, a boy and a girl. Porter would have settled for whatever they were given.

He and Kat had grown up close, but not in-each-other's-pockets close. She had stood by him at the funeral. Alternated with Mum to have him round for dinner so he wasn't alone with his thoughts every night. How could he tell her that seeing her and his brother-in-law, Tony, playing happy families with Tom and James sometimes gave him a hollow queasy feeling like someone had scooped out his insides, shaken them like a martini and poured them back in? As much as he loved them all, they were a flash-forward to what he and Holly could have been. Should have been. Kat would tell him not to be so stupid. And she'd mean it, too. That wouldn't make it any less of a painful reminder.

'I know, Mum. I know. Dad round?' he asked, changing the subject.

She shook her head. 'He's popped out to get a new lawnmower. Shouldn't be long, though, if you're not in a hurry to get anywhere.'

'I'm done for the day,' he said, plucking two cups from the cupboard, knowing that he was far from finished. He wouldn't be heading back to the station, but the questions he still had after the visit to the Locke house were like ticks under his skin. If he could manage more than the five or six hours' sleep he'd been getting by on, a clearer head might help make sense of what he'd learnt today, and what he still needed to find out. He felt tired, and not just from chasing a good night's sleep. The effort of trying to be a good copper as well as a good son, brother, uncle, felt like it demanded more than he had in him to give on days like today. He owed it to them to try. All of them. Natasha Barclay was on that list now as well. Each needing him to be something different for them.

It was the ones missing from that list that weighed the heaviest. Husband. Father. Deep breath. Push it all inside. He'd deal with it later when he went home after Anderson's leaving drinks. Alone.

Porter stared at his reflection in the bathroom mirror. Holly used to tell him he had 'rugged good looks'. He knew she meant it as a compliment, but he always equated the words with the notion of something worn or weather-beaten. There were still very few lines on his face, but he was sure that most of them had appeared in the last eighteen months. He flicked the stray strand of hair that had crept towards his eyebrow back into place. A hasty shave had left matching blooms of red either side of his chin. He licked the tip of his finger and rubbed them away, but they were back within seconds. Better to let them clot and he would sort them out in the gents' toilet when he arrived.

It had been a long few days, and the couch plus TV combo had whispered sweet nothings in his ear while he ate a hurried dinner from a tray on his lap, but he had given his word that he would be there tonight. He opted for a plain black V-neck sweater, mainly because he wouldn't have to iron it. His mum used to iron his dad's socks, never mind the rest of the wardrobe. He was more of a 'hang it up till you need it' kind of guy. The faint creasing on every shirt in sight made him think of Holly. That was one habit that she had tried and failed to break him out of.

He glanced over to his bedside table, eyes lingering on the picture from their wedding day. Facing each other, her with a hint of a smile, looking up into his eyes, both oblivious of the camera pointed at them. He'd come close to putting it in the drawer a few times. Looking at it brought back the sights and sounds of the day, bittersweet pleasure and pain in varying degrees.

He heard a low throaty rumbling, and looked down to see Demetrious the cat weaving in and out of his legs.

'Be with you in two seconds, buddy.'

He slid his phone into one pocket and his wallet into the other. Demetrious raised his purring another notch on the Richter scale. Even the bloody cat made him think of her. Holly had rescued him from the local shelter, claiming she needed company when he was working long shifts. He never did learn how to say no to her.

'OK, OK, I get the hint. Let's go.'

He headed into the kitchen, the cat keeping within a few paces, herding him in the right direction. He opened the cupboard door and looked blankly at the meagre array of tins and packets.

Shit, the shopping! Bugger!

He had forgotten to swing by Tesco on the way home. That meant there was no milk for cereal or tea in the morning, either. He spotted his contingency plan and grabbed a tin of sardines in brine, drained them in the sink and dumped them into the blue plastic bowl on the floor.

Demetrious gave one suspicious sniff, then forgot all about Porter and only had eyes for dinner. Porter topped up the neighbouring bowl with water from the tap, and left Demetrious to it. He left the small lamp on by the side of the sofa and headed out, hoping it would not be too late a night.

The hooded glow of the desk lamp made shadow puppets of James Bolton's hands against the far wall as he folded his arms, staring at the back of Alexander Locke's chair. His boss hadn't spoken since acknowledging the knock on the door, but the rich hint of cigar smoke he wore like aftershave confirmed he was there.

'Well, James,' said Locke, breaking the silence as he spun his chair round. 'Imagine my surprise to find two police officers in my house when I got home today.'

Bolton stared impassively, not sure if this was a cue for him to ask a question. He opted to stay silent, and Locke continued after a brief pause.

'You know how much I hate surprises.' Locke gave a slight shrug, leaning forward to plant his elbows on the desk. 'Especially ones that were meant to have been dealt with. Years ago.' His voice rarely rose above a conversational tone, but Bolton had known him long enough to sense the edge to his words. He had long since lost count of the situations he had dealt with for Locke over the years and was none the wiser.

'Natasha Barclay?' said Locke, settling back into his chair with a creak that could as easily have been his joints as the leather of the seat.

Bolton paused, only for a second, and nodded. Now he understood the undertone of displeasure. 'What about her?'

'It seems she didn't vanish as completely as we thought, or as you told me she had. The police found her, well, a part of her: her hand. It was in the freezer at her old flat. Mind telling me how it got there?'

Bolton didn't know for sure but he could make an educated guess. 'Olly?'

'Are you asking or telling?' said Locke.

'A bit of both, I suppose.' Bolton shrugged. 'Don't know for sure but that was more his style than mine. We sent the finger to her dad like you said, made him realise how serious the situation was. My guess is Olly kept the hand in case Barclay needed telling twice.'

'How convenient for you he's not around to dispute that.'

'Be easier if he was,' said Bolton. Truth be told his world was a better place without Davies in it. Questions were asked when Davies was found slumped in his car, but nobody had dared ask Bolton to his face.

'Somehow I doubt you actually mean that,' said Locke.

'What did they say?' asked Bolton.

Locke gave him a terse summary of the visit from Porter and Styles. Bolton took the stubby remains of a packet of chewing gum from his pocket and popped two pieces in his mouth, crunching through the eggshell exterior as he listened. When Locke finished, he fixed Bolton with a stare that could have wilted flowers but the big man met it without blinking. Locke's patience lasted three whole seconds.

'Well?'

'Well, I don't think that we have anything to worry about. As far as we knew she was long gone then and she still is now. If I were you I'd just tell them that you don't know where she is—'

'Which I don't,' Locke interrupted.

'There you go, then, and there's no one around to contradict you.'

Locke scowled but gave a slight nod of agreement. 'I want you to speak to Finch. He was close to Oliver. See if he remembers anything.'

Bolton grunted in acknowledgement. He'd do it – he always did what Locke asked – but was fairly sure it was a waste of time. Finch had crawled inside a bottle of single malt when his wife left him a decade ago, and had rarely come up for air since. Bolton was more than capable of filling in the blanks for Locke himself, but he wasn't likely to do that any time soon. That would mean admitting he'd had ears on Davies for years, bugging his house, keeping one step ahead of him in the battle to be Locke's right-hand man. He'd heard a great many things of interest from titbits of gossip about business Davies had on the side. He had been quite the chatterbox in the safety of his own home. He'd chattered still more that night when Bolton's shadow had risen up from its hiding place in the back seat of his car. Chatty right up to the end, bargaining for his life, right up to the point when the loop of wire arced over his head, slicing through his neck like cheese wire through a wheel of cheddar, not long after the mess with Natasha.

It had been part business, part personal. Bolton hadn't wanted any competition for the number two slot. Not that Davies had been real competition, but Bolton wasn't one to leave things to chance, and he genuinely didn't like the man. This situation with Natasha Barclay was as if Davies was getting his own back. Stirring trouble from beyond the grave. He genuinely had no idea that Davies had stashed her hand in the freezer. As it turned out, a single finger was all they had needed to send her father a message. Stupid bastard should have gotten rid of the rest straight afterwards. The irony was not lost on him that, in killing his rival, he'd caused the hand to stay there all these years instead of being disposed of.

He grunted a goodbye to Locke and headed out to find Finch. He'd sort it. God knows he'd sorted worse than this. If he was honest with himself, and he had to do it over, he'd still get rid of Olly Davies, and to hell with the consequences.

* * *

By the time Porter arrived, the night was in full swing. Rosie's was an Irish bar halfway between the station and Hyde Park, and a popular destination for a quick drink or five after a long shift. He spotted Styles, bottle of Bud in hand, by the bar, talking to two detectives he recognised from the drugs squad, Anderson and Whittaker. A quick scan showed at least a dozen more faces he knew, as well as a few that he was just on nodding terms with. Porter made a beeline for Styles, who had just delivered a punchline by the sounds of the laughter coming from his audience of two.

'Better late than never, boss,' he said, slapping a greeting on Porter's shoulder and holding up four fingers to the passing barmaid to refresh their bottles.

Porter greeted Anderson and Whittaker with a quick handshake, and took a long, slow swallow from the Bud that Styles passed over his shoulder.

'Thought you were a no-show for a while there, Porter,' said Anderson. He was a big man, two hundred and fifty pounds at least, his brown dome of a head completely bald.

'Nah, had to turn up to check the rumours were true and you are actually retiring this time.'

When Anderson laughed, his whole body shook, especially the shoulders. It reminded Porter of the way a jack-in-the-box bounced up and down. Anderson's first attempt at retirement had been the subject of banter in the office for three years now. He had been all set to pull the plug, when his wife upped and left him, taking half of his retirement fund with her. It seemed that the prospect of spending every day with him hadn't been that appealing after all, and he hastily withdrew his paperwork. A mild heart attack six months ago had changed that, though, and this time he promised there would be no false starts.

'Scout's honour.' Anderson held his index and middle fingers up to his head in mock salute. 'This time I'll go and stay gone.'

They toasted his impending departure, bottle necks clinking together like crossed swords, and listened to him talk about the golf courses he would tour round when he had no clock to watch.

By the time he had finished his fourth beer, Porter felt his earlier reservations about coming out start to melt away. Anderson was dragged away by a couple of the younger detectives to drink a shot of tequila with them at the other end of the bar. Whittaker went with him for moral support, saying that shots were a young man's game and he had better chaperone his partner, whose words had started to develop just the slightest of slur around the edges. Porter felt the warm glow seep through his body as he drank, loosening the grip of the long day at work, one finger and one bottle at a time.

He and Styles rehashed the visit to the Lockes, and made plans for how they would tackle the next week's tasks. Porter caught movement over Styles's right shoulder and looked over in time to see Simmons flash a smile and a quick wave his way. He returned it with a tight-lipped smile of his own, and Styles whipped his head round to look behind.

'I can have a word with the DJ if you like, to make sure he remembers to play a slow number at the end of the night?'

'I've told you before,' said Porter, using the end of his bottle as a pointer towards Styles, 'relationships at work are more hassle than they're worth.'

Styles shook his head and opened his mouth to speak, but Porter continued.

'I mean, you're my partner, for Christ's sake. It would never work between us. Let's just pretend this little proposition didn't happen, and we'll say no more about it – besides, you can't dance for shit.'

He had timed it perfectly and Styles had to clamp his lips together as he laughed to avoid the mouthful of beer he had just taken shooting back out.

'Well played, boss,' he said, inclining his head in acknowledgement of a line well delivered. 'Can I ask you a serious question, though?' His face told Porter he meant it, and it wasn't a set-up for a punchline. 'All joking aside, she's a lovely girl, and you two don't work together any more, strictly speaking. Are you not tempted, not even one little bit?'

Porter shot another glance towards Simmons. She had turned to the side now and was listening to whatever anecdote the small wiry detective whose name escaped Porter was telling. He tried to find the words that wouldn't make him sound like a coward; instead, he just shook his head.

'I'm out of practice, she's too young, I'm too old, work gets in the way – take your pick.'

'To address your points one at a time,' he began, counting out on his fingers. 'Bollocks, bollocks, bollocks and bollocks.'

That got a smile from Porter, and he took a swig from his bottle. 'Maybe.' He shrugged. 'I dunno, mate, the idea of going on a date with someone, it feels weird. Feels like I'd be cheating on her. I know that sounds ridiculous, but that's how it feels in here.' He tapped his palm against his heart.

'You know she'd slap you for saying something that daft, don't you?'

Porter smiled wider this time, a real smile, one that showed teeth. 'She probably would,' he conceded. 'She probably would.'

'No probably about it,' agreed Styles.

'I'm sure I'll get there eventually,' said Porter. 'Just takes time.'

He glanced over again. Simmons was gone.

The next bar they went to was even busier. The Duke of Kendal sat on the corner of Connaught Street, and put Porter in mind of a giant slice of architectural pie, the way its angled front pointed into the street. It had just reopened under new ownership, and the flyers promising a free shot for every customer bearing them had done their job admirably by the size of the queue. Porter stood nursing his seventh bottle of Bud – or was it his eighth? He would have to grab a burger or pizza on the way home to kick-start the recovery process. He felt a tap on his shoulder and looked round to see Simmons slotting in beside him at the bar.

'Evening, guv,' she said with a wry smile.

'Evening, Simmons,' he said, raising his bottle by way of greeting.

She swatted his words away with one hand. 'Just Eve will do, or Evie, if you like, seeing as we're off the clock.' She had a glow to her cheeks that could have been make-up, or it could have been the drink; he couldn't decide.

He smiled. 'Alright, Eve, Evie.' Three seconds that could have been three minutes ticked by as she looked up at him. 'Good turnout for Anderson.'

Way to go, smooth talker, breaking that awkward silence. Might as well ask her if she comes here often.

'Mm, like this lot needs an excuse for a piss-up.'

'I'll drink to that,' he said, taking another swig from his bottle.

'So . . .' She drew out the last vowel into at least three syllables. 'You around Monday? We could grab a coffee and you can tell me how it went with the Lockes?'

'What about now? I can—'

'Nope. No shop talk on a night out,' she said with a shake of her head.

'OK, OK. It can wait till tomorrow,' he said, holding his hands up in surrender.

She clocked the suds at the bottom of his bottle held against his chest.

'Buy you another?'

Had she moved in closer, or had he just imagined it?

He looked down at the bottle. 'Um, no, thanks. I'm good. I should probably make a move, early start in the morning and all that.'

She lowered her eyes, and the space between them returned.

'Yeah, good idea. Probably won't be too long myself.'

She made her excuses and headed off to the toilet, with a promise to find him tomorrow at work. Porter drained the last from his bottle and made his way over to Styles.

'I'm gonna hit the hay. Catch you Monday.'

'Can't tempt you with one for the road?'

Porter shook his head. 'Nah, I'll just cramp your style. You kids have fun.'

'No worries, boss. I'll grab the cuppas on the way in and see you there.'

Porter spent the next few minutes working his way around the splintered group until he had said all his goodbyes, including a promise to Anderson to meet him for a final coffee before his last day. He headed outside, trading the buzz in his ears from the bass of the speakers for the drumbeat of rain on the road outside. He paused under the awning and looked off to the right just in time to see the sole taxi pull away from the rank. He sighed and pulled his phone from his pocket, but hesitated as he heard the voice.

'Didn't have you pegged for a smoker, guv.'

Porter spun round to see who had spoken, and saw Simmons leaning against a doorway two doors down from the bar, cigarette in hand.

'They wouldn't let me smoke by the entrance,' she said, pointing at the bouncers outside the doorway. 'Come on, get under here before you get soaked.'

He looked up at the sky, realising that he had wandered beyond the protection of the black canvas. He felt the raindrops, fat and heavy on his head and sweater. Half a dozen quick strides and he was in the doorway with her.

'Want one?' She held an open pack of Marlboro Lights towards him.

He waved them away. 'No thanks, don't smoke. I was just going to call a cab when you shouted.'

'It was hardly a shout.' She laughed. 'You're not that easily startled, are you? Although, you did look a bit lost for words when I suggested that last drink.'

He was suddenly aware of how small the doorway was, and how little space separated them. He could smell her perfume, mixed with a waft of smoke that drifted up from the cigarette she held by her side.

'I know we're doing coffee on Monday morning,' she said, moving an inch closer, body language made bold by drink, only an inch, and she filled his field of vision now. 'But the offer of a drink still stands, you know, I mean another time . . .'

Before he could answer, she closed the remaining gap and kissed him hard, her forward momentum bringing their lips crashing together, and for the briefest of moments he felt her tongue tickle against the edges of his mouth, a cocktail of red wine and tobacco. Time froze for the briefest of seconds, the longest of moments, before he placed his hands on her shoulders and gently moved her back.

'Evie, I . . .' He stopped. Couldn't find the right words. Confusion. It had felt good. 'I don't know—'

She placed a finger on his lips to silence him. 'S'OK. My bad. I just thought maybe . . .'

She drew back, six inches first, then six more. The inches seemed like miles now. She smiled like an embarrassed teenager and turned her face to the side, hiding behind a cloak of hair.

'Sorry. Little too much to drink. Can we . . . ?'

'It's fine,' he said. 'Honestly, I'm flattered, it's just that . . .'

How do you explain to someone that you're still in love with a ghost, or that you don't want to cheat on a memory? He was trying to work out how to explain it, or even whether it was worth explaining at all, when he was saved by the sweeping headlights as a taxi pulled into the rank. He was surprised how quick they had gotten here, until he remembered that he'd never actually made the call.

'Ladies first,' he said.

'Nah, you take it. I'm going to head back in for one more,' she said, dropping her cigarette to the floor and grinding it with her heel. 'Unless you're going to take me in for littering?'

They both smiled, out of relief at the easing of tension as much as anything.

'We still on for a catch-up on Monday morning, then?' she said.

Porter nodded, and made a dash for the cab. He didn't look back at the doorway to the bar until he was safely in the car, but she had already retreated back inside. The only shapes he could make out beyond the rain-smeared window were both over six feet tall, the dark, unmoving golems that were the bouncers.

He gave the driver his address and slumped back into the seat, running his fingers through his damp hair. He exhaled loudly.

Jesus, didn't see that one coming.

'Rough night?' asked the cabbie, a hint of Jamaican lilt in his voice.

Porter nodded. 'You could say that.'

'Woman trouble?'

'Kind of,' he said; then added, 'It's complicated.'

Part of him dreaded any uncomfortable tension he knew there must surely be when he saw her on Monday, but who was he kidding? There were far worse ways to end an evening. It might well have complicated things, but those complications were his to wrestle with. His issues, not hers.

CHAPTER EIGHT

Porter had sat across from murderers, thieves and gangsters and not batted an eyelid. He felt out of sorts and out of place today, though, as he watched the dozen or so turf wars amongst the five- and six-year-olds for supremacy of the soft-play kingdom. He guessed at best that he'd had four hours' sleep last night, and his hangover was lurking dangerously close to the surface. Kat looked down at him from behind a curtain of rope netting on the second storey of the soft-play. She waved him up to join them, but he shook his head, pointing to his coffee – a poor excuse, but it was all he had to cling to.

Harriet came back from the toilet just as he was making his excuses, and tutted loudly as she sat down.

'Go on,' she urged. 'Get yourself in there for a few minutes at least. It'll do you good.'

'To get beaten up by a gang of kids faster than I could shout "ASBO"? That'd do wonders for my self-esteem.'

'Do you have to make a joke of everything?' She shook her head, but smiled all the same. 'I want you to promise me you'll play with the boys at least once before you leave.'

Porter held up two begrudging fingers to his temple. 'Scout's honour.'

Kat bounced up and out from a sea of balls she had landed in and hopped over to his table. She slung herself into the chair next to him, breathing loud, but not hard.

'You're up, bro. I need to tag out for a spell,' she said, slapping his thigh. 'Two minutes. I promise.'

'Clock's ticking,' she said, tapping an imaginary watch. 'What's new with you, then?' She peeled away the stray bits of fringe that were matted to her sweaty forehead.

'Not much,' he said. 'Busy at work, still. You know how it is.'

'I know you need to get out more. Let your hair down now and again.' She leant forward, ruffling his mop of hair like she would a toddler.

'I do get out,' he said, getting defensive. 'I went to a leaving do just last night if you must know.'

Kat rolled her eyes. 'Doesn't count if it was just the work crowd. Unless . . .' – she looked sideways at him through slitted eyes – 'there are any hot young ladies on the force?'

Porter blushed, looking away, and Kat stabbed a finger towards him. 'Aha! I knew it. I need a name, age, rank and star sign.'

'His name's Brian, aged forty-two from Watford, and he's a Virgo,' Porter shot back.

Kat screwed up her face, sticking her tongue out. 'Well, if you won't help yourself, let me help you. Girl sitting at your nine o'clock is single. Sarah, aged twenty-nine. One daughter, Sophie, a little sweetie. She's never been married, and . . .'

'Woah, easy tiger,' said Porter, both hands up in surrender. 'I'm all good, sis, honestly.'

'What about the brunette in the ball pool?' she said, ignoring him. 'Anna, thirty-one, no kids, she's just here as a semi-responsible adult with her nephew?'

'Jesus, you don't give up, do you?'

She shook her head proudly. 'I'm like a dating version of the Terminator.' She held out a hand to him, putting on her best Arnie accent. 'Come with me if you want to love.'

That one really tickled him, and he came dangerously close to spitting out a mouthful of coffee. He had just managed to rest his cup back on the table when he heard the twins yelling his name. He turned towards the sound just in time for them to barrel into his legs.

'Unclejakeunclejakeunclejake!' Two excited voices blurring into one.

'Hey, you two. Having fun?'

'Will you come and play with us?' said Tom.

James butted in. 'We're playing king of the castle and Matthew's dad is helping him. You're bigger than his dad so we might win.' They both jumped up and down, slapping his legs like rhythmically challenged drummers.

'I'd love to stay and continue the chat, sis, but duty calls,' Porter said with a shrug.

'This isn't over,' she called after him.

He knew he'd taken the coward's way out. Knew he couldn't dodge the issue for ever. He waded carefully through the ball pool, convinced he'd step on a submerged child any moment, and up into the heart of the soft-play. A small boy wearing a fierce expression began launching plastic balls at him from the top of a plastic slide. Matthew, he presumed. Tom and James charged fearlessly past him and began clambering upwards. Porter followed them, his promised two minutes turning into ten, then fifteen. The worries of the previous week were a long way away, at least for now. When he finally clambered back out, he realised that he was actually enjoying himself, smiling. That didn't happen often enough these days.

Styles swung by Saint Agnes' Catholic School first thing Monday morning on his way to the station. The buildings were shrouded behind twin barriers of trees and grey railings. Groups of chattering children swarmed through the gates, leaving parents waving at their backs. Styles identified himself to a teaching assistant shepherding the kids through the front door, and was pointed inside to the front desk. The receptionist Styles spoke to answered in a lethargic tone, but that quickly changed to flustered when he explained he was a policeman. The poor woman stammered an apology and went off to find Mr Palmer, the teacher who headed up the alumni association responsible for coordinating events for former pupils.

Mr Palmer peered at Styles through glasses as thick as a telescope lens when he came through the door two minutes later, nervy as if the receptionist was playing a prank on him by saying a police officer was waiting for him. He listened without interruption while Styles explained why he was there, and promised to email across a list of pupils from Natasha's year, along with the contact details they had for them.

Styles thanked him and headed off to meet Porter at the station. When he arrived, he saw Porter slouched in his chair, arms crossed, staring out of the window as he slowly dragged a thumb back and forth across his stubble.

'Simmons in yet?' asked Styles, reaching for his cup.

'No, she's running late, but I spoke to Gibson. Sounds like there's going to be some action tonight. Seems our inside guy is due to pick up a fresh consignment later this evening. He's going in wired up, but there's going to be a team outside.'

He had seen his boss talking to Simmons on Friday night through a window blurred by rain. He saw how awkward Porter looked at the mention of her name now, and decided to skip any cheeky comments about the two of them. Porter could handle almost anything you threw at him, but this was his weak spot, and Styles knew to leave well alone. It didn't affect his work, at least not that Styles could tell, but he hoped for Porter's sake he managed to get his head around the idea that life without Holly was possible eventually.

'I thought no one was going to make a move until we had something on Bolton and Locke?'

Porter shook his head. 'They're going to be there just in case. Sometimes Bolton is around, sometimes he isn't, but if it's just Carter and Patchett, then it's look but don't touch. What about you? Any luck with the school?'

'Yeah, they're sending over what they have, so we can start calling around this morning.'

'Good stuff,' said Porter, taking a sip from his cup. 'I've had another idea as well.'

'Careful, that's your quota for the week used up in one go.'

'I'd throw a few more into the mix as well, but I know you struggle to keep count once we get past two,' said Porter, without missing a beat. 'So I was thinking, Nathan Barclay had no family apart from his daughter and ex-wife, nobody else to speak to about what kind of guy he was. He ran that company for a long time. I know he sold up over thirty years ago, but there's a chance that there could still be some people working there from back in his day.'

'Maybe,' said Styles thoughtfully. 'What's your plan?'

'I say we go to Atlas and tell them we're investigating the disappearance of the former owner's daughter, ask if she ever visited her old man at work – that kind of angle. In the meantime, we see what we can find out about the man himself. What was he like to work for? How did he react when he had to sell up? How well did he handle the pressure?' Porter counted the questions out on his fingers as he went.

'Sounds good to me. We might as well head over now. Even if the school sends through the info straight away, there's a good chance most people will be at work. It'll be easier to catch them when they're finished for the day.'

They both stood, and Styles grabbed the car keys from his desk. It would be a long shot sniffing around Atlas, but as long as they stuck to their story of investigating Natasha Barclay there should be no ripples to knock Simmons and Gibson off course with their case. Piecing together a profile of a man from more than three decades ago wouldn't be easy. Quite the opposite, but Nathan Barclay was the only one they had any reason to suspect, even if it was based solely for now on the ambiguity of his last words.

Styles couldn't imagine what it must have felt like for Barclay's world to come crumbling down around him; first his marriage, then his business, to the point where he felt like he only had one way out. He had known people crack under less pressure, had seen it first-hand on the cases he had worked. Had that pressure built up to the point where its release was so forceful, so unbridled, that he had lashed out and hurt his own flesh and blood? Styles felt a sense of sadness wash over him at the thought. Either way, he doubted that justice could truly be meted out. If Barclay was responsible, he would never see the inside of a courtroom, never have to live with the hurt he had caused. If he was innocent, then Natasha's disappearance was just another layer of tragedy heaped upon a family that had already suffered through more than most, and his investigation would be right back where it began.

He could tell from the way Porter was acting that the case had gotten under his skin. The notion that someone could have met an untimely end and not had anyone make a serious effort for over thirty years to find them clearly did not sit well with him. Nobody had ever been convicted of Holly's death, either, and maybe Porter saw this one going the same way. The ease with which the Lockes had accepted Natasha's disappearance without question clearly bothered him, too, and made him even more determined that somebody should speak up for Natasha. Somebody needed to be held accountable for whatever had happened to her, and if her own family wouldn't do it then it might as well be them.

It was almost noon by the time they pulled up outside the main gates to the warehouse, and the intensity of the sun in the cloudless February sky offered false hope of warmth as Porter and Styles both shielded their eyes from its glare. The dashboard display showed it was a brisk four degrees outside the comfort of their car, although the stiff breeze would cut that in half.

Atlas had a number of premises dotted along the river, so they had opted for the one listed as the company's headquarters. The warehouse reminded Porter of an airplane hangar. Its appearance bordered on military; the drab olive green of the walls reminiscent of a hundred other buildings from his army days. The only break in the monochrome exterior was the Atlas logo stamped on each side. It stayed true to the Titan from Greek mythology whose name they had taken, the sculpted ivory-coloured form of a man, crouching and straining under the weight of the planet that sat atop his heavily muscled neck and shoulders. Porter couldn't help but notice the historical inaccuracy. Atlas holding up the earth was a common misconception. His grandfather used to read him stories when he was younger, tales of heroes, of Odysseus and Agamemnon. Achilles and Hector. He remembered thinking Atlas had been given a bum deal, condemned for ever to bear the weight of the heavens on his shoulders, not the earth upon which he stood, as many thought. Porter fancied he'd gotten a better bargain nowadays, now that the earth was home to some seven billion people. He wouldn't want that weight on his shoulders.

They pulled up to the unmanned security barrier; Porter leant out of his window and pushed the button to speak. He waited patiently until a woman's tinny voice squawked out from the intercom, shattering the silence. They identified themselves and the voice directed them to the visitor's car park by the left-hand corner of the building, telling them they'd see a sign pointing the way to reception there. They followed the directions and found themselves inside a room that was the very definition of minimalistic. There was a chest-high counter running three quarters of the way across, punctuated by a hinged hatch to allow access, with two moulded plastic orange chairs set against the wall.

On the other side of the counter stood a woman that Porter pegged for mid-fifties. She reminded Porter of one of his former schoolteachers in her crisp, white blouse and sensible navy blue skirt, the way she peered out at him over the thick black frames of her glasses with a look of permanent disapproval. When she opened her mouth to speak, he half expected the same static and crackle in her voice that had filtered through the intercom.

'Good morning, Officers,' she said in a disappointingly normal tone. 'I've called Mr Awad; he's the site manager. He should be here any minute. Please, have a seat.'

She smiled and gestured to the chairs that were as hard and unyielding as they looked. Thankfully, Mr Awad arrived less than a minute later, rescuing their backsides from any prolonged discomfort. If Simmons was right about Locke, men like him operated on a cocktail of reputation, respect and a healthy dose of fear. If he was even half the character he was being painted as, Porter imagined at least some of the men who worked for him would have heard a rumour here and a whisper there. He wondered whether Awad was one such man as he came around the counter towards them.

Awad was a short, balding man, around the same age as the receptionist. He wore a pair of faded green overalls, suggesting he was a hands-on manager, but a white shirt and tie peeked out over the top of the zipper pulled up to his chest. He subconsciously wiped both hands on the front of the overalls, and extended one of them towards Styles, who happened to be standing closest.

'Rafi Awad,' he announced, blinking quickly through his small wire-framed glasses. 'I'm the site manager.' His eyes contradicted the confidence in his tone as they flicked nervously from Styles to Porter, over and over again. 'Mary tells me you gents are with the police?'

'That's right, Mr Awad,' said Porter, taking the lead. 'We're investigating a missing person's case. The young lady in question was the daughter of the former owner, Nathan Barclay.'

'Oh, that was well before my time,' said Awad, a little too quickly for Porter's liking. They hadn't even hinted at the direction of their questioning and already he was trying to distance himself from whatever they were looking into.

'But you are aware that Mr Barclay used to own Atlas?'

'Yes, but that was over thirty years ago. I don't see what—'

'When did you start working here?' asked Styles, cutting across him.

'Let me see, I started off as a forklift driver back in '89, so been here over twenty-five years now,' he said with a hint of pride.

'Is there anybody here who would have been employed when Mr Barclay was in charge?' asked Porter.

'There's a few old-timers, but what has that got to do with—'

Porter held up a hand to silence him. 'As I explained at the start, Mr Awad, his daughter, Natasha Barclay, is missing. Obviously, Mr Barclay hasn't been around for some time to speak to, so we need to look at anywhere she might have frequented, her father's place of work being one.'

'Well, there are two that spring to mind,' said Awad, rubbing his chin thoughtfully, 'There's Willy Thompson. He drives one of our forklifts. You might try Alec Brookes as well. I'm pretty sure he was around then, although it's that long ago I really doubt . . .'

'Thanks, Mr Awad, if you point us in their direction that'd be great,' said Porter tersely. He was getting tired of Awad ending every response with a dismissive remark of his own.

Awad checked the shift rota and quickly determined that Willy Thompson was back there in his forklift somewhere, and wouldn't clock out for another three hours. Alec Brookes was on a day off, and Styles jotted down contact details for him so they could call by on the way back to the station rather than make another trip back to the warehouse.

Thompson was a short, barrel-chested man with a ruddy complexion. Both forearms had an eclectic mix of faded tattoos that continued upwards, part of the collage disappearing up into his sleeves. His gut bore witness to a sedentary lifestyle, almost touching the steering wheel of the forklift as he shuffled out of his seat to meet them. He had worked for Atlas since 1980, and had seen Nathan Barclay around plenty, but never exchanged more than a few words with him.

Styles showed him a copy of a picture they had taken from Natasha's flat. She wore a knee-length cotton dress, white with black polka dots, which threatened to billow up around her Monroe-style. One hand pinning the hem to her thigh, the other holding onto a wide brimmed straw hat. Happier times.

Thompson shook his head. Styles segued into questions about the debts and the takeover. Had Barclay spent more time than usual at work? Did he seem stressed by what was happening to the business? Thompson answered in short clipped sentences with vague recollections of nothing being out of the ordinary. When Porter and Styles climbed back into their car five minutes later, they didn't feel they knew Nathan Barclay any better. He was a good man to work for by all accounts, but they had gleaned nothing significant about the man himself.

'You think he was holding back?' asked Styles.

'Hard to say,' said Porter. 'He looked nervous, but it is a long time ago, and people do feel naturally uncomfortable when we land out of the blue. Fancy a trip to see the other guy, Brookes, before we head back?'

'Might as well,' said Styles. 'Can we grab a coffee on the way there, though? Caffeine withdrawal is kicking in.' He held up a hand, exaggerated forced tremors making it practically vibrate. They pulled away without giving the warehouse another glance.

A pair of seagulls swooped down into the almost empty car park, and began waging war over a half-eaten sandwich. The victor hopped closer to the warehouse with his prize, while the loser pecked at the crumbs left behind. The door opened so slowly that neither of them flinched, continuing to devour their respective spoils. Awad watched the sun glint off the rear windscreen as the two officers drove away. He lifted the mobile to his ear, feeling the familiar nervous fluttering in his stomach that he did every time he had called the number, and this time was no different.

Alec Brookes lived in a modest first-floor flat on Keyes Road in Dartford. There had been no answer at first and they were about to give up when he ambled up the stairs carrying a Tesco carrier bag, loaf of bread peeking out, half squashed. Porter ran over the same explanation for their enquiries as he had given at the warehouse, and Brookes grunted an invite for them to follow him inside. He offered to put the kettle on, but they both held up the Starbucks cups that had been hiding in plain sight by their sides.

'He was a good man,' said Brookes, settling into an old brown leather sofa, with a cup of tea so pale it could pass for milk. 'Always good to me.' He had a puffiness around his eyes, the whites tinged with the slightest blush of pink. Porter wondered if he had not long been out of bed, or if he'd hit the bottle hard the night before. He glanced around the living room; the plate speckled with toast crumbs, the newspaper from the previous weekend, the ashtray filled with butts smoked right down to the filter. Doubtful that there was a Mrs Brookes.

'What can you tell us about him, Mr Brookes?' asked Styles.

'He worked hard to build that business up after his dad died, I can tell you that. Even slept there a few nights when we had big shipments that needed to go out. He'd roll his sleeves up and sweat alongside the rest of us.' Brookes had that faraway look in his eye now, the one somebody gets when they're seeing past events as if they were present day.

'Did you ever meet Natasha?' asked Porter. 'Did she ever come to the warehouse?'

'Once.' He nodded. 'Couldn't tell you when, exactly, but there was once. I think she was fresh back from a trip somewhere and she came to surprise him. Lovely girl.' His voice trailed off and he sipped his tea to fill the silence.

'What about when he lost the business, Mr Brookes? How did he seem when that happened?' asked Porter.

'Lose it?' said Brookes with a sardonic chuckle. 'That's one way to put it.'

'How do you mean?' asked Styles.

Brookes sat back against the couch and looked down at the cup resting on his leg. 'Look, I need that job. I might not like the man, but he pays well, and . . . well, c'mon.' He pinched a fold of wool by the collar of his faded blue jumper, pulling it out slightly from his chest. 'I'm not exactly gonna find a job in an office wearing a suit any time soon, am I?'

'I take it by "the man" you mean the current owner, Mr Locke?'

'He didn't lose it. It was nicked from him at that price, however you dress it up. Thirty years Mr Locke has owned that place now,' said Brookes, the corners of his mouth turning down in distaste. 'Thirty years and he's barely even been to the site, let alone spared two words for anyone there.' He shook his head. 'Now, Mr Barclay, there was a proper gaffer.'

'Mr Brookes, anything you say to us is in confidence. We're not going to report back to anyone at Atlas, least of all Mr Locke. What can you tell us about when the business changed hands?'

Brookes blew on his tea, watching the surface vibrate and the ripples break against the side of the cup. The seconds stretched out. He sighed, the decision made.

'I know he was in bother, money-wise, you know? His dad had built that up from nothing. After he took over, we were busier than ever.' He smiled, remembering the good times. 'As much overtime as you could handle. My bookie saw most of that. Only ever saw Mr Locke there once before all that' – he gestured with his hand – 'stuff happened.' His face hardened at the mention of Locke.

'What happened when Mr Locke came by?' asked Porter.

'Wasn't just him.' Brookes shook his head. 'Him and his boys turned up. Little 'n' Large, we called 'em. Don't get me wrong, they never laid a finger on him. Didn't have to.'

'How do you mean?' asked Styles.

'They just stood and talked in his office. Whatever they said to him in there did the trick, though.'

'In what way?'

'Scared the shit out of him, it did. Didn't have to be a hotshot copper to work that one out. It was written all over his face. You ask me, he was persuaded to sell up.' He made quotation marks with his fingers at the mention of persuasion, the gesture echoing the sarcasm in his voice.

'When did that take place?' asked Styles.

'A week before he did himself in, maybe a day or two either way. Little 'n' Large came back one more time, a couple of days after, but Mr Locke wasn't with them that time.'

'Little and Large? You mentioned them before, who are they?'

'Mr Locke's boys, James Bolton and Oliver Davies. They'd popped by a few times before to see Mr Barclay. They start showing up, not long before all that shit kicked off with that Bembenek fella, as it happens. Just seems like they turned up and bad things started to happen.'

'What can you tell us about Mr Bembenek?'

Brookes shrugged. 'Just what they said in the papers. Never knew the fella myself.'

'What about Mr Locke's men you mentioned, Bolton and Davies?'

'Never had much to do with them myself, but you hear things.'

'Like what?' prompted Porter.

'Like they weren't the kind of lads you want to get on the wrong side of. Mr Bolton comes around from time to time. He's in charge of site security.'

'Do you know anyone who's gotten on their bad side?' asked Styles.

'Nah, like I say, I hear things, but it's all "a mate of mine knows a guy who" type thing. Bolton was meant to be handy with his fists back in the day. Probably still is now, for all I know.'

They carried on the verbal dance for a few more minutes, but Brookes had nothing more specific to tell them. They walked to the door, promising him that his name wouldn't be mentioned in any conversations they had with anybody at Atlas. They shook hands and stepped out across the threshold.

'I hope you find her,' said Brookes. 'Terrible thing, what happened to her dad. That's enough for any young girl to handle, let alone getting into any bother herself.'

Porter nodded. 'I hope so too, Mr Brookes. Thanks for your help.'

Alec Brookes retreated into his comfortable oasis of clutter. Porter and

Styles trotted back down the stairs in silence. Brookes hadn't given them anything solid, but a few of his comments had made Porter more than a little curious. Had Barclay gotten on the wrong side of Locke or his men, as Brookes had put it? Had he already been suicidal or was there something about the confrontation with Locke that had taken him to the edge and beyond? Most of all he longed to have been a fly on the wall over thirty years ago, and to know what had put the fear of God into Barclay that day. There were two men still alive who could answer that question, of course, but he didn't expect Locke or Bolton would give up the information any time soon.

CHAPTER NINE

By the time they got back to the station, Styles had an email from St Agnes' with an attachment that had contact details for the ten members of Natasha Barclay's class that were active in the alumni network. They split the list down the middle and started calling.

It was a little after three in the afternoon, and as expected they found themselves mainly talking to answerphones. They had agreed in advance on a suitably vague voicemail to leave, saying only that they needed to speak to the person in connection with a case that had a connection to St Agnes', and left their desk numbers for them to return the call.

They did manage one success each. Porter spoke to a Jonathan Stone, who was happy enough to answer his questions, and did remember Natasha, but said they had moved in different circles. He hadn't seen or spoken to her since they were eighteen, and had moved to Manchester after finishing university. He was no longer in touch with anyone else from school so Porter thanked him for his time and ended the call.

Styles had a little more luck. He managed to speak to a woman called Rebecca Arnold, who used to be in the school swimming team with Natasha. They hadn't been best friends but had been close enough to invite the other to birthdays and hang out after school on occasion. She was out of town, but gave Styles her train times for coming back if someone could meet her for a chat at the station.

'It's not much but it's better than nothing, I suppose,' said Porter when Styles was finished recounting the call. 'Coffee while we decide what's next?'

Porter went to get the drinks while Styles called home. He was coming back through the cafeteria door, when he almost collided with two people striding down the corridor. Coffee sloshed against plastic lids. He looked up and saw Simmons and Gibson, equally as startled by his sudden appearance.

'Shit, sorry, Evie.' He caught himself, and hoped Gibson didn't read anything into his use of her first name. 'Mike.' He nodded a greeting towards Gibson. 'Sorry, didn't see you there.'

'No worries,' said Gibson.

Porter turned to face Simmons. 'I came to see you this morning but you were still on your way in. Have you got a few minutes now?'

'We're just on our way to meet Owen Carter.' She saw his blank look and added, 'Our man in Atlas.'

'Ah, OK. I'll maybe catch you later, then.'

'I need to pay a visit before we go, so you two catch up and I'll see you down at the car,' said Gibson, gesturing towards the gents' toilet.

Simmons shrugged. 'OK, see you there.'

Gibson trotted away, leaving the two of them sharing the awkward silence. Simmons broke it first.

'We don't have to do the Locke catch-up now if you're busy,' she said, pointing at the two cups he held.

'These? No, no, these are just for me and Styles. I've got a few minutes now if you do? Here, have mine,' he said, offering her one of the cups. 'I can pop down and get another one later.'

'Thanks, but I'll take a rain check for now. Besides, Nick's a good guy but I wouldn't want to come between him and his caffeine.' There was that smile of hers again, framed by a dimple either side.

'OK, well, how about you give me a shout when you guys get back?'

'I'd better get going, but yeah, let's catch up later.'

'Yeah, of course.' He moved to the side to let her past. 'You can give me the rundown of how it goes out at Atlas as well.'

'It's a date,' she said, with a cheeky grin. 'Don't worry, guv, just a figure of speech.' She was past him and around the corner before he had a chance to reply.

He watched her go, standing for a moment even after she had disappeared around the corner. *Not a good idea*, he told himself. She was a junior officer, and he had seen enough workplace flings go wrong to fill a whole season of *The Jeremy Kyle Show*.

So we're considering a fling now, are we?

He felt like giving himself a slap, but with both hands holding hot coffee, that wouldn't end well. He settled instead for a long, drawn-out sigh. He didn't know what it would actually take to get him to the stage where he felt free to even think about letting himself get close to someone again. Wasn't sure he even wanted to, but Styles was right about one thing: Holly wouldn't want him to wallow like this, not for so long. She'd tell him to stop moping around and get back to living his life. Knowing it and doing it were two different things entirely.

The sun hung low, lightly kissing the horizon. But for the dashboard showing the temperature outside to be a brisk 5°C, it had all the hallmarks of a glorious Mediterranean-style evening, the kind that finds people outside enjoying a nice Chianti, or sipping a cold beer. The Atlas warehouse sat on a bend in the Thames, just along from Rainham Marshes nature reserve. Simmons had already promised herself a trip back to spend some time there when all this was over. Mike Gibson killed time during stakeouts by chattering endlessly, and one day he'd painted such a vivid picture of watching the peregrine falcons taking their prey on the wing that she'd googled it after work, and sat mesmerised by a video of one swooping down on a flock of pigeons like a kamikaze pilot, and the explosion of feathers that followed. It seemed incongruous that a place like that was just down the road from a row of warehouses where men like Bolton and Patchett plied their trade.

Gibson nudged her, pointing as Owen Carter got out from his car and walked into the Atlas warehouse. They had parked two hundred yards away along Coldharbour Lane in their unmarked gunmetal grey BMW, with three identical units spaced around the site at a similar distance. Fifty yards further back, and parked facing the other way, was a faded red van. The logo on the side advertised C. J. Errington & Son, Plumbers, and housed the mobile listening post that would receive and relay the live feed from the hidden microphone Owen Carter had pinned underneath the collar of his coat. Last but not least, they had eyes on Patchett himself; a long range lens was trained on his office window from the rooftop of a neighbouring warehouse. They needed to see the exchange take place, as well as hear it, if they were going to hang him out to dry.

Carter glanced back in their direction as he disappeared inside. The car was silent except for the thud of Carter's footsteps on the hard concrete floor, relayed over the radio. The plan for tonight was simple in theory. Carter was due to collect his monthly delivery from Patchett, which he would then sell on through a handful of dealers he used. They would get Patchett bang to rights on tape, and that would give them enough ammunition for a tap on his home, office and mobile. Whether they could follow the same route up through Bolton and on to Locke was another matter, but she would settle for Patchett tonight and worry about the rest later.

A low rumble sounded on the audio as Carter cleared his throat, followed by a squeak that sounded like a door opening.

'Hiya, Andy, how's tricks?' Carter's voice was clear as a bell.

Gibson looked at Simmons and winked. 'Here we go.'

'I'm good. You're late.' Patchett's voice was throaty, like gargling with gravel, a side effect of his forty-a-day habit.

'Yeah, sorry about that,' said Carter. 'Traffic was a mare.'

Simmons hoped that Carter didn't look as nervous as he sounded.

Patchett grunted in response. They made small talk for the next few minutes about the previous weekend's football scores, and Carter asked Patchett about one of the other men from the warehouse who was nursing a broken leg after coming off worst in a collision with a forklift. Carter said something about the weather and Patchett cut him short, having reached his tolerance level for inane chatter.

'Enough of that crap. How was business last month?'

'Good, yeah, business was good,' said Carter. 'Sold out, in fact.'

'Well?' said Patchett expectantly. 'What you got for me?'

They had agreed to let Carter hand over the money from the previous month's sales so as not to arouse suspicion. There was a series of rustling noises and a thud. In Simmons's mind, Carter had dropped the brown envelope, heavy with cash, onto a surface, maybe Patchett's desk.

'Bravo team, what are we looking at?' whispered Simmons into the silence. Bravo was the designated call sign for the team with the camera.

'Patchett's counting the money,' the reply crackled back, sounding louder in her ears than it surely was in reality. 'He's just pulled a rucksack from under the desk.'

They had briefed Carter at length this morning. Gibson had drilled into him exactly what they needed to see and hear to make it a clean operation. That list included seeing the merchandise during the exchange.

'Carter's opening the rucksack. He's pulling something out.' The few seconds of silence that followed were heavy with anticipation. 'Bravo to all units, we have confirmed sighting of the product, repeat, confirmed sighting of the product.'

Patchett's voice cut over the top of Bravo unit. 'What the hell are you doing? Put that shit away. Anyone could walk in.'

'Soz, Andy, I'm half asleep. Been a long day.' The sound of the bag being zipped up again, followed by a sigh that could have come from either of them.

'It's little mistakes like that that end up getting people in big trouble, man.'

A loud tapping interrupted the conversation, and made Simmons jump. A woman's voice came next.

'Mr Patchett, he's here. He just pulled up in the car park a moment ago.'

'What do you mean, he's here? He's early. He's never early.'

'Well, he's here. He's on his phone outside, and he sounds angry.'

Simmons looked up towards the warehouse in a flash. Who the hell were they talking about?

Shit, what did we miss?

She had been so fixated on the conversation that she had been staring at the glowing LED lights of the radio. When she looked out of the windscreen, she had the ghost of the numbers still stamped in her retinas. They floated in front of her until she blinked repeatedly to banish them. A hulking figure paced back and forward in front of the building. Even from here, she could tell he was well over six feet. A bald pale head stood out in contrast to the black knee-length coat that whipped back and forth around his legs as he walked.

Simmons scrabbled around for the small pair of binoculars in her lap without taking her eyes off the man, although with his size she suspected she knew who she would see. He quickly came into focus and she nodded to herself.

'Hello, Mr Bolton,' she said under her breath.

Gibson gave a low whistle. 'Could be a little unexpected bonus for us here,' he said to Simmons, then clicked the button to speak to a wider audience. 'All units be advised, an additional target has arrived on-site.' He gave a quick description of James Bolton, although Simmons doubted it was necessary. They had all seen his picture pinned up on the wall back in the investigation room, and you didn't see many who had the height and width to fill a suit the way that Bolton did.

She adjusted her position by millimetres, and focused on the car. Another man sat motionless in the driver's seat, another face she recognised.

'We've got Daniel Stenner in the car as well, but he looks like he's made himself comfy for now.'

Stenner was another name on the chart they had built which sat on the wall in their investigation room back at the station. It mapped out a mixture of those they knew were involved in Alexander Locke's organisation, and those whom they merely suspected. Stenner was Bolton's driver, gopher and general shadow. He was clean as far as a criminal record went, but as with many of the names on their wall Carter had spoken of him as a man who was more than willing to break the rules, as well as break anyone who tried to make him stick to them.

'Hope we don't have to stick him in a line-up at any stage,' she said to Gibson, training her binoculars back on Bolton. He looked puzzled. 'Imagine having to find another five his size to stick beside him.'

They both shared a brief, nervous laugh, cut short as Bolton stopped his pacing and disappeared inside with a face like thunder.

* * *

'Expecting company, Andy?' asked Carter.

'Not yet, I wasn't,' snapped Patchett. 'Do us both a favour and make yourself scarce.'

Carter nodded. 'No worries. See you around.' He scooped up the rucksack and swung it over his shoulder. He could feel the beads of perspiration prickling against his back as they soaked into his shirt. Thank God he had kept his coat on so Patchett couldn't see any sweat patches. He could always blame the coat for overheating, anyway. He had been convinced from the second that he walked in that Patchett would know something was up. It was written all over his face, screamed aloud by his stiff body language.

Why the hell did I let them talk me into this? Shit!

He mumbled a farewell to Patchett, who gave little more than a grunt in reply, and had just reached for the door when it swung open. Even before he registered who it was, the bulk that filled the doorway made him stop dead in his tracks. He looked up, and was met with a flat dead stare in return.

'Mr Carter,' James Bolton practically growled, in a voice low enough to rival Barry White. 'Going somewhere in a hurry?'

Carter instinctively looked in Patchett's direction, cursing himself for doing so in case Bolton saw the fear in his eyes.

Stay cool. Act normal. Just look him in the eye and answer him.

Carter gave what he hoped was a confident smile, though it felt more of a nervous grimace. 'Me and Andy had just finished up. I was gonna head back home.'

'Stick around,' said Bolton. 'Might have a job for you. I'll come find you after Mr Patchett and I have had a little chat.'

Bolton brushed against both sides of the doorway as he squeezed through. Carter stepped back to let him past.

'I'll hang round outside, then,' he said as cheerfully as he could muster.

'You do that, son.' Bolton smiled, a strange thing to see, with all the creases on his face in the right place but none of the emotion behind it. He slapped the door shut in Carter's face with a hand the size of a hardback novel, without saying another word.

Carter stared at the door for a second, contemplating whether to try and eavesdrop, as much for his own nosiness as those he knew were listening in, but thought better of it. James Bolton was not a man you wanted questioning your intentions, let alone doubting your loyalty. He swallowed hard and retreated to the relative safety of the reception area to take a load off his feet until Bolton was ready for him.

A heavy silence descended on the interior of the car, punctuated only by Carter's slightly ragged breathing.

'I don't like this, guv. Not one bit.' Simmons chewed nervously on her bottom lip. 'Bolton doesn't bother with the likes of Carter. Why would he line him up for a job now?'

'If it gives us something solid on Bolton, who cares?' said Gibson. 'Bravo team, have we got eyes on Bolton and Patchett?'

'Eyes on both,' crackled the response. They had lost the audio, of course, without Carter, but a visual was better than nothing at this stage. 'Bolton is doing the talking. Patchett is just sat there with a look like he's shitting his pants.'

'All units stand by. Nobody moves until Bolton clears the scene and I give the word.'

Simmons heard a shuffling noise, and realised it was Gibson bouncing his leg up and down on the seat. The nervous anticipation that came with a stakeout was infectious. She realised her own breathing had fallen into sync with Carter's, which echoed through the car's speakers. Looking across at Gibson, she saw he had closed his eyes like he was meditating.

Zen and the Art of the Stakeout.

Time stretched out for what seemed an eternity before Bravo unit chipped in with an update.

'Both subjects are on the move. Patchett standing up and Bolton going for the door.'

As their transmission ended, Simmons heard a door opening and footsteps growing heavier as they approached Carter.

'Let's take a drive, Mr Carter. We can talk on the way.'

Silence followed by a rustling noise, then footsteps receding. Simmons turned to Gibson with a puzzled look.

'Is it just me or is the sound getting fainter?' Regardless of whether they were leaving at the same time or together, she still expected to hear at least one set of footsteps consistently. She raised her binoculars again to focus on the door. It opened and Carter stepped out, followed closely by Bolton.

'Shit! Where's his bloody coat?' Without the mike on his jacket, they had lost their one and only audio source. Carter was like a silhouette in his light grey sweater against the backdrop of Bolton's black overcoat.

'The son of a bitch has double-crossed us,' spat Gibson.

Simmons shook her head. 'Something's wrong, guv. He looks even more nervous than when he went in. What did we miss?'

Let's take a drive, Mr Carter. We can talk on the way.

Carter had made his fair share of mistakes over the years but as he stooped to get into the passenger seat, he wondered if helping the police would be his biggest and perhaps last. From stories he had heard, he knew Bolton had a low tolerance for anyone who got out of line.

Bolton had suggested the drive, and then held a finger to his lips with one hand, the other reaching down and turning over the collar on Carter's coat to reveal the mike, like a caterpillar on the underside of a leaf. He had mimed the action of removing the coat to Carter and held his hand out for the offending garment, laying it on the chair and pointing towards the door that led outside.

The cool air attacked Carter's armpits in that brief walk to the car, and made him all the more self-conscious about the rubbery feeling of sweaty skin upon skin. He had no idea how Bolton knew about the mike, let alone where to look. He saw a man get out of the driver's side, and climb into the back seat as they approached. He recognised the face, Daniel Stenner, one of Bolton's right-hand men, and went to get in the back seat beside him, but felt a tap on his shoulder and saw Bolton nodding towards the front passenger seat. Bolton climbed into the driver's seat, and the Mercedes visibly rocked side to side as he adjusted his position.

'That's better, don't you think?' he said as he started the car.

Carter looked at him blankly, his mouth hanging slightly open, unsure how to respond.

'We can speak freely now, without our uninvited guests. Well' – he paused and looked at Carter – 'uninvited by me anyway.'

Bolton turned the car around and cruised out past the raised security barrier. Carter sat still, head fixed front and centre, but all the while his eyes scanned the buildings and rooftops for any sign of his watchers. Would the watchers become his saviours or was he in this on his own now?

'If I were in your shoes I'd be wondering two things right now,' said Bolton, glancing over. 'How did he know I was miked up, and what the hell is he going to do about it?'

Carter opened his mouth to speak but Bolton cut him off.

'In answer to the first point, that's none of your fucking business, but suffice to say that I know everything that happens in my world. As for the second point, well, Mr Carter, that largely depends on you. You see, I know about your predicament.' He casually rattled off the facts of the case the police had against Carter. 'So you see, I understand you were put in a difficult position. It would have been better for all concerned, however, if you had kept your fucking mouth shut and asked to see Mr Jasper.' Charles Jasper was the solicitor who handled all legal matters for Locke & Winwood.

'Mr Bolton . . . sir . . . look, I—'

'I'll let you know when I want you to speak, Mr Carter.' Bolton's voice rumbled low like thunderclouds. It didn't rise above a conversational volume, but the unspoken menace in his tone meant it didn't need to be any louder. 'I said we'd talk on the way there. I didn't say you'd be allowed to do any of the talking.'

Carter sat back in his seat. He glanced in the wing mirror and saw no sign of anyone following them. Had they even seen him leave, or were they still listening to his jacket sat alone on a seat? Like he had been for most of his life, he was on his own.

'I have a proposition for you. One that reflects your previous loyal service to the firm.'

'Whatever you need.' Carter nodded vigorously as he clutched at the lifeline. Bolton turned to look Carter in the eye as they stopped at a junction, and silenced him with a glance so forceful it may as well have been a slap across the face. They had taken a series of rapid-fire twists and turns, so that even though they'd driven for less than five minutes he had lost his bearings. The sprawling mass of storage units and warehouses could be like a maze for the uninitiated.

'Simple. I need two things from you,' said Bolton. 'I need you to promise me you've had your last conversation with the police.'

'I swear,' Carter said. 'Those bastards won't get another word out of me.' He grinned in relief.

'Secondly, I need you to deliver a message for me.'

'Just tell me what and who to and it's done.'

Bolton nodded. 'All in good time.'

He pulled the car over to the kerb outside a four-storey brick warehouse. The sign over the door advertised Taylor Fisheries, but there was no sign of life inside. The metal shutters were pulled firmly down on both the ground-floor windows. Horns rang out from the nearby Thames, boats rumbling a greeting to each other in low bovine bass notes.

'Upstairs.' Bolton nodded towards the door. 'We'll be five minutes and I'll drop you back at your car when we're done.'

They got out of the car, and Stenner slid into the driver's seat. Bolton pulled a bunch of keys from the pocket of his coat. Carter looked back along the road they'd just driven up, unsure if he wanted to see the officers that had been his shadows for so long now. Would their appearance hurt or hinder his chances of getting out of this in one piece, bearing in mind that Bolton knew anyway? It didn't matter either way; all he saw was an empty street with sheets of scattered old newspaper being prodded along the pavement by a lazy breeze.

The drying sweat on his back gave him a chill that tiptoed up his spine, and Carter followed Bolton into the gloom of the doorway.

Simmons sat bolt upright in her seat as Gibson pulled over to the kerb. He had positioned the front end of their car so the building in front shielded it from the road the three men had disappeared down a minute ago. Simmons was out of the car and at the corner in a flash with her back pressed to the wall. Gibson swore under his breath.

'Get back,' he hissed.

She risked a glance past the edge of the wall and saw the car parked outside a whitewashed building with blue lettering that was too far away to make out. She could make out a shape inside the car, but it looked like just one man, not three.

'They've gone inside,' she whispered back over her shoulder. Gibson had come up alongside her.

'All three of them? Into where?'

'I didn't see anyone actually go in, but the car is parked outside and I'm pretty sure there's only one of them left in it. Looks like Stenner. Can't make out the name on the sign, but it's the white one on the right-hand side.' She shuffled back to swap places with him so he could see. She heard tyres and looked to her right. Two of the other units had followed them, leaving one car plus Bravo unit on the rooftop watching Patchett.

'How do you want to play it, guv?' she asked.

'We sit tight.' Gibson looked around. 'Get the others to pull into the alley over there in case they come out fast and head back our way. Move ours as well. I'll keep an eye.'

Simmons did as she was told, and a minute later the street was deserted again. She told the other officers to wait in their vehicles with the key in the ignition in case they needed to pursue, and she went back to where Gibson stood glued to the wall.

'Any sign?'

'Nothing. Swap with me a second while I check in with Bravo.'

He peeled away from the wall and she peered around the edge once more as he whispered into his phone. The doorway was around a hundred and fifty feet away, and the dark blue door looked firmly shut. She looked up at the storeys above it. Each of the other three floors had a matching pair of large windows, turned into mirrors by the angle of the sun. No more than three minutes had elapsed since the men disappeared inside, but it felt like the longest wait of her life.

She heard the engine of the car rev up and it jerked away from the kerb, still with the solitary figure inside.

'Car's gone, guv. Bolton and Carter must still be inside. What do we do?'

Gibson's answer came low and urgent over her shoulder. 'We stay with our man, and stay on Bolton.'

What the hell are they doing in there? Is Carter still our man, or is he playing both sides?

Carter followed Bolton towards stairs. Most of the light inside came through the windows even though Bolton had flicked a series of switches when they came in. The bulbs shone feebly and left the darkness in the furthest corners unscathed. A large cargo door at the rear of the ground floor was so rusted that it could have been painted brown. Four parallel lines of workbenches sat in the centre. That must have been where they gutted and scaled the fish. Carter sniffed the air. There wasn't even a trace of telltale fishy odour. He was pretty sure no fish had passed through that door for a good few years.

Bolton took the stairs two at a time without looking back, and Carter had to practically trot up them just to keep up. Neither of them had spoken a word since they came inside. When they reached the top of the final staircase, Bolton led him through a doorway with twisted hinges hanging from the side that had long since given up their grip on the door itself.

He walked over to the large window in the centre of the wall that faced out to the front street and stood there, hands clasped behind his back, a lord surveying his manor. Carter stopped just inside the room. An old wooden desk and steel grey filing cabinet sat in the corner next to two plain wooden tables. Scattered around the room were a minefield of cardboard boxes, their once uniform brown exteriors discoloured with splashes of mould.

'First things first, give me a hand moving these,' said Bolton, motioning to the nearest pile of boxes. 'This place will be flats in twelve months and I need to clear all this shit out.'

Carter nodded and followed Bolton's lead, carrying them one at a time over to the wall nearest the door. They weren't too heavy, but his fingers went through the bottom of several, where the cardboard had turned to mush. He wished he had a pair of gloves like those Bolton wore, but had to make do with rubbing his hands together, sending a shower of card fragments raining to the floor.

It took almost ten minutes, and Carter had just placed the last box on the floor when he heard a scraping noise. He turned to see Bolton with his hands on one side of the old desk.

'Grab this,' said Bolton.

Carter did as he was told and they manoeuvred it over towards the large window that looked out over the road.

'Here will do,' said Bolton, when they were four feet away from the panes.

Carter hurried back over to fetch the matching chair and had just reached it when Bolton spoke again.

'Do you know what makes a business successful, Mr Carter?'

Carter stood mutely, unsure whether he should speak, let alone what to say. Bolton saved him the trouble.

'It's the people. With the right people you can achieve anything.' He motioned for Carter to join him. Carter wasn't about to argue. He left the chair and strode over eagerly to where Bolton stood. 'You need people with the right skills, but if you've not got an engaged workforce, you've lost the game before you start. Do you know what I mean?'

'Engaged? I, um . . .'

'What I mean is that they have to understand what role they play, and why the business needs them to succeed. You have that and the sky's the limit. You don't, and, well . . .' He turned to face Carter, 'Your employees start to make poor decisions, like talking to the police.'

'Mr Bolton, I—'

Bolton held up a shovel-like hand. 'Of course we're not running your bog-standard business here, Mr Carter, but there are similarities. In both scenarios, you might be hauled into a room with your boss to explain yourself. Difference is, in our line of work you might not leave the room.'

The blood drained from Carter's face. Bolton was a big man. Correction, he was like Goliath to Carter's David. Maybe he could outpace him if he made a run for it. The primal part of his brain was telling him to do just that, but his legs had turned to lead.

'As I said before, though, I'm a reasonable man.' Bolton turned so he was facing Carter now. 'And if you deliver this message for me I guarantee you'll leave this room in one piece. Can you do that for me?'

Carter nodded, like a child eager to please its parent. 'Course I can, Mr Bolton. Just tell me what I need to say.'

Bolton smiled again. 'Say?' His laugh bounced off the walls and reached the corners that the weak light from the bulbs could not. 'I don't need you to say anything.'

Carter's forehead crinkled in confusion. He was still frowning when Bolton grabbed his hand. He felt something smooth slap his palm. His fingers closed, an automatic reaction at first, before Bolton's meaty paw covered his hand and squeezed his fingers into the pad of his thumb.

Pop.

Carter looked down in surprise at his hand. He saw the blood welling between his fingers before the pain sliced through him. Bolton released his grip and reached up, grabbing Carter by the collar of his sweater in one hand, and stooping to reach through Carter's legs with his other. Carter's eyes were still fixed on his own hand. His fingers parted slightly, shards of glass glistening wickedly from between the gaps. He saw the swirling metallic thread of a light bulb fitting sticking out past his little finger.

What the fu—

Bolton plucked him off the ground as easily as a child plucking a flower and lifted him in one smooth motion above his head like a barbell. It happened so fast that Carter didn't make a sound. His arms windmilled and his mouth gaped open like a fish. Bolton held him there for a second, no more, then, bunching his heavily muscled shoulders, he launched Carter horizontally at the window.

There was no life story flashing before his eyes, just one glimpse of memory. When he was a child, they'd had a family trip to Blackpool and he'd ridden on the rollercoaster. The feeling of weightlessness had made him wide-eyed with excitement, and his eyes widened once again, but this time in surprise. The somersaults his stomach turned as he flew gave him a queasy feeling, a long way from the thrill of the fairground.

He did a quarter turn before impact, his back smashing into the point where the upper and lower sash met. Time and damp conditions had long since weakened the wood, and it crumbled, the two halves of the window frame bursting outwards like they were made from papier-mâché. The noise was deafeningly loud after the relative silence that had preceded it, but Owen Carter heard nothing except the wind whistling in his own ears, and soon not even that.

James Bolton looked out through the splintered frame, down to the road below. Carter had landed with arms and legs splayed out, like a child making snow angels in winter.

'I did promise you would leave in one piece,' Bolton muttered to the empty room. He saw movement off to his left down below, figures running towards the broken lump of flesh and bone that used to be Owen Carter.

'Message delivered. Job well done, Mr Carter.'

Simmons almost missed it. After nearly fifteen minutes of inactivity, she stood up straight behind the wall and rotated her neck in an effort to banish the stiffness. Moments after she resumed her position, she saw the window burst outwards a split second before the crash reached her ears. She watched, helpless and horrified, saw the arms doing a frantic front crawl in mid-air, looking for purchase but finding none. She heard the sickening thump even from that distance, then silence.

Gibson's voice roared in her ear and broke the spell. 'Go, go, go!' He raced past her and out into the street. She fell in behind him, her fitness letting her keep pace despite her shorter stride. A flash of movement caught her eye and she glanced upwards just in time to see a shape in the window before it pulled back. It happened so fast she couldn't be sure, but from the size of the shadow, it had to be Bolton.

Gibson reached the door ahead of her and pulled out his ASP telescopic baton. Simmons followed suit. He pointed for her to spread right when they went in and he would do the opposite. She nodded agreement, fighting to control her breath after the sprint, but revelling in the adrenaline rush that made her heart feel like it was trying to leap out of her chest. She glanced back at the corner they had sprinted from. No sign of the officers from the other units. They had been sat in their vehicles and might not have even heard Gibson's shout. Best case, they were a good twenty seconds behind them. Gibson held three fingers up and mouthed the countdown.

Three . . . two . . . one . . .

They burst through the doorway, and she broke right. She took in the room in a series of sweeping glances. The long benches. The big cargo door at the back, partially shrouded in darkness. The staircase off to the left where Gibson now stood by the first step, looking upwards. He motioned her towards him and pointed up the stairs. She ran across to join him and they opted for speed over stealth. Gibson shouted as they raced up the first flight.

'Police, anyone in the building stay where you are and do not move.'

They reached the doorway on the landing and went through it in the same order they had entered the front door, Gibson leading the charge. Simmons didn't see the blow that floored him so much as hear the impact, a sickening meaty thump. Whatever had hit him dropped him mid-stride, and he was halfway to the floor so that she almost tripped over him with her momentum. As it was she managed to grab on to the door frame with one hand and keep herself upright, but her leg had become tangled in his as he went down.

She instinctively looked down towards him, her eyes tracing his fall. The black shape started in the periphery and exploded from nothing, like the Big Bang, to fill her vision in a nanosecond. She tried to raise her baton to block it, but seeing Gibson felled like that had short-circuited her reactions and the best she managed was a half-hearted block at chest level. An arm snaked around her neck, clamping a palm against the back of her head and pulling it forwards onto the door frame with such astonishing speed and force that she was powerless to resist. In that final moment, the one thing that registered was surprise, not at being blindsided by her mystery attacker, but that she was calm and felt no fear.

CHAPTER TEN

Porter was about to call it a day when the call came in. He and Styles bolted for the door along with four other detectives who happened to be sitting at desks nearby. With lights and sirens, they made good time and screeched to a halt twenty yards from the Taylor Fisheries building. The first officers to respond had already set up a cordon around the door and a section of the road outside. Porter glanced over to the left, where a young constable stood next to a crumpled form of a man. There was no mistaking him for anything other than deceased. His head was tilted to face Porter, his eyes wide in surprise, in denial right to the end.

Porter dismissed him for now. He could wait; he wasn't going anywhere. An ambulance was blocking his view of the front door. Its rear door was open, and he could see there was nobody inside it yet. He sprinted around it and into the building, stopping so abruptly that Styles nearly ran into the back of him. Paramedics were making their way carefully down the stairs, carrying a stretcher.

'Evie!'

The lead paramedic looked up at him. 'Look out, gents, coming through.'

Porter and Styles retreated through the door and the paramedics bustled past them. Porter looked down and felt his stomach lurch when he saw her face. Her eyes were closed, the right side of her face was an angry palette of purples and blues, ballooning up to an alarming size. They had dressed what looked like a deep gash on her face. It ran from halfway down her forehead to her eyebrow, and continued another two inches from beneath her right eye down her cheekbone. There was no movement; she lay deathly still on the stretcher as they prepared to lift her into the ambulance.

Jesus, is she dead?

His stomach did another flip until he noticed the misting of condensation on the inside of the oxygen mask that waxed and waned with each breath. He turned to Styles.

'She's alive.' He looked up at the paramedic who was stepping out to close the doors and head to the driver's seat. 'How bad is she?'

'Could be worse,' he said, hustling past them. 'Vitals are strong, but she's been out since we got here. Hard to say much for sure till we get her back to base.'

'Where you headed?'

'Darent Valley A & E, if you want to follow?'

Porter nodded. He knew the way, but he also knew they'd not let anyone near her while they assessed her injuries. He wanted to have a look inside first, and he'd head straight there afterwards. He motioned for Styles to follow him. They heard footsteps up on the floor above them and headed straight up to examine the scene.

Porter was moving at pace as he reached the first-floor landing, and almost walked head first into a man coming the other way. He pulled up short of a collision and saw Anderson with a startled look on his face.

'Jesus, Porter, watch where you're going.'

Whittaker was right behind Anderson, and put his hand out to stop himself becoming part of the pile-up. Porter ignored Anderson's comment and looked through the doorway. Mike Gibson's body lay just beyond the frame, his feet no more than twelve inches past the threshold. He had fallen with his head turned away from them so Porter couldn't see his face. A crimson halo surrounded his head, his hair, greying but still with a sprinkling of the dark brown it used to be, now had a liberal splash of red at the base of his skull. One arm lay flat against his body, the other tucked underneath. Porter looked back at Anderson, who just shook his head.

They stood like that for a moment, not meeting each other's eye.

'What happened?' said Porter finally.

Anderson gave them a rough and ready account of what had happened at the warehouse, and how they had ended up here. He explained how they had been waiting in their cars when they heard Gibson shouting, and how he and Simmons had already disappeared inside the building by the time they rounded the corner.

'By the time we got inside it was all over. Bolton was gone, the other guy, Stenner, had already shot off in the car, and Carter was roadkill. We heard a car start up somewhere out back, but it was gone before we got out there. Found Gibson exactly where you see him. The paramedics checked him for a pulse but . . .' His voice tailed off.

'What about Simmons? Where was she?'

Anderson pointed to the floor just shy of the doorway. 'She was in a heap on the floor. From the looks of it she'd cracked her head on the doorway' – Porter saw the dark red stain on the frame where she must have connected with it – 'and she fell backwards out onto the landing. Think she might even have tripped up on Gibson.'

'What makes you say that?' asked Styles, finding his voice for the first time since entering the building. It would be embarrassing for Simmons if that was how it had gone down. Whether it would have made a difference to the outcome for Gibson was debatable, but had her clumsiness meant that a suspect in the death of a police officer had been able to flee the scene?

'Her foot.' Anderson gestured with his hand towards where Gibson lay. 'It was in between where his legs are now, slightly under the material on his trousers by the ankle. She was lying back here, mainly on the landing.' He gestured back through the door towards the stairs. 'I'm thinking she heard whatever happened to him, came up fast and came a-cropper.' He pointed at the door frame. 'Position of the mark on the frame is consistent with her height.'

'And what exactly happened to him?' asked Porter.

Anderson shrugged. 'Other than the fact the back of his head is caved in, your guess is as good as mine. Bolton and Stenner are nowhere to be seen.

There's a fire escape leading down the side,' he said, pointing at a door in the far wall, 'but by the time we checked for signs of life with these two, and cleared each floor, there was no sign of anyone else. We're fairly sure Bolton came in here with Carter, but he didn't come out the front, I know that much, so that's our best guess for now.'

Porter looked down at Gibson again. His thoughts immediately went to the picture on Gibson's desk at work, a family shot with his arms around his wife, and their sons like bookends to their left and right. They would have to be told.

Pity the poor bugger who pulls that duty.

'What about the building?' asked Styles. 'Why here?'

'No idea,' said Whittaker, speaking at long last. His face was pale, and a sheen of sweat on his brow hinted that he was still struggling with what they had stumbled into. 'We've not come across it before, but we can check it out at Companies House when we get back.'

'Any idea what they used on Gibson?' asked Porter.

'Over there.'

Anderson pointed a few feet past where Gibson's body lay, to a piece of wood around four feet long. Even from where he stood, Porter could see the wispy strands that clung to it where a jagged edge had torn a clump from Gibson's scalp when it had connected. The hairs of the light grey clump were bound to the wood by a congealing streak of blood. The contrast of the colours and the way the tuft stuck out reminded Porter of a fly-fishing lure.

Porter stared for a few more seconds, soaking in the scene. His eyes lingered once more on Gibson, then the door frame, feeling his anger rising. He clenched and unclenched his fists.

'Come on, then,' he said, addressing the three of them. 'Every extra minute that bastard is left to strut around town is an insult to Mike and Evie.' His use of the officers' first names somehow made it even more personal to them than it already was. 'A man his size can't be too hard to find, even in this city. Let's bring him in.'

They left one of the uniformed officers from downstairs to guard the scene on the first floor. Anderson and Whittaker had been working the Locke case for six months solid and had a good handle on Bolton's usual haunts. He gave Porter and Styles addresses for Bolton's office, as well as for the few businesses they knew he owned. He split a further eleven possibilities between the other officers who were outside on the street, opting to keep Bolton's home address for himself and his partner.

They agreed that whoever located Bolton would call for backup before attempting any arrest. After what had happened to Gibson and Simmons, nobody wanted to take any chances. Course of action agreed, each pair of detectives peeled away towards their own cars.

Porter slid into the driver's seat and had the engine growling impatiently, already in first gear and ready to pull away, before Styles had even reached the handle. He glanced through the windscreen to where Carter lay on a carpet of broken glass and splinters. Someone had covered his body with a sheet now, but his outstretched hands still peeped over the top edge, like a child playing hide-and-seek. The second his partner's door closed, Porter hit the accelerator and the car jerked forward.

Simmons had been hunting for a way to put Bolton, amongst others, behind bars for drug trafficking, and had been willing to put herself in harm's way to do it. The irony dawned on Porter, as he drove, that it would be the harm she had been willing to risk that would see him arrested. He just prayed that she would pull through to see it happen with her own eyes.

The hunt for Bolton bordered on anticlimax. Detectives Booth and Thomas found him in Oyster Bay, a Chinese restaurant that he owned, and the first on their list of three addresses. His car was parked outside, and he and Stenner were sitting there bold as brass at the table in the centre of the restaurant. He was halfway through a plate of Singapore chow mein that could feed a family of four when the delegation of six officers walked in. Anderson and Whittaker took point, with Booth and Thomas bringing up the rear, sandwiching Porter and Styles in between them. Porter was straining at the leash to lead the charge, to be the one to confront Bolton, read him his rights, but he held back. It was more Anderson's right to claim the collar. Bolton was part of his case, Simmons part of his team.

Bolton didn't look up or acknowledge their presence as they wound their way between the tables towards him, even when Anderson moved close, practically touching the cloth on Bolton's table.

'James Bolton?'

Bolton stabbed his fork into the centre of his mountain of food and twirled it, his fork accumulating noodles like a stick gathering candyfloss. Only after he had heaved it into his mouth and started to chew did he look up. He smiled and tapped his lips with the fork, grunting as he worked his way through his mouthful.

'Sorry, Officer, my mum always told me it's rude to talk with your mouth full,' he said once he had finished. 'Apologies, but if you're after a table we're booked solid. You'll have to come back another night.' He gave a smile that had all the warmth of a ventriloquist's dummy.

Porter glanced involuntarily around the room. There were several dozen tables, all bar two of them empty. A young couple sat at the table by the window, oblivious to the scene that was unfolding, eyes only for each other. Four young men occupied a table in the far corner, suit jackets slung across the backs of their chairs, top buttons undone on their shirts and ties with knots that had relaxed a few inches below the collar.

Anderson nodded and returned the smile with an equally cold one of his own. 'Business is booming, Jimmy. We'll call ahead next time and book. In the meantime, why not get them to pack up your food to go, and you can finish it down the station while we have a chat.'

'Sounds like he's asking me out on a date, Mr Stenner, not very politely I might add. I preferred it when he called me James. What do you think, should I play hard to get?'

'Don't flatter yourself, Jimmy, you're not my type. I'm not in the mood to fuck around today, though. James Bolton, you're under arrest for the murders of Owen Carter and Michael Gibson, and the attempted murder of Eve Simmons.'

Bolton sat back and looked impassively up at Anderson as he recited the rest of the statement. When Anderson was finished, Bolton plucked the napkin from his lap and dabbed his lips before laying it on top of the remnants of his meal. Porter looked on, reminded of the sheet he had seen draped over Carter.

'You're making a big mistake,' he said, his eyes moving slowly, deliberately, from one officer to the next. 'In every sense of the word. However, never let it be said that I don't cooperate with our fine boys in blue.'

Bolton put his hands up in mock surrender and stood up slowly, before extending his wrists towards Anderson, who grabbed them as roughly as he could, trying to pull Bolton away from his table. He might as well have been tugging on a towrope anchored to a vehicle for all it moved Bolton. The big man just smirked and watched with a bored expression as Anderson cuffed him.

They repeated the process with Stenner, and Booth stepped forward and did the honours with his cuffs. He and Thomas manoeuvred Stenner towards the door. Whittaker, in the meantime, came to the opposite side of Bolton and put a hand on his left arm, while Anderson took the other. As they steered him out past the silent stares of the restaurant staff, Bolton spoke over his shoulder to the restaurant manager.

'Make the call, please, Mr Lau.'

A smartly dressed Asian man moved away from the kitchen door at the back of the room and picked up the phone that sat behind the bar. Porter and Styles brought up the rear as the convoy of officers herded their suspects out into the street, looking left and right as they pushed them down into the waiting cars. It looked an impossible task to squeeze Bolton through the door frame and into the back seat, but they managed. Porter glanced back through the window. Beneath the reflection of the street, he could still make out the manager, more animated now that his call had clearly connected. His free hand gestured towards where Porter stood.

Porter wondered who was on the other end of the phone. He doubted it was Locke. The manager wouldn't be quite so animated and demonstrative with the man himself. Whoever it was, he had no doubt that the message would filter through to Locke quickly enough.

Let's see how he reacts now that we've got his big Dobermann locked up.

Bolton sat opposite Porter, looking as calm and unhurried as a man waiting for his main course at a restaurant. It wasn't the first time he had seen the inside of a police interrogation room and it showed. His relaxed posture oozed apathy. Next to him sat Charles Jasper, who had arrived at the station minutes after them. The lawyer, or an associate of his, had clearly been the target of the call that the restaurant manager had made, and Jasper had ushered Porter and Styles out of the room for twenty minutes while he conferred with his client. With Jasper as his shield, Bolton had yet to utter a word since arriving at the station.

Styles pushed a button to start the recording, and nodded at Porter, who walked them though the standard opening, his eyes never leaving Bolton, who stared back blankly.

'So, Jimmy, let's dive in head first. You were in the Taylor Fisheries building down by the river earlier today. What brought you to that neck of the woods?'

'Business, and Mr Bolton will do just fine.'

'What kind of business, Jimmy?' said Porter, sticking with the informal version of his name in the hope of needling him.

Bolton shook his head softly at the weak attempt to antagonise. 'Manners cost nothing, Detective. My business there is property. I own the building and wanted Mr Carter to gut the place for me so I could develop it.'

'So you agree that you were there with Owen Carter and Daniel Stenner at approximately 5.30 p.m.?'

'Mr Stenner drove me and Mr Carter there, yes.'

'How do you know Mr Carter?'

'He's an employee at Atlas. I run security for Locke & Winwood. Atlas is part of Locke & Winwood. It's my job to know who we employ.'

Porter changed tack. 'So now we've established the three of you were there, how about you tell us what you were doing when Owen Carter decided to do a swan dive through the top-floor window.'

Bolton just smiled and Jasper jumped in. 'Detectives, we are willing to stipulate that my client and his associate had arrived at the scene with Mr Carter, but that is as far as we go. Neither Mr Bolton nor Mr Stenner entered the premises, and had left the scene before the incident you are referring to took place.'

Porter snorted a laugh. 'You're trying to tell me that Owen Carter was just having a bad day and threw himself out of that window?'

'No, Detective, I'm telling you that your own officers at the scene have confirmed that my client's car was no longer parked outside when they entered the building. They have in fact confirmed that it left some ten to fifteen minutes before the incident occurred, ergo there is no evidence to suggest that either of them were at the scene at the time of the incident.'

It always bothered Porter how trivial a state a lawyer could reduce a situation to. Calling it an incident made it sound like a minor fender bender, or shoplifting. Two men had lost their lives and Simmons was fighting for hers, or at least he hoped she still was. The thought that she might lose that fight, while he sat here unaware, squatted in his mind front and centre, and he had to struggle to concentrate. Jasper's casual offhand references were starting to get a rise from him, and he felt a dull thud in his temples. He took a deep breath to even himself out, and fixed Bolton with a steely glare, even though he was addressing Jasper.

'So what you're asking us to believe is that your clients' presence at a murder scene mere minutes before two people were killed, and a third seriously injured, is a simple case of coincidence and nothing more?'

'I believe the term you're looking for is circumstantial evidence, but essentially, yes, that's exactly what I'm saying, Detective. We are confident you will find no physical evidence linking either of my clients to the scene. In addition, Mr Lau, the manager of the restaurant you arrested my clients in, can confirm their time of arrival, which is consistent with having left the Taylor building ten minutes before these events took place.'

'That's bullshit and you know it,' snapped Porter. 'Ten minutes is a small enough margin of error that they could have left after killing Carter and Gibson and floored it to get there. Hell, for all we know, Mr Lau is just earning his keep by saying they arrived when they did.'

Jasper shrugged. 'I'm just recapping the facts, Detective. There's no speculation or conjecture in what I've just said. It's supported by your own officers' eyewitness accounts. You can't place my clients inside that building, let alone laying a hand on Owen Carter or your officers. Nobody actually saw them enter. Now please tell me, do you have anything else to substantiate these charges?'

Porter let out a loud sigh and sat back from the table. He hated to admit it to himself, but Jasper was right. They had nothing solid yet linking Bolton to either of the murders, or the attack on Simmons, apart from his gut instinct screaming that the big man was guilty as sin.

'Well, Detective, anything else to share with us?' said Jasper, raising his eyebrows.

Porter wanted to ask Bolton about Carter and Patchett, about the drugs that they knew and could prove were moving through the company. That was off limits for now, though. They couldn't prove Bolton's involvement in that any more than they could prove he was a murderer, not yet anyway. All that would do was confirm any suspicions that both Bolton and Locke might have, that they had been compromised. There was a chance they already knew about the leak. Perhaps Bolton had killed Carter to cut the flow of information to the police. That would definitely be motive enough, but they needed something more concrete to make a case, and avoid the Crown Prosecution Service getting jittery about going after him on circumstantial evidence alone.

Finally, Porter spoke. 'We have nothing further to ask at this point, Mr Jasper, although we will most likely want to speak to both of your clients again once we've completed a thorough examination of the crime scene and the bodies. We'll be taking statements from Mr Lau and the other officers at the scene, so if there're any discrepancies you can rest assured we'll be in touch. We're also hopeful that Detective Simmons will be able to give her account of what happened soon.' He looked at Bolton as he said her name.

'If that's all, then, Detectives' – Jasper looked from Porter to Styles – 'I'd ask that my clients be released without charge, and allowed to leave until such time as you uncover any evidence actually linking them to any of these events.'

Porter terminated the interview and nodded at Styles, who ended the recording.

Bolton and Jasper got up to leave, and Porter reached for the door handle to let them out, but stopped before turning it.

'Don't you be going too far now, Jimmy. I have a feeling we'll be speaking again soon.'

'Always a pleasure, Detective,' said Bolton, moving close so that Porter had to tilt his neck a few more degrees to maintain eye contact. 'Do give my regards to your colleague if she wakes up.' There was the tiniest emphasis on the 'if', just enough to make Porter dig his nails into his palms to control the anger he felt rising.

It was Bolton who broke away from the stare, and Jasper filed out after him. Porter followed them out into the corridor. He and Styles watched as the diminutive Jasper scurried after Bolton, the difference in their sizes almost comical.

'Well, what now?' asked Styles.

'Now?' Porter turned to face him. 'Now we go and see Simmons. Until we know what the crime scene techs found at the scene, she's our number one play. There's a good chance she knows what happened in there. Let's go and see if she's awake yet.'

Bolton's words echoed in his mind.

If she wakes up. If . . .

Sometimes the smallest words carried the heaviest of weights.

Porter stared through the window on the intensive care ward. Simmons looked so small in the midst of the machines that surrounded the bed, tubes and wires swarming around on all sides. Her hair, usually pulled back in a ponytail, made a dark frame for her eggshell-white face. A plastic tube snaked along her arm and in through her mouth, chest rising and falling courtesy of the nearby ventilator. He hated hospitals. Their scents and sounds. Squeaky rubber floors and lemon-scented hand sanitizer.

He had no idea how long he had been staring for when he felt a tap on his shoulder and saw Styles gesturing towards a doctor coming towards them.

'Detectives, I'm Doctor Rose.' He was a tall thin man in his early fifties, with short-cropped grey hair, and bony shoulders that made it seem the hanger was still stuck down the back of his white hospital coat.

'DI Porter, and this is my partner, DS Styles.' Doctor Rose smiled warmly and shook hands with them both. 'How is she doing, Doctor?' asked Porter.

Rose sucked air in through his teeth while he decided how candid to be. 'She's sustained a serious head injury, and we found some bleeding on her brain so we had to take her straight into theatre.' He saw the grave look on Porter's face and held up a hand. 'We've managed to stop the bleeding, but we won't know for sure how serious the damage is until she wakes up.'

'When is that likely to be?' asked Styles.

'Hard to say.' Rose shrugged. 'It's an inexact science, I'm afraid. She has swelling around the area of impact, internally and externally, that will take at least a few days to go down. I know you're keen to speak to her, but I wouldn't count on doing that for a few days at least.'

Porter felt disappointed and elated at the same time. On one hand he desperately needed the help she could give him. He wanted to be out there chasing down his man, but at the same time, the thought that she could be sat up in bed talking in the next forty-eight hours gave him hope.

Rose continued with his diagnosis. 'There's a chance with head trauma that her memory of the event may be fuzzy, or even not there at all. She also has a depressed fracture of the cheekbone and orbital socket. She'll most likely need surgery for that, but that's relatively straightforward and can wait until the swelling has subsided. Has anyone contacted her family?'

Porter nodded. 'Her parents are on their way back from a holiday in Spain. They should be here first thing in the morning.' He glanced over Rose's shoulder and saw Anderson and Whittaker walking towards them, carrying cups of canteen coffee. Rose made his excuses and left to carry on his rounds, nodding to the other two detectives as they joined Porter and Styles. They all stared through the window as Porter summarised the doctor's comments for them.

When he finished, none of them spoke for a moment. Through the glass, the muted *ping* of the ECG echoed on endless repeat, punctuating the background hum of the ward. Porter felt an uncomfortable dose of déjà vu wash over him. The machine Holly had been hooked up to had kept the same rhythm, all the way to the end. The same sense of irony struck him now as it had then, that the very noise that signified a heartbeat, and confirmed life itself, could also be a countdown to the inevitable, depending on whether you were glass half empty or half full.

'This is so fucked up,' muttered Anderson. 'They didn't have this coming, either of them.'

His sympathy clearly didn't extend to Carter. Porter glanced at him and saw a thin veil of pink overlaying the white of his pupils; had he been crying?

'What's our play, guv?' asked Whittaker.

Porter tore his eyes away from Anderson and rubbed a hand on the back of his neck. All the tension of the day seemed crammed into a spot just above the base of his skull that throbbed with all the signs of a legendary headache to follow.

'Our play . . .' His voice tailed off as his mind teemed with a hundred unanswered questions. 'Our play is we hit these bastards with everything we've got.' But his words rang hollow in his own ears. The fact that they had released Bolton and Stenner told him what they had wasn't enough. He saw that reflected in the eyes of the three men looking back at him.

'I say we speak to Superintendent Campbell tomorrow. We ask to lead on Mike's murder, and Evie's assault. We ask him to pool resources and share what we have across the two cases, this one and the drugs angle.' He half expected Anderson or Whittaker to object; at the very least, to stake their claim to lead on it. Simmons was one of theirs, after all, but they stayed quiet for now.

'First thing is to see what they find at the scene. We should have that tomorrow, right?' He looked at Styles, who nodded confirmation. 'Maybe that puts one of them in the same room as any of the three victims. In the meantime, we hit them all where it hurts, in the pocket.'

'How do you mean?' asked Whittaker, looking puzzled.

'I mean we get in their faces, make it hard for them to do business.'

'We can't do that yet, guv,' said Anderson, shaking his head. 'They don't know we're on to them. If we start hanging round for no good reason they're going to suspect and just shut up shop.'

'You really think they don't know we're looking at them?' Porter asked incredulously. 'Why kill Carter if they didn't think he'd crossed them? Why were we on the scene that quickly if we hadn't already been watching? They aren't stupid, more's the pity. Besides, we'd not be investigating trafficking, we'd be looking for a murderer. We'd be looking for a cop killer.' He paused to let his words sink in. 'We have every right to be in every one of their buildings, speaking to anyone we damn well please to find who did this. Who mentioned drugs? If we happen to stumble upon something in the course of that then so be it.'

Whittaker chipped in. 'And in the meantime they'll shift little or no product, with us sniffing around.'

'Exactly,' said Porter. He could feel his pulse quickening as a plan started to form. 'Styles, first thing in the morning I want you looking at everything Locke owns or has ever owned. I don't care how low-profile this bastard has been. Nobody can operate for this length of time without making a single mistake; it's just that no one has been looking in the right place, that's all.'

Styles nodded. 'What about our case with Barclay? We putting that on hold for now?'

Porter shook his head. 'I can't put my finger on it yet, but Barclay selling out to Locke doesn't feel right. Whether that sent Barclay over the edge and he hurt Natasha, or whether she got caught up in the middle of whatever was going on between them, I don't know. Either way, I say we work both cases. There's too many roads leading to Locke for them to be just coincidence. We can pick up where we left off tomorrow on that one too.' He checked his watch: ten-thirty. 'Go on, all of you get some sleep and we hit this full steam ahead in the morning.'

Pep talk done, he looked back at Simmons. He saw from the corner of his eye that the others had started to wander towards the exit. He watched her for a moment longer, the rhythmic rise and fall of her chest. For a second he was back at Holly's bedside, waiting for the flicker of an eyelid that never came. His eyes started to mist around the edges, and he blinked tears away before anyone could see. The lack of arrest, the absence of someone to blame, still festered in a dark corner inside like an unlanced boil. Her death had left a blank space in his life, and no direction in which to channel his anger.

Blink.

His mind snapped back to the present. This was not Holly. This time, things would be different. This time there was a face to funnel that rage towards. He turned and trotted to catch up with Styles.

I'm coming for you, Jimmy.

* * *

'You've got to believe me, boss. I had no idea he was peddling bad gear, let alone talking to the coppers.' Andrew Patchett's usual low grumble of a voice had snuck up an octave in protest.

'I don't *have* to do anything, Mr Patchett. I do, however, believe you. If I didn't, you'd have been booked on the same one-way trip as Mr Carter. What about that lanky streak of piss he hung round with? What's his name again? Thick as thieves, those two. You found him yet?'

'Jono Murray? Yep, picked him up this morning. Daft bastard went round to Carter's place to pick up what was left of that shite they were selling. Useless fuckers had been cutting it with anything and everything they could find in the bathroom cabinet.'

'Where is he now?' Bolton squeezed his knuckles, popping them like bubble wrap.

Patchett jerked his head towards the far wall. 'Through there. Think he's lost a stone in sweat since we brought him in. He's bricking it.'

'Let's go and have a little chat, then, shall we?'

Bolton let Patchett lead the way. He knew his way around the Atlas warehouse well enough, but he wanted Murray to see Patchett first. To think he had a reprieve, that it was just to check he was still there. Patchett led him down a long corridor, stopping at the last door on the left, and pulled a small key ring from his pocket.

This mess with Carter didn't worry Bolton. He could do without the hassle, but he was fairly sure Locke would buy a line about Carter having a go at him. He ran through the worst-case scenario. He would never willingly move against Locke out of loyalty for what the man had done for him over the years. But by the same token, he had always imagined his boss would have drifted off into a retirement villa somewhere tropical, and left him to run the show. Was it so wrong for him to want a bigger piece of the pie while he waited? The only person he'd seen play second fiddle for a longer stint was Prince Charles. He would have been tempted to leave a roller skate neat the stairs at Buckingham Palace long before now if it was him.

Patchett was his man, not Locke's, and he trusted him as much as he did anyone. Never completely, but enough. Brainless fools like Carter and Murray were another matter. Disposable but dishonest. The irony of what they had done wasn't lost on him. To skim from him, the way he was skimming from Locke. It was just plain greed to cut other shit in with the product, though. Greed that brought Carter to the attention of the police. Greed that put Murray in the chair in which he now sat.

Bolton smelt him before he saw him. The kind of ripe sweat it took days to cultivate, and a half-dozen washes to get out. Jono Murray had always reminded Bolton of a sulky teenager, even now in his thirties. Face permanently set in a scowl, as if the world owed him a living. Always had an answer for everything. Bolton looked down at where Murray sat tied to a plastic chair. Not so fucking cocky now, was he?

Murray tried to put a brave face on when he saw who had entered the room. He looked up at Bolton, smile as fake as the knock-off Armani jeans that hung off his spindly legs. Add those to a Nike T-shirt two sizes too big, and he could make for a cracking scarecrow. Bolton nodded to Patchett, who closed the door, and moved to stand in front of it.

'Mr Bolton,' Jono Murray said with a forced lilt. 'This is all a mix-up. I didn't have nuffin to do with whatever Owen had going on.'

Everything about him repulsed Bolton. The faint brown sweat-rings under his armpits. The way that everything he said came out half-sniggered. The fact that he had the balls to try and get one over on him. He ignored the double negative in what Murray said, and bent down so he was in the younger man's face, inches away.

'Of course you didn't, Mr Murray. That's why you went back to clear out the stash as soon as you heard what happened to your little pal.'

'Nah, nah, you've got it all wrong, boss. I was gonna bring that to you, see. I heard him talking. Knew he was up to something, so I guess he got what was coming. I'm your boy, though. I was gonna come straight to you with it.'

'Of course you were, son. Course you were.' Murray flinched as Bolton patted him on the knee, then stood up. 'That's why you'd packed yourself a bag isn't it. You were going to come to see me, then pop off for a little break somewhere for a bit of R & R?'

'I was just gonna pop and stay with my mum for a few days. She's not getting any younger, you know, bless her.'

'And she's lucky to have a son like you,' said Bolton, wandering over to a desk by the far wall. He took his jacket off, settling it on the back of the chair as carefully as if he was dressing a mannequin in Harvey Nics' window. He unbuttoned both cuffs with his back still to Murray.

'So I was wondering, when can I get back to work, boss?' said Murray, aiming for chirpy, but sounding pleading.

'What about visiting your poor old mum?' said Bolton. 'You've forgotten about using her to try and talk your way out of this one, haven't you?' He turned round, shook his head, sighing as he approached Murray. 'I wish it was that simple, son,' he said, rolling his sleeves back to just below the elbow. 'You see, Mr Carter had been talking to the wrong people. Who's to say you won't do the same given half the chance? Maybe you have already?'

Murray's head started to shake side to side, like he was watching tennis on fast forward. 'No, no, no. Not me, boss, I wouldn't. I would never—' The open-handed slap caught him across the cheek, toppling him like a bowling pin.

It boiled down to fear and respect. People respected Locke. They feared men like Bolton. They didn't make an enemy of him. That's the difference between him and Locke, he thought to himself. He'd take fear over respect any day.

'Just like you would never mix in baby milk or fucking talcum powder into my perfectly good cocaine?' Bolton growled. 'More to sell. More to line your grubby little pockets with.'

The side of Murray's face glowed pink, eyes watering. A trickle of blood mingling with snot snaked out of his nose and down his face. 'That was Owen. That was all Owen,' he whimpered. 'If you're worried I would say anything to Mr Locke, you needn't. I—'

Bolton's foot shot out and connected with Murray's chin, snapping his head back. 'You'll be lucky if you can manage a confession to your fucking priest by the time I'm finished with you, son.'

Murray's eyes rolled back, mouth opening, blood lining the gaps between his teeth. Whatever sound he was trying to make, it was stuck halfway down his throat and all he could manage was a choking rattle.

'Boss?' Patchett spoke for the first time since they'd entered the room. 'Hate to stop you in full flow, but he can't talk if you break his jaw. How else will we find out who he's talked to?'

Bolton stood over Murray now, one leg planted either side of his chest, watching it heave up and down like a bellows. He didn't bother turning round as he spoke to Patchett. 'This isn't about whether he's talked or not. He stole from me. Where would I be if I let that kind of thing slide? I'd be on the floor underneath somebody's boot like this little shit here.' Bolton placed the sole of his shoe on Murray's neck. 'Now I suggest you don't interrupt me again.'

Bolton looked down at Murray, at his eyes, pupils dilated to the size of five pence pieces. He drew his knee up to chest height, put all his weight into it, and drove it down with a sickening crack on the bridge of Murray's nose. He stepped back, admiring his work. He noticed a splash of blood on his shoe, and wiped it against Murray's T-shirt. What had started out as a white top was now speckled with red like a Jackson Pollock painting. Fear trumps respect every time.

CHAPTER ELEVEN

Deciphering a dream could be like trying to translate a foreign language after hearing it for the first time; the images had an echo of familiarity, but the true meaning hovered tantalisingly out of reach. Other times you ended up dreaming about something you saw on the news before you turned in for the night. Porter woke with a start after a dose of the latter.

Simmons had been in her hospital bed where he had left her last night, but the room was different. It had no door, only an enormous window. He had stood, nose practically touching the glass, breath flowering and fading on the surface. Holly fussed around her in an old-fashioned white nurse's uniform, tucking in the bed sheet, checking vitals. He called out, but neither of them reacted. He smacked the flat of his palm against the glass so hard it stung; not so much as a flicker of eyes in his direction.

He looked at the clock by his bed: 5.14 a.m., barely worth trying to get the last half hour before his alarm caught up with him. His subconscious still clung on to that raw feeling on his palm even now that the dream had evaporated. He looked at his left palm, half expecting to see it glowing pink from the impact, but only a pasty white hand hovered in front of him. He slipped on a pair of shorts and stumbled off in search of breakfast. Demetrious watched from the comfort of the sofa as Porter ambled past like a Neanderthal man, arms dangling by his side and feet dragging to make a *swish, swish* against the laminate floor.

He opened the fridge, staring blankly at the pitiful amount of milk he had left, barely enough to cover the bottom of the container, and decided to head to the twenty-four-hour garage down the road. He swapped his shorts for jeans and a black fleece, opting for the five-minute walk over a lazy drive.

The girl at the checkout smiled at him as he placed his basket in front of her. She had worked here as long as he could remember, and reminded him of someone, but he couldn't quite put his finger on it. She had a badge clipped near her collar with *Sam* stamped on in bold black capitals, and her black hair was scraped back from her face into a tight ponytail. Her eyes did a little dance; left, right, up, down, as she looked at him. He wondered for the first time since he got up whether his hair was sticking up at odd angles, and felt himself blushing at the thought of how he must look.

'Early start?' she asked cheerfully.

He looked up, startled, as if he'd not seen her there. 'Afraid so.' He forced a quick smile. 'Not as early as yours, though.'

'Mm,' she murmured in agreement as she packed his items into a plastic bag. 'I usually do lates but I'm helping a friend out, and the overtime doesn't hurt either.'

'Yeah, I thought I'd usually seen you on a night-time rather than this ungodly hour.'

She laughed. 'The joys of working for a twenty-four-hour shop.'

He went to pay but realised he only had a five-pound note, and with the extra things he had grabbed on the spur of the moment he was twenty pence short.

'Guess I'll have to pop one of these back,' he said.

'I'll let you off. You can pay the extra next time.'

'You're sure?'

'I won't tell if you don't.'

'That's very kind of you, thank you.'

He smiled and headed out into the still-dark morning with its whispers of faint traffic. He glanced back through the glass shopfront as he walked past, hoping she hadn't noticed the flush he felt in his cheeks. That was more conversation than he usually dared strike up with women he didn't know, but no reason to get self-conscious. Damn Styles and his non-stop piss-take. She was just being friendly. It was her job to be polite, so why was he left wondering if she was flirting with him? He wondered if he'd ever get to the point of flirting back. Wondered if he wanted to. What was the worst that could happen?

He considered that for a moment as he climbed back into his car. The worst scenario wasn't that he might not be ready for what it could lead to. Worst case by far would be if Styles found out. That would give his partner ammunition for weeks – months, even – but it made Porter smile all the same.

It wasn't that he wanted to end up a lonely old man, but the idea of being with someone, of feeling that way about anyone other than Holly, stirred up such a conflicted knot in his stomach, that he wasn't sure he could ever unpick it.

Porter was at his desk with the day's inaugural coffee by six-thirty. He sipped it slowly as he watched the darkness outside evaporate, as if God was turning up the brightness on his celestial TV.

He silently berated himself for the way he had handled things yesterday. Going after Bolton that quickly had been a mistake, although it had been satisfying to haul him in. It wasn't that he thought they'd tipped their hand by questioning him. Porter was certain that Bolton and Stenner knew they had been under surveillance. Maybe Patchett had too. What other reason was there for Carter to have ditched his coat unless he'd been persuaded to do so by one of the others? Persuaded, coerced: made no difference. He had let his anger get in the way of building a case, they all had, but today was another day.

He planned to call and check on Simmons around nine, and he had arranged to meet Natasha's school friend, Rebecca Arnold, around lunchtime. She had been away for a few days visiting a friend, but was due back into King's Cross around noon. He drained the last of his coffee and spun away from the window to face his computer. He fired up Google and set about tracking down anything he could in the public domain about Alexander Locke, Nathan Barclay and James Bolton. There was very little about Barclay and Bolton, but after reading the first few articles on Alexander Locke, things took an unexpected twist.

Locke might have kept a low profile as far as the law was concerned, but he had featured quite recently in the local press, half a dozen times in the last twelve months to be precise, as well as a string of older search results. It seemed he had a reputation as a local philanthropist, donating undisclosed sums to a number of charities. There were pictures of him in front of a community centre he'd helped fund the rebuilding of, a shot of him with a local MP at a fundraiser for a nearby kids' football team. The third one he read stopped him in his tracks. Locke was wearing a traditional-style tuxedo, flashing his pearly whites for the camera. He looked every inch the successful businessman, but it wasn't Locke that made him catch his breath, it was the man whose shoulder his arm was around.

Shit, that's all we need.

Porter leant back, arms crossed, resting his chin in one hand while he took in this latest development. The picture on his screen showed Locke arm in arm with the deputy commissioner, Adam Nesbitt, at a fundraiser of some sort. The last thing they needed if they ever made an arrest was for a picture like this to surface in the tabloids. The deputy commissioner attended dozens of these events, and probably wouldn't even remember posing for the picture, but that wouldn't bother the journalists. They would sink their teeth into that and gorge on the story for weeks. He'd have a word with Superintendent Campbell when he came in. The politics of the job could be like quicksand if you weren't careful, and if it surfaced some other way, making Campbell look bad, he'd make Porter pay somewhere down the line.

Porter looked up to see Styles coming through the door. He reminded Porter of a basketball player or a high jumper: he was all limbs, zigzagging between desks like an NBA shooting guard dribbling around his opponents.

'Bit keen today, aren't you? You'll show the rest of us up. Did you bring an apple for the teacher as well?'

'Couldn't sleep. Had an interesting morning already, though.'

Styles stopped short of continuing his usual brand of sarcastic comebacks, perhaps sensing the seriousness of yesterday still hanging over them. 'Share the joy; what have you found?'

Porter spun his monitor around and Styles gave a low whistle.

'Friends in high places, I see,' he said, walking around to his desk and taking a seat opposite Porter.

Porter shrugged. 'Doesn't change anything, but we could do without the complication. OK, I figure the day pans out like this. Rebecca Arnold is due in at King's Cross at noon. See how far you can get digging into Locke's financials. We've only really looked at him in connection with Barclay so far rather than in his own right. After speaking to Alec Brookes, I wonder how kosher Locke's non-drug-related business practices are. If he was strong-arming Barclay in any way, then we run that down in relation to Natasha. Did he just threaten Barclay, or did he extend that to his family as well?'

'What about Bolton?' asked Styles. 'Do we speak to him again? Might turn up the heat a little more?'

Porter shook his head. 'You saw what he was like yesterday. If we haul him in again straight away, he'll sit there looking smug and not say a bloody word. Let's see what we get back from the crime scene report first. Might make our job easy if he left prints all over, but no sense rushing it like we did yesterday. He'll keep.'

'Any word from the hospital on how she's doing?'

'Not yet. I'll give them a call now, then I'll give you a hand with the financials. It's about time you showed me how you decipher that stuff.'

Styles grunted an acknowledgement and started pecking away at his keyboard while Porter picked up the phone. The ward sister he spoke to sounded weary. He guessed she was coming off the night shift rather than being the cavalry relieving those that had worked through since yesterday. She told him Simmons was still stable and was due a further assessment at ten o'clock. There was no sign of her waking up, but he hadn't expected that just yet. He extracted a promise of a call if anything changed, and let her get back to the dozens of patients more deserving of her attention.

He would give anything for her to be sitting upright and chatting away, not only for her own personal wellbeing, but because he was desperate to hear her side of what happened in the Taylor Fisheries building. Had she seen what happened to Gibson? Had she seen Bolton? He prayed she would remember some or all of the frantic charge up the stairs, although he couldn't pin all his hopes on that. The doctor had said there was a chance she might remember nothing. He knew the right thing to do for the time being was to assume she had nothing to give them, and pursue all other lines of enquiry to get something more concrete.

His thoughts darted back to the photo of the deputy commissioner. That was one mess he would gladly follow Campbell's lead on, but one situation he couldn't walk away from was the intersection of the two cases after yesterday's maelstrom of events. Anderson and Whittaker would likely welcome his help with their case, not least of all because their team was lighter by two after yesterday. Locke was a big fish, though, and whoever landed him would have their moment in the limelight. Porter didn't give a damn about the backslapping that came with closing a case, and his worry was that Anderson would want to keep his own hand on the rudder but didn't have the stomach for what lay ahead. Anderson had been a good detective in his day, but he had peaked with the Spice Girls in the nineties and any fire that had burnt in his belly was more of a glowing ember these days. The time to tiptoe around Bolton had passed, but Porter worried that Anderson would want to continue the softly-softly approach to keep fishing for Locke.

Porter decided he would talk to Campbell about it. Emotions always ran high when anything happened to an officer, and they needed a show of strength, a message to any and all onlookers that the full force of the law would crash over you like a tidal wave if you dared raise a hand to one of theirs. Men like Bolton and Locke would read anything else as a sign of weakness, and that was the last thing they could afford right now.

He checked his watch. Almost three hours until he was due to meet Rebecca Arnold. The thought of meeting her triggered a mental leap to Natasha Barclay. An image of her face from one of the pictures they had taken from her flat floated accusingly to the surface in his subconscious, smiling at him across the decades. His eyes flicked guiltily to a folder on the edge of his desk, then away again to where the photograph in question lurked inside, and he scolded himself for barely giving her a second thought since yesterday. He was usually good at compartmentalising, too good sometimes, but Bolton's apathy in the interview room had bordered on amusement at times, and made Porter bristle with anger.

He looked down to see his right hand had taken on a life of its own and curled into a fist at the thought of the big man, and he forced himself to relax. Bolton would slip up, make a mistake, if not now then eventually. His sort always did, and when that day came, Porter would be waiting. He was nothing if not patient, and for a man like Bolton, he would wait as long as it took.

Porter had joked about learning to decipher the financial side of Locke's business, but after more than two hours of patient explanations by Styles, he decided that he would happily let his partner keep the mantle of translator for this particular foreign language. He grasped most of the basics, but when Styles started explaining some of the finer points of corporate takeovers to him his eyes just glazed over.

Luckily, he didn't need to be a financial whizz to understand the scale of Locke's empire. Including the parent company, it spanned fifteen separate companies. They laid claim to an empty meeting room and transferred everything they uncovered onto a whiteboard. Each company had its own box, complete with the type of business, date and price of purchase and previous owners. Slowly but surely, a wide-based pyramid formed, with Locke & Winwood as the tip. Porter popped the top back on his marker pen with a loud *click* and stepped back to admire his work, Michelangelo surveying his Sistine Chapel.

'Whatever else he is, he's a shrewd businessman,' said Styles, very matter-of-fact. 'He runs the show end to end. No outside input unless absolutely necessary.'

Porter came around the table to where Styles sat and slid into the empty chair beside him so they both faced the board, interviewers getting ready to interrogate their suspect.

'How do you mean, end to end?'

'Look at what it is they do.' Styles pointed to the leftmost box and worked his way across. 'He's got four separate haulage firms: Atlas down south, and the others all at major ports. Each of those locations has a sister company nearby that owns the warehouse space for storage. His site security and vehicle maintenance are all handled by another offshoot. Basically it's all done in house—'

'—so there're no outsiders to stumble across something they shouldn't,' Porter finished the sentence for him.

'Exactly. There's got to be legit stuff going through these as well, but they'll have trusted people on the inside at each place who can mark any special shipments and make sure they get handled the right way.'

'So if it's such a close-knit family, how do we get past that, then? We can't exactly charm our way in.'

'Shame there's no way of knowing which ones are the more interesting shipments,' said Styles.

'There's not much we can do at this stage even if we did – no probable cause.'

'Now, now, guv, you're not usually so quick to admit defeat. What if we received a call from a concerned employee saying that a particular truck from Atlas, for example, had been stolen earlier that day? We'd be compelled to pull them over to check it out.'

Porter smiled. 'Since when did you turn into such a scheming little bastard? You're meant to be Sherlock, not Moriarty.'

'Glad to see you've finally come to terms with me wearing the deerstalker in this relationship.'

Porter swatted the jibe away with a wave of his hand. 'I'm all for being creative, but when we bring any of them in again, it has to be done right. If Bolton comes back in here, the only way he leaves is still in cuffs and on his way to a cell.'

Styles nodded. 'Amen to that.' He pointed back at the whiteboard. 'I want to spend a bit more time on this later as well. Something doesn't feel right about the way he's bought the others out.'

'Such as?'

'I'll need to do a bit more digging, and none of them came as cheaply as Atlas, but Locke bought them all for a fraction of what you'd expect the market value to be.'

'You're saying he's not just got an eye for a bargain?'

'I'm saying that there's enough smoke and mirrors around the Atlas takeover to suggest the slump in business was engineered. Maybe he makes a habit of driving the price down in his own unique way. Maybe Barclay wasn't the only business owner to get a visit from Little and Large?'

'That's a lot of ifs, but fine, check it out. Might be interesting to see if any of the others who sold out ended up like Barclay. I wouldn't mind a chat with them if they handled their own buyouts better than he did.'

They lapsed into silence as they studied the chart for few more seconds. Porter couldn't decide if it looked more like a pyramid or an iceberg. If it was the latter, and this was just the tip, Porter wondered just how far the rest of Locke's empire extended below the waterline, and how many others like Barclay had underestimated it, and sunk without a trace.

Superintendent Campbell was on a call when Porter knocked on his door, but waved him in, holding up a finger to signal he wouldn't be long. Porter stayed standing until Campbell finished his call and told him to take a seat. Porter perched himself on the last few inches of the chair. He never felt entirely comfortable around Campbell, and didn't want to draw out the conversation any longer than he had to.

Campbell was a big man in a little man's body. He tried too hard on all fronts. Too loud. Too gregarious. Too officious. His pale, pasty face was the result of too much time in the office, too little exercise, and the last few years had seen him turn into the bigger man, quite literally, but just not in the way he would have wanted. He was starting to grow jowls, and it was almost worth pissing him off to see them wobble like the last turkey bitching about Christmas. Rumour was that he'd been a decent copper in his day, leading the charge against some of the city's biggest drug dealers and gangs, but Porter had only ever known him wedged behind a desk.

'Morning, Porter, what can I do for you today?' he asked in a self-important tone.

Porter had prepared a sales pitch to try and tie the Natasha Barclay case together with the investigation into yesterday's events. That meant annexing the drugs angle as well. With Bolton being a key suspect in Gibson's death, any move against him could affect their strategy to take down Locke and his organisation.

Campbell listened without saying a word, peering at Porter over steepled fingers. When Porter finished, there was a brief silence while Campbell considered the options. Finally, he spoke.

'I'll be honest with you, Porter, what you're saying isn't totally without merit but I'm not convinced. What about Anderson, for starters? He and Whittaker have put a hell of a lot of hours into the drugs angle and, besides, Gibson and Simmons are their people. You could argue they have more skin in the game. I can guarantee Superintendent Milburn won't let it go easily when the time comes to make any arrests.'

Roger Milburn was Campbell's peer and headed up the drugs squad. He was a no-nonsense old-school copper, fiercely protective over his people and their cases, and would almost certainly put up a fight.

Porter shrugged. 'We've got three murders now, guv. They're stacking up, and no disrespect to DI Anderson, but he's got no experience running a murder investigation.'

'Three?'

'Yep, three. I want to officially treat Natasha's disappearance as suspected murder. No way she's walked away after injuries like that. We've already got two solid suspects in Bolton and her father. We already have motive if it turns out to be the dad, and we can place Bolton inside her flat so he's still a contender. Think of the headlines if we can close this one after this length of time. It's about time we got some good press.'

'And if we don't close it?'

'Then nobody even knows. Nobody reported her missing. The press doesn't know about it, and the only people that might care, the family, don't seem to give a shit. It's win-win on that front.'

'What about Gibson and that other chap, Carter? Anderson was there on the scene.'

'He was, sir, that's true, and no disrespect' – Porter made a show of looking around for eavesdroppers even though he knew the door was shut – 'but that was a massive balls-up. No way should Simmons and Gibson have been allowed to charge in on their own like that. Anderson's cut corners in the past, and there's a chance he might do so again here to make sure no mud sticks to him. Besides, worst case, if we can't nail anyone for Carter, maybe it was an accidental death and doesn't even hit the murder stats?'

Porter hated himself for appealing to Campbell based on office politics and public opinion, but it was the best way to play him from experience. Campbell was a pen-pusher who lived and died by the crime statistics. Closed cases were his currency, and Porter needed his blessing to merge the two. He sensed that Campbell was wavering and played his trump card.

'Besides, Anderson will be wandering off into the sunset in three weeks, and we need continuity. He'll just be passing on to someone else then anyway, so why not me, now? He and Whittaker can stay involved on the drugs side, but I really want this one done right, and that means me taking point.'

Campbell stroked his chin thoughtfully for a full five seconds before giving an answer. 'Alright, Porter, I'll speak to Milburn and see what we can agree. We can call it a joint task force or something like that. Now what was the other thing you wanted to speak to me about?'

Porter had deliberately waited to get Campbell's support before he mentioned the picture of the deputy commissioner posing with Locke. Campbell's face visibly paled when Porter told him what he'd found.

'Who else knows about this?'

'Just me and Styles for now. I'll be briefing Anderson and Whittaker later today.'

'See that it goes no further for now,' said Campbell. 'I'm sure there's nothing to worry about. The deputy commissioner attends dozens of these things every year, but leave that with me. Do not move against Locke before I've had a chance to see if we're exposed in any way.'

'Understood, sir.'

'And I want daily updates. I'll call you later after I've spoken to Milburn. Now if that's all, I've got a meeting in five minutes.'

Porter thanked him and headed back downstairs to grab coffees for himself and Styles. He tried to leave the politics to others when he could, but if doing it this way meant he led on both cases, and helped keep Natasha in the spotlight as well, then it was a means to an end. He guessed it was the same in the private sector. There would always be those jostling for position instead of focusing on the task at hand. He classed himself as more of an idealist. High rates of case closure were good, but not because it was a numbers game. It was good because the higher the number, the more people paid for their crimes, the more families would feel justice had been done, and the more people Porter could look in the eye and say he had done everything in his power to make things right.

He knew that kind of approach could well cost him as many allies in the long run as it would gain him, but it was the only way he could keep doing the job. His gut told him that the picture of Locke with Deputy Commissioner Nesbitt was probably innocent enough, but he knew that if it wasn't he couldn't let that pass. He would pursue things to a conclusion, let the chips fall where they may, and politics be damned.

Porter stared up at the roof of the revamped King's Cross Station while he queued for a drink at Leon. It swirled up and out from a central steel stalk, as if the glass ceiling had sprouted from the earth, metal branches criss-crossing back and forth to weave a canopy. He wondered what the same architect could do with the station at Paddington Green given half the chance, and a fraction of the budget. He shuffled to the front of the line, paid for his coffee and wandered back towards the tables out front. A shoal of young children shot past, trailing wizards' robes behind them, chattering about Platform 9 ¾, and a stray wand nearly put paid to his coffee before he'd managed a sip.

Rebecca Arnold only kept him waiting five minutes. She was a slender woman, mid-fifties, wearing a knee-length quilted black jacket, fastened right up to her chin, with her cheeks pink after a brisk walk from her train. Her short, pixie-like hair was cut like Demi Moore's character in *Ghost* and she looked down at him with eyes questioning as she approached, even though he was the only person at the tables.

'Miss Arnold?' Porter asked, rising to greet her.

'Mrs Arnold.' She held up her left hand, a diamond no bigger than a match-head placing a sparkling exclamation point on her statement. She gave a smile that melted into embarrassment. 'Sorry, I didn't mean that to come out as snappy as it must have sounded.'

Porter returned the smile. 'Not at all, Mrs Arnold. I'm Detective Inspector Porter. Thanks for taking the time to meet me. Can I get you a drink?'

She shook her head. 'No, thank you, Detective. I'm on a bit of a detox. No caffeine for a month.' Porter pondered that for a second: his idea of hell.

Rebecca Arnold unzipped her coat as she sat, revealing a plain cotton blouse and charcoal grey skirt underneath. Porter guessed at bank cashier, although he was as good at guessing professions as he was at guessing women's ages. Being wrong about the latter was far more likely to make enemies of his subjects, so he tended to keep his thoughts on both to himself.

'So you're probably wondering what all this is about,' he said as he sat back down.

She nodded nervously in agreement. 'The officer I spoke to said it had to do with Natasha. Is she alright?' Her tongue darted out to moisten her lips.

'That's what we're trying to find out, Mrs Arnold. I'm afraid she's missing, and we're looking for people she may have been in contact with.'

Rebecca Arnold shrugged, eyebrows and shoulders moving in unison with the gesture, and frowned. 'Like I said to the officer on the phone, I've not spoken to her since my final year at uni. We're literally talking back in the eighties here.' She raised a hand to stifle a squeak, somewhere between a laugh and a grunt.

'That may be so, Mrs Arnold,' said Porter calmly, 'but for all we know you could still have been one of the last people to see her. No one has seen her since April 1983.'

Her eyes widened and parallel lines of surprise scored her forehead like sheet music. 'She's been missing since the eighties and you're just looking for her now?'

'Nobody had reported her missing, Mrs Arnold. We didn't know we needed to be looking.'

'And now they have?'

'Something like that.' Porter sighed. He had to stop her asking her own questions and keep to his agenda. 'Because it's so long ago, anything you can tell us about her could be useful. Things like what kind of person she was, who she hung out with, anyone she fell out with, friends, boyfriends, those kinds of things.'

She uncrossed then recrossed her legs, giving herself time to think. Porter had other questions to ask, but he waited her out, giving her time to revisit a decade long gone.

'She was . . .' she began slowly, searching for the words. 'She was a cool person to hang out with. We were close for a while, first because of the swimming team, but after that we stayed friends outside of school until I went off to university. We used to hang out on weekends, sneak into clubs, you know, the kind of stuff teenagers do.'

'What about her family?' Porter prompted. 'Did she talk much about them?'

She gave a knowing smile. 'Yep, more of a rant when it came to her stepmum. Thought she wasn't good enough for her dad. She was a proper daddy's girl from what I remember, even though he spent more time at work than at home. I tried to call her after I heard about, you know . . . what happened to him.' Her voice faded away to a murmur.

'You said tried; did you manage to reach her?'

She shook her head. 'No, no I didn't. I called her place, called her a few times, but she never answered. I went round to see her when I came back for the Easter holidays but she was never home when I called round.'

Rebecca Arnold looked up at Porter. 'Are you honestly telling me she's been missing since then?' There was a slight tremor in her voice now.

'We've not found anyone that she has been in contact with since around that time. What about other friends or boyfriends?'

'Why do I feel like you're not telling me everything?' she asked accusingly. 'Do you think something has happened to her?'

'There's not a lot to tell at the moment, Mrs Arnold,' Porter lied. 'But the more we find out about her, the more chance we have of figuring out where she went. So, any friends or boyfriends you can tell me about?'

There was no way he was about to tell her that they had her long-lost school friend's hand in an evidence bag. He needed calm recollections, not thoughts scattered by a grisly revelation.

'She had a steady boyfriend for a year at school, Tom Wilton, but they broke up before our final year and she played the field for a bit after that. I was always the one they would come and talk to in the bars, but it was so they could get to her. Not that I'm complaining. There were plenty to go around.'

'Anyone in particular you remember?' he asked. Porter started to feel like a broken record, and longed for her to just give him a straight answer without any rambling recollections.

'She did have a thing for the bad boys,' she began, a half smile turning the corners of her mouth upwards. 'There weren't loads but she knew how to pick them. There were a few I remember. One reckoned he was in the SAS, and kept disappearing for weeks saying he was on a mission. The other one wasn't the best looker, but kind of hard to forget. He was that big that we joked he probably had a beanstalk in his back garden. Her dad and stepmum didn't approve, mind.'

Porter opened his mouth to ask his next question but stopped, mouth open like a goldfish. Rebecca Arnold gave a curious smile.

'Detective, are you alright?'

He nodded slowly, choosing his words, not wanting to get his hopes up.

'The last one you mentioned, do you remember his name?'

She looked away and up at the ceiling, as if there would be a clue lurking by the light fittings, swirling her fingers in a circular motion as she searched for a name.

'John, Jim, Joey . . . something like that. Couldn't say for sure, it's been a long time.'

'Did he have a scar here, by any chance?' he asked, tracing a line from the edge of his jaw into the cleft of his chin.

She shook her head. 'No, I'm pretty sure he didn't.'

'Pretty sure, or certain?' Porter practically barked the question at her, his impatience starting to show.

'Certain.' She leant back, her expression showing the slightest hint of frostiness at his tone.

'I'm sorry, Mrs Arnold. I didn't mean to snap like that. It's been a long few days.'

'Who's the man with the scar?'

'Nobody. What about . . .' He stopped short of asking her about the SAS wannabe when something else occurred to him. 'Mrs Arnold, could you excuse me for just a minute.'

She nodded, and he grabbed his phone from the table, logging in to his email. He found the attachment he was looking for, and scrolled through a few pictures. When he found the one he wanted, he put the phone down and spun it to face her.

The black-and-white photograph onscreen showed a man who looked to be in his mid to late twenties, with an angry face like a bulldog chewing on a wasp, and a military-short haircut. Some people were like a rabbit in the headlights when they had their mugshot snapped. This man just looked bored. She looked at it for a few seconds then smiled, her whole face brightening as she looked up, like a pupil eager to please their teacher.

'This is him. Where on earth did you get this?'

Porter waited until they were all seated before he spoke. Styles was the last man in, and slid into the free seat between Anderson and Whittaker.

'C'mon then, Porter,' said Anderson impatiently. 'What's so important we've had to put lunch on hold? I've only had a bowl of that granola crap all day.' He patted his gut as he winked at Whittaker, and Porter grimaced at the ripple of flesh beneath the shirt. 'Girlfriend reckons healthy eating will trim me down and give me a new lease of life in retirement.'

Porter held his phone down by his side. It was turned inwards against his leg to hide the screen. He saw Styles looking down at him, and realised his knee was bouncing up and down, but Porter kept his poker face on, tapping a rhythm out against his leg with the handset.

'I've spoken with Rebecca Arnold, and things just got interesting,' he said with an enigmatic smile.

'Who the hell is she?' asked Whittaker.

'She's a classmate of Natasha Barclay.'

'Your hand with the missing body?' asked Anderson. 'What's that got to do with our case? We'll help if we get time, but we really need—'

'They're linked beyond doubt now. He's the link.' He whipped his hand up to chest height fast enough to give the man in the picture whiplash.

'Is that who I think it is?' said Styles softly.

Porter smiled. 'How many other six-foot-five arseholes do you know? Bolton knew Natasha Barclay. Mrs Arnold puts them together twice in the weeks leading up to Barclay's suicide; the same time frame anyone last spotted Natasha. She's pretty sure Natasha took him home after a night out.'

'I can see it's an old pic, but he looks different as well – I mean, not just younger.'

'It was taken when he was hauled in for assault back in the eighties. He got jumped on by four blokes in the nick and ended up with a nasty slash from a razor blade across the chin. That's where he got his attractive scar, but this was before that.'

Anderson cleared his throat. 'All very well and good, but how exactly does that help us with Bolton? So he knew her? Big deal. You saw what happened when we dragged him in with no proof. All this proves is that she didn't exactly play hard to get if she put out after two dates.'

Porter shot him an irritated glance and Anderson's throaty chuckle died away. Attitude like this was exactly why he didn't want Anderson with his hands on the steering wheel. Some people had their glass half empty. Anderson's had a massive crack running down the side for good measure.

'I'm not suggesting we run out and arrest him now, you daft bastard. We already know from his prints that he's been in her apartment. He could spin that any number of ways, but now we have proof that he actually knew her personally. Think it through, though. Locke uses Bolton to intimidate Barclay. He also ends up talking the daughter into bed, and soon after that Barclay sells up, eats a bullet and she goes missing. You honestly think that was just coincidence?'

Anderson just shrugged.

'Bullshit,' snapped Porter. He could feel the blood rising to his cheeks, hear the edge creeping into his voice, but he wasn't going to let Anderson's indifference infect the case, or his need to solve the puzzle. 'Whatever he did, he did it for a reason. Who knows what he wanted? Maybe it was to get some kind of leverage over Barclay, maybe it was just an extra little "fuck you" from Locke.'

'I agree it's not just coincidence, guv,' said Styles, 'but how do we work backwards to figure out what the hell happened? I mean, it's not as if Bolton is just going to give us a kiss and tell, is it?'

Porter sighed. This was the part of the case still shrouded in a swirl of mist, and the harder he stared at it, the more impenetrable it became. 'We start by going over the crime scene report again; question any anomalies, anything that looks out of place or doesn't sound quite right. If we can place him in her flat the day she went missing, we can bring him back in.'

'We can't move on him yet,' protested Anderson. 'What about Locke? What about doing things right?'

Porter glared at him. 'If you'd done things right, we wouldn't have one officer dead and another fighting for her life.'

Anderson flinched as if he'd been slapped, and Porter instantly regretted it. 'Look, I'm sorry. That was harsh. What I'm trying to say, though, is if we get him for something he did way back then, it takes the pressure off us to pin what happened yesterday on him. Don't get me wrong,' he added, 'I'll see him done for that as well, but it buys us time to work that case and gets him off the streets.'

'We can still work the drugs angle as well,' Styles piped up.

Anderson looked at him and sneered. 'So, what, then? We never needed Bolton all along, and just jump straight up to Locke? Is that what you're saying?'

'No, but think about it. We already have the other guy on tape – Patchett? If Bolton gets taken out of the picture, Locke will need someone else to step in. Whoever that is will work with Patchett, so you turn Patchett just like you turned Carter.'

'And look how well that worked out,' mumbled Anderson under his breath.

'Didn't quite catch that,' said Porter, the tone of his voice a clear warning to Anderson that he need not bother repeating it.

'Nothing. Doesn't matter.'

Porter gave a grim smile then looked over at Styles. 'OK then. While we're all together, do you want to give an update on what you found with Locke's little financial dealings?'

Styles nodded and quickly summed up what he'd uncovered about the various companies Locke had snapped up over the years. He gave an overview of each purchase, mostly from memory, but snuck an occasional glance at the notepad in his lap. The businesses centred around four ports at key locations. Besides London, Locke operated in Grangemouth near Edinburgh, Grimsby on the east coast and Milford Haven nestled in the west, four points on a skewed compass. At each of these hubs, as Styles christened them, Locke had his own storage, his own transportation, and his own private security teams. The other three businesses were nothing to do with that industry: two restaurants in Dartford and a gym near Gravesend.

They all listened intently as he painted a picture of an empire that had grown from a sapling to a network of companies whose reach sprawled across all of mainland Britain. Locke had a knack, it seemed, of snapping up struggling businesses for a fire-sale price, and turning their fortunes around. That wasn't the only thing that each purchase had in common, though. All three businesses at the hub in Grangemouth had been privately owned by Alastair Reece. The Reece family had sold out to Alexander Locke after Mr Reece was killed in a road accident back in 1999. The east coast arm of the business in Grimsby was purchased after the owner, Martin Murphy, was killed in a hit-and-run after a night out in 1993. Wales was different. George Evans had lost his biggest customer in 1998 after a series of warehouse fires sent their confidence plummeting and his insurance premiums through the roof. Mr Evans's last known address showed he had stayed in Wales but moved north to Caernarfon after he sold up.

Styles closed his notebook and leant back to signal to his audience that his show and tell was done for now.

'Brings a whole new meaning to hostile takeover,' said Porter.

'How the hell has nobody picked up on this before now?' asked Whittaker.

'Don't care,' said Porter. 'What matters is that we have now and it ends here. You two take Murphy and Reece. See if anyone who worked the cases is still around, any of the family we can speak to. Styles and I will take Evans, and I want to have another chat with Mrs Locke, on her own this time.'

'Yes, boss. Anything else while we're at it? Shine your shoes, make your tea?' said Anderson, a whininess creeping around the edge of his words like a petulant teenager. 'I've got a better idea. How about you let us do our job and worry about your own case. We've worked too hard to just—'

'Really?' Porter cut him off. His tolerance for Anderson's excuses slipped away in an instant. 'Six months and the best you have – sorry, my mistake, *had* – was a low-level warehouse fella so small-time he barely registered on the scale of criminal intent. And you really think this is a pissing contest so I can get to shake hands with the chief constable and steal your headlines?'

Anderson glared at him, but Porter hadn't finished with him yet.

'If we have evidence that James Bolton is guilty of murder, I'm damned if he gets to keep walking round no matter what else he's done. I can place him with Natasha now, and I guarantee you he will have fucked up somewhere else as well. If I can pin whatever went down at her flat on him, or the scene from yesterday, then he's going down for that.'

He'd nearly said '*then he's mine*', but making it clear just how personal this was starting to feel wasn't the way to get cooperation from the other detectives.

He sucked in a deep breath and tried a different tack. 'Look, we both want the same thing, but you don't put one copper in the morgue and another in intensive care and get a stay of execution. If we can pin even one of those on him, then maybe he rolls and gives us Locke to strike a deal for himself.'

'Whatever. Let's just get on with it,' Anderson grumbled. 'But get one thing clear: you're not my boss. You don't order me around. I was closing cases when you were still squeezing spots, so less of the attitude and we'll be just fine.'

Porter just looked at him for a few seconds until Anderson broke the stare, and headed out with Whittaker in tow, looking slightly embarrassed by his partner's reactions. Porter waited till they were both gone before closing the door and slumping back into his seat.

'All the ladies love a bad boy, guv. Does this mean you want to start playing "bad cop" in our next interview?'

Porter gave him a gentle rap on the shoulder with his knuckles and smiled. He thought of Simmons lying in her spider's web of wires and tubes. Granted, there was nothing between them, not really. Nothing had actually happened.

Maybe a little flirting, at worst? Worst? Best? He couldn't decide what it was or what he wanted it to be. He couldn't focus on that right now, but the idea that somebody he cared about could slip away at any time, without there being a damn thing he could do about it, stoked a fire that had only been embers since Holly. Even if it was only platonic, the concept of protecting those who couldn't protect themselves was why he had joined up in the first place. Even though they couldn't bring Bolton in yet, he felt in his gut that it was only a matter of time.

All the ladies love a bad boy.

Had that been Natasha's mistake? The odds of her being alive were slim. He hoped that it had been quick for her. Maybe she hadn't even seen it coming. Bolton didn't strike him as a man much given to mercy, though. If he was involved, then it didn't bode well for her, and maybe she had been her old man's Achilles heel. Had losing her as well as the business tipped the scales and made his choice for him? Porter didn't know what choices he would make if given the same circumstances, and hoped to God he never found out.

CHAPTER TWELVE

An arctic front still claimed squatter's rights even now with March only a week away. Slate-grey clouds balanced precariously on the peaks, scowling down at the valleys below, and splashes of stubborn snow speckled the higher ground like dandruff. The A5 sliced through the heart of Snowdonia National Park, following paths sculpted over four hundred million years by the crushing weight of ice.

It was the kind of scenery that would make even a hardened city dweller stare in contemplative silence. Porter had spent nine years in the army, and had experienced the Welsh scenery first-hand on several training exercises, but without the creature comforts of a heated car interior. He smiled grimly at the memory of squatting behind the remnants of a drystone wall, blocks scattered like Jenga pieces, jealously guarding a fire from the savage wind, boiling water for a cup of tea he would savour like a fine wine.

They spent most of the drive to George Evans's house walking through the possible outcomes as far as Natasha Barclay was concerned. They both dismissed the notion that Natasha might still be alive. It would be hard enough to survive that kind of traumatic injury altogether, let alone without the support of your friends and family. The original theory that Barclay killed her himself still had merit. The fact that he might have been pushed to his limits and beyond to be able to do that by Locke systematically dismantling his world would not change that fact.

After interviewing Rebecca Arnold, there was an equally good chance that Bolton was their man. Bolton had a stake in Barclay selling out. Who was to say how far he would have gone to make sure that happened? There was also the possibility that it was for himself, and that he'd simply lost his temper with her. Porter knew he had that in him, that ability to cross the line and do what others could not stomach. Had Natasha said or done the wrong thing, flirted with another man in front of him? Could it have happened in the heat of the moment?

The last scenario they considered was that it was someone else entirely, someone that hadn't even made a ripple on the pond, let alone a big splash like Bolton. Porter conceded it was possible but unlikely. Bolton was still the prime suspect for him, although everything about the case against him still felt flimsy. They had a witness to place him with Natasha, and had his fingerprints in the apartment, but he could already picture the sneer he would get from Charles Jasper if they dragged Bolton in again with nothing more than that. They'd no doubt argue that he'd gone back there after a few drinks, had a drink, maybe more, and left promising to call her the next day. The perfect gentleman.

At this stage, their best chance of a conviction still lay with Simmons waking up and positively identifying him as her attacker. As for Locke, there was nothing to verify that he either knew what Bolton had planned at the Taylor building or that he'd sanctioned it himself. Nor was there anything to link him directly to the avalanche of narcotics that flowed through his network. Their best shot at him, as of now, resided in an old farmhouse three miles from Caernarfon.

According to the report Styles had dug up, George Evans had suffered in more than just the financial sense. The last fire had been at an overflow storage site near Haverfordwest, and Evans had been on-site when it happened. He had gone back into the building to help one of his men who had been overcome by the smoke, and ended up with third-degree burns across his right shoulder and down onto his bicep.

They drove through Caernarfon itself and came off the main road, crossing the River Seiont just before it made its final loop towards the mouth to empty its contents into open water. Evans lived in an old farmhouse with whitewashed walls and a thatched roof. Smoke seeped lazily from the chimney, dancing on the breeze and disappearing into nothing. A Land Rover was parked under a nearby oak tree, its white paint camouflaged behind splashes of mud dried black and a layer of dust from long hours of use.

They had made a decision not to call ahead. People had a tendency to suddenly remember urgent commitments and not be around to open the door when you told them your arrival time in advance. Porter rapped four times in quick succession and stood back from the door, looking around as he waited. As close to Caernarfon as it was, the house had a secluded feel to it, set back from the main road with a line of trees casting a protective arm around the west side and a line of wooden fencing to the east. Porter preferred the ebb and flow of the city, the life that pulsed through it with all its sounds and smells. It had a vitality all of its own, from the low rumble of the Underground and the indeterminate murmuring of large crowds of people to the symphony of scents assaulting the nostrils at places like Borough Market. That was his world.

A blurred silhouette moved behind the opaque glass door, and a key scraped then squeaked in a lock. The door swung open to reveal a man six inches shorter than Porter. He guessed him to be in his late sixties, wearing an old green sweater and dark blue jeans. His once rusty brown hair had a frosting of white around the edges, and the beard that exploded from his chin reminded Porter of Gimli the dwarf from *The Lord of the Rings*.

He stared at them from beneath eyebrows almost as dense as the beard, and raised them like two arching caterpillars in an unspoken question.

'Mr Evans?' said Porter.

'I am he,' Evans replied, with a curt nod. His voice was low like an idling car engine, with the unmistakable sing-song lilt of the Welsh accent.

Porter quickly introduced himself and his partner. 'We'd like to ask you some questions about a case we're working on. It involves a number of companies and individuals, some of whom you've done business with in the past.'

Evans held Porter's gaze as he spoke. 'Son, I've not worked a day in nearly twenty years. Just enjoying my retirement. I think you've wasted your petrol coming here.'

'That's when we're taking about, Mr Evans,' said Styles. 'Nineteen years ago. You sold the three companies you owned to Locke & Winwood.'

Evans whipped his head around to look at Styles, eyes narrowing as he stared. 'You've got some nerve coming round here asking questions now. Where the bloody hell were you when I asked for help years ago?' He still spoke in a low grumble, but the sparks of anger coming off his words were unmistakable.

'Sorry, Mr Evans, I wasn't aware that there was any police involvement when you sold up,' said Porter.

'There wasn't.' His voice rose a shade higher now, lifted by the anger. 'But there bloody well should have been. Useless bastards didn't lift a finger. Said there was nothing they could do. No evidence, apparently. Well, they didn't look that bloody hard, I can tell you.'

'Well, if you can spare us the time, Mr Evans, I'd be more than happy to hear your version of events.'

Evans eyed him suspiciously then shrugged. 'What the hell. I've got nothing better to do, and I'm not scared of that bastard. Not any more.'

He turned and made his way back inside the house, gesturing for them to follow.

'Scared of who, Mr Evans?'

Evans shouted back over his shoulder as he turned a corner at the end of the short hallway. 'Of Alexander bloody Locke, that's who.'

Porter and Styles sipped politely at mugs of steaming milky tea while Evans sat across from them at a large oak kitchen table and told them what he remembered. He had taken over from his uncle after working there for twenty years, and turned a small family business into one of the biggest in the area. He had been in the early stages of the most lucrative contract they'd ever had, when a spate of warehouse fires had led to the very same customer exercising a get-out clause and leaving them with hefty insurance premiums to pay, and no sign of new business to replace the lost revenue.

'He didn't stop there, though,' said Evans.

Porter interrupted. 'You say "he" – are you saying that Mr Locke was responsible for the fires, Mr Evans?'

'I can no more prove that than I can prove that God exists, but with some things you don't need proof, you just believe and know in your heart. He might not have struck the match, but he did this to me, as sure as night follows day. He did this.'

'What makes you so sure?' asked Styles.

'I was warned,' he said simply. 'I was warned that I'd regret turning down his offer.' His eyes had lost some of their focus now, not seeing the kitchen table, but looking back and seeing things as they had transpired, seeing Alexander Locke.

'What was the warning, Mr Evans?' said Porter softly, not wanting to break the flashback, just steer it in the right direction.

'He offered me peanuts,' said Evans, 'nothing near its real worth. I said no, of course, but he wasn't put off and next time he brought his muscle. Two of them came with him, one big bloke and one little. Made me the same offer again, and said that he wouldn't be so generous if I made him stretch to a third. I told him that wasn't how negotiation works. I told him that when your offer is rejected, you're meant to up it. You know what he said to that?'

Porter was caught mid-sip with his mug to his lips and a mouth of warm tea, and couldn't speak, but he shook his head slightly to prompt Evans.

'He laughed at me. Actually laughed in my face, him and his two babysitters. Found it hilarious, they did. Then he looks at me and asks me what the hell made me think that anything was up for negotiation? The bloody cheek of the man.' Evans shook his head, still bristling at the disrespect all these years later.

'And then what happened?' prompted Porter.

'First fire was a week after that. No one got hurt, thank God.' Evans made a quick sign of the cross. 'But we lost everything in the building. Cost me a bloody fortune, even with the insurance. Second one was only two days later. Third one the day after that. Fire Brigade said it was faulty wiring, but I had those places checked regularly. There was bugger all wrong with that wiring!'

He was practically shouting now, every other word sending tiny grenades of spittle arcing out. Then his voice grew quiet, his story moving into the eye of the storm, his recollection calmer now.

'Third one was what got me.' He rolled up his sleeve. 'I'd worked late and was just finishing up when it started. Ripped through the place like a tornado. No way was that the wiring. A fire moves that fast it's had help, you know what I'm saying?' He looked at them both for affirmation. 'I was just stood watching my life go up in smoke when I heard Danny shouting. Lazy sod had been having a sly snooze off in a corner, and woke up coughing.'

He grabbed the cuff of his right sleeve and started to pull his arm back up it as he spoke.

'I didn't even think. Just ran back in. Suppose if I'd stopped and thought about it I'd probably have been too scared to do anything. I found him quick enough and we were nearly out. I could even see the door. There was a container on a shelf off to my right, God knows what was in it, but it went up with a bang and next thing I know my bloody shirt is on fire.'

He had pulled his arm completely out by now, and lifted the hem of his jumper up over the side of his chest until his shoulder and arm were exposed. The scars were old, and had long since lost their vivid red glow. What was left behind was a faded pink, in contrast to his natural pale freckled forearm. Its contours rose and swirled in places like leathery brushstrokes. The disfiguration extended part way across his chest, then stopped suddenly in a thicker tidemark of scar tissue.

'Locke came back the day I got out of hospital, to offer his sympathies, if you can believe that. Looked me in the eye and told me I was lucky my buildings didn't have thatched roofs like my house. Told me how those old thatches take like kindling and go up in seconds.'

His face was flushed with anger now. The pent-up hatred for Locke had lain and festered for almost two decades, but it bubbled to the surface now.

'The bastard told me I should get the wiring checked at home so the farmhouse wouldn't go the same way. I didn't tell Anne about that last part, God rest her soul.'

Evans looked off to the left as he spoke, and Porter followed his gaze to see a photograph of a younger Evans with his arm around his bride. He was unmistakeable in his suit, his beard just as prominent, she with a simple white dress and a modest bouquet of roses.

'She's no longer with us?' asked Porter.

'No,' he said with a shake of his head, 'but that was nothing to do with Locke.' The anger in his eyes gave way to a more youthful sparkle, a reflection of good times long gone but still remembered. 'Cancer. She died four years ago. She's the reason I sold up in the end.'

'How do you mean?' asked Styles.

'I didn't have much to start with, Detective, so losing the business didn't leave me any worse off, and I still ended up with some money to show for it, although not as much as I deserved.' He gave a bitter chuckle. 'She was all that really mattered to me, and he wouldn't have stopped. I knew that then. Wouldn't have stopped until there was nothing left, and I couldn't risk anything happening to her. Couldn't have lived with myself, especially not after some of the things his two meatheads said.'

'Out of interest, Mr Evans, are these the two men you're referring to?'

Porter pulled two pictures from his jacket pocket, one of Bolton, the other of Davies, and placed them on the table in front of Evans.

Evans nodded grimly. 'That's the bastards right there.'

'And what was it they said?'

'The little one, had a face like a weasel with beady little eyes, he did, he told me what would happen if I insisted on holding out.' Evans grimaced as he tapped the picture of Oliver Davies. 'Told me a story about another chap that had apparently tried saying no to Mr Locke.' The name was spat out rather than spoken. 'This other fella was like me: self-made man, hard worker, family man.' A tremor crept into his deep voice now, the slightest of vibrations behind the words. 'Told me in a fair amount of detail what would happen to Anne if I didn't sign it over.'

Evans rubbed at his eyes. Porter saw the fire in them mixed with frustration and fear. Fear for what he would have subjected his wife to if he hadn't done as he was told.

'Don't get me wrong, if they laid a finger on her they'd have had to put me in the ground to stop me. I would've done anything for my wife. She didn't want me to sell.' Evans looked back at the wedding photograph as he kept on talking, confessing to her now what he couldn't tell her years ago. 'If I'd told her about the threats she'd have made me go to the police, and somehow I didn't get the impression that would be the last I'd see of those three if I did. I couldn't take that chance. Couldn't risk them coming for her when I was at work. They didn't strike me as the kind of men to make idle threats.'

Porter's head buzzed with the familiar excitement that came when strands of a case started to come together, to coalesce into something more solid. 'This man they told you about, did they tell you anything else about him? His name? Where he was from?'

Evans looked back from the picture at the two detectives, licked his lips nervously, and shook his head. 'No. No name.'

Porter realised he had been holding his breath as he waited for the answer, and let it out loudly.

'But they showed me a picture. The little one had it with him. Showed me a picture of what happens to people who say no to Mr Locke.'

'What was in the picture, Mr Evans?' asked Porter.

Evans stood up and went across to a wooden dresser tucked into an alcove. He opened a drawer and rummaged around inside. When he turned around, he was holding a tattered brown envelope. He walked slowly across to where they sat and slid it across the table towards Porter with a soft whisper, and took his seat again.

'See for yourself.'

'What's this? Is that . . . ?' Porter's voice tailed off. Evans finished the sentence for him.

'The man that said no. They told me to keep it as a souvenir. Thought about taking it to the police, at first, but there'd be no proof they gave it to me. Probably no easy way to find out who the chap even is. I don't know why I kept it, to be honest. I only looked at it one more time, a year after it all happened, to remind myself that I made the right choice not ending up like him.'

Porter lifted the flap up, so old that there was no hint of stickiness where the adhesive used to be, and drew out the single photograph from inside. He recognised the surroundings before he even looked at the face. The jacket, folded neatly so as not to crease it. The single sheet of paper positioned squarely on top of the garment. Finally, he looked at the face. Nathan Barclay's eyes were closed; his head hung forward, lips slightly parted. There was no mistaking his peaceful expression for that of a man taking a power nap, though. You only had to look at the dark spray on the cabinet behind him to know his eyes wouldn't be opening again.

Porter passed the picture across to Styles. Nathan Barclay's suicide had just become a lot more interesting.

Alexander Locke watched Charles Jasper scuttle across the driveway and climb into his car. He heard the rustle of fabric from behind him, where James Bolton reclined against the sofa. The big man took up half of the available space on the three-seater, and looked around the room as if he was casing the place. Locke didn't often allow people who worked for him into his home. Bolton had only been here twice before, and with good reason. Men like James Bolton drew trouble to themselves like one of those ultraviolet lights that lures in flies. Sometimes that trouble was from business rivals; other days, like today, it was the authorities. Locke felt himself becoming irritated at Bolton's indifference to the mess he'd contributed to, even now, days after the shitstorm at Taylor Fisheries.

'What the hell have you got to say for yourself, then?' Locke snapped at him, cracks showing through his usually cool demeanour.

Bolton sighed, rolling his eyes like a naughty child. 'Storm in a teacup, boss.'

'I'd hardly call a dead police officer a storm in a bloody teacup. What happened in there?'

'Mr Carter just got too big for his boots is what happened. Tried to do to me what I ended up doing to him.'

Locke scoffed. 'Carter? That scrawny little shit tried to take you out?'

Bolton shrugged. 'I know, the cheek of it, eh? Thinking he could catch me with my pants down. I ask him to help me shift a few things around and next thing I know he's swinging a two by four at me. He charged me, I clipped him, and he ended up smashing through the window.'

Locke couldn't help but wonder what a clip from Bolton would feel like. He'd seen a few men on the wrong end of one over the years and it never ended well for them.

'And the officers?'

Bolton folded his arms and sank back into the sofa. 'Not my doing, boss. Soon as I saw Carter take a dive I was out of there. He must have had backup there, and they ended up tangling with the coppers.'

Locke studied him for a moment. His gut told him Bolton was holding back. Then again, he'd proved his loyalty so many times over the years, Locke couldn't bring himself to doubt him completely. He was about to ask for more detail on Carter's failed attack when he heard the crunch of tyre on gravel from outside. Had Jasper forgotten something? Whoever it was came in without bothering to knock, or ring the bell. Locke heard footsteps marching towards them down the corridor and was surprised to see Gavin Barclay storm in, cheeks flushed candyfloss pink. With his rumpled suit and prematurely receding hairline, he looked about as threatening as an angry accountant as he strode over to Bolton.

'You,' he spat out. 'What did you do to my sister?'

Bolton glanced over at Locke, who in turn looked mildly amused.

'Hmm?' Gavin jerked his head forward to emphasise his prompt, but it fell short, looking more like a nervous tic.

'You do know I was seeing your sister for a bit before she went missing, don't you, Gav? You really want to know what we got up to? You get off on that kind of thing?'

Gavin screwed up his face and flinched backwards. 'What? That's not what . . . You know fine fucking well what I meant. And you,' he said, turning to face Locke. 'You're no better. Why did you do it? Sending this fucking ape after her. Then calling your slimy lawyer to get him out.'

Gavin turned back to see Bolton rising from the sofa, unfolding himself, filling the room as he stood.

'Cool your jets, boy. That's no way to speak to the man.' Bolton, almost at his full height now, reached out, putting a cautionary hand on Gavin's shoulder.

'You were never good enough for her. Get your fucking hands off me,' he spat out. Gavin reacted without thinking, lashing a hand out towards Bolton, only reaching his collarbone. More of a slap than a punch, and about as damaging as a moth fluttering at a lightbulb. As it landed, the anger melted from Gavin's face, replaced by shock that he'd actually laid a finger on Bolton. With Locke still just a spectator, Bolton swatted Gavin with a backhander that could fell a tree, sending him sprawling backwards over the coffee table. Gavin spun as he fell, landing face down, and Bolton was on him in a flash, grabbing Gavin's left wrist in a vice-like grip, extending the arm and pushing the hand down towards the forearm. Locke heard a soft snap, like dried twigs. Gavin's squeal was high enough that Locke expected the neighbourhood dogs to come running.

'Enough, James. Leave him be,' said Locke.

Bolton looked disappointed as he released his grip and stepped back. Gavin rolled onto his back, clutching his hand to his chest and whimpering like a wounded animal.

'What the hell have you done to him?' a woman's voice shrieked.

Locke looked over to the door and saw Mary rushing across the room to kneel by Gavin's side. Bolton held up both palms in a *nothing to do with me* gesture. Locke felt the last of his patience dissolving, with all of them. Bolton, with his 'lash out now, ask questions later' approach. Gavin, who was just one of life's punching bags; always had been, always would be. As for Mary, she was hardly a saint. Locke knew that she was more in the know than she let on. If she knew half of what he suspected, it would make Gavin see his mum in a whole different light. Mary glared up at both of them, a lioness protecting her cub.

'He came charging in here full of hell, yelling his head off about his sister, and took his chances throwing a cheap shot at James,' Locke snapped. 'He's fine. He just needs to calm down, that's all.'

'Let me see that,' she said to Gavin, lifting up his wrist. He winced, sucking air in through gritted teeth. 'I think you've broken his wrist,' she snapped at Bolton. 'He's going to need this seen to. I'll drive him to A & E myself. I wouldn't want either of you to put yourselves out.'

She helped Gavin to his feet. 'You're a bloody animal,' she said to Bolton. That was the equivalent of swearing by her standards. The two men watched in silence as she ushered him out of the room and out into her car.

Bolton held his hands up as if to say *what can you do*. 'You saw it, boss. He went for me. I just reacted.'

'Just like with Carter, eh?' said Locke. 'Twice in the space of a few days. What are the odds?'

CHAPTER THIRTEEN

Porter patiently waited his turn. Superintendent Campbell's verbose outpourings tended to be more of a soliloquy than a two-way conversation, and Porter knew from experience there was little to gain by interrupting.

'So let me get this straight.' Campbell shuttled back and forward between his desk and the window as he spoke, his voice slow and measured, as if dealing with a small child. 'He masquerades as a pillar of the community by making large charitable donations, to causes endorsed by our very own deputy commissioner, no less. Hell, he even rubs shoulders and shakes hands with the man. A man who can end both our careers with a wave of his pen, and now Locke is a murderer as well?'

'What I'm saying, sir, is that we need to consider this new evidence and where it might lead the investigation.'

Porter's pace and pitch was equally as regulated. Campbell had a stubborn streak in him and this wouldn't be the first time he'd waved his bureaucratic wand, inadvertently grinding a case to a shuddering halt simply because it wasn't how he had seen things playing out.

'And the new evidence, is there anything else to consider, or is it just the information from the Welsh chap and that picture?' He waved a hand in the direction of the Polaroid they had taken from George Evans.

'Just, sir? It's an eyewitness account of how a member of Mr Locke's organisation confirmed that Nathan Barclay died because he didn't want to do business with Locke; an account given while in the presence of Mr Locke, I might add. Now, I'm not saying it's enough to bang them all up just yet, but if we can—'

'I admire your passion, I really do. One of ours is lying in the hospital and you want to hit back. I'll tell you how this will be played back to us by his solicitor, shall I?'

Porter clenched his jaw, swallowing a quick retort, and bristling at the phrasing Campbell was using.

One of ours. Admire my passion?

The man had some nerve. He'd been fast-tracked since he joined the force, and had served the vast majority of his career from behind the safety of his desk. If they were all on the same team, all had a common goal, why did it feel like Campbell was more concerned with how things might look instead of getting the right result?

Campbell resumed his pacing as he spoke. 'This Mr Evans, we only have his word that Davies handed him the picture for starters. Only have his word that he ever met with Locke under those circumstances, let alone as confirmation of what was said between them. As for this . . .' Campbell held up the evidence bag with the picture in it. 'Without any corroborating evidence as to how he came by it, they'll strongly suggest that we investigate how he managed to get his hands on a crime scene photograph.'

'That's the thing though, sir, it's not a crime scene photograph. Well, I know it's a picture of the deceased, but . . .' Porter sighed loudly. 'But it's not one he could have just come across, or even taken from us.'

'And how can you be so sure, Detective?'

'Evans says he was out of the country on holiday when Barclay died and it checks out. He's willing to make a statement confirming how he came to possess the picture.'

Evans had confirmed he would come in if they needed him to. With his wife gone, he had readily agreed at what he saw as a chance to turn back the clock and stand up to Locke.

'It's still one man's word against another, Porter, and I'll remind you again, it would be the word of a man who hands out money to good causes and shakes hands with our top brass, so I'll ask you again, how can you be so sure?'

'Because there's something wrong with that picture, sir. It's not one of ours. Whoever took that picture was there at the scene, but it wasn't us.'

Campbell sneered as he studied the picture again. 'You showed me the original yourself when you made your pitch to run both cases, Detective. It looks like the same picture to me, right down to the jacket and the note.' He tossed the bag onto his desk and it skittered across the surface until it hit his keyboard.

The arrogance of the man was unbelievable. He was so sure of himself that he couldn't see what was right in front of him. Porter hoped his polite smile didn't look as fake as it felt. He reached across and drew the photograph towards him, picking it up and turning it to face Campbell.

'If it's one of ours, sir, then why are there no evidence markers at the scene? This one was taken before we even turned up.'

Campbell's face reddened as he snatched the picture back from Porter and sat down. Even though there was no audience to witness the glaring error, Porter had a feeling he would pay for embarrassing his superior like that somewhere down the line, but right now he didn't give a damn.

Porter listened while Anderson and Whittaker relayed what they'd found out. Whittaker had spoken to Martin Murphy's son, Callum. The car that had struck Murphy was found abandoned a few miles away in an alley. The owner had reported it stolen the day before and no one was questioned, let alone charged. Callum Murphy hadn't been involved in the business, but confirmed that his dad had been approached by a potential buyer from London a few weeks before the accident. His mum had been in favour of selling up and enjoying early retirement, but Murphy had flatly refused to entertain the idea. Callum didn't have any knowledge of the would-be buyer and his mother had passed away two years earlier, so there would be no way to confirm that Locke had made the original offer, short of Locke himself offering up the information. Whittaker had thanked him for his time and left it at that.

Anderson went next. He read from his notes in a flat, almost disinterested tone. He'd spoken to Alastair Reece's widow. Reece had been fanatical about his bikes, his pride and joy being his Harley Davidson chopper. She had been the last person to see him alive after he had headed out early one Sunday morning for a ride to blow away the cobwebs. She had been worried when he hadn't returned several hours later and wasn't answering his phone. They found him an hour later, his bike having struck the central reservation barrier which sent him sailing over the opposing lane and onto the grass verge. There were no eyewitnesses, and Reece was pronounced dead at the scene.

One of the officers who attended the scene had found an errant smear of blue midway up the jet-black petrol tank, the only suggestion that his accident may not have been a solo venture. The paint matched up to that used on the powder-blue Ford Focus, one of the most popular cars on the road at the time, and virtually untraceable.

Reece, too, had been approached with an offer for his businesses, according to his wife. Unlike Murphy, Reece had given it serious consideration, but had ultimately turned it down. He had made a passing comment to her about the buyer not being a man he wanted to do business with but hadn't elaborated. Her husband had been in the ground less than a week when Locke made an approach. She was left with two young children and no idea how to run a business that size, so had taken his offer without hesitation.

Porter could feel the excitement building as he listened. He knew that none of this was enough to build a case against Locke, or any of his associates. There wasn't the slightest provable fact in any of it, but it settled the question in his own mind about the kind of man Locke was. He had been willing to concede the possibility, however slim, that Bolton, Davies or both had been operating their own sideline without Locke's knowledge. The circumstances surrounding the expansion of Locke & Winwood made that impossible in Porter's opinion.

He made a mental note to dig out details of the local officers that worked each of the deaths and see if they could add anything. He would have to tread carefully, and not mention his suspicions about Locke to any of the locals. He didn't want them getting excited at the prospect of a suspect in an unsolved death, and word getting back to Campbell just yet that two more murders might be pencilled in against such a pillar of the community.

Porter stood up and turned to face the other three detectives. He gave a summary of their trip to Wales, ending the account by producing the photograph from a nearby folder, like a magician pulling a rabbit from his hat.

'That's all very well and good, but what can we make stick?' said Anderson, folding his arms over a chest that made his shirt strain at the buttons, the centre line parting at each one to reveal a flash of brown flesh.

Porter decided to let Anderson's pessimism go by without a challenge this time.

'From all of that? Nothing at the moment. We can speak to whoever investigated the deaths and the fires, but it's that long ago they might not even be on the force still, let alone able to tell us anything useful.'

Anderson's features softened ever so slightly, as if that was what he wanted to hear.

Jesus, he really doesn't have the stomach for a big case before he cashes his chips out.

Porter kept his thoughts to himself and just shrugged in acknowledgement. 'We might be able to use it to rattle Locke or his boys, though, put them on edge. People under pressure make mistakes. Maybe we let a few details slip when we pay a visit to Atlas and see if it gets back to them?'

'Speaking of which, how are we slicing that up?' asked Anderson. 'We can do the drive-bys on Atlas while you two check up with the locals on those cases if you like?'

Porter nodded. 'Yep, thanks mate. That'd be good.'

Maybe he was judging Anderson too harshly if he was offering to do the legwork. That would give him and Styles a chance to work out where they went next with Natasha's case, and he hadn't had time to track down Will Leonard for the report on the scene at Taylor Fisheries.

His phone vibrated and he glanced down at the screen. It was a text from Campbell.

In my office when you have 5.

Had he spoken to Milburn already? When Campbell had recovered from his embarrassment at misreading the photograph, he had dismissed Porter, promising to ring Milburn straight away. In Porter's experience, Campbell rarely tended to be the bringer of good tidings, and almost never this quickly. He excused himself and headed to find out, mentally preparing his plan B if the answer wasn't in his favour.

Porter debated sending Campbell a reply saying he had left the building and was tracking down Will Leonard first, but thought better of it. No sense in delaying potentially bad news, and if Campbell found out he had fobbed him off, he would be even harder to win round. No sense swimming against the tide unnecessarily.

The door was slightly open, but Porter knocked anyway. Campbell was staring intently at paperwork on his desk, and spoke without looking up.

'Come in, have a seat. I'll just be a second.'

Porter sat as instructed and waited patiently for Campbell to finish. Porter didn't know how he could do it. He couldn't think of anything more soul-destroying than having budgets as your number one adversary, instead of the actual lawbreakers they were here to police. Someone had to do it, he supposed, and was just thankful it wasn't him. He would rather follow Anderson into the sunset than chain himself to a desk.

Campbell finished whatever he was reviewing and scribbled an intelligible signature at the bottom like a child's doodle.

'Ah, Porter.' He sounded almost surprised to see him even though he'd sent the summoning text.

'You wanted to see me, sir?'

'Yes. I've just come off the phone with Milburn. We've agreed to run a joint taskforce taking what happened to Gibson and Simmons into account. Anderson will still lead on the drugs angle. You and Styles will follow up on Gibson, Simmons and that other chap. You'll do daily briefings for myself and Superintendent Milburn at the end of each shift to make sure there's no unnecessary overlap.'

Porter didn't react. It wasn't exactly what he wanted but it was enough of a happy medium for him to work with. He would rather be setting the direction for the case as a whole instead of part of it, not for any personal gain, but to put it simply he just didn't have the confidence in Anderson that his superiors did.

'What about our other case, sir, Natasha Barclay?'

'What about it, Porter? That can wait, quite frankly. This takes priority.'

'But, sir, the links between them are—'

'The links between them are weak and circumstantial, Porter.' Campbell's voice cut across Porter's. 'We have no body, no firm evidence apart from that which points to her own father, which by the way you're now suggesting may not in fact be a suicide, the more I hear.'

Porter opened his mouth to speak, but Campbell wasn't finished. His voice reminded Porter of the whiny drone of hedge trimmers.

'We've got two murders to solve already without turning a perfectly good suicide into a third, and adding a missing person on top. What we need is to close the book on whoever attacked our officers, and to establish how far up this drug ring goes.'

Porter stared at Campbell now with undisguised contempt.

A perfectly good suicide?

Had he really just said that? That was as clear an indication as to where Campbell's priorities lay as any Porter had ever witnessed.

'Until I'm convinced otherwise, we do not go anywhere near Alexander Locke. That's one political applecart I don't intend to upset unless or until we absolutely have to. For now, Bolton is our chief suspect, and I expect you and your team to focus all your attention on him and his associates. We get the evidence and we bring them in, but not before. I don't want that prick Jasper looking that smug again. Ms Barclay has waited thirty years for somebody to ask where the hell she's gotten to. I'm sure she can wait another week or two until we clean up this mess. Are we clear?'

Porter swallowed down a dozen more colourful career-limiting responses, and nodded slowly.

'First briefing five o'clock today, then, please.'

Campbell smiled and held Porter's gaze for a few seconds before turning his attention back to his beloved paperwork. Porter saw it for the dismissal it was and headed out to find someone to vent to.

Styles held out a mug as Porter walked past, like a caffeine version of a marathon runner visiting a water stop. Porter slowed as the cup changed hands, and completed his circuit of the desks until he reached his own and sat to face his partner.

'Well? Did the Man from Del Monte say yes?'

Porter's mouth twitched at the corners, stopping short of a full-blown smile.

'Yes and no.'

'Oh, you know how I love it when you go all cryptic and mysterious.'

This time Porter couldn't help but smile. He quickly filled Styles in on his conversation with Campbell.

Styles shrugged. 'You win some, you lose some. Could be worse. So we're shelving Natasha for now?'

Porter shook his head. 'No, we can work both. As long as we make enough progress on the murders to keep Campbell and Milburn happy, we can use whatever spare time we have to crack on with Natasha.'

'Since when do we have spare time?' scoffed Styles.

'We'll make it work,' Porter said simply.

'But Campbell said not to bother Locke while—'

'Campbell said not to bother *Alexander* Locke. He said nothing about his wife,' said Porter, a look on his face like butter wouldn't melt.

Styles tutted loudly. 'I bet you weren't disciplined enough as a child. You've got a naughty streak in you a mile wide. Did your parents spare the rod?'

'I'm just taking the man at face value, albeit quite literally.'

'What's the angle, then? We've already been to see her twice.'

Porter took a loud slurp from his mug. 'You saw how nervy she was last time, and how she clammed up as soon as his lordship came home. She knows more than she's told us, maybe not enough to crack the case, but she knows something. Maybe she even knew about Natasha and Bolton? Maybe she and Daddy disapproved of their blue-eyed girl sleeping with the stepdad's help and made her break it off with Bolton? Maybe that's what triggered the argument and struggle at her place?'

'That's a lot of maybes,' said Styles, leaning back, arms folded behind his head. 'And "crack the case"? Really? Has anyone actually used that since Columbo?'

Porter scrunched up a scrap of paper from his desk and flung it at his partner's head. Styles ducked easily out of the way and grabbed at a folder on his own desk. Porter flinched instinctively, but Styles leant forward and handed it to him instead. Porter eyed him suspiciously as he took it. Styles feigned a hurt look.

'So cynical. As if I would reduce myself to your level? Some of us would rather be doing police work. While you were off sucking up to Campbell, I paid Will Leonard a quick visit and got you some light bedtime reading.' He picked up an identical folder of his own, holding it up to Porter like a referee showing the red card.

'Crime scene report?'

'Yep. That plus a little extra bonus, but have a look at the report first.'

Porter opened the file and scanned through Leonard's summary. A single blow to the head had killed Gibson. He'd likely been unconscious before he hit the floor. Face-planting on the hard concrete had broken his nose and fractured a cheekbone, although he was beyond pain by then. The blow had been delivered Babe Ruth style to the base of his skull, causing a fracture and cerebral haemorrhage.

Carter had died from a full bingo card of injuries: head trauma, massive internal bleeding and punctured lungs where two broken ribs had driven through them like stakes. No real surprises there. Porter read on but stopped suddenly mid-paragraph and looked up at Styles.

'You've got to be fucking kidding me?'

'Hang fire, you must be ahead of me.'

'No way could that have been a bloody accident!' Porter spat out angrily.

'Eh?' Styles was confused, but read on, and ten seconds later realised what had brought the outrage to Porter's voice.

Cause of death for Carter was obvious. Gravity plus a concrete road tended to only end one way. What was less obvious were Leonard's observations on how Carter came to do his Icarus impression. Fragments of a lightbulb had been found embedded in his hand, with the pale grey threaded section four feet away on the road. This, plus the arrangement of furniture on the third floor of the building, had led Leonard to surmise that one possibility was that Carter had been changing a bulb and had simply fallen backwards while standing on the desk to reach the fitting.

'Death by DIY?' Porter gave a sardonic laugh.

'I know he's got to consider all options, but that's stretching it a bit, surely?'

'More likely that things got rough and Carter smashed a bulb to use as a weapon.'

'I'd want something a damn sight bigger than a lightbulb if that big bugger was charging at me,' said Styles.

Porter shook his head in disbelief. He knew it would only piss Leonard off if he tried to poke holes in what he had written. The report wasn't Leonard trying to give them a definitive answer. Bolton had left no prints behind, Porter assumed thanks to a pair of gloves, so Leonard was just interpreting the physical evidence he could see and laying out provable possibilities.

It left them without a solid reason to haul Bolton back in. Their only real chance as it stood was for Simmons to wake up and give an eyewitness account of what happened, but that could be days yet. That wouldn't bother Milburn that much at this stage, and by extension Anderson, as it gave them a longer window to progress the drugs case, but it pissed Porter off. It made him want to lock Bolton in a dark room until he confessed, but knew Campbell and Milburn would make him pay dearly for it.

Styles noticed his partner's darkening mood. 'Don't you want to know what your little bonus surprise is then?'

Porter had forgotten about the secondary comment Styles had made a minute ago.

'What? Oh, yeah, come on then. It's got to be better news that the lightbulb theory.'

'Well, it's nothing to do with this scene, but Leonard did find something unusual back at Natasha's place.'

Porter's expression changed, alert and inquisitive again in an instant. 'What is it?'

'Well, it turns out that when he ran tests on the blood from her carpet, there was a bit of an anomaly. They took the full slice of carpet to test. Turns out that Natasha wasn't the only one to blame for the spillage. He found another blood type mixed with hers. Barely a trace, but enough to test.'

'Who?' Porter was all business again, his mini-rant forgotten.

'Swings and roundabouts. We know it belongs to another person, but that person isn't in the system, not for DNA, anyway.'

Porter had been expecting a name, and sat back again with a loud sigh.

'I can tell you whose it isn't: our favourite customer, Mr Bolton. He gave a sample with a previous arrest. Course we still have his fingerprints there, but they're not quite so damning.'

'I'm sure he'll be delighted to hear that.'

'I never promised you a conviction from it, but it's something, at least, something more than we had this morning, anyway.'

'Yeah, I know. I'll stop whinging now.' He drained the last half inch of coffee from his mug, and leant forward to place it in his desk when he froze, still gripping the handle.

'Jesus, I must be getting old. I nearly missed that.' A smile crept slowly across Porter's face.

'Missed what? The desk with the cup? Even a blind quadriplegic could manage that one. You want a gold star?'

Porter shook his head. 'Careful who you mock, young man. You've missed it as well.'

'Come on, then, put me out of my misery.'

'We can't rule out Bolton, but we can rule out Barclay.'

'How so?'

'We don't have a sample for him per se, but it would have shown up as a familial match if it was his, so whoever she struggled with it wasn't him.'

'Then what the hell was he apologising for in his note?' said Styles.

Porter shrugged, but that didn't really bother him that much right now. As far as he was concerned, that put Bolton squarely in the frame for Natasha. As much as he wanted to pin the others on him as well, he had to fight the urge to go and find him straight away. He knew he would get a slap on the wrist from Campbell if he did. He could live with that, but it was his own desire to make sure Bolton went down for all three deaths that won out.

It might only be a small step forward but it felt like the most progress they'd made in days.

They took a call each, Porter speaking to the local police force in Grimsby, while Styles tracked down the investigating officer in Grangemouth. Both cases had hit a dead end quite quickly and just gathered dust since. They were alike insofar as there being no witnesses to either death, and no real leads to speak of. The car that had hit Martin Murphy had no usable prints apart from those belonging to its owner, who had been at a football match with friends. The officer Styles spoke to in Scotland told him that they had checked local garages within a fifty-mile radius for any powder-blue Ford Focus in need of any bodywork or paint work. The only two they had tracked down were a result of separate incidents, each with another party, who could confirm how and where the damage was sustained.

'What time can you get here for tomorrow morning?' he asked Styles.

'Any time, really. Emma's up and out for yoga in the morning, so whenever. What you got in mind?'

'Thought we might try third time lucky with Mrs Locke, if you're game? Maybe park up early somewhere round the corner and wait till he heads out to work so there's less chance of him interrupting us.'

'Can do.'

Porter figured Locke would head out by nine at the latest. They could wait till then, speak with Mary Locke and be back at the station by mid-morning.

'I'm assuming, with you being a master of interrogation, that we're not just going to ask her outright what she's hiding. What's the plan?'

'We've been fairly gentle so far,' said Porter. 'I think it's time we throw a few surprises into the conversation and see what we can flush out. If she's hiding nothing, we get nothing, but I bet you a bacon butty on the drive back that we don't leave empty-handed.'

'Yeah, what the hell, let's do it. Maybe she'll even confess and make it the best three quid I'll have ever spent.'

Friday morning's sky was a rumpled duvet of grey cloud as far as the eye could see, and a veil of diamante raindrops studded the windscreen. They had been there for almost an hour and the clock on the dash read a little after eight. They had no idea what time Locke left for work and hadn't wanted to take any chances of running into him as they parked up. Porter had reached for the lever to wipe the droplets away, but Styles had stopped him. The rain would blur the shapes inside the car to passers-by, while they knew which car to look out for, even with their rain-blurred vision.

Porter outlined his plan while they waited. They'd asked her last time if Natasha had been involved with anyone. That had been just before Locke had returned home. They'd allowed themselves to get distracted and left without an answer to that, for starters. She had seemed on the verge of unburdening herself, of what he didn't know, but he was convinced she had something that could help them, however small.

'I say we ask her straight up about Bolton as well.'

'You sure about that, guv? What if she tells her hubby and he tells Bolton?'

'Worth the risk,' said Porter. 'Besides, there's worse things we could do than rattle a few cages. Other than that, let's just play it by ear depending on what she says.'

Styles opened his mouth to speak when an arc of light swept around the corner of the street that led to the Locke house. Through the dawn half-light they could see the outline of a body in the driver's seat as a jet-black Mercedes swung around the corner and headed away from them to God knows where. There was no mistaking the car, even in the gloom. The licence plate, L0CK3, was probably worth more than their unmarked car. They decided to give it ten more minutes to be sure before driving slowly up to the house.

The house looked deserted apart from the light outside the front door. As they got closer, though, Porter made out a faint glow coming from behind the living room curtains. It took Mary Locke a full minute before her voice came over the intercom. She sounded cautious, although Porter guessed most people would treat any pre-breakfast callers with suspicion. There was a hesitation while she decided whether or not to let them in. Porter stared intently at the metal grille of the intercom box, willing it to let him in.

The gate clicked open, probably because she couldn't think of a reason to refuse them, or maybe just out of good old-fashioned British manners; Porter didn't much care which. She appeared in the doorway wearing a pair of navy blue cotton jogging bottoms and a matching fleece, zipped up to the neck, hair tied in a short ponytail and make-up immaculate as usual. Porter was beginning to wonder if she slept upright so as not to ruffle her appearance.

'Do you have any idea what time it is, Detective?' she said with a shrill tone in her voice.

Porter saw it for the rhetorical question and expression of annoyance that it was, and left it unanswered when he responded.

'I'm sorry, Mrs Locke, but there have been a few developments and we need to ask you some follow-up questions.'

'You've just missed my husband. Maybe it would be better if you came back this evening when you can speak to him as well?'

Porter smiled politely. 'No need, Mrs Locke. You should be able to help us just fine. May we come in?'

She pursed her lips but relented and stood back to let them in. They followed her through to the now-familiar surroundings of the living room and took the same seats as last time.

'I can only spare you five minutes, I'm afraid,' she said, her fingers fiddling with the zip of her fleece. 'I'm heading out to meet a friend. We go power walking twice a week.' She gestured towards her pristine white Nike trainers that looked like they'd not trodden a path since leaving the box, as if to justify her less than formal choice of outfit.

'That's fine, Mrs Locke. We appreciate whatever you can spare.'

Porter kept the smile lingering as he talked. He wanted to relax her as much as possible in order to maximise any reactions if their questions threw her a curveball.

'So, first off, last time we spoke I lost track of my questions a little when your husband turned up.' He shrugged, the clumsy detective cleaning up from his previous visit. 'We had just asked if Natasha had a boyfriend, or had been dating anyone around the time you saw her last. Is there anyone you can remember? Anyone who might have seen her more recently than you or your husband?'

Her expression changed, barely noticeable, but something passed across her face that he couldn't read.

'After you left the last time, my husband and I spoke for quite a while, about what you'd found, what you asked. I must apologise, but when I said the last time I saw her was around the time her father died, that wasn't actually the case.'

She gave a weak smile, and Porter and Styles shot each other a quick glance.

'Having the police turn up on my doorstep with bad news must have muddled my brain more than I thought. I did see her a few times after that. I took a few trips over to Poland, you know, just for a break. I stayed in a hotel and she came into Kraków to meet up.'

'And you only remembered that after we left?' Porter tried his best to keep any sarcasm from his voice, but felt like he failed miserably.

'Yes, that's right.' She nodded rapidly as she spoke. 'It was just two trips across, only for a few days each time. We met for dinner and wandered round the town for a while.'

'So how long after her father's death was this?' asked Styles.

She shrugged. 'Three months, maybe six. I don't know exactly. It was a long time ago.'

'I thought you said you two didn't really get on, Mrs Locke?'

'We didn't, but you know how it is, I had to try. With her father gone, she didn't have much family left, and we were family still, Gavin and I. We were all the family she had.'

'Where did you stay when you went to see her?'

'Oh, just some hotel off the main square,' she said, crossing her legs, trying to look relaxed, and failing miserably. 'It's years ago. The name escapes me. Does it really matter?'

Porter gave a patient smile, the sort you might use on a five-year-old after they ask *why* for the ninth or tenth time. 'You'd be surprised how helpful even the smallest of details can be, Mrs Locke. Is there any way you can check?'

She rolled her eyes. 'It was a lifetime ago, Detective. I wouldn't have a reason to keep that kind of information this long.'

Porter could tell she was getting impatient by her dismissive tone. He pulled out a small black leather notebook from his jacket and scribbled down a few words about the location of the visits, and approximate times.

'Do you really think that's relevant to the case, Detective?' She craned her neck upwards in her best giraffe impression to see what he jotted down.

Porter nodded. 'Anything that goes towards piecing together her whereabouts is helpful. What did she say about where she was living and working?'

'Just that it was a school somewhere outside the city. She didn't seem to want to share any more than that, and it was such a long time ago.'

Porter was getting a slightly defensive vibe from her. That could be because there were things that she didn't want to say, or simply that she felt under pressure because she couldn't remember more details. He couldn't decide which, and decided to change direction again.

'So back to what we mentioned before, we're interested in speaking to anyone she might have been involved with before she left for Poland. Does anyone spring to mind?'

'She hadn't really had a boyfriend since school, Tim, or Tom something . . .'

'Tom Wilton?' asked Styles.

She thought for a second then nodded. 'Yes, Tom Wilton. Lovely boy he was.' She stopped, and gave him a puzzled look. 'How do you know about Tom?'

'We spoke to an old school friend, Rebecca Arnold. Anyone else, even someone she might have just dated a few times?'

She ran a palm back over the tightly drawn hair all the way through to her ponytail. 'No . . . nobody springs to mind. Not that I know of, anyway.'

'What about James Bolton?'

A twitch of an eye, a flutter of eyelash, an extra second's delay when she spoke. Porter knew he had struck a nerve somewhere deep down.

'He works for my husband, Detective.'

'We know that, Mrs Locke.' Porter left it at that and waited her out.

She looked sharply away to the window and her ponytail danced in annoyance. 'You want to know if Natasha knew him? I'm assuming the fact you ask means you know he did.'

'And what was the extent of their relationship?'

'Relationship?' she scoffed. 'There was no relationship. She tried to flaunt him in front of us, Alexander and me. Silly little girl, trying to rebel and show how grown-up she was.' She looked back at them, anger in her eyes and her voice. 'As far as I know they dated, if you can call it that, for a week, maybe two.'

'How did your husband feel about that? Her dating the staff?'

'Alexander said she was big enough to make her own decisions. She wasn't his daughter, just as she wasn't mine. He barely gave it a second thought. I suggest if you have any questions about it, you speak to Mr Bolton himself. Now if you don't mind, Detectives, I really do need to head out.'

She stood quickly and stared at them until they followed suit.

'Thank you, Mrs Locke, we'll be in touch if we have any more questions.'

'Hopefully not, Detective. It's a long way for you to drive and there's really nothing more I can think of to tell you.'

Unless you suddenly remember something later like you did with your Poland trips.

Porter kept his thoughts to himself, and smiled instead. He'd love nothing more than to continue the chat down at the station. See how aloof she was in an interrogation room. Four walls, a digital recorder and a mild dose of claustrophobia had a way of unsettling the most confident and self-righteous of people. He could imagine the look on Campbell's face if he marched her in there, though. What he'd give for a boss that actually had his back. One that trusted him without worrying about pissing off the very people they were investigating. She ushered them out with a curt goodbye and no sooner had they turned their backs than the door clicked firmly shut behind them.

'Well, that went well.' Styles kept his voice low in case it travelled back to the house and through an open window.

'You believe the story about the trips to Poland?' Porter asked as they reached the safety of the car.

'If you're calling it a story, then I'm guessing you don't?'

'Just seems a little convenient that she remembered after she spoke to her husband, a man who employs our chief suspect and has a vested interest in keeping him out of jail.'

'Playing devil's advocate, it's a lifetime ago, and she had just been told that her stepdaughter is most likely dead.'

'A stepdaughter she didn't have much to do with. Hmm, might be nothing, but I need you to check out her story when we get back. See if we can check if she left the country in the six months after Barclay's death, and if so, where to.'

'Not sure if we can go back that far, but I'll give it a go.'

Porter had noted her reaction to the mention of Bolton's name with interest. For a woman who claimed to have a strained relationship with her stepdaughter, there had been a definite reaction, and not a positive one. For all he knew it could have been Natasha's fling with Bolton that had driven the final wedge between her and her stepmum. There was something there for sure, but he couldn't quite decide how best to approach the problem of getting her to open up.

He decided to focus on Bolton himself. They could head back to Natasha's apartment block later in the day and see if any of the older residents recognised a photograph of him. It was a long shot, and maybe not even necessary as they had his prints to place him there, but Porter hadn't been back since the day they found Natasha's hand. The absence of hard evidence was making him feel like he was wading through treacle towards an unclear goal. He hoped a trip back to her place might shake something loose, some connection he had yet to make. He had agreed to meet up with Anderson and Whittaker after lunch, and the briefing with Campbell and Milburn wasn't until five.

'We need to make a few pit stops on the way back,' he said, turning to Styles.

'How many you got in mind?'

'Four. I want to take another look at Natasha's place. It was all a bit chaotic last time. Just a quick look around. After that, I want to swing down by the river and poke my nose in at Taylor Fisheries. There has to be something there. It all happened so fast from what they say, so he can't have planned a perfect crime scene. Last one is to pop in and check on Simmons. I know they said they'd call if there was any change, but it doesn't feel right ignoring her until they do.'

If they do.

Styles nodded, and they lapsed into silence for a few seconds before he spoke again. 'I thought you said four stops?'

'Ah yes, almost forgot. We may not have got much, but we didn't leave empty-handed, so mine's on white bread with no sauce, thanks.' Porter smiled as his stomach seconded the motion with a low rumble.

They got their sandwiches to go from a greasy spoon cafe, and demolished them quickly as they drove. Porter's shirt was a crime scene in its own right, crumbs in his lap and a stray spot of grease the only signs that a sandwich had even existed.

Natasha Barclay's flat was eerily quiet compared to their last visit. The swarm of crime scene technicians poring over every surface had long since moved on to pastures new. Only the bald patch where the carpet had been cut away to file as evidence, and the dried blood on the wall, gave any hint of what had taken place.

What the hell had actually happened?

Lovers' quarrel? Drunken fight? Something more planned, premeditated? Had she even known the kind of man Bolton was? He knew it was dangerous to discount the possibility of a third party being involved, but he saw it in Bolton's eyes. He couldn't back it up with any evidentiary proof, couldn't elicit a confession from Bolton, but there had been something in the big man's smirk at the station. Something that taunted Porter, dared him to come after him. Not that Porter needed any encouragement, but he had to take something else to Campbell, something new, to be allowed to put Bolton in a room again.

The flat felt like it had resumed its slumber, like a coma patient after the hopeful flicker of the eyelids has passed. The lines etched into the layers of dust would soon be filled, like tyre tracks with fresh snow. The curtains were still open, the dated decor looking even more surreal in the cold light of day than it ever had hiding in darkness.

Porter didn't even know what he hoped to find. He wondered if he'd made the trip back as a reminder that Natasha counted just as much as those who had died more recently. He wouldn't let her be forgotten for another thirty years, not by her family, and not for the sake of Campbell and his crime stats.

They poked around for another five minutes but found nothing. They had similar luck with showing Bolton's picture to the older residents. They managed to get an answer at two doors, but both neighbours shook their heads, blank looks in their eyes.

They opted to visit the warehouse down by the river next, saving a visit to the hospital for last. Porter squinted, focusing on the road as the wipers cleared their twin cones, only to be sprayed with a fine mist again in seconds. There was something vaguely hypnotic about the monotony of the *swish squeak* as they worked tirelessly, and they rode most of the way in silence.

The entrance still had a line of police tape across it when they pulled up, but there was no one guarding the front door. Porter guessed that now Will Leonard had filed a completed report, it would be deemed that any and all relevant evidence had been gathered, leaving the rest of the interior and its contents as not relevant to the investigation.

Styles was closer to the entrance when they parked up, and stooped under the tape, lifting it with his index finger as he did. It looked almost comical to Porter. Styles, with his height, would have been just as comfortable stepping over it like a slow-motion hurdler, but he followed him in without comment or wisecrack.

It was as if Porter was seeing the inside of the building for the first time. He closed his eyes and tried to picture it from his previous visit.

Simmons, mask covering her face, a blur on a stretcher. Gibson, facing away, stretched out like a toppled mannequin.

He silently cursed his own inattention to detail. Sure, he'd seen the crime scene photographs, but they were taken after the story had unfolded. He operated best on the sensory overload that came with a fresh scene. It worked with the adrenaline as a catalyst, fuelled him, made him sharp. He'd been distracted this time, looked at it all through the subjective lens forced upon him when greeted with a colleague fighting for her life on a stretcher. Distracted when he could least afford to be; he felt like he was letting her down, letting them both down.

He turned in a slow three-sixty circle, taking it all in. The report had found no evidence of any recent activity on the ground floor prior to Tuesday's events, so he headed upstairs, Styles following close behind. The stillness of their surroundings served to amplify the chorus of creaks and groans as they made their way up the old staircase. The first floor and the doorway into the room beyond looked strangely bare without the body in situ and those in attendance documenting what they saw. The dark tattoo of blood on the floorboards was the only indication that anything bad had ever happened.

There hadn't been any prints found on the murder weapon. The length of wood hadn't matched any of the fittings in the building. The assumption was that it had been left over from a storage crate or something similar, but the identity of who had wielded it remained a mystery. Porter remembered Anderson mentioning the fire escape as a possible exit point for anyone who had been in the building, and wandered over to look. The door was locked, but he peered out of a nearby window and saw a fire escape angling downwards, hugging the side of the building. A narrow alley ran the length of the row of buildings and ended in a T-junction, one branch joining the main road they had parked on, the other a mirror image for the road layout that served the buildings behind them. It would have been a simple matter of exiting via the fire escape and taking the right fork, away from the oncoming police officers. Of course, the locked door would pose a problem, but for someone with a key, someone who owned the building, for example, it would be no issue at all.

Thanks to the chaos surrounding their first visit, they hadn't made it up to the third floor to see where Carter had fallen from, and they headed there next. A series of large wooden boards had been fixed in place to plug the gap where the glass once was. There was a small heap of shards that caught the light. Not much to show for a window that size, but then again most of the glass had rained down after Carter and broken into even tinier pieces when it met the tarmac.

There was ample light coming through the remaining windows, and Porter noted the position of the desk underneath the light fitting. While Styles paced the edges of the room, Porter climbed up onto the desk and stood up. He looked over his shoulder, then up at the fitting.

'I just don't see it,' he said, addressing no one in particular.

He thought back to the crime scene photographs and realised what had been niggling him. The position of the body had been such that Carter's head had faced the direction that Simmons had approached from. If he had stumbled backwards off the desk and into the window, surely he would have fallen straight backwards and landed with his head and feet more or less at a right angle with the building, rather than at parallel to it?

Styles came over to peer out at the street through the remains of the shattered window. Porter dropped down to sit on the desk and repeated his concerns aloud for Styles to chip in his thoughts.

'I agree,' he said simply. 'Anything other than Bolton helping our friend through the window is entirely too coincidental. Our problem here won't be proving it wasn't an accident, though, it's still placing Bolton inside the building. There's a good chance that . . .'

He stiffened, and his voice tailed off as he stared through the window.

'What? What you thinking?' Porter prompted.

'I'm thinking I hope that's what I think it is,' he said, leaning and pointing off to the right.

Porter slid off the desk and waited for Styles to step aside, then peered out to see what all the fuss was about.

The road was quiet, although the hum of machinery could be heard from a nearby factory. 'Where am I looking?'

'Right up there.' Styles pointed again, his arm indicating a line of sight above street level, and Porter followed his direction. He narrowed his eyes, still unsure what he was meant to be looking at, until he focused his attention a little higher to allow for the slight difference in their vantage points. Lamp posts were evenly spaced long the road, with one every hundred feet or so. Most of the other buildings on the street were one or two storeys, and the lights atop the curved neck of the poles looked down upon the rooftops. The one closest to them on the opposite side of the street, however, was slightly different from its neighbours. A small dark shape clung to the top of the pole just below the light.

'What is it?'

'I'm guessing it's some sort of CCTV,' said Styles, without taking his eyes off it. 'We can check with whoever worked the scene to make sure they've got their hands on the footage. Whether it shows anything worthwhile is another matter, but with a bit of luck I think we may have just found a way to place Mr Bolton where we need him to be.'

They swung by Darent Valley Hospital for their last stop, and saw a man sitting by her bedside as they entered the room. He held her right hand encased between his, his head bowed, his lips trembling ever so slightly. Their footsteps gave them away and the man's head snapped up, aware that he was no longer alone.

'Hi there,' said Porter, apologetic at disturbing the private moment. 'We work with Evie. Are you a relative or a friend?'

The man nodded and stood, smoothing out the creases in his pale blue sweater as he did. Porter guessed he was in his late fifties, his hair so grey it could pass for white. His face showed the strain of his bedside vigil, and Porter wondered how many of the creases in his forehead and around his eyes had been carved deeper by the worry of the last few days.

'Alan Simmons. I'm her father.' He held his hand out over his daughter's bed, and Porter and Styles took turns to introduce themselves. 'Please, have a seat.' He motioned to a trio of chairs stacked in the corner of the room.

They positioned a pair of chairs on the opposite side of the bed, rubber legs scraping on the hard floor like nails on a blackboard.

'How is she? Any update from the doctors?' asked Porter.

Alan Simmons looked back to his daughter as he answered. She looked peaceful despite the dressing that covered most of the right side of her face. Porter could still picture the wound, raised, angry. The bruising had darkened into swirls of indigo and dark mustard yellow, but it would start to fade in the next few days.

'No change.' He said without taking his eyes off her. 'Were you there? Were either of you there when it happened?'

Porter shook his head. 'No, sir. We only arrived on the scene after we got the call.'

'Can you tell me what happened? Are there any suspects?'

'We don't know everything yet, but we've got a few leads we're looking into.' The words sounded even more cliché aloud than they had in his head. 'We'll find who did this.'

Alan Simmons gave a tired smile. 'I want to believe you, Detective, I really do.' He reached out and patted her hand. 'I tried to persuade her not to join. I know it's not a time for "what ifs". Did you know she studied sociology at university?'

Porter shook his head. He realised he didn't know an awful lot about her outside of the job and felt bad for it.

'Always wanted to help people. She was going to be a social worker. She changed her mind, though, and once she had there was no talking to her. Always was a stubborn one, my Evie. Always determined once she set her mind to something.'

Porter couldn't help but smile. He had seen first-hand how hard she went after something she wanted.

'Anyway, she loves what she does. That's all you can ask as a parent, for your kids to be happy.'

He bowed his head again, weighed down by the helplessness of the situation, slowly stroking the back of his daughter's hand. Porter felt like an outsider, and looked at Styles, gesturing towards the exit with a flick of his head. Styles nodded agreement, and they stood up.

'Sorry to disturb you, Mr Simmons. We'd best get back to the station.'

Alan Simmons nodded and stood, following them to the door. He shook hands with them both, and Styles headed off down the corridor, but when Porter tried to pull his hand away Simmons kept the grip, resting his left hand lightly on top, and leant in towards Porter.

'She talked about you, Detective. She said you were a good man and a good detective.'

The surprise showed in Porter's face. He wondered in what context his name had cropped up.

'Have you ever lost somebody close to you?'

Porter nodded. 'I have, yes.'

Alan Simmons said nothing, waiting for Porter to fill the silence. But Porter hated talking about Holly to anyone, let alone a stranger. It was private, personal, and sharing that side of himself wasn't his style. He hesitated, Holly's face flashing in his mind. He saw something of his own grief reflected in Simmons's eyes, and before he had time to think about what he was doing, he started talking.

'My wife, Holly, a couple of years ago. Hit-and-run on her way back from a parents' evening at school.'

'You have children?'

'No, she was a primary school teacher.'

Alan Simmons's face softened, as if he sensed his own pain mirrored in Porter. 'Did they find who did it?'

Porter shook his head. 'No, they, uhm . . .' He cleared his throat, glancing over his shoulder to see how far Styles had got. 'There were witnesses, but the car had been stolen. No one saw the driver. Found the car abandoned the day after.'

Porter felt his face redden. This was the most he'd talked about her in over a year. Simmons was nodding his head gently, acknowledging the effort it was taking to share the memory.

'I'm sorry to hear that, Detective. That must have been even harder to take.'

Porter nodded at the understatement. 'We even lifted prints from inside the car, but we didn't get a match. Whoever they belong to has never been caught.' He stopped abruptly, not sure where to go from there. Evie Simmons was still alive. The last thing her father needed was to hear a sob story about someone he'd never met while his daughter battled for her own life. What else was there to say? That things would be OK in time? They didn't feel that way for him, but Alan Simmons needed hope, not hopelessness.

The two men lapsed into silence again. Porter shifted his feet, uncomfortable at having opened up to a man he'd only just met. Simmons spoke after a few seconds.

'Well, I sincerely hope you're there when they do.'

Porter chewed on his bottom lip as he considered what that would feel like. He'd imagined that moment so many times. He didn't know what worried him more, the thought that they might never slip up, or what he might do if they did, and he had a chance to look them in the eye.

'Funny thing about being a parent,' Alan Simmons continued. 'You feel every bump and scrape in the playground like it was you that had fallen. Imagine how this one measures on that scale.' He inclined his head towards his daughter. 'If you're as good as she thinks you are, I'm sure you'll find him. When you do' – he leant in closer still, all the softness gone from his voice – 'I wouldn't judge you if you chose to stop being a good man, because the man that did this to my daughter doesn't deserve the kind of justice a good man would offer.'

He released his grip and backed away into the room, leaving Porter in the corridor, wondering what kind of justice he would give to the man driving the car that killed Holly, and whether James Bolton deserved any better.

CHAPTER FOURTEEN

Porter had promised Anderson and Whittaker they would be back at the station for 2 p.m. for both pairings to update each other before they went to Campbell and Milburn, but they weren't at their desks when he and Styles walked back into the room. He checked in the two nearby interview rooms while Styles went to get coffee, but found them both empty.

Porter spotted Constable Chris Reid, one of the younger officers, slouching back in a chair. Reid was in his early twenties, boundless energy for the job and a desperate desire to make a good impression on the more senior detectives. Porter explained the situation around the camera, and Reid nodded eagerly. Task successfully delegated, Porter went back to his desk to check his voicemail while he waited, and had just put the phone back in its cradle when Styles reappeared.

'Forget your coffee?'

Styles shook his head, and Porter could tell from his expression that something was bothering him.

'Everything OK?'

'Anderson and Whittaker are upstairs.'

'I wondered where those lazy bastards were hiding.'

Styles shook his head again. 'Something's going on. They're in with Campbell and Milburn.'

'Already? We're not meant to brief them for another three hours.'

'You think they're sucking up to make sure their case gets priority?'

'No idea, but whatever it is they can at least do it to our faces. C'mon.'

Porter jumped up and followed Styles upstairs. They found the four men two floors up, in a meeting room usually reserved for the high and mighty rather than the rank and file. Anderson was the one talking as they approached, miming his thanks to the thick glass wall. Whittaker sat ramrod straight in his seat, looking a little unnerved. Campbell and Milburn sat at the opposite end of the table, listening intently as Anderson spoke, like two presiding judges.

All four turned at the same time as Porter and Styles approached the door and knocked. Porter saw Campbell beckon him in with a wave of his hand. Anderson's mouth was half-open as if paused mid-sentence as they turned to face the two detectives.

'Sorry, sir, I thought we'd arranged our briefing for five,' said Porter, opting for tact over terseness. The latter wouldn't win him any brownie points with his superiors, so he kept any animosity towards Anderson in check for his own sake. 'My apologies, we were out following up a few leads.'

'Our briefing is at five, Detective, but we do need to speak to you now, as it happens,' said Milburn. 'Something has come up today that involves you, both of you. Please, take a seat.'

Porter had never worked directly with or for Roger Milburn, but he knew him by reputation. Word was that he ran a tight ship, and didn't tolerate anyone who didn't give absolute loyalty to him and the team. Milburn reminded Porter of a politician more than a police officer. His smile, when it broke free, reminded Porter of a shark, all teeth on show but without any real warmth in the rest of the face. He looked at Anderson and Whittaker, searching their faces for any clue of what it might be about, but found none.

They sat opposite the other two detectives, with the senior officers at the head of the table. He glanced again at Anderson and Whittaker, but they didn't meet his eye.

'Would you like us to go first, sir? I can give a quick update on where we're at?'

A flash of pearly white from Milburn. 'We'll get to that shortly, Detective. First of all, why don't you tell us why you deliberately disobeyed a direct order from a commanding officer.'

There was no cordiality in his tone or his words. Porter's head swam with possibilities, and he opened his mouth to speak, but Campbell jumped in before the first word could escape his mouth.

'What we would like to know, Detective Porter, is why, after I specifically instructed you to leave Mr Locke out of the picture, you visited his house this morning?' His tone was softer than that of his peer, but still with an unmistakable frosty edge.

His question took Porter by surprise. He knew he was playing fast and loose with the rules by visiting Mrs Locke this morning, but they hadn't told anyone where they were going, and had only left her a little over five hours ago. How the hell had it gotten back to Campbell so fast? He didn't have time to consider the routes the information might have taken before Campbell became impatient and paraphrased his own question.

'Well, Detectives, what were you doing at Mr Locke's house this morning?'

He addressed them both this time, but Porter answered before Styles felt compelled to. His partner was one of the most intelligent people he knew, but he was still wet around the ears when it came to dealing with office politics.

'We were finishing up an interview with Mrs Locke, sir. We didn't get the opportunity to finish it a few days ago, and needed to ask her a few more questions to get background on her stepdaughter.'

'And by collecting background, you of course mean accusing one of her husband's employees of being complicit in her disappearance?'

Porter lowered his gaze for a second as he sifted through the possibilities. The only one that made sense was that Mrs Locke had called up and complained after they had left.

'Sir, I don't know what she said exactly, but we were very respectful, and as soon as she asked us to leave we—'

'She didn't say anything. *He* did, or should I say his solicitor did on his behalf, asking why we're harassing his wife and accusing his staff without proper cause or foundation.' His tone was no different to that he used in day-to-day conversation, but the way he enunciated reminded Porter of a schoolteacher.

'I then had the pleasure of a call from Deputy Commissioner Nesbitt, asking why we're aggressively pursuing a case with so little evidence, against a man of Locke's standing. That puts me in a difficult position, Porter. I either back your play and look like a fool for doing so with insufficient evidence, or I tell him you operated against explicit instructions and look like I can't command my own men. Which would you have me do? That's a rhetorical one, by the way.'

Campbell paused for breath and glanced at Milburn, who wore a relaxed smile, presumably thinking about his own stock rising as Campbell fought to defend his own name.

'Sir, if I may?' Porter hoped to mitigate whatever censure was coming by sharing his observations about the inconsistency at the crime scene, and the possibility of footage of the street. If he could convince them of the case against Bolton for Gibson and Simmons, he might be able to trump their desire to use the big man as part of the drugs case. The publicity that would come of jailing a cop killer was something surely even Campbell couldn't pass up. Locke was all theirs as far as he was concerned but every instinct he had screamed out that Bolton was their man for both of his colleagues, as well as Natasha.

'No, Detective, you may not.' Milburn took over now. 'While you and your partner have been harassing Mrs Locke, your friends here' – he gestured towards Anderson and Whittaker – 'have been doing some worthwhile police work.'

Porter looked over at the two drugs squad detectives again. Whittaker was looking at an imaginary spot on the wall, an uneasy look on his face. Anderson, unless Porter was much mistaken, looked pleased with himself, betrayed by the corners of his mouth twitching like a tic.

'Mr Locke and Mr Bolton met with them earlier when they visited Atlas. Mr Locke is astounded that he or any of his associates are suspects, and has offered us full access to his properties to inspect as we see fit, as a show of good faith. In addition, Mr Bolton has requested we check his phone records as a means of clearing his name. Turns out that based on the location of his phone, he had in fact left the premises and was seven miles away in a Chinese restaurant. That plus the statement from the manager means he's clear. It means you do not touch him.'

His last four words were spoken slowly for emphasis, as if for the benefit of a small child. Porter stared at him hard. The phone location meant nothing where a man like Bolton was concerned. He could have easily slipped it to someone else to drive it there for him. He employed the manager of the restaurant. It was paper thin, and Milburn knew that as well as he did, but it served to put Bolton off limits for the murders, and in play for the drugs. Milburn didn't give a shit how Bolton went down, as long as he did, and as long as he and his team got the credit for it. Porter's stomach knotted in anger. The fact he could sell out his own for personal gain put him almost on par with Locke as far as he was concerned, but he couldn't let the animosity show. Milburn had the ability to make life difficult for him. Very difficult indeed.

'Are we clear, Detectives?' Milburn addressed the question to all four men.

He heard the others murmur an acknowledgement, and tried not to speak through gritted teeth when he gave his own.

'Good. I'm sure I don't need to tell any of you the consequences for going your own way on this one.'

A flash of shark-like teeth, and Milburn closed the notebook he had in front of him. 'Let's reconvene at five, then.'

Short of placing Bolton at the scene from any camera footage, Porter knew he was fighting a losing battle, and bit his tongue. They stood up to leave when Milburn asked Anderson and Whittaker to stay behind for a few minutes. Porter didn't bother looking back as he left. He knew Anderson would be gloating on the inside, and didn't want to give him the satisfaction of seeing a hint of frustration. The job was hard enough at times when you only had the criminals to fight against. Internal enemies were something he could do without. He shot Styles a look to keep him quiet until they were safely back downstairs, and mentally prepared the rant that his partner would patiently sit through.

Styles sat quietly and bore the brunt of Porter's anger. The door to the small room was closed, but Porter still kept his voice down, knowing that the sound would carry, but also careful not to misdirect his anger towards his partner.

'So what now? Do we toe the line? I'm guessing we have to?'

'The only thing that might make a dent in their stubbornness is that camera footage,' said Porter, sitting back in exasperation. 'We place Bolton there and they can't ignore him.'

'Let's hope Reid gets it sooner rather than later, then.'

They both looked up at the same time to see Whittaker walk through the door. He saw the glare Porter shot him and immediately raised his hands, palms out in surrender.

'Whoa there. I had nothing to do with that little ambush upstairs.'

'I notice you say "I" and not "we".'

Whittaker gave a pained smile. 'Let's not go there. I know he can be a prickly bastard at times, but he's my partner, and we're all on the same side.'

'Not all of us,' muttered Styles.

'Look, we didn't ask Locke to call up. We were there when his wife called him. He was pissed. He hid it well, but he was pissed. Called Jasper up straight away and asked for a restraining order.'

'He did what?' Porter almost exploded with anger and incredulity.

Whittaker shrugged. 'I'm guessing Jasper advised against it for now, or we'd have heard about it upstairs.'

Porter shook his head in disbelief. 'He's got some bloody nerve.' He was about to launch into a rant about Locke, when it hit him. 'So let me get this straight, Locke just happened to turn up at the same time you two paid a visit? I thought he hardly ever showed his face on-site.'

'No idea. He and Bolton were in the office already when we got there.'

'So what happened, then? I'm assuming they weren't exactly overjoyed to see you there?'

'Didn't seem too fazed, to be honest. He's either not our man, or he's got some balls to put on a front like that.'

'And he's just going to let us stroll around wherever we want without a warrant? I can only assume he's already cleaned house. What did he say, exactly?'

'Dunno, I wasn't there. I went for a snoop around while Anderson stayed with him to make sure he couldn't call anyone.'

'And where's Anderson now?'

'Toilet, I think.'

'So what did you find, then?' asked Styles.

Whittaker shook his head. 'Nothing, but we're going back with dogs this afternoon. They still think it's the murders that we're looking into for now, though.'

'By which time they'll have shifted anything that was there and thrown a shitload of bleach down to cover any scent,' said Porter. 'It's like he's one step ahead. He's not daft. He knows it's not about the murders. Why else would he be opening his doors up other than to throw us off the scent?'

'How about you two, anyway?' asked Whittaker. 'What was it you were trying to tell those two upstairs?'

Porter gave him a summary of their morning. Whittaker listened intently, eyes widening at the mention of a camera.

'I never spotted it,' he said, looking embarrassed. 'How long before we can have a look?'

'No idea. I'll check with Reid in a minute.'

'Be careful, Porter. I hear good things about you, but Milburn isn't a man to get on the wrong side of. This one's his platform for the next step up, and I wouldn't want to be the one who fucks it up for him.'

'Consider me well and truly warned.'

'I didn't mean it like that.'

'I know, I know.' Porter instantly felt bad. He hadn't thought for a second that Milburn was delivering a warning as such, but the need to constantly look over his shoulder to see what his own people were doing was making him snappy. 'Sorry, Jon. Do me a favour,' he said, changing the subject to thaw the atmosphere. 'Ask Anderson to give me a shout when you see him. I want to know more about how it went with Locke and Bolton while you were sniffing around.'

'Sure thing, will do. See you at the funeral tomorrow, yeah?'

'Yep, will do.'

Whittaker left them alone, and Styles headed to the bathroom, promising to send Anderson Porter's way if he was still there. Porter wandered back to his desk and sat down in his chair with a heavy thump. He was long overdue a holiday. He hadn't done anything with his leave allocation since Holly, other than use a few days here and there to fix a few things around the house. He decided there and then, once these cases were clear he would take a few days. To hell with it, he would take a week. He'd strap his mountain bike to the back of the car, pack up his fishing gear and head to the Lake District. He closed his eyes and leant back in his seat. The decision made, it couldn't come soon enough.

He stood up again and walked to the window adjacent to his desk, touching each ear to a shoulder, smiling at the satisfying *click* of the vertebrae. The street below was a patchwork of shadow and light, an artistic collaboration of sunlight and cloud. He stared at the herd of cirrus clouds meandering across the sky, remembering playing the game with his mother as a kid: spot the face in the sky. The two on the left were narrow triangles that met at the apex, joined together to form a bow tie.

He looked down and saw Anderson's familiar bald head dodging between two parked cars, phone clamped to his ear. He lifted his hand to rap on the glass, but let it fall back to his side. There was no way Anderson would hear him with the noise of the street. Trust him to be scurrying off when he was needed.

Porter picked up his phone and called Reid. The young officer answered on the third ring.

'Where are we at getting that footage?'

'Turns out it's not a camera per se,' said Reid. 'It's a meteorological monitoring unit. They have them all over the place these days.'

'So we can tell if it was raining but not who was there?' said Porter, sarcasm getting the better of him.

'N-no, sir. There is something we can use,' Reid stammered, not knowing how to respond to his senior officer's mocking comeback. 'It doesn't just monitor the weather. I checked and it's part of a network of weather stations across the country called Weather Watch UK.'

Reid paused to see if that rang any bells with Porter but heard only static on the line.

'If you go to their website you can click on hundreds of stations across the country and see the weather at each location.'

'Wait a minute,' said Porter. 'Do you mean as in get a weather report, or we can *see* the weather, as in actually see it?'

'Actually see it, sir.'

Porter clenched his fist and thumped his desk twice in triumph. 'That's the best news I've had in a long time, Reid. How soon till we get it?'

'Not till tomorrow, sir. A word of warning, though, it's not going to be a continuous feed.'

'You mean it's not always on?'

'I mean it takes a frame every three seconds, so it'll be like watching a series of still photos, like old-fashioned CCTV.'

'Reid, as long as it shows us the Taylor building, that won't bother me one bit. I'll take my chances. Good work.'

He caught the tail end of a nervous thank you from Reid as he took the receiver away from his ear. He didn't want to get his hopes up too much until he saw the footage, but it was about time something swung their way, and he allowed himself a cautious smile.

CHAPTER FIFTEEN

The rain that had fallen for most of the last twenty-four hours stopped just after breakfast in an act of celestial goodwill, and the clouds went from grubby lumps of dirty cotton wool to a cleaner, slightly off-white; nature's own *Fifty Shades of Grey*. The road wound into the cemetery and splintered off into a hundred paths leading to a thousand tombstones.

Porter had limited experience of funerals, and he was keen to keep it that way. Over a hundred mourners had gathered to pay their respects to Mike Gibson, including his wife and two sons. Porter had met her four or five times before on work nights out, enough that she recognised him through the blur of tears and gave him a weak smile when he arrived. He hadn't known what to say to her as he walked past, so settled for a clichéd 'Sorry for your loss.' There wasn't time for much more than that as a relative – Porter guessed her father, from his age – shepherded her towards the chapel, protective arm around her.

Deputy Commissioner Adam Nesbitt was in attendance, moving slowly from handshake to handshake, weaving through the knots of black uniforms. He reminded Porter of a politician working the room. Porter himself merited no more than a nod and a smile before Nesbitt moved on to speak with Superintendent Campbell. Porter didn't need to be able to lip-read to know he figured in the conversation. Campbell's not-so-subtle glances in his direction told him all he needed to know. He'd worry about that if and when it came back to bite him.

Porter slid into a pew at the back of the chapel next to Styles, and watched as Gibson's family were ushered into the front row. He had taken his place there once. Next to Holly's parents. Confused from the conflict of comforting reassurance from others that despite your loss you're not alone, but all the while longing for them to leave so you could let the grief wash over you and be done with it. Porter tried to let his mind wander, think about something other than funerals. Anything would do. He thought of Natasha, but that darkened his mood even more. Mike had quite the crowd, but Natasha had no one who even cared enough to look for her. Who would she get? The last funeral he had been to was the father of a friend. You could count the mourners that day on two hands, including the priest, and that had somehow amplified the sadness of the occasion. Even though he had only ever seen Natasha in photographs, he couldn't help feel that she deserved better than that.

Porter forced himself to focus on the picture of Mike Gibson that sat atop the coffin. Today was about Mike. Not Natasha. Not Holly. Even thinking her name in a place like this brought back the all-too-familiar hollow feeling in his stomach. His mouth felt dry, as if he'd had a few the night before, and he felt himself start to fidget in his seat, desperate to be anywhere but here.

He forced himself to sit still, fixing his gaze on the photo as the priest worked his way through the service, right up until the curtains whirred along the rail, obscuring it from view. He filed out into the aisle with the others, feet shuffling in frustration, needing to get out into the fresh air and away from all this.

'Plans for the day, then, guv?' said Styles, once they were outside.

'We see what Reid has for us when we get back. No point planning too far past that, yet, cos that could change everything.'

Styles nodded. 'It could, but – and I don't want to rain on your parade here because there is a but – if it only shows a frame every three seconds, we might come up empty-handed even if he was there.'

'What do you mean "if he was there"? Of course he was there. He's—'

'Whoa, easy tiger.' Styles raised his hands in surrender. 'I agree. I'm just saying there's a chance that he did whatever he did in however many seconds of nothingness between frames.'

Porter was painfully aware of the odds being stacked against them, and didn't have a concrete plan beyond that, but decided to cross that bridge when they came to it.

'Emma's invited you round for dinner on Sunday. Roast beef and all the trimmings, if you can make it?'

'Let me check my packed social calendar, but there's a good chance I'll be free.'

'So that's a yes, then?'

Porter smiled and nodded. He spotted Anderson breaking away from the crowd, making a beeline for his car. 'Hang on, let me grab Anderson for a sec before he vanishes again.'

He half-walked, half-trotted down the road that led back to the main gate of the cemetery, and was within twenty feet of Anderson when he reached his car.

'Anderson, you got a second?'

Anderson turned around, keys in hand. Porter saw what looked like a roll of the eyes as he clocked who was chasing after him, but was too far away to be sure.

'I'm on my way back to the station. Can it wait till then?'

'It'll only take a minute.'

Anderson glanced from his car and back to Porter, weighing up his options. Porter slowed his pace, but kept moving towards him, as if closing the distance might sway the decision. Anderson shrugged and relented.

'Fine, whatever, as long as it's literally a minute. Places to go, people to see and all that.'

Porter stopped when he drew level with the tail end of the car, and slid his hands into his pockets. He gave Anderson his best 'we're on the same side' smile.

'Just wondered how it went with Locke yesterday? We didn't get a chance to talk about it.'

Anderson reached into his jacket pocket and pulled out a crumpled pack of Marlboro Lights.

'What do you mean? Jon ran through that with us in the briefing yesterday. Not much more to say other than what he told you, really.'

He shook a cigarette out and placed it in his mouth, fumbling for his lighter with his free hand.

Porter kept his smile in place. 'We did, but if you remember, he said you guys had to split up for part of it. Said he went for a wander round the warehouse floor while you stayed with Locke and Bolton.'

'Yep, and?' Anderson said curtly, the cigarette between his lips now, dancing with every word.

'And I'm wondering what they had to say for themselves. From what Campbell said yesterday, Locke sounds fairly confident that we'll find nothing.'

Anderson drew the smoke into his lungs and turned his head a few degrees, firing a smoky dart over the roof of his car. 'Yep, he certainly does, but if it's there we'll find it.'

'That's the thing,' said Porter, taking a step closer. 'I was thinking about that, thinking about why make the offer. He must be confident there's nothing to find, at least nothing anywhere we know to look, anyway. Then I got to thinking about Carter, and why he ditched his mic, and how Bolton seemed to have his getaway planned that day.'

'So what are you saying, then?'

'Not sure, really. I'm just thinking out loud, but when someone is a step ahead it tends to be cos they know what's coming.'

'You're thinking Locke has someone on our side of the fence?'

Porter arched his eyebrows. He had, as it happened, but wasn't ready to voice any suspicions yet. 'I was going to say maybe he has a man following one or more of us, so he knows when we're coming for him, but that's an interesting point you bring up. Guess anything's possible.'

Anderson shot a quick glance first over Porter's shoulder, then his own. He moved closer now so they were only a foot apart. When he spoke, his voice was low despite there being nobody else within twenty feet.

'I didn't want to say anything in the room yesterday, but I think you could be right.' His eyes continued to scan the surroundings as he talked. 'About a month ago, I ran into a guy I arrested years back for dealing. He looked more nervous than he should so we started talking about reasonable grounds for a rummage through his pockets and his rucksack. He of course swears blind there's nothing to see, and asks if I'm interested in a little information instead of a wasted search, as he puts it.'

Anderson paused for another drag on his cigarette. Porter glanced behind. The mourners had drifted away now, and he saw Styles leaning against their car over by the gates, hand to his head, presumably holding his phone.

'So I was expecting the usual bullshit of rumours of some deal coming up that he'll give me on a plate, but then he springs it on me. Says there's a big outfit based down by the river, someone we've never heard of. Someone with a copper on the payroll.'

Porter's eyes widened. It had been nothing more than a theory in his mind, one he hadn't even shared with Styles yet, not through any mistrust but because he couldn't quite convince himself it could be true.

'And what did he tell you about this copper? Can he describe him or her?'

'He went one further than that. He gave me a name. Well, a first name at least.' Anderson took one more hit of nicotine before flicking the remaining stump, end over end, to the ground. He squashed it with his heel and dragged his foot back and forth a few times to finish the job. 'He said the guy's name was Mike.'

'Mike? As in our Mike? Mike Gibson?'

Anderson's eyes widened in alarm. 'Keep it down,' he warned. 'I can't prove it, but I had noticed Mike acting a little strange lately.'

'Strange, how?'

'Strange as in the way he worked the case at times. Nothing solid I could pin down, but you just get a feeling when something's not right, you know? My guy says he saw him twice with Bolton. I showed him a pic and he ID'd Mike. Next time I saw Mike I asked him a question about the last time he interviewed Bolton, and he started telling me about when we'd questioned him about an assault. Not enough evidence for it to bring him in and charge him, of course, but Mike swore blind that was the last time he'd spoken to him.'

'And you think what, then? That they killed him because they thought he was playing them? Double-crossing them?'

Anderson just shrugged. 'No idea, and I could be way off the mark here. I've not even told Jon, it's that tenuous. But yeah, maybe following them to that building was no accident. Maybe that was their plan all along. Maybe they'd had a falling-out, or maybe Mike had a crisis of conscience, who knows? Either way, that could explain why they killed him, but didn't finish the job on Simmons.'

As much as Porter wanted to discount the possibility of one of their own turning on them out of hand, the objective part of his brain kicked in. It would explain why they'd known about Carter's mic, why they were opening their doors for inspection now. They would have moved everything that Gibson knew about in case he was double-crossing them. How compromised might they still be now that Mike was dead and not feeding them any more information?

'We have to take this to Campbell,' he said finally.

'And say what? We have an anonymous tip one of our team was dirty, but absolutely nothing to back it up, a copper who, by the way, we've given the all-singing, all-dancing funeral to for dying in the line of duty. I'm sure that'll get me in his not-so-good graces alongside you. No bloody thank you.'

Porter chewed on his bottom lip. He knew Anderson was right, but it was the proverbial rock and hard place. If he told Campbell, there was a good chance it would be dismissed out of hand, with no supporting evidence and the alleged conspirator dead. If he didn't, and it came out later in the investigation that it was true, it could hurt them. Correction, he thought, it could hurt him. By then there was a good chance Anderson would be sitting somewhere sunny collecting his pension.

'I don't know,' he said finally. 'Let me think about it. Who's your guy, the one who pointed the finger at Mike?'

Anderson shook his head. 'I promised I'd keep his name out of it unless we needed him to testify, and Mike's not getting arrested any time soon.'

'What if it was true and Mike wasn't the only one?'

'Then that's a whole other problem that none of my sources have flagged, so I won't be losing too much sleep about it. Now, if you don't mind, I've really got to get going.'

Porter nodded and promised to keep the revelation, if it had enough substance to qualify as that, to himself for now. He watched as Anderson drove slowly through the gates and accelerated away towards the main road.

Styles had finished his call and was waiting in the car. 'What's Anderson's craic, then? Anything to report?'

Porter hesitated before answering. 'Nothing worth repeating. Come on, let's get back.' He rarely kept things from his partner, and it wasn't a question of trust, more that it felt wrong to even hint at something that dark at Gibson's funeral, and it was only hearsay, a throwaway remark made by a criminal trying to curry favour with an officer. He filed it away as something to look at later, and gazed out of the window as they pulled away.

Porter had known Gibson mainly by reputation, but what he had heard was all good. He knew there would be a strong push to bury it either way, regardless of whether any case against Locke or Bolton held up, no pun intended bearing in mind Gibson's untimely ending. Any acknowledgement of corruption inside the department, even when rooted out and exposed to the light, did more harm than good. That push would come from Milburn, and Campbell would support him in return for a favour to be cashed in further down the line.

Rooting around in the mess left behind wouldn't change the outcome for Simmons or Gibson, but Porter wasn't sure he could balance his own personal scales if he left it alone. Doing nothing would somehow cheapen the sacrifice that his colleagues had made. Whether they would do it for him or not was another matter, but he had to believe that they would, had to believe that doing the right thing still meant something. If it didn't, then what was the point in doing what they did?

He decided it was too early in the morning to be getting so philosophical, and let it go for now. It would be easier if he could talk to Anderson's source, but he didn't expect a change of heart there any time soon. There had to be another way to approach it. Whether he could figure that out in time to make a difference in the case was another matter, but he'd give it his best shot.

'So here's an interesting little revelation for you,' said Styles.

Porter looked up from his screen. Three strong cups of coffee and a croissant that tasted marginally better than cardboard had done nothing to kick-start his creativity. This morning had left him feeling sluggish, present day priorities in a tug of war with bittersweet memories; Porter stuck in the middle, unable to focus. He stared back at Styles for a few seconds before realising his partner was waiting for a response.

'Sorry, I was miles away. What did you say?'

'I said she had a good poker face.'

'Eh? Who? What are you on about?'

'Mrs Locke. She had a good poker face.'

'What the hell are you talking about? Spare me the build-up.'

'She lied to us. About her trips to see Natasha.'

That got Porter's attention, and he sat forward, leaning both elbows on his desk. 'What do you mean, she lied? What have you got?'

'According to this' – he pointed at his screen – 'in the six months following Nathan Barclay's death, Mrs Locke did leave the country twice, but I'm fairly sure she didn't go anywhere near Poland.'

'How do you know that? Where was she? Can we prove it?'

'One question at a time,' said Styles, holding his hands up to fend off any more. 'I know because I checked. She was in New York and Paris. Yes, we can prove it.'

'Checked, how?' Porter was intrigued, but sceptical. As much as he abhorred the concept of terrorism, it had made tracking international travel much easier, both inside the European Union and beyond. They were talking about three decades ago, though, a time when kids could visit the pilot in the cockpit and you could carry a bottle of water through customs without security jumping all over you. He was pretty sure passenger manifests wouldn't stretch back that far.

Styles tapped a finger against his nose and winked. 'Friends in low places. Mrs Locke booked flights using a Visa card both times. I know a man who can dredge up all sorts from my days back in financial, even from thirty years ago.'

'She could have paid cash,' Porter ventured.

'She could have, but you don't believe that any more than I do.'

Porter sat for a moment, mind racing before he spoke. 'Give me specifics.'

Styles flipped open his notebook and recited the dates he had scribbled down for each trip. As well as the dates, there were a number of transactions at each destination consistent with a fortnight in New York and a three-day stay in Paris.

'There's no doubt she was there. Question is, why lie? Also, did she lie to her hubby, or does he know where she really was?'

The silence hung between them as they stared across the desk at each other, the hint of a smile creeping on both faces confirming the shared thought.

'OK, what do we do now?' asked Styles. 'She's off limits unless we get Campbell on board. I'll back you if you want to try again so soon, but . . .' The way he let the sentence trail off told Porter everything he needed to know about his partner's desire to take it to Campbell again so soon.

Porter opened his mouth to speak when it hit him. 'We go and see her,' he said.

'Just like that?' said Styles. 'And your grand plan for not getting us both hauled in front of Campbell and Milburn is . . . ?'

Porter shook his head. 'She won't talk, not this time. Think about it. She's cornered by her own lie.'

Styles looked blankly at him, so Porter continued, speaking slowly, checking out the strength of his argument as he went.

'First off, we have her lying to two police officers investigating her stepdaughter's disappearance and probable murder. Why would someone lie about that unless they had something to hide? Secondly, if she lied to Locke as well, she's going to have to try and spin the same lie to him if we call her out on it. She's hardly going to call him up this time and say "Honey, I just fed the nice officers a line of bullshit which makes me a potential suspect. Could you make a few calls and clean this one up for me?", now is she?'

Styles shrugged. 'Maybe he knows about it.'

Porter barked a short laugh. 'You think after everything we know about him he's that sloppy? Anything's possible, I suppose, but I seriously doubt it.'

'What are we saying, then, that she had something to do with Natasha disappearing, and made up these trips to cover her tracks so Locke wouldn't suspect her?'

Porter felt a tightness forming across his shoulders from hunching over a desk for too long, and rubbed at it with one hand. 'Honestly? I don't know. Maybe. We know they didn't get on. We know she's hiding something. People make bad choices in the heat of the moment. It would explain why she had Locke call up the deputy commissioner. Maybe she's trying to scare us off.'

Styles held Porter's gaze for a moment while he crunched the possibilities in his mind. 'What the hell, let's do it. You're right: whatever happened, she's part of it one way or the other. That's the only way this makes sense.'

Porter shook his head this time. 'I'll go. No sense in us both getting a kicking over it if I'm wrong.'

Styles rolled his eyes. 'Oh yeah, cos of course I'm "that guy" who lets his partner fall on his sword. Do me a favour.' He stood up and pulled his jacket on. 'Come on, then, if we're going to tilt at windmills we might as well do it before rush hour kicks in.'

Porter flirted with the idea of trying to talk him out of it. If it did blow up in their faces, he saw no sense in them both suffering, but he knew Styles was stubborn when it came to backing him up. Porter wouldn't have borne a grudge if his partner had taken the out offered to him, but deep down he'd known it would be refused point-blank; that's exactly what he would have done.

He patted his pockets, listening for the jangle of keys, but spotted them peeking out from underneath a folder on his desk. He had no idea what truths lurked behind Mary Locke's lies, but thirty years' hibernation was enough; it would end today.

CHAPTER SIXTEEN

Mary Locke's anger was a tangible thing that crackled through the airwaves and shot out from the intercom speaker. The quiet, submissive tone of previous visits had been replaced with an abrupt, clipped reply that brooked no argument.

'Sorry, Detectives, but I'm under strict instructions not to admit you, and to contact my husband immediately. I believe he's spoken to your superiors.' Her words were coated with a smug glow of immunity.

'I believe he has, Mrs Locke, and you're well within your rights to do that. Before you do though, I'd take a moment, and consider how your husband, and my superiors' – he placed heavy stress on *superiors*, merely the proverbial messenger begging not to be shot – 'would take to finding out that you lied about your trips to see Natasha.'

A tremor of anger rippled through her reply, but it rang false in his ear. 'How dare you call me a liar? Just you wait until my husband—'

'Mrs Locke, excuse my being blunt, but you provided false information to officers investigating an alleged murder. We can prove that you didn't take trips to Poland to see your stepdaughter when you claim to have. As to why you felt the need to give us that information, I can't say, but I'd much rather discuss it face-to-face, unless you're happy for your neighbours to listen in as we chat through your intercom.'

Silence, not even the hiss of static through the speaker. Porter and

Styles stood motionless, staring at the intercom, willing her to respond. Every second of silence that slipped past could be a second on the phone to her husband. Finally, after moments that felt like eons, a noise made them both look up sharply. The front door opened, and Mary Locke came out. She locked the door behind her and looked furtively both ways to neighbouring houses. She looked directly at them, but walked to the Range Rover parked off centre and got in without a word. The reflection of the sun off her window as she closed the door dazzled Porter and he shielded his face with a forearm, hearing and feeling the rumble of the gate opening as he rubbed at his eyes.

They had called her bluff and lost. Whether she had already called Locke, or would call him when she was safely away from them, it didn't matter. The first domino had fallen and the rest would soon follow. Her engine revved as she crept out of the gate. The stars had cleared from his vision now. He saw the sun glint off her Jackie-Onassis-size sunglasses as she pulled onto the road and drew level with them.

When she stopped abruptly it took him by surprise. The driver's side window purred as it lowered. She spoke without turning her head, eyes staring along the road in front, or at least he assumed they were; it was impossible to tell behind her dark glasses.

'There's a coffee shop about five miles from here called Hutton's, near Harrow. Do you know it?'

He nodded, then realised she wouldn't see the gesture. 'Yes.' He cleared his throat. 'I know where it is.'

'Meet me there in an hour.'

The window whirred back up and she accelerated away. Styles turned to Porter and cocked his head to the side.

'What just happened? I thought she was going to do a vanishing act there.'

'That's what we detectives call catching a break, son. I knew it. I knew she was holding out on us.'

'Holding out what, though? That's the question.'

'I haven't got a bloody clue.' Porter laughed. 'Let's go and find out.'

* * *

She was ready to talk, reluctant but ready. Porter didn't understand the need to wait an hour and wondered what could be so pressing, so they opted to follow her in the absence of anything more productive. There was also a tiny part of him that thought she might make a beeline for her husband, and he wanted to be in position to head her off if that looked likely.

They had kept a safe distance of at least three cars behind, but she showed no signs of being aware of a tail, let alone trying to evade them. She drove west through Stanmore. Porter wondered if she was heading to their rendezvous early and just wanted time to compose herself with whatever she wanted to talk to them about, but she went past the turn-off and on towards Northwood.

After another five minutes, she turned south towards Ruislip. Porter was beginning to think she had spotted them after all, and was leading them on a pointless loop back towards their intended meeting place. They were nearing the village, tucked in two cars back behind a red Mini Cooper that made Porter think of *The Italian Job*, when he saw her signal left onto a street marked Reservoir Road. Neither of the two cars between them followed suit, so after Porter made the turn, he eased off the accelerator to avoid catching her up.

The straightness of the road ahead made him even more cautious. As much as he didn't want to risk losing her around any bends, there was now nothing but a hundred yards of road in between them.

Styles sensed his hesitation. 'Let her go. It's a dead end up ahead.' He tapped the screen on the satnav.

Porter slowed to fifteen miles an hour as they passed the gate on their right that lead to a lake called Ruislip Lido. Originally a reservoir built to feed the Grand Junction Canal back in the 1800s, it was known nowadays for its artificial sandy beach, speckled with towels and picnic blankets in the summer months. It was bare today, though, a couple strolling arm in arm its only occupants.

Up ahead he saw her brake lights winking as she came to a stop, and he quickly pulled over to the kerb. He reached across Styles to open the glove box, and then remembered he hadn't replaced the compact binoculars he'd broken several months back. He made do with leaning forward in his seat and narrowing his eyes in a squint as the stick figure in the distance exited the

Range Rover, its lights giving a rapid double flash as she locked it. Instinct from Porter's previous life in the army registered it as two dots, the letter 'I' in Morse code. He smiled at the memory.

He heard the click of a camera shutter, and turned to see Styles resting his iPhone on the dash. He had zoomed in far enough to be able to identify Mary Locke, but not so much that the picture had surrendered to grainy vagueness. Porter nodded his approval at the improvisation.

'I'm not just a pretty face,' said Styles, his eyes fixed on the image on screen. 'And I'm guessing she's not just here for a breath of fresh air, so worth taking a few snaps to establish her whereabouts, and whoever she might be here to meet.'

'You think the hubby might put in an appearance?'

'Your guess is as good as mine, but I'm going to go with no. I think you called it right first time. Whatever she knows, she doesn't want him knowing.'

Mary Locke headed straight for the treeline at the end of the road. As soon as she was out of sight, Porter started the car up again and drove slowly past the Range Rover. The only other people in view were an elderly couple coming out of the Water's Edge pub, and a woman coming towards them with a pushchair. She had come from the direction Mary Locke had headed. A dull green gate marked the end of the road and the start of Ruislip Woods. Despite the branches that reached down to obscure the path, several of the gaps in the foliage shifted from green to red and back again as Mary Locke's coat refused to be camouflaged.

Porter swung into the car park on the left and they walked back down to the entrance. The trees that crowded the gate opened up into a clearing. The path hugged the treeline on the right, and they could see her, red coat seeming to glow every time she stepped from shadow to sunlight.

'You think we should be laying a trail of breadcrumbs?' said Styles.

Porter smiled but said nothing. They kept pace with her, careful to maintain their distance while keeping hers in their line of sight. Each time she vanished, they quickened their pace. The path forked ahead and she bore left, away from the lake. The trees grew thicker on their left, a solid wall of greens and browns, oak and silver birch. Porter checked his watch. They had been walking for almost ten minutes at an unhurried pace. He guessed they had covered half a mile, maybe a touch more.

Suddenly she veered left and vanished from view. They broke into a fast walk that made Porter think of the Olympics, how he'd chuckled at the swinging hips of the long distance walkers, how Holly had mimicked their swaying steps around the living room. He pictured the serious look of concentration as she turned a hard right angle in each corner; remembered tripping her up so she collapsed across him on the sofa. He struggled to embrace these glimpses of happier times. They left him with an empty feeling somewhere inside, reminding him that whatever it was, his heart, his soul, it hadn't fully healed.

That feeling stayed with him as they reached the point they had last seen Mary Locke. Five paths converged, spreading outwards from the centre like spokes on a wheel. Shadows coated the route she had taken, a protective cloak of green allowing only a fraction of the light safe passage to the ground. They could still make her out ahead. The gloom had turned the red of her coat into a rusty hue as she picked her way along the path.

Porter turned to his partner, his voice a low whisper. 'I say we take a side of the path each and stick close to the trees in case we need to take cover.'

Styles nodded and pointed off to the left. Porter nodded and moved to the right. They carefully picked their way along the edges of the path, careful to avoid making too much noise by doing anything as clumsy as stepping on fallen twigs. They both froze as the figure ahead took a sharp right off the path and into the thick combination of trees and undergrowth, glancing back the way she had come as she turned. Neither of them dared move, unsure as to whether they had been spotted, or whether they'd blended into the shadows. Porter looked across at Styles and gave a shrug. His partner replied by wiggling his hand palm-down to signify a maybe.

Porter waited a full count of ten before risking a glance ahead. Nothing. He took a chance and crossed the path to where Styles hunched behind a large oak.

'Three options,' he said, counting them off on his fingers. 'We head back to the car, we head in there after her, or we walk past where she dodged off the path and keep walking but see if we can see where she's at.'

'How about option four?' said Styles. 'We hide out here and wait for her to head back. One of us follows her back towards the cars, the other has a nose round up there and see if we can figure out what she's doing. Worst case we'll be at the cafe five minutes behind her.'

'If she shows.'

'If she shows,' agreed Styles.

Porter thought about that for a moment, then nodded. 'Alright. Let's get set behind there.' He pointed to a large bush to their left. 'You pick her up when she goes past and I'll take a look.'

They settled down to wait, and a few minutes later heard a crunching of leaves from the direction she then came from. Porter stared at the leaves in front of him, willing them to part enough to let him watch her walk past. The footsteps grew louder, and were accompanied by snatches of colour on the other side of the bush. Porter frowned. The colours were wrong, and a second later a man wearing a light blue waterproof jacket walked past, hands jammed in pockets, strains of music, audible but not identifiable, leaking from his headphones.

Mary Locke made them wait another five minutes, her footsteps quick and light. She was past them in a flash of colour, but Porter put a hand on Styles's arm and counted a full ten seconds before letting go and stepping out onto the path. She had already reached the junction of the five routes and Styles headed after her without a word.

Porter watched him go before turning and breaking into a jog towards the spot he'd fixed in his memory earlier. She had left the path a few yards past a large stump on the right-hand side. The relatively flat top, and absence of trunk anywhere in sight, suggested it had been felled rather than fallen; a long time ago, judging by the top, worn smooth. He glanced down the path again in time to see Styles disappear round the corner. He figured he had ten minutes before Mary Locke reached her car, so that gave him five minutes to look around if he wanted to get back in time to follow her to the cafe.

Porter scanned the trees and bushes ahead. He stood still, listening for anything that could signify another person nearby but all he heard was the faint noise of traffic in the background, punctuated by the chatter of unseen birds. As they had waited for her to pass them a few minutes ago, an idea had started to form. What if she wasn't here to meet anyone? What if she was here to hide something, leave something behind? She had been carrying a large handbag that could have concealed any number of things, maybe something relevant to Natasha.

He looked up into the branches and slowly worked his way down. The thick canopy of leaves meant that the diluted sunshine had to work even harder to suck up any rainwater that made it down this far. There was no surface water, but the soil looked far from dry. He squatted down for a closer look, and saw the tread of a shoe in amongst the dark ridges of mud. Another, less clear, but a similar enough size to be from the same shoe, lay just ahead of it. A small shoe. A woman's shoe. He was on the right track.

Porter kept to the right of the prints and followed them beyond the first line of trees. He paused twenty feet in when they seemed to end abruptly, but saw they started up again a few feet further on. He glanced back over his shoulder but the path had vanished behind a screen of leaves. Time check. He had three minutes left of his allotted five. The tracks stopped suddenly by a huge oak. The trunk was so large that Porter doubted he could circle it with his arms. Branches, too many to count, reached upwards, clawing against each other, competing for sunlight. He did a lap of the tree to see if she had gone further in, but the ground either side was untouched. He squatted again and looked at the marks closest to the tree. Two outlines sat side by side, as if she'd stood on the spot for some reason.

Satisfied this was as far as she had gone, Porter did another circuit of the tree, less concerned now about scuffing her trail. He walked slowly, staring at the base. The roots rippled outwards like octopus's tentacles, but the soil was undisturbed. If she had left anything behind it wasn't here. The only thing that broke the monotony of rough bark was a patch of snowdrops on the far side, shaped like a giant teardrop by what light and rain could battle its way down to help them grow. He looked at his watch. Time to head back or he'd risk losing her. He spun a last lazy circle before retracing his steps back to the path.

Damn it! What the hell was she playing at?

It started as the vaguest of notions but grew in an instant, then hit him full force, and if he was right this would change everything.

They spotted Mary Locke sitting in the far corner when they got there. It was a bright, homely place; the big glass front unobscured by curtains or signage allowed the sunlight access to all areas. It wasn't the kind of place she could hide in a dark shadowy booth at the back, but Porter assumed that burrowing herself away in the corner made her feel somewhat more secure.

They were the only customers, and the waitress intercepted them before they'd pulled chairs out from the table. They both ordered black coffee in cardboard take-out cups. There was no telling how quickly the clandestine meeting might end. Mary Locke didn't rise to greet them, didn't even look up from her cup, head bowed and glasses resting just above her hairline. Porter caught a whiff of peppermint from her teabag as she submerged it repeatedly on her teaspoon, like a witch on a ducking stool.

'I don't know if . . .' When she spoke, it came out thick with emotion and she coughed twice, clearing her throat and starting again. 'I don't know if I can give you what you need.'

'What do you think we need, Mrs Locke?'

'You say you can prove I didn't go to Poland. What do you mean by that?' she said, deflecting the question.

'Exactly that. We know you travelled abroad to two destinations on the dates you told us about, but Poland wasn't one of them.'

'I don't appreciate being called a liar, Detective,' she said, a flash of defiance in both her voice and in her eyes as she looked up.

Porter nodded slowly. 'Then I suggest you don't tell any that we can easily disprove.' He met her gaze and held it until she looked back down at her cup. 'Before we get on to Poland, why don't you tell us why you went to Ruislip Woods, Mrs Locke.'

She stiffened, then opened her mouth to speak but only managed fragments of words. 'I . . . What do mean . . . I don't . . .' She regained composure and went on the offensive. 'Have you been following me? You have no right.' She stopped short of shouting, but the shrillness of her voice made the waitress glance over.

'We have every right, Mrs Locke,' said Porter in a calm voice, trying to keep things level. He'd shared his theory with Styles on the journey from the woods, and they'd agreed to tackle things head-on. If they were wrong, they were already in a world of trouble with Campbell anyway, but Porter refused to let go of the feeling that they were on to something; if they could just apply the right pressure to the right place.

'Now, unless you want me to go back to those woods with the dogs and a forensic team, and make you fully accountable for whatever we find there, you need to start talking to me.'

Silence followed the ultimatum, broken only by the shuffling of feet, the waitress bringing them their coffees, scraping her soles on the tiles as she walked. She set them on the table and turned away with a smile but no conversation. Porter watched Mary Locke through the fingers of steam stretching upwards from his cup, as he waited her out.

'Mrs Locke, you asked us here to talk,' said Styles in a soft voice that a psychiatrist would have been proud of. 'Whatever it is you need to get off your chest, you know it's the right thing to do.'

She stared a moment longer, gaze fixed on her cup but not seeing it. When she looked up, her eyes were tired and damp with tears. 'None of this is right,' she said in a quiet voice, bottom lip trembling. 'None of it. I did not kill Natasha, Detective. I would never hurt her.'

'But you do know what happened to her, where she is.' Styles's tone told her he wasn't expecting a response, merely stating a fact.

She nodded, drawing her cup towards her, cradling it with both hands. Porter glanced at Styles with a look that urged silence. She was at the edge of the precipice. He was willing to bet she was more likely to take the step of her own accord than be pushed over by any verbal battering.

'You know about the tree,' she said finally. 'You followed me there. You know about the tree.'

Porter nodded. 'I saw the tree. Did you plant the snowdrops?'

She looked almost relieved at his words. 'I was there that night,' she said, ignoring his question about the flowers. 'I didn't see it happen. Didn't even see her face, but I knew it was her. After what happened with Gavin the other day, I . . . well, I couldn't live with myself if I stayed quiet and let him get taken from me as well.'

Porter's heart was beating so hard he fancied it was visible through his shirt, but he sat perfectly still, not wanting to disrupt her flow. Whatever the reference to Gavin was, it could wait.

'It was an accident, I'm sure it was. I don't think anyone would have hurt her on purpose.'

'What was an accident, Mrs Locke?' asked Styles.

Porter glared at him, but Styles's gaze was fixed on Mary Locke. They'd agreed on the way here that he would lead, as the senior detective. *Just let her tell her story.* He willed his partner to shut the hell up. The seconds didn't so much tick by as crawl. Porter was ready to jump in with a prompt to undo the damage when she spoke again.

'It was stupid. I was so stupid. I knew he wasn't good for her.'

Styles cut in again when she paused for breath. 'Who is "he", Mrs Locke?'

Porter tried not to let his frustration show, but extended his leg under the table and gave his partner a tap across the shin, not too hard, but hard enough. Styles tensed, but said nothing, and gave the slightest of nods. Message received.

'James Bolton. I managed to convince myself that she was old enough to make her own mistakes. See who she wanted to see. He had a reputation with the ladies before they got together. He was . . . is a charming man in his own way.' She seemed not to have been distracted by Styles's interruptions, and Porter breathed a sigh of relief. 'If she hadn't been mixed up with the likes of him this might never have happened. And to think I thought it was Alexander up to no good.'

'What do you mean by that?' said Porter.

'It was nothing, really. Just me being stupid. There had been calls late at night. He always had the odd one, but it got me thinking. Then he got one, late one Saturday night. Said that he had to go out. That he had business to take care of.'

She reached down into her bag and pulled out a paper hanky. It looked far from fresh, speckled with fluff from its residence wedged deep in the bowels of a bag that probably cost as much as Porter's suit.

'Of course, I convinced myself he was lying,' she said with a wry smile. 'Part of me wishes he had been. I sometimes think, if only there had been another woman these last thirty years could have been so different.'

She folded the hanky twice, dabbed at the corner of her eyes and contemplated a road not travelled. 'I'd probably have stayed with him regardless. He has a way of getting what he wants. Anyway, this time I followed him, convinced I'd pull up outside a hotel somewhere. Have to watch as he met up with some tart ten years younger. But instead he ended up at Ruislip Lido, off in the car park along from the pub. That's where . . . where I . . .'

Her face crinkled at the pain of remembering. Porter was torn between gentle prompts and letting her work through it in her own time. He had dozens of questions fizzing round inside his mind. She seemed to be pointing the finger at Bolton, but Locke was still mixed up in there somehow.

'There were three of them waiting for him. James, Oliver and some other chap I didn't recognise.'

'That's James Bolton and Oliver Davies?' Porter was fairly sure, but it didn't pay to assume too much. She nodded. 'And this other man, what can you tell us about him?'

She shrugged. 'I've never seen him before, or since. Dark hair is all I can remember. They were all standing by the car. Alexander got out and they talked for a few minutes. He was pointing at them, all of them, like he was annoyed at something, and that's when I saw her. They opened the boot, and lifted her out.'

'Lifted who out?' Porter asked. It was like prompting a five-year-old to get to the point, but with traumatic memories, the storyteller tended to blur the edges of unpleasant parts without a little steering.

'I never saw her face. She was wrapped in some sort of blanket, and I couldn't risk getting too close, but I'm sure it was her. I'm sure it was Natasha. I saw her hair hanging through the end of the blanket. She always had beautiful hair.' Mary gave a wistful smile.

'How can you be sure it was her from that, Mrs Locke?' Porter asked.

'Poland,' she said, closing her eyes.

'Poland? Where you told us you'd visited her? How does that tie in?'

'We had an argument not long after she was . . . after she disappeared. Her name was thrown into it, and I said I'd had a letter from her. That she had left because she couldn't stand him. And that I was going to see her for a few days. Stupid, I know, but I just had to get out of there. The thought of what had happened to her . . . I felt suffocated. I wanted to see his reaction. He doesn't give away much, as you've seen. But when I said that he looked surprised. That's when I was sure that she was never coming back. I'm sure he had me followed. I'm pretty certain I saw one of his men near my hotel in New York. I guess he thought I might be having an affair. He knew I was lying about where I was, so it stood to reason that I might be lying about who I was with. He knew damn well it wasn't Natasha. I'm sure he only reminded me the other day because he wants me to feel like a fraud telling you the same story.'

'So you've known all these years? What about the police, Mrs Locke? Did you call the police? Did you try and tell anyone what had happened?'

'And say what, Detective? I had no way to make sense of what I'd seen, who had done what. I couldn't prove a thing. All I would have done would be to put myself and Gavin in danger. He might have taken Alexander's name, but he's still just a stepson in my husband's eyes.'

Porter's brain scrambled to make sense of what she was saying. Was Alexander Locke a part of what had happened to Natasha, or had they gone to him afterwards asking for help to cover it up, whatever *it* was? There was still the matter of all the other shit he was linked to. Bolton too. He was still firmly in the cross hairs for this. Davies was long dead, but who was the third man Locke met with, and where did he fit in? Porter had been so sure that Locke had been the one behind everything. Had he just been blinded by the need to call someone, anyone, to account for Natasha, and now for Gibson and Simmons too? He parked this for now, and steered her back on track to the night at the woods.

'I was afraid to get out,' she continued, 'afraid that they'd see me. I could see them talking. They split up then. Alexander and the other man went into a pub by the car park. James and Oliver carried Natasha off into the trees.'

She looked confused now, reliving the moment, seeing shapes join with the darkness and disappear, but not knowing exactly what she was watching.

'I . . . I was worried about her. I tried to follow them . . . I couldn't see where I was going very well. All I could see was a torch up ahead, and sometimes not even that. I never knew exactly where they stopped. I couldn't risk them knowing I was there. I gave up and went back to my car, nearly got lost on the way, but I made it, just.'

'Wait a minute,' said Porter. 'What about Natasha? What about the tree? How did you find the tree?'

She shook her head and spoke slowly. 'I don't know where they took her, Detective.'

He leant in closer still, words somewhere between a whisper and a hiss. 'Why did you go to that tree? Are you honestly trying to tell me I won't find her there? Cos if you are, I'm not buying it.'

'You think I wanted to leave her out there, with them? God only knows what they did to the poor girl, but if they'd found me there . . . Do you honestly think the fact I'm Alexander's wife means that there wouldn't be any consequences? If you do, then you don't know men like these.'

'So let's assume for a minute I decide to believe you, what the hell does the tree have to do with any of this?'

'Part of me thought I'd dreamt it when I woke up the next day. I rang her, tried going round: nothing. I went back to the woods the day after. I tried to remember where they went, I found the last place I could remember, that part where the paths cross.'

Porter assumed she meant that five-way nexus they had followed her through earlier.

'From there I just couldn't . . . it was impossible. I kept losing the path, imagining I was going to trip across her just lying there.' She closed her eyes, gave a sad shake of the head. 'All I know is that they took her in there and she never came out. The tree was just . . . I saw the flowers, and they were the only thing I found. Everything else was just greens and browns and blacks, and there they were. Beautiful. Perfect.'

Porter felt his previous excitement fading, replaced with a pounding in his head. So close. He had felt so close. She sat straighter in her seat now, expression and body language rediscovering some of its former poise.

'Do you know what it's like to live for thirty years with a secret like that, of them doing . . . whatever they did? Now do you see why I said nothing? Did nothing?' She prodded herself in the chest with a stiff finger. 'I can't prove anything.' One prod per word. 'I couldn't save her. I couldn't find her. If they would do that to her, what do you think they might do to me? To my son? Just because I'm married to their boss doesn't mean they wouldn't do whatever they had to, to save themselves.'

She paused for a moment. 'My husband can be a hard man, Detective. He wouldn't have got to where he is by going easy on people, but he would never condone hurting Natasha.' A little strength crept back into her voice. 'Never.'

She stared at Porter, daring him to contradict her. He didn't believe for a second that Locke was squeaky clean, but he begrudgingly conceded to himself that she could be right about this much. If it had been Natasha, it sounded like whatever happened had already taken place before he drove out that night – not that this would condone any part in covering it up. James Bolton had been involved with Natasha not long before she disappeared. They could prove he had been in her flat. Was he so focused on nailing Locke that he risked overlooking the glaringly obvious? Violence followed James Bolton. Had for years. If even half the stories about him were true . . . One thing at a time. Focus on what happened to Natasha, for now at least. Whatever Locke was up to, his time would come, and soon. If Porter could take his right-hand man out of action, that would be a big *fuck you* to Locke and his whole operation.

Decision made, he took a deep breath. Refocused on Natasha. 'So the tree is what, then, nothing?' Hope seeped away like a slowly shrinking balloon as he said it.

A firm shake of her head. 'It's something, to me at least. There's not a day that has passed I haven't wondered if I could have done something that night, or any of the days that followed. It was somewhere to go when I hated myself for being weak. Somewhere to go to say sorry. Somewhere I could find again if I needed to.'

That made sense. The tree stump he had used himself as a marker – it had guided her back time after time, year after year, for apology after apology.

'I looked for a sign, any sign of where she might be. But after a while, it was enough just to be there.'

Porter sat back, calculating odds of success from what they had. 'Mrs Locke, we need to find her. We need you to make a statement and we'll go back there and find her.'

She looked alarmed. 'A statement? No, I can't . . . He would . . . You don't understand. If James knew I was talking to you, even like this . . . I've told you what I know. If I hadn't and you'd found her anyway, it would have looked like I'd put her there myself, but I can't do any more than that.'

Her hand shot forward and covered his where it rested on the table; the other went to her mouth. Eyes already wide, pupils growing in fear like zoom lenses.

'No one can know about this. About me, I mean. Go there. Find her, but you can't use my name.'

'It's not that simple, Mrs Locke.' Porter sandwiched her hand with his free one, firm but reassuring. 'We need you. Without you we have no one identified at the scene. Without you there was no girl hauled out from the boot of a car, no drive to the woods. Without you they all give a story they agreed thirty years ago about meeting for a pint, and that's if they even admit to being in Ruislip at all. Nothing changes. Do you understand that?'

'I understand that if he knows I've talked, we're not safe. Me or Gavin. I've told you everything I can, it's up to you what you do with it, but please keep me out of it.'

She pulled her hand back and stood up, chair legs rattling as they scratched backwards. She took out her purse and dropped a ten-pound note on the table by their coffee cups.

'I have to go. Please don't tell anyone we talked. Especially not my husband. If he knew I'd been there . . . that I'd talked to you . . .' She paused. 'It would make things very difficult for me. For my marriage, and my son.'

She slid her glasses down from her head to hide the pain in her eyes, and left without saying another word. Porter watched her reflection in the mirror above their table, and wondered if his best chance – scratch that, *Natasha's* best chance – to end this mess had left with her.

Porter and Styles kicked around a handful of ideas on the way back to the station. If this were any other case, they would have scooped Bolton up, sealed him in a box-like room and verbally sparred until he cracked. That wasn't an option here, though. Campbell was the gatekeeper to any of that after the dressing-down he'd given them. He wouldn't be easily swayed on the say-so of a witness who, on reflection, had seen nothing concrete, nothing provable. It would be different if they found her first. If they could find Natasha, go to Campbell with a body . . . but that brought with it a logistical nightmare. Styles had googled Ruislip Woods on the way to the cafe; they stretched over seven hundred acres. Even with a vague sense of where Mary Locke had led them, they had as much chance of winning the lottery this weekend as they did of stumbling across Natasha.

It was a little after two by the time they parked and headed upstairs. The lunchtime exodus meant most of the other officers had migrated to the cafe downstairs, or headed out for something more edible than the usual in-house offering. The debate in the car had reached a stalemate. Porter wanted to convince Anderson and Whittaker to join them for a speculative poke around in the woods. Styles preferred to chip away at Campbell, hoping Mary Locke's version of events, as difficult to prove as it was, would convince him to send a canine unit out.

A Post-it note caught Porter's eye as he dropped into his chair, block capitals scratched deep into the surface, sticky strip barely clinging to his screen. He didn't recognise the writing but then he noticed it had been signed by its author, Reid, the young officer who had been chasing up footage from the weather station. Porter grabbed the phone and punched in the extension number Reid had scribbled down.

It only rang twice before he answered. 'Reid speaking.'

'Reid, it's Porter. Just seen the note. You got anything for me?'

'Ah, yes, sir. I'll be right up.'

Porter went to ask him what it was, but heard the click as the line went dead. He didn't have long to wait. Reid came bustling in less than a minute later, almost colliding with Styles, who was heading out to the bathroom. Reid held a hand out to Porter, who looked at him blankly at first, waiting for him to speak, until he saw the memory stick.

'Do you want to tell me what's on here or is it a surprise?' he asked, plugging it into a spare slot at the base of his PC.

'It's not the best quality, sir, and the delay between frames makes it a bit jerky, but see what you think.'

Reid reached across and double-clicked on the icon that appeared. Windows Media Player sprung to life and after a few seconds of solid black, a street scene snapped into view. The image was far from sharp, but the wide-angled fish-eye lens showed both sides of the street peeling away from the road, perspective slightly distorted. The time in the corner read just before 3 p.m. According to the report Anderson had filed, the shots they were watching were two hours before they had charged into the building. It was like watching stop-motion animation. Cars were there on one shot, gone the next. The few people he saw advanced along the street in leaps of twenty feet. Reid dragged the cursor across the scroll bar, and the images flickered, strobe-like, as he travelled through time.

The clock read 17.05. A black Mercedes appeared at the top of the screen, taking three frames to pull up outside Taylor Fisheries. Two men exited the car. There was no mistaking Bolton. The only place he would blend in would be the gorilla cage at the zoo. Porter noted the second man getting out of the passenger side: Owen Carter.

The two men disappeared inside and the car vanished soon after. The stop-start motion made for a painful viewing experience, and Porter motioned for Reid to skip forward to the action. He fixed his eyes on the window, waiting for the explosion of glass and splintered frame.

When it came, it was like a magic trick. Carter hovering in the air one second, on the ground the next. Porter saw figures appear from the far right corner, advancing quickly towards the building. He swallowed hard as he recognised Simmons, keeping pace with Gibson; he leant forward, grabbing the mouse to pause it, as if that would stop what was to come.

'Wait,' said Reid. 'Go back a bit. Nope, not that far . . . Here, let me.'

Porter surrendered control of the mouse. Reid dragged the marker on the progress bar back a few millimetres, the image frozen with Carter on the ground.

'There.' He stabbed a finger towards the gaping hole that used to be the window. 'Look there.'

Porter stared at the darkness inside the window frame, at the amorphous blob, more grey than black, centred within it, but he could no more identify the person than he could stop Simmons's charge. He knew it was Bolton, but knowing it and proving it were different things entirely. They could prove Bolton went into the building, now, though, that was something, and maybe even enough to get Campbell's sign-off to bring him back in.

Reid's finger twitched again, the picture advanced to the next frame, and Porter froze, eyebrows arching upwards. The figure was leaning forward, looking out onto the road. He hadn't noticed it on the first run-through; his attention had been fixed on Carter. It leant into the daylight, taking on shape, the unmistakable shape of James Bolton.

'Well halle-fucking-lujah,' said Porter, slapping Reid on the back hard enough to make his finger slip on the mouse button. The footage started rolling again. Simmons and Gibson, the Charge of the Light Brigade, but Porter was already halfway to the door.

CHAPTER SEVENTEEN

Porter stood back from the desk and waited as Campbell watched the clip for a second time, pausing on the frame that showed Bolton looking out, surveying his handiwork. Campbell stared at it, leant in closer, sat back and sighed.

'I'll call Milburn. He's not going to like it, but we have Bolton at the scene. We have him on record lying to us. Bring him in. Send a team to the woods as well. We've got enough to bring him in without the girl, but the more we have on him the more likely he is to give us Locke if we offer him a deal.'

Campbell looked and sounded almost disappointed, but nothing could dampen Porter's excitement, not even a selfish bastard like Campbell.

'I'll get right on it, sir.'

He turned to leave, but Campbell wasn't finished.

'Don't think this is over, Detective.' Porter stopped, looked back at Campbell with a confused frown. 'You crack on and get after Bolton now, but when this is all settled, you and I' – he gestured from Porter to himself and back again – 'will have a conversation about obeying orders from your commanding officer. More to the point, what happens when you don't.'

'Sir?' Porter feigned ignorance, knowing full well what Campbell was getting at.

'I made it clear that Mary Locke was off limits. I *did* make it clear, didn't I?'

'Yes, sir, but I—'

Campbell held up a hand. 'No buts, Porter. Now, go on, do your job. This'll keep till later. And remember, it's Bolton we're bringing in. There's nothing but hearsay on Locke for now. Stay away from him.'

Porter gritted his teeth, imagining how satisfying it would be to squash Campbell's face up against the monitor, Bolton's pixelated image still frozen on it. To show him close up just how good he was at his job. He'd face a dozen Campbells to put away one Bolton. Fuck him. Let Campbell do his worst. He tried to convey all this in a look. One long, gritty stare. But Campbell already had his head down, fixated on the case file on his desk, and Porter's defiant look was wasted on him.

Porter left without another word. Styles was grinning as Porter approached his desk.

'Did our esteemed leader like what he saw?'

'Ha!' Porter gave a low sarcastic laugh. 'I'm not so sure that he liked the fact that we were still chasing Bolton, but I told him that Reid was already looking at the camera when we were warned off. Not much he can say to that.' He stopped short of sharing Campbell's warning of the dressing-down looming once Bolton was in custody. He'd take one for the team and keep Styles out of it. No point in telling him. Styles would only try and take his share of the blame.

'So we're good to go?' said Styles.

'Yep. Let's get cracking. There's a million and one things to organise for tomorrow.' He saw the confused look on Styles's face and realised that in the excitement at the thought of arresting Bolton, he had missed a step out.

'Campbell has given the thumbs up to try and find Natasha first. We'll head to the woods first thing Monday. We've got him, though. No matter what we find or don't find next week, we've got him.'

Styles nodded. 'What time do we start?'

'First light.'

'Does Mrs Locke know?'

Porter shook his head. 'Nothing to know yet, but she'll find out soon enough if we get lucky.'

They both sat back in their seats at the same time, lapsing into silence, thinking about the conflicting emotions tomorrow could bring, equal parts hope and tension, searching the woods an inch at a time. Porter didn't relish the prospect of raking through the leaves and mud all day, but every inch searched was an inch closer to bringing Natasha's killer to justice, and for that he'd wade through a damn sight worse than woodland.

The raindrops that evaded the canopy tickled Porter's face. A ripe, fat one hit him smack in the middle of the forehead as he looked up. Pointless to wipe it away when he knew there would be more to follow. Yesterday and today, they had arrived at the woods around dawn. Two long days of expectation giving way to frustration.

Campbell had insisted on meeting him here the first morning, but had made his excuses after an hour and hadn't been back since. Something about a committee to attend and budgets to review. He'd be back sharp enough if they found something, though. Couldn't have the rank and file claiming too much of the credit for an operation he'd sanctioned, however grudgingly.

Porter found the snowdrops again at the first attempt, and they'd started from there, radiating outwards in a grid. He looked back at them now, still visible even at a distance. They stood out proudly, surrounded by mud the colour of discarded coffee grounds, their bowed heads a white blemish on a dark canvas. He'd naively thought they were more than just Mary Locke's marker. That they were the *X* that marked the spot. No such luck, though. The dogs had breezed past them as if they weren't even there.

He looked around for Styles and saw him behind a line of trees, their trunks thin and straight like prison bars, walking slowly alongside the officer in charge of the ground-penetrating radar device that always reminded Porter of a chunky lawnmower. He felt the insect-like buzz of his phone. Voicemail from his mum. Why the hell had it not rung first? He tapped the screen to call her back, but the handset never made it to his ear.

Styles was at least forty feet away and facing the other direction, so Porter couldn't hear what he was saying to the officer beside him, but the body language told him all he needed to know. A hurried pat on the shoulder, head twisting left and right, searching for Porter, finding him, summoning him with an excited flapping of the hand.

Porter picked his way through the tree roots that clawed at his feet, pushing aside the low hanging branches that whipped back angrily at the space he left behind. By the time he reached Styles three others had beaten him there, and they stood around the GPR like vultures round carrion, looking expectantly at the ground. No carcass to pick at, just mud, churned up to the consistency of cake mix by the elements and heavy boots.

Porter broke the silence. 'Well? What have we got?'

The officer with his hands resting on the GPR cleared his throat. 'Something worth digging for, guv. Could just as easy be a bird under there, a dog even. More than likely will be, but we'll soon see.'

He dragged the GPR backwards, took a roll of police tape from his backpack and started marking out an area roughly six feet square. Porter took a step back, heard the buzz of an insect. No, not an insect. He looked down, realising his phone was still in his hand, his mum's voice a faint tinny squawk as she tried to get his attention. He lifted it back up, took a step away from the circle and spoke without taking his eyes from the square of dirt inside the tape.

'Hi, Mum . . . No, I haven't listened to it yet . . . Yes, I knew I'd rung you back, but . . . No, listen, Mum, I'm going to have to call you back. Something's come up.'

He ended the call and leant against the nearest tree, watching as two officers began carefully scraping away the earth inside the taped perimeter. He'd seen paint dry faster, but knew they had to take it slowly for fear of missing something. They worked in relative silence, and apart from the occasional screech of a radio, the stillness of the trees made it seem that even they were holding their breath, waiting to see what would be uncovered.

A little under ten minutes and two feet of soil later, Porter saw the officer closest to him stop, bending down to peer at something. Porter squinted, trying to make out what he was looking at, but all he could see was damp, spongy soil. The officer reached down, swiping a short bristled brush across a patch of ground by his foot. Porter's toes bunched and uncurled inside his shoes, nervous energy that had to escape somewhere. His impatience got the better of him.

'What have we got?'

The officer straightened up, twisting round towards Porter, his feet staying planted in the mud. 'It might not be her, guv, but it's a someone, not a something.'

Porter stepped closer and peered at the ground, and saw what he was talking about. A curved grey dome streaked with dirt. A single eye socket staring blindly up at him, the other still buried. Teeth, stained the same colour as the rest of the skull. He looked up at the faces around him, saw a few of them nodding gently. They'd have to run tests, of course. Prove it was her. Surely it had to be, though, didn't it? He didn't like to jump to conclusions, but to come looking for her, only to find someone else? That only made sense if Locke had used his wife to feed them false information, but if that was the case, who the hell would he want them to have found? Fuck that. It was her unless or until someone proved otherwise.

'Come on, then,' he said. 'She's been down there too long already. Let's get her out of here.'

NATASHA – APRIL 1983

Natasha closes her eyes as she inhales. Feels the sweet sting of smoke tickling the back of her throat. She tolerates Mary's husband for her brother's sake, but there's only so much of his Lord of the Manor attitude she can stomach without a ciggy break. She has barely touched her Sunday roast before escaping into the back garden, but then again who can blame her? Alexander's money can buy clothes fit to grace a catwalk, but doesn't, it seems, stretch to cookery lessons. Mary tries, bless her, but her Yorkshire puddings are as tasty as papier mâché, beef so overcooked Natasha expected it to turn to ash when she touched it, and all doused in gravy the colour of muddy water.

It's the way he talks to her, she decides. That's what rubs her patience raw like sandpaper. He talks to her like she's on the payroll. Does the same with Mary, as well, but she just nods and accepts it. She decides there and then to make other plans for next weekend. Mary's voice drifts through the open kitchen window, and Natasha retreats around the corner of the house, along the path towards the side gate. Her stepmum knows she smokes but Natasha can't be bothered with the tired look of disapproval Mary wears every time a cigarette goes near her mouth.

Another deep drag, but the quiet crackle of smouldering cigarette paper is drowned out by the low rumble of an engine from the front of the house. She hears a car door open and close, and footsteps stomp their way across the drive. The echoes of the bell reach her even here, and she hears voices. Blurred and indistinct, she can make out one word in three or four. She sidles closer to the gate, both voices now have owners. Alexander Locke is one. The other makes her eyes widen in surprise. James. Mixed emotions. She misses him a little. Her fling on the wrong side of the track. Sleeping with the help, so to speak. If she's honest, she let it happen just to see Alexander's reaction as much as anything. There was something deliciously naughty about being on the arm of a man that most people fear.

She lets the smoke curl from her mouth of its own accord, almost afraid to blow it out in case they hear her. Ridiculous, she knows, but her chest tightens as she listens, words becoming clearer. She screws her eyes closed to concentrate, as if that will amplify their words, but she's not sure she wants to hear any more. All she can think of is her father. Of what Alexander has just told James to do to his warehouse. To him if he doesn't play ball. If he doesn't sign the papers. She needs to warn him. Wonders what he's done to piss off Alexander. She can't face going back inside, but knows she has to. She can hardly stroll through the side gate with those two stood out front.

Her hand is shaking as she stubs the cigarette out in the soil by her feet. Natasha folds her arms protectively across her chest and heads back inside. She mutters her thanks to Mary, musters a terse smile for her brother, Gavin. She doesn't want to have to walk past the two men at the front door, and heads for the toilet, locks the door and mouths a silent scream to herself in the mirror.

Oh my God! Oh my fucking God!

What if James is heading straight there now? What if he gets there before she can warn her dad? There's a payphone five minutes down the road. She'll call him first, and the police second if needs be. Whatever it takes to stop this from happening.

CHAPTER EIGHTEEN

Porter felt his mouth go dry as Will Leonard came through the door and headed over towards him. He'd cashed in some brownie points in persuading Leonard to rush the tests through, and studied the approaching face for a hint of the results, but Leonard gave nothing away.

'Hey, Will,' said Porter, trying to remain calm. 'That was quick, even for you.'

'Most people go for the flattery before they ask the favour.'

Porter couldn't bring himself to beat around the bush. 'Well? Is it her?'

Leonard nodded. 'It's her.'

Porter clenched his fists. 'I knew it. I knew it,' he said, more to himself than anyone else. 'Thanks, Will. I owe you.'

'That you do. If only my credit was as good with my bank. Anyway, I'll leave you to it.' He turned and made a beeline for the door, Styles coming through it seconds after Leonard had exited, as if one man had just pulled off the greatest quick-change act ever. He saw the look on Porter's face as he came closer.

'Well?'

'It's her. Let's see if Anderson and Whittaker are about. Never hurts to have numbers with a man like Bolton.'

They found Whittaker at his desk, mouth full of Mars bar and a smear of brown below his bottom lip. He crumpled the wrapper and hit the three-pointer in the bin against the wall.

'Too bloody right I'm in,' he said after Porter filled him in. 'Anderson just nipped for a cuppa. I'll give him a call and see you downstairs in five?'

They talked tactics while they waited for Anderson and Whittaker. They circulated Bolton's licence plate to all units on duty. They had his home and business addresses to split up and work through. At last, after all the frustrations of the last few days, Porter felt the familiar buzz that only came with the business end of a case, when everything started to converge on one point, one person.

He wasn't at his home, and the unit that went to the Oyster Bay restaurant reported back that he wasn't on the premises. Porter hadn't expected it to be quite as straightforward as the first time, but he was pleasantly surprised when a call came over the radio to say his car had been spotted outside a health club he owned. Porter checked the address. They were a little over ten miles away, and agreed to meet in a pub car park around the corner.

The traffic seemed to melt away. Porter wasn't superstitious by nature, but he'd take any good omens at this point, and smiled to himself as he saw two unmarked cars already there, side by side, as they pulled up to the rendezvous point. The two officers who had called it in got out when they saw Porter's car approach. He'd not worked any cases with them before but knew them by reputation. Sandford and Clarkson were plodders, not exactly setting the world alight, but dependable. Porter gave each of them a brief handshake as Anderson and Whittaker got out and joined them.

'When did we last see him?'

'No one's actually seen him, but we spotted his car outside. We've had eyes on it since then and it's not budged, so he's in there somewhere.'

'OK, follow my lead. You two stay on the front door when we go in. Styles and I will head inside and find him.' He turned to Anderson. 'Anderson, you and Jon take the back. We don't want him bolting, but if he does you'll be there to scoop him up. Any questions?'

A shake of heads all round. Porter licked his lips nervously.

'Let's get the party started, then.'

They rounded the corner and crossed the road together. The black Mercedes was parked nose-first against the wall. As they neared the entrance, Anderson and Whittaker peeled off and headed around the left-hand side of the building. The glass doors parted with a whisper as they approached and Porter checked over his shoulder to make sure Sandford and Clarkson were behind him.

A receptionist sat behind a counter off to the right. She couldn't have been more than twenty, and her bright *how can I help you* smile faded into confusion when she saw Porter approach, warrant card out at arm's length. She picked up her phone when Porter explained who he was looking for. He reached out a hand and pushed hers, and the receiver, back down.

'It's OK, no need to announce us. Where is he?'

She'd last seen him going into the gym area of the club, and directed them through double doors off to the side. They found it easily enough, following the whir of fitness machines and upbeat music piped through speakers. The smell of sweat hung in the air as they crossed the divide from the freshness of the corridor into the stuffiness of the gym. It dwarfed the one Porter used at the station. Mirrored walls stretched the length of the room, men making entirely too much eye contact with themselves as they strained with weights bigger than their egos.

Porter motioned for Styles to move down the right and he headed left. The room was an L-shape, the far leg of it disappearing round to the right. They attracted a few glances from the gym-goers but most were too busy preening in front of a mirror as they worked out. Of the dozen or so people he saw, only two of them were women. They both pounded out a beat on side-by-side treadmills, earbuds in, eyes front, ignoring the posturing alpha males.

The hidden leg of the room came into view slowly as Porter edged along the wall. Four exercise bikes lined up in a stationary peloton. A man in his forties pedalled furiously, rocking side to side as each leg extended, a bloom of sweat staining a grey Nike running vest.

No sign of Bolton. He turned to Styles, who shrugged back at him. Porter scanned the room. The only other door was marked *Fire Exit*, one with a horizontal push bar to open it. Styles came over to join him.

Porter spoke into his handset. 'This is Porter. Be advised subject is not in the gym. He may be trying to exit the building. Proceeding through fire exit towards rear of the building.'

He pushed the bar down and the door swung open with no resistance, revealing a corridor with an identical fire exit door twenty feet away at the far end. He burst through it with Styles close behind, and almost ran straight into Anderson. They quickly disentangled from one another, and Porter stepped back.

'Nothing?' he asked.

'No sign,' said Anderson.

'Sandford, Clarkson, anything?' he barked into his handset.

'Negative, guv,' Sandford squawked back.

Whittaker stayed on the fire exit, and Sandford on the front door, while Porter led the others on a room-by-room search. Bemused customers and staff members watched as they opened every door and looked around every corner. Porter had to laugh despite his frustration when he saw Clarkson look under a desk. A man of Bolton's size would be more likely to wear it like a tortoise wears a shell than squeeze underneath it.

Five minutes and another chat with the receptionist later, they stood out front. Porter stared at his own distorted reflection in the sleek black Mercedes.

'He knew we were coming. That's the only way. He knew we were coming.'

'How could he, guv? We had the exits covered before we went in. Maybe he just left his car here while he went somewhere else?' said Sandford.

Porter shook his head. 'Nope, the receptionist saw him go into the gym about twenty minutes before we got here. If he left, he left out the back door, but he did it before we got here, and the only reason he would do that is cos he knew we were on our way.'

'But how could he know? Has he got someone watching us?' asked Clarkson.

'Fuck knows, but he did,' said Porter.

They headed back to their cars to split up and work through the remainder of the list, leaving Sandford and Clarkson to watch Bolton's car. Porter thought back to Gibson's funeral. The conversation with Anderson. The grass who gave up Mike's name, however unsubstantiated. First Carter's wire, and now this? If there was someone else on the inside, then he or she would keep the lowest of profiles after everything that had happened. It would be hard enough to track Bolton down without their every move being compromised. A man with Bolton's connections and money could hide for months – years, even – without that kind of help.

Porter felt the onset of a headache and rubbed at his temple. The day had started with so much promise, and now things were grinding to a halt again, derailed by an unseen adversary. He could only fight against what was in front of him. There had to be a way to draw his opponents out.

They were half a mile away from the station after a fruitless afternoon when it came to him, and he smiled.

Porter took the stairs two at a time in an effort to catch up. He reached the landing just as the door to the main office drifted closed, but he could see Anderson on the other side, and yanked it open.

'Anderson, you got a second?'

Anderson turned and shrugged. 'Yeah, what's up?'

'Out here?' Porter gestured towards the corridor behind him.

Anderson followed him out and stood, arms folded, resting on top of his gut. Porter wondered if he could rest a pint glass on it the same way.

'What's up?'

Porter looked both ways and leant in, the universal gesture of *just between you and me*. 'That guy you mentioned, the one you told me about at the funeral. Can you talk to him again? I think we need his help. There's no other way Bolton could have known we were coming.'

'What, you still think they've got another one in their pocket?'

Porter shrugged. 'You got a better theory as to how he got out of there before we showed up?'

Anderson stared blankly back at him. 'Maybe we're chasing shadows. Maybe there's no big conspiracy and he just got lucky.'

'Yeah, maybe, but that's more maybes than I'm comfortable with. What's your guy's name? I want to see if he'll talk to me about Mike. Maybe there's something else he heard, something he doesn't think matters, anything that might help us.'

Anderson shook his head. 'I gave him my word I'd keep him out of it unless we need him on the record.'

'Then get him on the bloody record,' said Porter, trying to keep the frustration out of his voice and failing miserably. 'Look, can you at least go and see him, ask if he'll talk to me. If he will, then great, but even if he'll only talk to you, that'd be something.'

'Sure.' Anderson sounded exasperated. 'If it'll shut you up.'

'Today?'

'Jesus, you don't want much, do you? My ex-wife was less needy than this. Yes,' he said, rolling his eyes. 'I'm knocking off early today anyway, so I'll go see him on my way home.'

'Cheers, Anderson. I appreciate it.'

Porter reached out and gave a friendly slap against the shoulder. He felt the soft, doughy arm under the shirt, and turned away, vowing never to let himself turn into a walking heart attack.

Porter busied himself with paperwork for the next hour. He'd barely eaten all day and his stomach growled like an ill-tempered dog. Styles offered to get him something from the canteen, so Porter gave him a five-pound note and instructions to bring back whatever had the highest meat content.

Styles had been gone less than a minute when Porter saw Anderson stand up, leaning his head to both sides, his neck cracking like popcorn in the microwave. He kept his head down, eyes focused on his screen, as the big detective lumbered past him.

'That you done, Anderson?' he asked without looking up.

'Yep, catching a flyer today. I'm owed a few hours.'

'Don't forget to ask your guy if he'll help out.'

'How can I forget with you asking every five minutes?' he asked. 'Yep, I'll ask. Let you know how I get on tomorrow.'

Porter waited until the door had closed behind him then counted to twenty, grabbed his car keys and headed downstairs. By the time he reached the exit to the car park, he saw Anderson fumbling with his keys beside his car, a ten-year-old Honda that hadn't truly been white since it left the showroom. Porter took his phone out and pretended to be studying it as two officers came in past him and disappeared up the stairs. He waited until Anderson's car edged out of its parking space, then walked quickly to his own car. He gave Anderson a five count to get clear of the building before pulling out into traffic. Rush hour was fast approaching, and the traffic was visibly thickening, the roads like arteries carrying the life of the city in both directions becoming congealed and sluggish.

He knew Anderson lived near White Hart Lane, but he didn't seem to be taking a direct route there at the moment. Porter stayed a cautious three cars behind; far enough not to be noticed but close enough to nip through any changing lights or navigate busy roundabouts. His plan was simple. He would tail Anderson to his informant. After they parted, he would stay on the informant but call Anderson. If the news was good and the guy was willing to sit down with them, then there was nothing to worry about, and he would leave it to Anderson to arrange the where and when. If Anderson told him that the guy wasn't willing to help, then Porter would follow him back to whatever rock he crawled under and try a little persuasion of his own; nothing physical, but Porter could be quite persuasive when he needed to be, and his need was as great now as it had ever been.

He followed Anderson through a series of turns onto the A10, and along as far as Stoke Newington, before he finally saw the Honda pull into a parking space ahead on the left. Porter didn't want to risk driving past. He didn't know if Anderson would recognise his car, but couldn't take a chance that he'd be spotted if he continued. He pulled sharply to the left with a flash of his indicator, and into a space a hundred feet behind Anderson.

It suddenly occurred to him that he didn't know what direction Anderson would walk when he got out, and frantically scanned the interior of the car, looking for something he could conceivably hold up to block his face. The best he managed was the service log from the glove box, but his fears were unfounded as he watched Anderson haul himself out and cross the road with something between a walk and a waddle. Porter shook his head. It was just as well the big man was retiring. He would have more chance of winning *The X Factor* than he would of passing another physical.

Porter waited to see which way he headed before making a move himself. He was ready to open his door when he saw Anderson vanish into a cafe with a Turkish flag draped in the window, reappearing a few minutes later with a plastic bag big enough to pass as an emergency aid food parcel. He hoped, for Anderson's sake, and that of his recently weakened heart, that he had help lined up to tackle it, maybe his mystery informant, maybe his girlfriend. He doubted that he would be spotted from this distance, but grabbed his hastily acquired logbook shield as extra insurance and peered around the edge to watch for the Honda pulling away.

From there it was a non-stop trip to the terraced house on Portland Avenue that Anderson had once shared with his wife. He had remortgaged to buy her out, and bored every detective in the building with the details of the divorce more often than Porter cared to remember. The postage-stamp-size front garden overgrown with weeds, and faded green front door, suggested Anderson wasn't exactly the house-proud type.

Porter checked his watch as Anderson fumbled with his key ring; quarter past five. He decided to give it until six, figuring the food would attract a visitor before it got cold. Whether it would be a visitor he gave a damn about was another matter. He was proved right less than ten minutes later. A woman walked past him and turned into Anderson's path, if you could call a six-foot strip of cracked concrete a path. She wore jeans tight enough to restrict her to a totter rather than a walk, low-heeled black shoes and a gingerbread-brown leather jacket that stopped at the waist. It didn't take a detective to work out this must be the new lady that Anderson had mentioned, the lingering kiss she gave him as he let her inside confirming it.

Porter cursed him under his breath and slapped a palm against the steering wheel. With a belly full of food and his lady-friend there, Anderson was going nowhere for the night. Why would the lazy bastard not play it straight? If he didn't want to put the squeeze on his source, then why not at least let Porter have a crack? He might only have less than a fortnight left on the job, but Porter would be the one left holding whatever mess he left behind while Anderson waltzed off onto a golf course for the next twenty years.

The rumble in his stomach almost registered on the Richter scale, and he wondered if whatever culinary delight Styles had chosen for him would be on his desk or in someone else's stomach. He glanced at his phone. He had flicked it onto silent when they went into Bolton's health club and hadn't switched the ringer back on. One missed call, one voicemail, both from Styles.

Porter looked over to Anderson's house one more time, the curtains now drawn. He clipped the phone into his hands-free cradle, dialled Styles and pulled out onto the road. Anderson would keep until tomorrow.

Anderson looked like he hadn't gotten much sleep, and Porter shuddered to think what the night might have entailed. He wore the same suit as yesterday, concertina folds across the bottom of the jacket from too many hours in a chair, and grunted a greeting at Porter as he passed.

Porter waited for him to finish his usual morning ritual that consisted of heading straight down to get a coffee, then chewing the fat with whoever would listen to him until it was time for a second cup. Only then would he be ready to fight the good fight. Porter had calmed down some since yesterday. He had decided that going in with an attitude would be counter-productive. Most detectives were protective of any sources they had on the other side of the fence, and if he got Anderson's back up then he would lose any chance he had of reasoning with him.

'You got a minute?' he said as Anderson traipsed past him, second coffee in hand, déjà vu.

'Yeah, what's up?' said Anderson, wincing as he took a sip from his cup before he realised it was still a few minutes away from drinkable temperature.

'Just wondered how you got on with your informant yesterday. Will he help us?' Porter had already thought his approach through. He couldn't very well say he knew the meeting hadn't happened, and wanted to give Anderson the chance to make his excuses.

'Yeah, it was a no go, I'm afraid.'

'Oh, he didn't show?'

'No, he showed alright, but he won't go fishing for us. Says he risked enough by telling me about Mike. He's afraid that if he starts poking around they'll get suspicious.'

Porter tried not to let the confusion show. 'Where did you meet him?'

'I bought him a pint at the Black Horse after work.' The Black Horse was a pub five miles from the station, five miles in the opposite direction to which he had driven yesterday.

'Just the one or did you make a night of it?'

'Nah, he wasn't talking so I left him to it after the one.'

'You should have said. If I'd known you were heading straight to the pub, I would have joined you.'

Anderson smirked. 'I'd have left you sat there as well. Had the missus coming round last night, and, no offence, but what she was offering trumps a pint with you and a petty criminal any day in my book.'

Porter smiled, but his mind scrambled to make sense of the lie. He knew that the meeting hadn't taken place, so why say it had? What did Anderson stand to gain by spinning him a line? Protecting a source wasn't uncommon, but lying to another officer was another thing entirely.

'Oh, I was talking to Campbell as well and he said something about Locke's missus having some dirt on him?' said Anderson.

'What?' Porter was thrown briefly by the change of direction. 'Oh, that. Yeah, maybe. I don't know yet. Listen, I've got to go, but I'll catch you later.'

Porter moved away before Anderson could respond, an uneasy feeling making his scalp tingle as he walked. He'd considered a dozen angles to the case already, but a fresh one squatted front and centre in his mind now. It was there and couldn't be ignored. He just prayed this one was as fruitless as the others.

NATHAN – APRIL 1983

He explains the family tree for a second time. That Natasha's mum is dead. That Mary is both her stepmum, and his ex-wife. The young sergeant nods, crosses out the last few lines with his pencil, scribbles some shorthand hieroglyphics on the page. Nathan feels the fool as he runs through it again. There's a good chance Natasha misheard. That Alexander was just mouthing off about him in general. They'd never exactly been best pals. How could you be, with the man who stole your wife? The man who wants to take over your business. A firm you've shed blood and sweat for. But not even Alexander is capable of this, surely?

Nathan has heard rumours. Stories told in hushed tones over a pint down at the Brown Badger on a Friday night. Tales that Alexander isn't the upstanding member of the community he seems to be. That's all he has them pegged as, though – tales. Stories embellished by a few pints too many. If Natasha hadn't already called the police after she spoke to him, he would have laughed it off, but this sergeant who had taken the call insisted on following it up.

He glances at his daughter, and is struck as ever by the similarity to her mother, God rest her soul. He feels the briefest of tugs at his heart. Knows that he would do anything for his little girl, even soothe away her unfounded fears over what she thinks she has heard. He reaches across, takes her hand in his and gives it a gentle squeeze.

The sergeant asks her to explain, again, exactly what she heard. She lets out a heavy sigh through pursed lips, like air escaping from a tyre. Tells him for a second time what she heard. Tells him that James will be giving her dad a choice. Sign or suffer. Something about shipments starting in two months, and that it has to be done by then. Nathan explains to the sergeant that Locke had made him an offer for his business the week before. Well below market rate. He stops short of telling the officer that he nearly took it. Doesn't tell Natasha that he's so deep in debt that he can barely breathe when he thinks about the numbers. He simply smiles and tells the policeman and his daughter that it's all some sort of misunderstanding. He tells them he'll pop round and see Alexander the following day and straighten all this out.

The sergeant lays his pencil down on the pad, and gives a gentle shake of the head. He tells Nathan these things are best handled by the authorities. He'll look into it first thing. Tells Nathan he isn't to approach Locke under any circumstances, and that they should keep this to themselves for now. Nathan leans back, arms crossed, and stares at the officer for a moment, then agrees to bide his time with a slow nod. Natasha looks far from happy. She's still protesting as Nathan ushers her down the steps of the station and into his car.

They're a hundred yards down the road by the time the young sergeant hustles through the door. They don't see him head in the opposite direction, towards a phone booth two streets away. He lifts the receiver, glancing both ways as he punches in a number from a scrap of paper.

The voice that answers sounds impatient. He identifies himself, short and to the point. 'You've got a problem.'

The man on the other end of the line listens to what he has to say. A few seconds of silence, then, 'Hmm. Interesting. Thank you.' A disconnected tone tells him the conversation is over. He makes his way back to the station, wondering what will happen to the father and daughter. He shakes his head to clear the thought. None of his business. Wouldn't want to be in their shoes though. No siree.

CHAPTER NINETEEN

'So are you going to tell me what we're doing yet, or do I have to play twenty questions?' asked Styles.

Porter kept his eyes fixed on the road as he spoke. 'I couldn't say anything inside in case anyone overheard, but if I'm right we're off to see Bolton.'

Styles's eyes widened. 'Just the two of us? Where is he? I'll tell Anderson and Whittaker to meet us there.'

'No,' said Porter, turning his head sharply, 'don't do that. Besides, there's no need, Anderson will be there before us.'

'So if you've told him, why won't you tell me?'

'That's just it,' said Porter gripping the wheel tight, knuckles blanching white. 'I didn't tell him. That's his Honda four cars up.' He nodded at the line of mid-morning traffic ahead.

'C'mon, cut the cryptic bullshit. What's going on?'

'It's Anderson. Anderson is the leak.'

'Jesus, are you sure?'

Porter thought for a moment. 'Not one hundred per cent, no, but I'm up in the nineties at the moment.'

He filled Styles in, starting with the conversation at Gibson's funeral, the lies about the informant intended to distract Porter by giving up Gibson as a dead end, and ending with a lie of his own.

'I told him I had a lead on a possible location for Bolton, but I needed to run something past Campbell first.'

'What kind of a lead?'

'That's kind of my point. There is no lead.'

Styles's mouth rounded into a perfect goldfish-style *ohhh.* 'So now we see if Anderson is headed to talk to people he shouldn't be talking to.'

'It was the only thing that made sense, the only way Bolton could have known we were listening in through Carter, or that we were going to pick him up at his club. I figured the only way to test it out was to feed him a line. Stands to reason he wouldn't make contact from his phone; too easy to trace if anyone looked. My guess was he'd either call from a payphone, or he'd go and see him in person, warn him off.'

'And?'

'And he was out the door within five minutes of me spinning him the lie. I watched him go across the road into the shopping centre and use one of the payphones, then jump in his car. That's when I came and got you. Best case he's leading us to Bolton; worst case, if it's someone lower he's meeting with, we snap a picture to confirm, then stick him in a room when he gets back until he gives us what we need.'

'What about Campbell? Does he know?'

'Not yet. That'll keep till we know for sure.'

'You know there's a chance that either he or Milburn will try and sweep it under the carpet, don't you?'

'At this stage I don't give a shit about what happens to that tub of lard up there,' he said, gesturing towards the Honda. 'All I want is justice for Evie and Natasha, and that means Bolton behind bars; Locke too if he ordered it. I'll worry about making sure Anderson gets what's coming to him after that.'

Styles nodded. 'Alrighty then.'

The rest of the drive was in relative silence, neither of them relishing the idea of taking in one of their own. They almost lost him once, but caught up thanks to a fortuitous set of traffic lights. Porter ran through a mental list of potential locations for Bolton, weighing each up against the direction they were headed. He glanced at a sign for a roundabout ahead: four possible exits.

Anderson's indicator flashed to show he intended to take the first and head left. Left would send him towards Gravesend.

'He's got some balls, I'll give him that.'

'Who, Anderson?'

'No, Bolton. Five minutes' time, you watch, we'll be at Atlas.' Porter gave a humourless smile. 'Size of that place, even he can find a corner to crawl into. Think about it, they must have hundreds of shipping containers out in the yard, never mind the warehouse.'

'So what's our play when we get there?' asked Styles.

Porter thought for a second. 'I've not figured that part out yet. Let's see what options Anderson gives us.'

Porter nodded with grim satisfaction soon after that. The roof of the Atlas warehouse poked over a treeline up ahead. There was only one car between them and Anderson now, so Porter decided to hang well back. He knew where to find him now if he lost sight of the Honda.

Anderson made the turning Porter knew he would, stopping for a few seconds at the barrier, its gate rising and falling like a clapperboard on a film set. Porter slowed to a crawl, pulling over to the kerb two hundred yards away. He reached over to the glove box and pulled out a small black pouch, ripping the Velcro flap open and taking out a compact set of binoculars.

'Aren't we the good cub scout?' said Styles. 'Been shopping?'

Porter grinned. 'Army and Navy store. Ten of your finest English pounds. I figure your camera will still zoom in enough to make an identifying shot if we need it, but I can focus better with these.'

He was about to get out of the car when Styles put out a hand to stop him. A dark four-by-four had appeared at the far end of the road, indicator blinking, preparing to turn to face the Atlas barrier. Porter snapped the binoculars up to his eyes, massaging the focusing wheel with his middle finger, melting the blurriness away. Even at this distance, even with the driver blocking part of the view, Porter could make out the hulking shape of James Bolton in the passenger seat. A confusion of shapes flashed across the lenses, and Porter peered over the top to see the four-by-four disappearing under the barrier.

'Ladies and gentlemen, Elvis has entered the building.'

'That who I think it is?' asked Styles.

'Yep. C'mon, let's see if we can get a snap of the two of them before they go inside. Shaking hands would be nice, but even just a side profile would do for now.'

They stuck close to the fence line, the angle of their approach and the closely grouped steel palisade fencing posts meaning that they could barely make out the outline of the warehouse until they got within fifty yards of the barrier. That worked both ways, though. Anyone looking out at the main road would see a flicker of shadow between posts at best.

Porter stopped behind a lamp post and Styles nearly walked into him. He raised his binoculars again, only squinting through one lens this time, pressing it up against a gap in the fence. The black car, he could see now, was a Land Rover, the dark green ellipse of the badge recognisable despite the distance. It pulled up next to the white Honda that Porter had begun to think of as more of a light grey with its film of grime.

'Quick, give me your phone,' he said to Styles, holding his hand palm up behind him, eyes front, like a relay runner waiting for the baton.

Styles slapped it into his palm and Porter brought it up, resting it on top of the binoculars. He kept one hand on them, pinched fingers spreading out to zoom in on the phone screen. With the cars parked side by side, the two doors opened like pinball flippers. Anderson got out first, Bolton unfolding himself from the passenger seat to tower above him. Porter hit record and the clock onscreen counted off the seconds. He'd give the proverbial right arm for sound as well, but the footage would be damning enough without it.

The two men exchanged the briefest of handshakes and disappeared inside, followed by Bolton's driver, who Porter recognised as Daniel Stenner.

'Call it in,' he said, no triumph in his voice despite the net closing. The fact that a copper was involved was bad enough. That he was partly to blame, even just by association, for what happened to Simmons and Gibson got Porter's hackles up. If you can't trust your fellow officers, then the world becomes an even darker place than he already knew it to be. He waited, watching the doorway through the binoculars until Styles placed the request for backup, then climbed back in the car to wait for the cavalry.

* * *

Anderson was used to being the bigger man in most situations, quite literally. He hadn't been south of two hundred pounds since Tony Blair won his first election, and the years that followed had seen slow but steady expansion, waistline creeping forward like a glacier. Even seated, James Bolton made him feel like David eyeing up Goliath. It wasn't just the simple maths, his height and weight. Christ, the man was big enough to have his own postcode. It was more the physical presence he exuded, the unspoken threat in a simple stare, the knowledge of what he had done, and might still do. Anderson watched in silence as Bolton sent Andrew Patchett packing from his office and took the still-warm vacated chair as his own, while Anderson made do with an older leather swivel chair, arms worn where a hundred elbows had rubbed.

'So, Detective Anderson, what news do you have to share that you had to drag me away from my little hideaway?'

His expression was somewhere between amusement and boredom, as if the manhunt for him was a game he could step in and out of.

'One of the other detectives, Porter, he got a tip where to find you.'

'And?' Bolton spread his hands. 'Should I be concerned? Was he on his way to slap the cuffs on me when you called?'

'I don't know. He wouldn't say. He needed to run it up the line first, apparently.'

'So you had me leave somewhere that might still be perfectly safe, on the off chance that some little shit on a street corner says he knows where I am? I pay you for quality information, Detective Anderson, not a half-arsed rumour. Anyway, as you know, people don't tend to feel inclined to speak up against me too often.'

'Owen Carter did,' said Anderson, regretting it as soon as he spoke the words.

Bolton scowled, eyes narrowing. 'Mr Carter was . . . unfortunate. He made some bad choices that didn't work out too well for him. You, on the other hand, have made good choices, so far.'

The last two words hung in the air. Had anyone else spoken them Anderson would have been on the offensive, asking if they were threatening an officer. He'd seen first-hand what Bolton was willing to do to a police officer, and asked himself, not for the first time, what the hell he had been thinking to do a proverbial deal with the devil. His deal had been struck with Alexander Locke, but in his own way Locke was more of a monster than the behemoth sitting in front of him.

A black-and-white photograph flashed across his mind. Post-divorce days, hazy drunken nights and bleary-eyed mornings. One small moment of weakness leading to one major lapse in judgement. A call to a number found online, the petite brunette at his door an hour later, the need for physical contact, fuelled by single malt, overcoming any hesitancy. The burning shame the morning afterwards, multiplied a hundredfold when Locke's man approached him soon after. The copied birth certificate saying she was fifteen. The feeling of falling down the rabbit hole with no means of return. The money he had been paid since had helped cover his alimony, but it was a sweetener, nothing more. They had him by the balls. He wasn't even sure they'd let him go when he retired. That was a bridge he would have to cross soon, but soon seemed like a lifetime away for now.

Anderson tried to placate him. 'You pay me to keep you one step ahead. I might not know where they're heading, but I know where they're not.' He tapped his finger against the armrest of his chair. 'Here. And if you're here then you're safe.'

'And you know this how?'

'Because this was one of the places I was sent to look for you, and because I called in the all-clear before you turned up. As far as the rest of them are concerned, I've searched this place from top to bottom.'

Bolton flashed a begrudging smile. 'Well, what do you know, maybe you're good value after all?'

Anderson gave a nervous laugh. He hated being beholden to anyone, least of all a low-life like Bolton, but he had to play the cards he was dealt till the end. Who knows, when he was strolling down a sunny fairway a thousand miles away, maybe an anonymous tip would get called in. Maybe some information on the less well-known aspects of Bolton and Locke's businesses would get spilt. Nobody on the force knew Locke smuggled immigrants in on some of his ships, for example. Yep, they'd regret treating him like an errand boy. Shame he wouldn't be able to take credit for it, but sometimes you have to be satisfied with having the cake, and take a pass on the eating.

He started to push himself up from his chair, but Bolton held up a hand.

'Not so fast. The boss wants a word with you before you swan off back to the station.' He looked up at Patchett. 'Call him. Tell him he's all clear to come in.'

Patchett nodded and started tapping at his phone.

Anderson sat back down with a meaty thump. 'He's here? Now?'

'Five minutes away,' said Bolton. 'He asked me to get you round here for a chat.'

'Chat about what?' Anderson asked, hairs prickling on the back of his neck. He heard Patchett mumbling into his phone, but couldn't make out what he was saying.

'That's for him to tell you,' said Bolton.

'Bit risky him being here if you are as well, don't you think?'

'We're safe here. You said so yourself, didn't you? He's close. Far enough away to be safe, though, if there'd been any bother.'

Bolton looked over at Patchett for confirmation. Patchett nodded. 'He's on his way. Five minutes. Ten, tops.'

Bolton gave a smile that would have passed for a grimace on anyone else, and switched his attention back to Anderson. 'Tell me about Detective Porter. He seems like a persistent sort.'

Anderson swallowed. He'd had his differences with Porter, sure, but he didn't wish the guy any actual harm. If he painted too flattering a picture, Bolton might see him as someone who needed taking out of the equation. After all, what's one more dead officer when you're already wanted for murdering the first? Maybe that's what Locke wanted to speak to him about? He gave Bolton a very brief summary of Porter, all the while wondering if this might be the last time he had to jump through the big man's hoops, or if he'd find safety in retirement. Safety, maybe. Salvation? Unlikely.

NATASHA – APRIL 1983

She sits with her hands curled protectively round a mug of tea that went cold ten minutes ago. Sue Lawley mimes the headlines from the muted TV in the corner, but Natasha is miles away, listening again to Alexander's words trickling over the gate to where she had stood.

Sign or suffer. See that he understands what not signing means.

She has never liked her step-father, but she's never feared him either. Not until today. She wishes that she had suggested sleeping at her dad's tonight. She worries about him at the best of times, let alone when he's been threatened. What were the shipments Alexander was talking about? What switch is flicked in some people's heads that makes them see the world through a violent lens like he must? Aside from for her dad's sake, she wishes she was there tonight for selfish reasons too. There's something comforting about knowing your parents are within earshot if you need them, although she suspects he is in greater need of her at the moment, even if he doesn't show it.

It's days like this that she wishes her mum was still around. Mary has tried her best over the years to fill impossibly big shoes. Still does, even though she's traded up and switched Nathan for Alexander. There's no substitute for the real thing, though. She's not sure whether her dad is working too hard or if it's just loneliness, but his salt and pepper moustache and the ever-deepening worry lines eroded into his forehead add a good ten years. She checks the clock above the fireplace. Quarter past ten. Tiredness washes over her like a wave and she closes her eyes. Just for a moment, she promises herself, then she'll head to bed.

She wakes with a start, sloshing cold tea into her lap. She swears under her breath, goes to stand up, but something makes her freeze. A noise from down the corridor. Something softly scraping. Cold tea forgotten, she treads softly towards the hallway. A *snick-snick* of metal on metal is coming from the front door. Her mouth flops open as she watches the handle on the front door twitch, wind a quarter turn like the hand on a clock. She feels like she's moving in treacle, paralysed with indecision as she processes what's happening.

The door opens an inch, then pauses. She fancies she can hear breathing coming though the gap, from whoever is in the corridor beyond. Realises she's listening to herself, short and shallow, all through the nose now, lips pressed tightly together. The world speeds up again before she can tell herself to move. Shapes barrelling towards her. She whirls and runs, feeling herself falling before the weight bearing down on her registers. A tangle of arms wrap around her legs. She pushes herself up on her palms, kicking out. Feels her slipper connect and something, someone, grunts in pain. Looks back and sees a man, face hidden behind a balaclava, scrabbling at her legs, pulling himself towards her.

Natasha doesn't see the blow until it's too late. The punch catches her on the cheek and her vision explodes into a thousand fireflies as her head collides with the wall. A coppery taste fills her mouth. Pressure on the back of her neck pushes her face into the carpet, nose grinding into the floor, mouth full of shagpile. Hands grab her wrists, yanking them behind her, and something is being wrapped around them. She is flipped over onto her back. Her eyes are watering from the impact against the wall, and she tries to blink away the blurriness. To decide if she's seeing double, or if there are in fact two masked men looking down at her.

She hears them talking despite the ringing in her ears. Two voices, two men. One of them speaks low, grumbling, complaining about her teeth splitting his knuckle. It comes from the bigger of the two men. She doesn't mean to speak out loud, just in her head, but she hears her own voice betray her.

'Why?' It doesn't even sound like her voice, thick and slurred.

His head whips down to look at her. He stares at her for an eternity, but doesn't respond. She doesn't need him to. Knows she's in more trouble than she can handle, no matter what their reasons. He reaches under her armpits and drags her up into a sitting position, back to the wall. He mutters something to the shorter man, and disappears off towards her bathroom. The short man looks like he's leering at her through the mask, coming in close, into her personal space. She can't see the face, but the look in his eyes gives her goosebumps.

Natasha figures if they wanted to kill her she'd be dead by now, but she can't bring herself to wait around to see what they want. She has no plan but moves anyway, knowing there might not be a better chance. She lurches forwards, slamming her head into his groin with all the power she can muster. Pain sets off depth charges somewhere in her brain, and she can't help but screw her eyes shut. She pushes back against the wall and up to her feet, stumbles past him as he crumples to his knees. She could weep with relief when she sees the front door still slightly open, and nudges it wider with her shoulder, blundering out into the corridor and pinballing off the far wall.

She hears shouts coming from back inside but doesn't look behind her. Doesn't waste time fumbling for the elevator button with her hands still tied, and charges through the door to the stairs. Her momentum carries her shoulder first into a wall, but she stops short of plunging down the stairs. Her chest is tight, and she wonders if this is what it feels like to have asthma. To have to fight for every breath. Halfway down and she hears the door above her burst open. Knows they're coming for her. She reaches the bottom. *Shit!* The door opens inwards. She spins round and gropes blindly for the handle. She sees the first man, the bigger one, round the corner of the stairwell above her, and the scream that's been building inside her since they burst into her flat rips out, echoing up every flight of stairs as she turns and runs out into the lobby.

Where are her fucking neighbours when she needs them? Never so much as look her in the eye, let alone say hello, but what she'd give to see one of their miserable faces right now. The door to the street is like the proverbial light at the end of the tunnel. Her heart feels ready to explode, like she's finishing a marathon, although she can't have travelled more than a hundred yards all told. She veers over to the left, pressing the release button with the side of her head that doesn't feel caved in. *Click*. Shoulder pressed to the door, she still expects to feel a hand around her neck any moment, yet the acoustics are deceptive, and his heavy footsteps are thundering all around her, but the chill night breeze hits her face, whispers that everything will be alright.

Natasha screams again as the man bounds through the door after her, and she lurches towards the street. Almost trips over her own feet and bowls into the back end of a yellow Ford Cortina. She looks along to her right, towards the shop on the corner, but it's closed. No cosy glow warming the pavement at this time of night. Her head spins like she's just got off the waltzer at the fairground. She turns to look the other way, and stops. Light fills her world, like a sun exploding, and she's weightless. Floating. Free.

CHAPTER TWENTY

It seemed like an eternity to Porter since Styles had put the call in, the minutes oozing by. He caught himself nibbling at the jagged edge of his thumbnail, something he hadn't done since he was a kid, and folded his arms to avoid further temptation. Thirty years in the making, and it would all come down to thirty seconds. Even just thinking about it, Porter felt his pulse quicken, fists clench.

He felt Styles knock against his arm, looked across and saw his partner gesturing towards the gate. He had been so fixated on the building itself that he hadn't noticed a dark saloon glide up to the gate. He didn't need to see into the car to know who was driving.

'You've got to be fucking kidding me,' he muttered.

'Well this just got interesting,' said Styles.

Porter flicked a glance at him, then looked back at the black Mercedes again. 'Because of course it was all a bit mundane up until now.' He leant forward, raising the binoculars and nudging them into focus on the driver's side window. Locke. What the hell was he doing here? Sure, he owned the place, but this couldn't be a coincidence, could it?

'So now what?' asked Styles.

Porter thought for a moment before he spoke. 'We wait for the others, then we go in. Nothing's changed.'

'We could wait till Bolton leaves, and move in on him wherever he ends up? Just playing devil's advocate for a second, though, what will Campbell say if we go storming in and—'

Porter shook his head. 'We have to have them both there, or Anderson might wriggle out of it. As long as Locke doesn't get in the way, or do anything stupid, he can keep for another day. Not even Campbell will have a problem with that.'

He hoped Styles believed his words more than he did himself. If there was even the slightest hint of the operation being anything but perfect, he knew from experience that Campbell would be quick to point the finger. He would be the natural target, but at this point all he cared about was hauling Bolton in. He'd deal with any bullshit Campbell cared to throw at him when all this was over.

The Mercedes pulled up by the main entrance, and Locke climbed out. He disappeared inside without so much as a glance over his shoulder. Home turf confidence. Porter shook his head softly. Not just confidence. Arrogance. The way his money and connections flowed around him like a cloak, deflecting suspicion onto people like Bolton. Not that Bolton didn't deserve all that came his way, and then some, but at least he was what he appeared to be. Locke was all facade, and Porter wondered what he'd be like if he was ever cornered. Wondered if he would regress to his East London roots without the trappings of wealth to protect him.

He sensed movement in his rear-view mirror, and saw four cars pull in behind. He was relieved to see one of them carried the team of authorised firearms officers. He got out to meet them halfway, and recognised the faces of most of the ten men that came towards him, but the one that stood out was Jon Whittaker. His expression as he approached Porter was inscrutable, his face pale and drawn. Porter felt for him. He wouldn't know where to start in that situation. All Hollywood movie bullshit aside, your partner was meant to be a rock, someone who would back you no matter what. To find out that yours had betrayed your trust and, even worse, had sabotaged an investigation that got another officer killed, was beyond the pale.

He nodded at him as Whittaker approached with the others, gathering around Porter in a semicircle. He quickly filled them in on what he knew and what he and Styles had observed. Styles had made the call to Whittaker direct rather than use an open frequency. They couldn't take the chance that Anderson was listening in. Whittaker had given a quick and dirty update to a disbelieving Campbell and Milburn before gathering all available officers and joining Porter by the warehouse.

'OK, it's a secure site, and that counts in our favour. There's a perimeter fence like this' – he tapped the rigid steel fence posts – 'all the way round, front and back. We send the van through first, and when I say through, I mean through. Locke's in there as well. He turned up just before you lads. He gets a pass this time, so be careful we don't give him any excuse to spit his dummy and call the deputy commissioner.'

He looked around and could see the excitement mingled with anticipation in the eyes of his audience.

'Just the AFOs first. We go through the barrier, pull back and leave the van blocking off the exit, then get your arses down here. The rest of you pile into the cars and we hit them like a fucking tsunami. No need for heroes, though. Stay in pairs when we get in, and let the AFOs clear the rooms first. We've got enough men here so if he won't come quietly call in your location and the rest of us will come running. Questions?'

A full round of headshakes, no words spoken.

'Right.' He checked his watch. Three minutes to noon. 'Let's give them a couple of minutes to get comfy, then we'll get the show on the road.'

Porter reached forward and touched Whittaker lightly on the arm as the other man moved back towards his car. Whittaker flinched and snapped his head around. Porter leant in, speaking softly so the others couldn't hear.

'This isn't on you, Jon. None of us saw it.'

'I know, guv, but thanks.' Whittaker gave a sad smile. That wouldn't be the last version of that he'd hear, a condolence of sorts. No matter how this played out, he was losing his partner. Correction: he'd lost him a while back. He just hadn't known it.

Anderson fidgeted in the hard plastic seat outside Patchett's office, where he'd been banished, while Bolton and Patchett stayed inside to talk. He spilt over the sides and the raised ridges dug into his thighs. It was barely noon but his stomach was gurgling its case for an early lunch. He heard Bolton's voice through the door, low like an idling car engine, followed by Locke's softer replies. He wondered how long they expected him to wait around like this, surprised he hadn't had a call from anyone checking his whereabouts from the station.

A glance at his watch. Five more minutes and he would head off. To hell with the consequences. He was still a copper and coppers deserved respect, even from the likes of Alexander Locke and James Bolton. The thought of a token victory, not waiting for another summons, of liberating his arse from the invasive rim of the plastic seat: decision made.

He stood, rubbing away the grooves the seat had scored into him, and headed back out to his car. The clouds hung low, smothering the city, squeezing colour from the day. The breeze kissed his forehead cooling the beads of sweat. He offered up a silent prayer in hope that the next six days wouldn't be like the last few, each stretching out longer than the last. He had cut a few corners over the years, but always with good intent. Six days then he was home free. Six days until he could leave all this behind. A man as resourceful as James Bolton could hide for eighteen years if he wanted. As long as he stayed out of jail for eighteen days, Anderson couldn't give a damn what he did next. He planned to be on a golf course in Florida with nothing more to worry about except whether a gator ate his ball.

He started the engine, but left it in neutral, fiddling with the volume on the CD player as the opening riff from 'Hotel California' drifted through the speakers, fingers dancing against the wheel. The timing was almost comical as he checked his rear-view mirror to reverse. Don Henley had just struck the last iconic beat of the drums to signal the end of the intro when they rounded the corner.

His lips got as far as mouthing *what the fu*—before his brain caught up. It processed the scene like a series of stills. The slight tilt of the van as it rounded the corner at speed. The three cars following the same swerving path, like Formula One drivers hugging the racing line. The split-second delay between seeing the barrier snap like it was made of papier mâché and the sound reaching his ears, a sharp report like a starter's pistol. It kick-started his survival instinct, and jerked him out of spectator mode.

His first inclination was to look for an exit. Twisting in his seat, fence to the left and right, protector turned captor. No way past the oncoming vehicles. No way forwards.

Fuck! Not like this.

His six days shrank down to six seconds, before he would be out of options, unceremoniously hauled from his car, face pressed to the warm bonnet, cuffs biting into wrists. He threw the door open, leaving the engine running, and bowled back through the door. He had one chance and one chance only. He had to reach the office before they did. Behind him, above the rumble of the Honda's engine, and the whine of the approaching motorcade, Don Henley sang on, blissfully unaware of events.

CHAPTER TWENTY-ONE

'When will you be back?' asked Patchett.

'A month, maybe two,' said Bolton, the decision made yesterday, long before Anderson's call. Bolton had argued against it. He had never run from anything or anyone in his life, and the idea of starting now incensed him. He looked across to where his boss sat in the corner, but Locke's eyes were fixed on his phone, and Bolton's half-scowl was wasted. Locke, smooth talker and pragmatist that he was, had won him over. He would stay at a villa Locke owned outside the town of Ponta Delgada, the largest town on São Miguel Island, which in turn was the largest island of the Azores. He had spent a week there three years ago at Locke's invitation, so he knew he would want for nothing. Locke looked after his own.

'How can I reach you if I need you?' asked Patchett.

'You don't. You need anything, you call Mr Stenner. He'll have a way to reach me.'

'You need me to do anything while you're gone?'

Bolton thought for a second and nodded. 'The other locations, I need you to show your face once a week. As far as anyone knows I'm off on a business trip, that's all. They find out anything else, I know it's come from you, and you and I will have a little chat when I get back.'

Patchett shuddered. He'd seen what a little chat with Bolton could constitute, and would do everything he could to never be involved in one.

'Yep, no worries. Done.'

Locke stood up, walking towards the window that looked out to the side of the building. 'If you two are quite finished your chit-chat, we have other pressing matters to attend to. Our friend Detective Porter, for one. I think—'

He stopped, mid-sentence. All three men glanced towards the door – a thud from beyond it, loud steps echoing. It burst open a second later, and Anderson filled the frame, sweat on his head like condensation, soaking through his shirt in a patch just above the upmost curve of his gut. Bolton stared at him, saw something in his eyes that reminded him of a cornered animal.

'I'll call you when we're done, Mr Anderson, and as you can see,' he said, folding his arms, 'we're not done.'

Anderson was breathing heavily. Even a short dash like the twenty yards back into the building took its toll. 'James Bolton,' he said, sucking in a deep breath. No going back now. Last roll of the dice. 'You're under arrest for the murders or Michael Gibson and Owen Carter, and the attempted murder of Eve Simmons.'

Bolton stared at him impassively. 'We're still a few months short of April Fools', Detective.'

Anderson's nerve almost failed him, but he continued. 'You do not have to say anything. But it may harm your defence if you do not mention when questioned something which you later rely on in court. Anything you do say may be given in evidence.'

Bolton shook his head slowly, the corners of his mouth twitching with half a smile. He looked to Locke. The older man shrugged, folding his arms. Bolton turned to Patchett now, a flick of his head towards Anderson.

Patchett was on his feet now, moving towards Anderson. The detective stepped in to meet him. He might have left his physical prime back in the mists of time that were the nineties, but some things were automatic, hardwired, and he moved with a speed that surprised even him, powered by adrenaline with a healthy dose of fear. Patchett aimed a punch at his head. Anderson slapped it off course with his right hand, reaching his left underneath and around to fasten on Patchett's wrist. Patchett paused for a beat, taken aback at the failure to land his blow. Anderson saw his chance and took it, driving a stiff jab with his now free right hand, connecting with Patchett's nose. Cartilage popped as the nose flattened unceremoniously against the cheek. Anderson was no Floyd Mayweather, but with his considerable weight behind it, the impact was still jarring.

He had no plan as such, so when Patchett stumbled backwards and toppled towards the wall, he felt a moment of elation. Arresting Bolton was the one hope he had. His line to his colleagues would be that he suspected they had a leak based on the fictitious claim of Mike Gibson as the inside man. He'd say he took it upon himself to infiltrate Locke's organisation, not knowing who in the force he could trust. He would pin his hopes on Bolton being old-school and keeping his mouth shut on everything, including him, and deal with whatever retribution Locke might try to mete out at a later stage.

He knew it was weak, but it was his only play. Deny, deny and deny again. Everything he'd received was in cash, untraceable, and that was under a board in his mother's attic. Ride out the storm, and maybe, just maybe, he could walk away from this.

A shout came from the hallway, Stenner's voice bellowing a warning.

'Coppers outside. Head for the back. Go, go, go.' Short, to the point.

If Anderson had moved fast, then Bolton was a blur. He was around the desk and in Anderson's face, the detective still distracted by Stenner's yell. Anderson felt, rather than saw, a hand that might as well have been a brick slam up underneath his jaw. It felt like the back of his head would touch his spine as it whipped back between his shoulder blades. He staggered back, bumping against the door frame. The hand came under the jaw again, this time pushing upwards and staying there, stretching his chin skywards. Anderson slapped ineffectively at the arm, but it was like trying to fell a tree with a flyswatter.

He couldn't see Bolton's free hand, but screwed his eyes closed, waiting for the punch that never came. Instead, he felt the briefest sting, followed by a tugging sensation just above his belt. It came again, and a third time before the palm withdrew, pressure released, and Anderson's head dropped forward, eyes opening. Bolton was gone. So was Locke. He heard footsteps, loud but growing fainter. A fog hung at the edge of his vision, eyes watering from the strike to his chin. Movement, a shape crossing from left to right. Patchett veered into sight, ruined nose poking through gaps in his fingers, wiping away blood as he ran.

Anderson shot out a hand to stop him, at least he swore he had, but Patchett ran on past unimpeded, disappearing around the corner, footsteps mingling with the echoes of Bolton's. The sound of raindrops, fat and heavy. His wheezing cough was the only noise in the empty room, empty save for him. The others would be inside any minute. He shouted to draw their attention, bring them to him, welcome him into their pursuit, but no words came out. He looked down, eyes widening with surprise, understanding, and finally acceptance. His hand reached down, pressed against his shirt, came away stained red.

Shouting from outside, a door banging, enough footsteps to pass for a centipede in Doc Martens, but Anderson could only slide downwards, his back against the doorjamb. His hands scrabbled at his shirt, pulling it up and out of his trousers, watching his life pulse away in steady beats of crimson. The fog rolled gently across his vision now, squeezing it into smaller and smaller tunnels, until they too winked out into nothing.

GEORGE – APRIL 1983

He swirls the glass in a lazy arc, ice cubes chasing each other around the bottom. The warm whisky fuzz usually spreads through him like melting butter, but not tonight. He's been on edge since making the call. The drunk at the end of the bar isn't helping. George glares at him for a full five seconds, but the man either doesn't see him, or doesn't care. His grey hair is all waves and angles. An explosion of burst blood vessels in his nose suggests he's no stranger to the booze, and his anti-Thatcher rant has all the logic of a five-year-old arguing against bedtime. The barman nods and smiles on autopilot, shooting a *what can you do* glance at George.

He hopes today's tip-off is enough to settle his account, but he knows that's probably wishful thinking. Knows he needs to figure out how to get a guarantee that he's free and clear. Now he's a copper he can't keep moving in those circles. He taps his glass against the bar, gives the universal *same again* nod. The barman looks relieved to escape the drunken diatribe for a spell. George fishes in his pocket, pulls out a fistful of shrapnel, pokes through it with his finger and stacks the right change on the bar just as his drink arrives.

He tells himself it's none of his business what will happen to the girl and her father. They might get warned off. Roughed up. He bows his head over the glass, starting to imagine that, and a whole lot worse. Pictures them coming in to make a complaint. Asking how Mr Locke had caught wind of them speaking to the police. Wonders if fingers will be pointed at him. He's careful to keep work and personal separate, but it wouldn't take too many layers to be peeled back to see that he's made some questionable choices as to who he plays cards with, and who he loses to on a regular basis. He tells himself the fact he's a copper protects him, debt or no debt, but he has no desire to put that to the test. He should have left that all behind him when he joined up. Should've. Would've. Could've.

What if they get more than a warning? More than a slap on the wrist? It's selfishness that pushes him up from his stool. Self-preservation. He should never have made the call. It could come back to bite him far too easily, but it's not too late. He knocks back his whisky in one gulp, welcoming the burn at the back of his throat, and heads out into the car park. There's nobody at the payphone and he taps in the number, clearing his throat as he counts the rings.

'Hello?' More of a snap than a greeting, but then again it was almost eleven o'clock.

'Hi, it's me. It's, uh, it's George.' He hates how weak his voice sounds.

'What do you want, George?'

'The thing I called about earlier. I, um, I was just thinking . . .'

'It's a little too late for thinking, George.'

'Oh, yeah, sorry for calling so late. It's just that . . .'

A soft chuckle cuts him off. 'When I say it's too late, I mean just that. It's *too late*.'

The emphasis on the last two words stops him cold. 'What have you done? What have you gone and done?' His voice rises, a worried edge to it.

'Goodnight, George.'

Click. The line goes dead. He stares at the receiver for a second then drops it, bolting for his car. The ignition coughs a few times, and starts grudgingly. He narrowly misses reversing into a bin, but puts it down to mild panic as opposed to whisky. He's driven in far worse states, another thing he adds to his *I must stop doing* list. The address she gave on her statement is around twenty minutes from here, but he shaves a couple off his time, thanks to two debatable amber lights and cornering like a Formula One driver. His is the only car on the road as he turns onto her street. Did she say number 42 or 62?

Condensation has crept across his windows as he's driven, and it's like looking through fog. He rolls down the window with one hand, steers with the other, squinting like Mr Magoo to see door numbers.

One minute the road is empty, the next she's there, like a magic trick minus the smoke and mirrors. George blinks and it's like snapping a picture. His headlights illuminate her like a leading lady. Her eyes are wide, mouth open, moving, but he can't hear what she's saying. A small smudge of something dark on her cheek. Make-up? Blood? Her arms are behind her back as if she's got a surprise for him. He flinches, spinning the wheel to the left as he slams on the brakes, but it's a futile gesture. The sickening *thud* that goes through him is off the Richter scale. The front bumper almost misses her. Almost. The corner catches her across the knees, chops her down, bounces her backwards off a dirty yellow car. He doesn't see her rebound, but feels a second impact towards the back of his vehicle.

From silence to chaos, and back again in seconds. The seatbelt has knocked the wind clean out of him and he gulps in a hungry lungful. He flings the door open and tries to get out but the belt pulls him back in. He stabs a thumb at the button and falls out onto the road. She is lying on her side, face mercifully covered by a veil of hair, torso twisted at an unnatural angle. George feels the hot bile scald his throat as it wells up, splattering on the tarmac, splashing his hands like warm rain.

Footsteps running towards him, skidding to a halt. He looks up, the confusion and bad lighting giving him a few seconds of grace before he sees their masks, and realises how well and truly fucked he really is.

CHAPTER TWENTY-TWO

James Bolton's feet moved fast, but his mind moved faster, jumping from one problem to the next. The crumpled lump of lard that used to be Anderson was already purged from his thoughts.

Evade and escape, in that order. If anyone got in his way, well, he'd deal with that when it happened. All coppers were smart-arses in his book, always thinking they were one step ahead. That applied in the interrogation room as much as out in the real world, so he knew they'd start by covering the exits and trying to flush him out. They'd expect a big lad like him to fight his way through their lines, which was precisely why he wouldn't do it.

Bolton was no fool. As big as he was, if they cornered him with enough bodies, he'd go down eventually, no matter how many he took with him. Even King Kong let go of the Empire State eventually. You didn't last long in this business without a healthy dose of paranoia, and with paranoia came contingency plans. He could have done without Locke to worry about. His boss was in good shape for his age, but they could have moved much faster without him. He toyed with suggesting that Locke stand his ground and wait for the coppers. They were here for him, not Locke, and he might even be able to buy them extra time. No, scratch that. There was a dead copper, at least he hoped Anderson was dead, in his warehouse. They'd not overlook that in a hurry, even if the copper in question was as dirty as a pair of wellies at

Glastonbury. Locke was in this with him for now whether he liked it or not.

Stenner was waiting up ahead, holding open the door that led to the warehouse. He was already vaguely aware of footsteps behind him. Could be Patchett. Could be coppers. No time to check.

'Boss,' Stenner barked as Bolton passed him.

Bolton turned, seeing a flash of yellow. Confusion gave way to understanding. The luminous work vests would fool no one close up, but from a distance they'd stand a chance of blending in. He handed one to Locke, pulling on his own as he ran, one arm in, the other flailing behind, searching for the sleeve, no time to stop.

Stenner made a beeline for the right-hand side of the building, Bolton and Locke not far behind. It faced off into the main compound outside, home to row upon row of shipping containers, stacked like Tetris blocks. There was a fire exit two thirds of the way along the wall. If they could reach that undetected they'd have a fighting chance.

A twitch of optimism at the corners of his mouth was cut short by the realisation, sudden, cold, like an ice bucket challenge, of a move forgotten. Bolton grasped at his pocket, coat trailing behind him as he ran, like a superhero cape. He thrust his hand in, fingers grasping at nothing but the lining. His pace slowed, remembering his mobile perched on Patchett's desk. *Fuck!* He tried to remember when he'd last cleared his email trash folder. A few days at least. There would plenty there he would rather the police didn't get to see. Then again, they were after him for murder. How much worse could it get?

If they could get to the rear of the building, there was a boat moored on the river they could use to get away. Bolton kept a spare key hidden on the boat for just such an occasion. Nothing else to be done. Backwards wasn't an option. Locke had drawn ahead of him and he picked up his pace again to catch up, shelves and aisles blurring past.

Porter burst through the doorway hot on the heels of two of the armed officers, Styles close enough behind to reach out a hand and touch his shoulder. Voices barking 'Armed police!' seemed to come from every angle. The reception area he remembered from their first visit was unmanned, and he placed both palms on top, swivelling his body sideways to vault over rather than waste time fiddling with the catch on the gate. A corridor led straight off the reception area to another door.

Porter chanced a look behind him to see who else had kept up with his charge. As well as Styles, who had himself just cleared the counter, two of the younger officers were coming through the main entrance. The door was unlocked and Porter found himself in another corridor, this one with two identical doors on either side, and a fifth at the end. The furthest door on the left was open, the light from the room carpeting the corridor and, more tellingly, the crook of an elbow jutting into the corridor by the base of the door frame.

Porter skidded to a halt, looking down, registering Anderson slumped, unmoving, then up, scanning the room for potential threat. Empty.

'Jesus, Anderson, what did you do?'

He crouched beside him, pressing two fingers to his neck for a pulse, taking in the scene as he waited for the familiar thud from the carotid. Papers had been scattered from the desk like oversized confetti. Anderson's once white shirt, now stained red like he'd spilt a bottle of wine down the front. Blood pooling on the floor in the V-shape of his legs, splayed out in front of him. Anderson had stuffed his left hand inside his shirt, a futile attempt to stem the flow that still ebbed weakly from the angry gashes the knife had made.

The fact that there was still a flow registered before Porter actually felt the pulse, weak as it was, more of a flutter than a beat. He looked around for something to use, and settled on his tie, sliding the knot part way down and off over his head. He bunched it up and pressed it to the wound. He felt Anderson flinch as he pushed.

'C'mon. Eyes open. Who did this to you? Where is Bolton?'

Anderson's eyelids yoyo'd up and down as he tried to focus. When he spoke it was barely a whisper. 'Locke. He's . . . they . . . gone . . . Locke.'

'Bolton,' said Porter, shaking his head. 'Locke can wait. We're here for Bolton. Where did he go?'

'He's here,' said Anderson, hair matted to the sweat on his forehead. 'Locke. He was . . . here.' His eyelids fluttered back down.

Porter used his free hand to gently nudge Anderson's cheek. 'Come on, mate. Talk to me. What happened?'

Anderson moved his head slowly back and forward, coughing with the effort.

'I tried . . . tried to arrest him. Didn't work out so good.' Anderson tried to smile but wore it more like a grimace.

Porter grabbed his handset, palm slick with sweat from Anderson's face, and barked his message to the team.

'This is Porter. Bolton confirmed on site. Be advised Locke is with him. Repeat Locke is with him. I want eyes on him ASAP, but Bolton is still the target. I need an ambulance here, now. Officer down.'

Anderson's head rolled slowly to one side, a stalactite of spittle dangling from his lip. Porter looked around frantically. He couldn't leave him here alone, but he was itching to get back in the chase.

'Dawson, here, take over,' he shouted to one of the officers who had caught up with him. 'Hold this here till the paramedics arrive.'

Styles had already moved past him. Porter heard him talking into his handset, low and urgent, as he checked the next room along. Porter stood up and went to join him, leaving Dawson crouching over Anderson. They checked the other three doors on the sides of the corridor, sacrificing stealth for speed. Nothing. Piles of cardboard boxes stacked too low to offer any cover to a man like Bolton. They'd all be searched eventually, but their priority today was the man, not his product.

The final door at the end of the corridor was locked. Porter took a few steps back, lifted his knee up to waist height, and tilted his hips forward, channelling all of his bodyweight into the kick. It landed flush beside the handle and the lock gave way. The door flew open, catching something unseen behind it and juddering back towards them. The loud crash faded, replaced by the low hum of activity in the warehouse beyond.

Porter placed a hand on the door frame and leant his head first to the right, then the left. No sign of Bolton. He stepped through into the warehouse itself, with Styles close behind. It reminded him of a trip to Costco, wooden pallets on the ground nestled underneath shelves bolted together, reaching up like the skeleton of a skyscraper towards the ceiling. They stretched off in both directions, punctuated by gaps that he assumed were aisles up which the forklifts he'd seen outside could drive to deposit their cargo.

Styles drew level with him, and he sensed more movement on his right, turning to see Jon Whittaker flanked by four AFOs, Carmichael, Palmer, Everett and Kaye, Heckler & Koch MP5s held at shoulder height. Porter whispered hasty instructions, sending Carmichael and Palmer scurrying away to the left with Whittaker, while Styles, Everett and Kaye followed him in the opposite direction. The right-hand path would take them to what he hoped was a central aisle, ploughing a furrow the length of the building. With two men hugging the left, and more down the centre and right, they would catch anyone lurking in the rows of parallel aisles from both sides, penning them in.

They reached the break in the towering shelves and turned a sharp ninety degrees, stopping abruptly to avoid colliding with two men slouching around the blind corner. They both wore hard hats and luminous vests, like bees that had lost their stripes. The man closest to Porter flinched and blinked like he was transmitting in Morse code. They spoke in tandem, words overlapping.

'Whoa, watch where you're going mate,' from the closest man.

The other, clipboard in hand giving him the pretence of authority, spoke in a haughtier tone. 'Who the bloody hell are you?'

'Police,' Porter snapped. He didn't recognise either man. 'James Bolton. Daniel Stenner. Alexander Locke. Where are they?'

They stared at him blankly, clipboard man breaking first with a shrug. 'No idea. You tried the office?'

Porter didn't dignify it with a response, pushing past them, breaking into a trot as he headed over to the right flank. A chaotic symphony of sound masked his steps, layered over the incessant hum of a busy warehouse: the *thunk* of a crate or pallet dropping into place, the monotonous beeping of a reversing forklift. They would cover his approach, but it worked both ways, his ears failing miserably to filter out the white noise, leaving him with nothing useful.

Porter reached the far wall ahead of Styles and turned to check the others were in place. A hundred yards away, Whittaker raised his arm, giving him a thumbs up. The shrunken figures of Carmichael and Palmer followed suit. Porter returned the gesture and they set off at a brisk walking pace, slowing down as they reached each junction, glancing along, seeing only familiar faces of other officers, and moving on.

From his brief glance up the wide valley of a central aisle that carved the building in two, Porter had seen that it ran the full length of the structure, smaller aisles feeding in from left and right like tributaries. Up ahead, an orange forklift proudly held a crate high above its body, an offering to the shelf above. The driver, unaware of the approaching officers, lowered it gently onto a ledge twice Porter's height, backing away, fork lowering like a retreating servant bowing to its master.

Movement to his left. He spun around, nervous energy coursing through him, but it was only Whittaker waving an arm to attract his attention. Had he seen something? Porter took a few steps towards him before Whittaker called out, 'Clear.' He pointed ahead.

Porter stared for a second, then realised the waving had simply been to attract his attention. He had been staring at the forklift and Whittaker must have thought he'd spotted something or someone. Porter cursed his own stupidity and gave himself a mental slap. He couldn't afford any distractions.

There was a chance, he conceded, that Bolton had made it out of the building. There could be any number of fire exits or other doors ahead. He would have to put his faith in the others who had stayed outside to check the perimeter. He prayed that wasn't the case, and that Bolton and Stenner were somewhere up ahead. He had the utmost confidence in those outside; his hope, his need, for Bolton to be inside was purely selfish. He wanted the confrontation. Instinct and adrenaline were in the driving seat now, a hunter and his quarry.

Lurking behind that desire to call him to account for his actions was a voice that whispered of the blurred lines between justice and revenge; to hit back against a bully who had hurt, maimed and worse. Porter only hoped he could keep the voice to a whisper when the time came.

Daniel Stenner's expression made Bolton look over his shoulder, expecting to feel a heavy hand grabbing at him. Nothing. Only a forklift nosing out from an aisle fifty yards behind him. He was level with Stenner now, right by the door. It was still closed in spite of Stenner's hand pumping the handle up and down. Even Locke looked uncharacteristically concerned. Then he knew why Stenner's eyes were wide in alarm, the first syllables of a curse on his lips.

No time for pleasantries, Bolton moved shoulder to shoulder with Stenner, a tap by his standards, but the contact sent Stenner stumbling sideways. He grabbed at the handle. It turned, the door moved. An inch of daylight, no more. A metallic clang, dull and hollow like an old church bell. He pushed again, sounding the gong for a second time. Again, shoulder to the door, grunting as he threw his full weight into it. He may as well have been throwing himself against the wall rather than the door.

He stopped, breath ragged through snarling lips, squinting through the narrow gap. What he saw made sense of his failure. Vertical grey ridges, a shade darker for being so close, the echoing chime as the door struck.

'Fuck,' said Bolton, drawing out the vowel.

'What? Can you budge it?'

'Some dozy bastard's gone and parked a bloody container against it.'

Bolton slapped a palm against the door, regretting it as it sent another chime bouncing down the aisles.

'Where now, then?'

'Plan B.'

'Which is?'

Bolton's face split into a maniacal grin. 'I'll let you know when I figure it out.'

Porter was so focused on the aisles that he didn't see the fire exit in his peripheral vision until he was past it. He checked his run and bounced back towards it, trying the handle. It turned, but the door stopped after a few inches. He put his eye to the crack, seeing metal draped in shadow, daylight lurking just out of reach. No way anybody left through here.

Styles moved a few paces ahead, signalling the all-clear. First Whittaker, then Palmer followed suit, the world's smallest Mexican wave. Porter looked up ahead, breathing short and shallow. There couldn't be more than six or seven more aisles to check. He sensed the end of the chase was around the corner, quite literally.

He moved quickly, expecting to see Bolton charging towards him round every corner, but met with disappointment after disappointment. Empty, all except for the third from last. A man in his forties, standard-issue luminous vest and hard hat balanced on his head, watched them nervously as they ran past.

Porter rounded the final turn, looking the full width of the building, seeing nothing but the other officers appearing a split second later. He swore under his breath and grabbed his handset.

'This is DI Porter. No sign of suspects inside. What's happening out front? Over.'

He looked behind him, back along the route they had run, the full length of a building eerily deserted for a place so alive with noise.

'Crawford here, guv.' Porter recognised the voice of the young PC. 'No sign of any of 'em. No one's tried to get out front.'

Porter turned a full circle, looking around as he tried to work out what they had missed. They had to be in here somewhere. He decided to retrace their steps, and signalled to the others to follow him back towards the front of the building, breaking into a trot. They were almost halfway back to the doorway that led to the offices, when Whittaker's voice burst over the radio.

'He's here. Left-hand side of the building. Bolton's here.'

They skidded to a halt, Styles ploughing into Porter's shoulder, knocking him against the corner of a shelf. They barely had time to separate when Porter heard the first shot.

Porter ran down the left-hand edge of the building, his jacket peeling away on both sides, threatening to wrap around his hands every time they brushed past. He knew Styles and the two AFOs were behind him. Their footsteps overlapped the beat of his own. He scanned ahead for signs of activity, saw figures up ahead. Crouching? Sitting? Hard to tell from here. There had been five shots, maybe six. It was hard to tell with the acoustics in a place like this. Nothing since, though.

He was within fifty feet now, and saw there were two men up ahead. One slumped against a stack of wooden pallets, the other kneeling over him. The man kneeling looked around at the sound of Porter's approach. It was Jon Whittaker, eyes wide, looking from Porter, then back to the man beside him. Porter slowed as he approached, seeing what had caused the panic on his face. George Carmichael was alive, barely. His eyes fluttered behind closed lids. His mouth a pale blue line, pursed in pain. Whittaker's tie was wadded in his hand, pressed just above Carmichael's collarbone, slick with blood. Porter fancied he could see more coming through the gaps in his fingers.

'Where's Bolton? What happened?' said Porter as he crouched down on one knee.

'Bastard was hiding between the crates. They all were. Came out of nowhere. Grabbed Palmer's gun and sent him flying before we knew what was happening.'

'Palmer? Where the hell is he, then?'

'Bolton got a few shots off. Carmichael went down, he nicked my arm with one as well, then they all fucked off down the far end. Palmer took Carmichael's gun and went after them.'

'Them? Locke and Stenner as well?' Porter noticed Whittaker's arm for the first time. The sleeve of his jacket was torn near the shoulder, ripped fabric matted with blood.

Whittaker nodded. 'Yeah.' He looked back at Carmichael. 'I should have gone after them as well, but I couldn't leave him, not like this.'

'It's fine, Jon,' said Porter. He turned to Styles. 'Tell the paramedics to get their arses in here once they arrive. You stay here. Take over from Jon. His arm's fucked. Get some pressure on there.' He saw the hesitation on his partner's face at the thought of being left behind, but Styles did as he was told. Porter motioned to Everett and Kaye to follow him up the aisle. Everett tapped Porter on the shoulder.

'If he's armed, guv, you'd better let us go first.'

Porter nodded and let them sweep past him, stocks of their guns pressed into their shoulders. They cleared the next three aisles before Porter spotted the doorway in the far corner of the building up ahead. He gave a low whistle to get the attention of the two AFOs and nodded towards it. They positioned themselves one either side, gave a silent countdown on their fingers from three to one, before Everett grabbed the handle and flung it open. Porter half expected a hail of bullets to fly in and ricochet around like pinballs, but there was nothing. Only the metallic *clang* as the door went a full one-eighty and hit the outside of the building.

Porter's breath roared in his ears, and he felt a suicidal urge to dive through the door first. Every second wasted was an extra yard between him and Bolton. He forced himself to wait until Everett and Kaye went through, but was close enough behind them to reach out and touch the back of their Kevlar vests if he wanted to. They both spun a tight semicircle, guns covering every angle as they took in their surroundings.

Porter whipped his head left to right, hoping for a glimpse of Bolton. Three articulated lorries were parked up to their right, rows of shipping containers stacked to the other side. They sat two, sometimes three high, narrow dark alleys disappearing between them. Where the hell were they? And where was Palmer, for that matter?

'Palmer, do you copy? What's your location?' Porter's eyes kept darting from side to side as he spoke. Palmer's voice came back almost immediately.

'Containers by the rear left corner of the building, guv. Could do with a hand.'

'On our way,' said Porter.

He kept pace with the AFOs this time, ignoring the sharp glance from Everett, and they had almost reached the first line of containers when he heard four more shots, grouped close together, like a melodic door knock. *Tap, tap-tap, tap*. They made their way into the alley, Porter sandwiched in the middle, Everett taking point, and Kaye covering the rear. Porter visibly flinched when he saw the boots sticking out past the end of the container, à la Wicked Witch of the East. *Please let that be one of them.* But he recognised the standard-issue footwear.

They reached the corner and saw Andy Palmer, face down. He had one arm tucked under his body, the other outstretched as if he'd been reaching out for something. Porter crouched beside him, feeling for a pulse, but fearing the worst as blood crept out from underneath Palmer and snaked its way towards Porter's shoes. Everett and Kaye moved past him as he pressed his fingers to Palmer's jugular, counting a full ten seconds. Nothing. Not a single beat. He let out an angry grunt and bounced back to his feet to follow the others.

Porter saw Kaye take a left up ahead, presumably following Everett as he was nowhere to be seen. What would he do if he were in Bolton's shoes? There must be another way out of here. They were armed now, or at least Bolton was, and if his plan was just to shoot his way out, he'd likely take his chances and head for the front door. A long, mournful bass note sounded from a boat battling its way along the river.

'The water,' he muttered. 'He's heading for the water.'

Porter looked around in frustration at the dull corrugated metal walls penning him in, remembering the river had been to his right as he entered the warren of containers. He came to the junction the others had disappeared down but they were nowhere to be seen. No time to waste. He bore right, speaking low into his mic.

'Everett, Kaye. They're going for the river. Repeat, head towards the river.'

Up ahead he could see the opposite bank of the river, the ash-grey water drifting sluggishly seaward. He burst out from between the last two containers, half expecting Bolton to be waiting for him, pistol sighted on his forehead, but it was empty. He heard footsteps and looked over his shoulder as Everett and Kaye joined him.

'You got eyes on 'em, guv?' Everett asked, his own eyes anywhere but on Porter, scanning for signs of a threat.

Porter shook his head, advancing across the concrete. They were penned in on three of the four sides of this concrete square. A tall wire mesh fence marked the boundary of Atlas property off to his left. The containers sat behind them, and the river blocked the way forward. He looked at the one route out that led back towards the front of the building. An obvious choice, but his gut still told him the river was the best bet. Twin metal loops sprouted from the concrete edge closest to the water.

Porter trotted across, motioning Everett and Kaye to follow. He slowed as he approached, hearing a low grumbling noise coming from down by the water. He stopped a few feet short of the edge, seeing the first rung of a ladder leading downwards. He peered over and saw a speedboat moored at a small wooden jetty. Stenner was at the wheel, with Locke sitting at the rear near the idling twin engines. Bolton was still on the jetty, hunched over a thick rope that coiled around a rusty metal loop protruding from the wooden boards. Everett and Kaye flanked Porter now, both sighting their guns on the men below.

'Armed police!' Porter shouted. 'Hands where I can see them. All of you. Now.'

All three snapped their heads around at the sound of Porter's voice. Bolton stayed crouched down, but glared up at Porter with a fierce scowl.

'Hands where I can see them,' Porter repeated. 'Don't make me ask again.'

'Or what, Detective? Are you going to shoot us? I'm not armed,' said Locke. Was there a tremor in his voice, or was it just distorted by the engine's low rumble? Porter couldn't tell.

'I'd rather not, Mr Locke, but that all depends on what you fellas decide to do next.'

Bolton started to straighten up and Porter sensed the men either side of him tense up, and saw why. A pistol, Palmer's Glock, dangled from his left hand.

'Put the gun down, Jimmy. It's over. We found her,' said Porter.

Bolton looked at him blankly. 'What's that supposed to mean? Found who?'

'Natasha. We found Natasha. Not even Jasper can help you talk your way out of this one, Jimmy, and that's before we even get started with the officer you killed back there. Then there's the two you wounded. Assuming that was you, of course, and not either of them.' He nodded towards Locke and Stenner. 'Why don't we all have a trip to the station and talk this through before anyone else gets hurt?'

For the first time he could remember, Porter saw surprise on Bolton's face. What was it he had said that got the response? Was it Natasha's name, or was it the mention of two injured officers? Did he think they were all dead?

'Natasha who?' said Bolton, but his face lacked the confidence his dismissive tone was aiming for.

'Natasha Barclay. We found where you buried her, Jimmy. You and your pal Olly. Me and my partner had a trip out to the woods at Ruislip. Oh, and did I forget to mention we've got you on CCTV chucking Owen Carter out the window as well?'

Bolton's hands stayed by his side but he turned slowly, angling his body sideways, looking at the two men in the boat then back to Porter. That last comment wasn't entirely true, of course. They had Bolton on camera, but all it showed was him watching, not actually doing anything. All the same, if it got a reaction then where was the harm? Shoes scuffed softly against concrete as Everett and Kaye fanned out, moving six feet or so either side of Porter, he assumed to make it trickier for Bolton if he decided to start shooting. Bolton looked back at the boat again, the Glock tapping a gentle tattoo against his thigh. When he turned back, Porter fancied he could see a hint of a smile in the crinkles around Bolton's eyes.

'Sounds like you've got me lock, stock and barrel there, Detective. I'd better come quietly then, hadn't I?' he said, voice dripping with sarcasm. 'There's just one thing that bothers me about all of those things I've allegedly done.'

'What's that, then, Jimmy?'

'Let's continue this at the station, Detective,' said Locke, rising to his feet. 'Mr Jasper can meet us there, and we'll see just how strong a case you have.'

Bolton cut in before Porter could respond. 'If it's all the same to you, boss, I'm quite happy chatting here for now.'

'Keep your hands where we can see them, Mr Locke,' Kaye barked.

Locke gave a tired smile, keeping his hands by his side, palms opening like a magician on the verge of a trick.

'You see, Detective,' Bolton continued, 'I've done some nasty shit in my time, most of which you fuckers, sorry, fine officers of the law, have no idea has even happened. Natasha Barclay was an interesting one, though.'

'Interesting, how?' asked Porter. Sweat pricked his back and forehead, but he resisted the urge to scratch at it.

'I didn't kill her, if that's what you're thinking. Sorry to disappoint,' he said with a shrug. 'No, it's interesting because I don't believe for a second you just happened to stumble upon her, not after all these years. Interesting because, the way I hear it, only four people knew where she was. Olly was one, but you couldn't have heard it from him. He's long gone, as is one of the others. According to you I'm allegedly another one, and I'm pretty sure you didn't hear it from me either. So if you're right that would only leave one person who could have led you to her.'

Bolton looked back towards the boat again, turning his body sideways this time instead of just looking over his shoulder. Porter couldn't see the gun any more, Bolton's left hand hidden from view now.

'Don't suppose you'd have any idea who that might be, boss?' Bolton practically spat out the last word.

'I haven't the faintest idea what you're talking about, James,' said Locke. 'Or him for that matter,' he added, nodding towards Porter. 'Now I suggest you stop running your mouth off. I'll call Jasper and we'll be walking out of the station within the hour.'

'Not this time, Mr Locke,' said Porter. 'This one'll take a little more clearing up, even for your little lapdog Jasper. Funny thing, though,' he said, brow creasing as he feigned deep thought. Locke was impatient now, and jumped into the gap he left.

'Come on, then, Detective. Dazzle us with your wit. What's so funny about you threatening me at gunpoint?'

Porter smiled, seeing it for the attempt at baiting him that it was. 'Not that kind of funny. No, the funny thing is that when I just told you that we've found the body of your wife's stepdaughter after thirty years, you didn't react. Nothing. You didn't even ask where she was. It's almost as if you knew we were going to find her.'

'That's a load of rubbish and you know it,' Locke snapped, the sharp edges of his usually precise accent blurring around the edges. *You can take the boy out of North London*, thought Porter. 'That's your proof that I know anything about this mess? That I didn't break down in tears?'

Porter shrugged. 'Looks like you need to convince your man here more than you need to convince me.' He tipped his head towards Bolton. The big man hadn't moved, head still swivelled, looking at his boss. Locke's eyes flicked to Bolton and back again. Porter couldn't see Bolton's face, but he wagered it wasn't exactly smiling right now. For the first time, Locke seemed uncertain of how to play the situation. He opened his mouth to speak, but Bolton beat him to it.

'Now?' he said, clearly looking at Locke, rather than Stenner at the far end of the boat. 'Now, after all I've done for you?' Bolton spoke through gritted teeth. 'You try and sell me out over a girl? Over a fucking girl, and one I had nothing to do with? You know fine fucking well I had nothing to do with that. Nothing.' His voice rose and fell again, like an engine revved.

'What have I just said, James? He's fishing. You of all people should be able to see through that.' Locke raised a hand, wagging a finger to emphasise his point.

Porter flinched as the first shot rang out, dropping to his knees instinctively. Another sharp *crack* followed right behind it, echoes merging, overlapping with a third. A fourth. *What the fuck? Why are they shooting?* Bolton was still facing away, and as much as Porter detested the man, shooting him with his back turned was unthinkable. It wasn't until he saw Locke spin around, falling away from him to the floor of the boat, that his brain started to play catch-up. The gun in Bolton's hand, still held low by his side, was pointing towards Locke. He had shot his boss, or shot at him at the very least. Porter thought Locke had been hit at least once, but couldn't say for sure now that Locke was obscured from view where he'd fallen.

Bolton whipped around, dropping to a crouch as he spun, moving faster than Porter would have believed possible for a man of his size. He'd almost completed the turn when Porter registered shots from either side of him. Everett and Kaye returning fire, shots popping like firecrackers in Porter's ears. Bolton grimaced, the arm holding the gun dropping as the bullets slammed into him. His own momentum kept him spinning around, past what would have been his firing line at Porter, and he staggered to the left as he fell.

Another noise cut through the ringing in Porter's ears as the engines roared into life. He saw Stenner hunched over the controls, partially shielded from the gunfire by a Perspex windscreen that wrapped around the front and part way down the sides of the vessel. He saw twin holes punched into it, kaleidoscopic cracks surrounding both, but Porter couldn't tell if Stenner had avoided the bullets that had made it through. The boat lurched forwards, taking with it what was left of Bolton's balance, sending him toppling over the side with about as much grace as a drunk at last orders.

The officers either side of Porter moved forwards in tandem, Everett squeezing off three more shots at the boat as it arced out into the river. Kaye kept his gun trained on the water where Bolton had landed with an explosive splash seconds before, the surface churned into a thick froth, the colour of the head on a pint of Guinness. Porter looked up towards the boat, a hundred feet away now and accelerating out of range. Still no sign of Locke. He saw Stenner glance over his shoulder, but his face was too far away to read the expression.

Porter looked back to the water by the jetty as Bolton broke the surface, floating face down, arms spread wide. He checked that Kaye had him covered before turning his back on the river to take the rungs two at a time on the way down, Everett following close behind. Bolton bumped gently against one of the wooden jetty legs as Porter reached the edge. He leant forwards, tapping Bolton's back twice and snapping his hand back, taking nothing for granted. No reaction. He reached under the nearest armpit and pulled upwards to flip him over.

'Christ, he's heavy.' Porter grunted with the effort. 'Give me a hand,' he said over his shoulder to Everett. The two of them grabbed a handful of fabric, flipping Bolton over, and he dipped back below the surface for a second as he was turned onto his back. 'Armpit each,' Porter said briskly, and they spun him round so his feet pointed out into the river, snaking their arms under and around, clasping on to his shoulders.

'On three?' asked Everett, and Porter nodded. 'One, two—' The *three* was replaced by a groan as they both pulled up and backwards, inching Bolton onto the rough wooden boards. They angled him round to lie him lengthways, and Porter knelt beside him. He saw Bolton's eyes move behind closed lids.

'Jimmy? Jimmy? Can you hear me? Hang in there, we'll get you patched up.' But no sooner had Porter spoken the words than he saw the blood on his own hands as he went to wipe them dry on his trousers. He looked back at Bolton, scanning for the source. The wet folds of his coat were wrapped around him like dark wings, and Porter couldn't see any tear in the fabric where a bullet might've entered. He remembered where he'd grabbed hold to pull him out of the river, and found what he was looking for. A ragged line of fabric at the neckline almost hid the wound. Porter carefully pulled the collar down an inch, wincing as he saw the trough of flesh that the bullet had carved out, blood still pumping out an angry red in contrast to Bolton's clammy pale skin. He felt Bolton twitch as he let go, cloth rustling back into place over exposed muscle, and looked down to see his eyes open a fraction. Porter heard Kaye's voice above him, calling for an ambulance, as well as calling in Locke and Stenner's escape. He clamped a hand over Bolton's neck to slow the bleeding, but it oozed between his fingers, and around the edges.

'Jimmy?' Porter leant in closer. 'You said he sold you out. Talk to me. Tell me what happened.'

A dozen possibilities bumped against each other in Porter's mind, like driverless dodgem cars. He struggled to believe anything Bolton said on face value. Maybe he had just been trying to shoot his way out of a tight corner, safe in the assumption that he couldn't talk his way out of the bodies back up at the warehouse? But why take a shot at Locke? Even if Bolton got banged up, Locke took care of his own. Bolton would have practically run whatever prison he ended up in. Unless . . . . unless there was something to Bolton's claim of being stitched up? It had been Mary, though, that led them to Natasha, not Locke himself. But what if she had always known the truth, that her husband killed Natasha, and had been covering for him all these years?

Bolton groaned, eyes half open now, darting round, unable to settle on anything, looking for a way out that wasn't there. 'Jimmy!' Porter's voice more urgent now. 'What the fuck just happened?'

Bolton's chest heaved up and down, thirsty for air as if he'd been running. His voice was barely a whisper, the gentlest Porter had ever heard him speak. 'Accident . . . . she was . . . didn't . . . didn't mean . . .' His body tensed, eyes doing a last barrel roll, mouth open, framing his last word. Porter felt Bolton's huge frame relax, tension melting out of his limbs as he gave up the fight. Porter stared at him, at the half-open mouth, wondering what might have come out of it if he'd had just a few more seconds. He checked for a pulse. Nothing.

'Fuck.'

He spat the word out as he stood up. He went to wipe his hand on his trousers again, the one that had been pressed to Bolton's neck. His palm was a watery red as if he'd been hand-painting, and he knelt down towards the water, wafting his hand back and forward like a modern-day Macbeth. He stood up and looked back at Bolton. *You got off easy*, he thought, *too easy*. He looked out at the river, the white snail trail churned up by the boat all but faded. Locke. Whether he had anything to do with Natasha now or not, not even he could wriggle out of the mess at the warehouse.

Porter told Kaye and Everett to stay with the body, and climbed the ladder. Where would Locke go? A man of his resources had likely planned for this day for years. Mary popped into his head. She was either Locke's unwitting accomplice for helping stitch up Bolton, or the big man's enemy for betraying him. Either way, Porter needed to speak to her, and there was no time like the present.

GEORGE – APRIL 1983

George has fallen headfirst down the rabbit hole and wonders if there's any way back. It's all he can do to scrape himself up from the tarmac and follow them inside. The bigger of the two men is a few feet ahead, the girl draped over his shoulder. Her hands dangle down, swinging loosely to pat him on the back with every step climbed. He hadn't even checked for a pulse before he scooped her up. Then again, with the angle she's been twisted at, maybe it's better if she doesn't have one, for her sake. Picturing how she had fallen, rotated at the waist like a discarded Barbie doll, gives him palpitations.

The smaller man brings up the rear, parking George's car, checking the street one last time, shutting the door behind him as he joins them inside her flat. The masks are off now, but he wishes they'd stayed on. He has the distinct impression that these two aren't a fan of policemen even under normal circumstances, and this evening is as far from normal as he's ever known.

He recognises the larger man as one of Locke's men. George has seen him at a few of the poker games, though he's never seen him play a hand. George doesn't know his name, only remembers people referring to him as the Big Fella. He looks like his mother hewed him out of a quarry rather than gave birth to him. He doesn't recognise the smaller man. The one with teeth like a Thames rat, eyes darting everywhere like flies looking for a place to land.

Big Fella nods towards the living room. 'Sit down, lad. We need to work this through.'

He disappears along a hallway, returning moments later with worryingly empty shoulders. He turns away to talk to Rat Face, and George can hardly make out a word. He sees Rat Face shrug, gesturing down the hallway where the girl must be. The big man grumbles like an outboard motor ticking over but steps aside. Rat Face heads to the open-plan kitchen, does a silent eenie-meenie-minie-mo along a row of kitchen knives. Slides a cleaver from the block with too much enthusiasm for George's liking. He scurries down the hallway and out of sight. George feels the sweat drying on his back. Smells his own vomit and feels his insides start to bubble like a witch's cauldron again. He swallows it down and finds his voice.

'Where is she? What have you done to her?'

Big Fella sighs and shakes his head like a disappointed parent to a naughty child. 'The question is what have *you* done to her, Sergeant?'

George swallows hard. Asks the question but isn't sure he can handle the answer. 'Is she . . . Have I . . . have I killed her?' He hears the fear in his voice but can no more put more steel into it than he can undo what's happened.

'She's seen better days, George.'

'Just bloody tell me!' he shouts back at Big Fella, desperate to know.

The big man narrows his eyes. 'I suggest you keep your voice down, George. We wouldn't want anyone coming to check out the noise, now, would we?'

George gets to his feet, moves towards the hallway, but is propelled back into his seat by a palm the size of a dinner plate smashing into his nose. Eyes cloud with tears, and he tastes the coppery trickle running over his lips, dripping onto the carpet. He's stunned into silence.

'You've done enough, George. Nearly fucked this whole thing up, but I'm an accommodating man. We can still make this work for everyone. Apart from her, of course,' he says, jerking his head in the direction of Rat Face's disappearance.

'What do you mean, make it work? Make it work how? I can't be involved in this kind of shit. I'm a copper.' This last part is practically a whine. He hates himself for it. Wonders if his nose is broken, or just banged up.

Big Fella tuts, walking across and leaning over George where he sits. He blocks out the light like a solar eclipse. 'That's exactly why you're going to do what we say, Georgie boy. If you want to stay a copper, that is. Mr Locke would prefer it if you did. Reckons you might come in handy.'

George listens as Big Fella talks. His eyes widen, head shaking slowly side to side as Big Fella tells him how the rest of the evening is going to run. Tries to block out sounds coming from somewhere out of sight. A bedroom? A bathroom?

Thunk . . . thunk.

The sounds are muffled but still solid and heavy enough to make him wince with each beat. He closes his eyes. Sees the snapshot of Natasha again. Eyes and mouth, concentric circles of alarm. Feels the swooping lurch of his stomach as if it's about to happen again. Knows it won't be the last time, and wonders how long he'll pay for what has happened tonight.

CHAPTER TWENTY-THREE

Locke's knuckles blanched where he pressed the damp cloth to his left bicep. The bullet had passed straight through. His arm had gone numb pretty quickly after the initial sting, but that was wearing off now, throbbing in time with the engines. They had weaved their way through a small armada of boats, but Locke was fairly sure none of them had paid enough attention to be able to place them if asked. In hindsight, Bolton shooting him had worked in his favour. Granted, he wouldn't have felt that way if he'd been hit anywhere more serious, but he'd been struggling to conjure up an end to the standoff that didn't end up with him in a cell, at least in the short term.

He couldn't work out how they had found the girl. Bolton had been right enough; of the men there that night, only three others knew exactly where they'd buried her. Bolton had served Locke well over the years, but he'd been making mistakes more and more lately. That mess at the Taylor Fisheries building had been a royal fuck-up. The latest and largest in a procession of fuck-ups. Grandstanding, pure and simple. He thought about Anderson. Dirty or not, they would never let Bolton get away with hurting a copper. If he'd been facing a few years for something minor, Locke was confident he could have bought Bolton's silence. But faced with life inside, offered the earth to name Locke . . . no, it had worked out for the best, he told himself. If Bolton had done his job all those years ago, he would have found that fucking hand in the freezer, and none of this would have come to pass.

'Boss?' Stenner's voice snapped him out of his daze. 'You ready?'

Daniel Stenner had finished winding the thick coil of rope around a wooden post, and winced in pain as he straightened up, reaching a hand out to steady himself on the side of the boat. Locke noticed for the first time since they fled the warehouse that Stenner was clutching his side, grimacing in pain. The dark stain on his blue shirt looked almost purple, blooming up from under his belt.

'You're hit,' he said, and Stenner nodded weakly. 'Give me that,' said Locke, keeping his makeshift dressing in place and holding out the hand of his injured arm. Stenner looked blankly for a second, then realised what Locke was after. He pulled the pistol from the waistband of his jeans and handed it over. Locke tucked it into his own belt, gestured Stenner to lead the way onto dry land. Small brown waves slapped at the side of the boat as the wake bounced off the bank and caught up with them, and he put out a hand to steady himself. He heard a rumbling, looked up, realising where they were as a plane swooped down towards London City Airport.

'Think I need to get myself to a doctor, boss,' Stenner said quietly as they stepped out onto a jetty not dissimilar from the one they'd left behind less than ten minutes ago.

'We'll see you right, Mr Stenner, don't you worry about that,' said Locke, planning three steps ahead. He'd seen a fisherman up on the riverbank as they made their way towards the shore, and guessed he wouldn't have carried all his kit there by hand. He might even have a phone, too. Transport was the first problem to solve. Once they were mobile, he needed to get to his house, to the duffle bag tucked away in his utility room. In it was everything he'd need to slip out of the country, for as long as it took to sort this mess out; maybe for good. He had no intention of making any detour past a hospital, but it served no purpose to tell Stenner that right now.

He told Stenner to stay put, and made his way up the steps. The fisherman was hunched forwards in a dark green camping seat, rod in hand like a giant garden gnome, and didn't react to his approach until he was ten feet away.

'Caught much?' said Locke, hands clasped behind his back, fingers wrapped around the pistol grip.

'Not a thing,' said the man, glancing across briefly. Locke put him in his sixties, with a weather-beaten face that spoke of a life lived under the open sky.

'Can't win them all,' said Locke, stopping five feet short of the chair. 'If they're not biting, I've got a favour to ask,' he said, bringing the gun around as he spoke. It shook with the tiniest tremor. Fatigue. He was too old for this hands-on bullshit. 'And I'd not think too long about your answer if I were you.'

Three minutes later, the river and the fisherman, still shouting obscenities, were in the rear-view mirror of the forcibly borrowed Volvo. Stenner sat silently slumped in the passenger seat, face as grey as the upholstery. Locke dialled a number on the fisherman's mobile phone from memory, flicking it on to speaker and placing it between his legs. It was answered on the fourth ring.

'Mary? Darling? I need you to listen to me carefully.'

'Alexander? What is it? What's wrong?'

'Listen and don't talk. They've found Natasha. They know it wasn't James. I'm coming home now, but we need to leave. Quickly.'

'Leave? To go where?'

'That doesn't matter right now. I need you to be ready.' The constant throb in his arm was like a second heartbeat, and every pothole the car hit sent fresh shockwaves of nausea through him.

'But what . . . will . . . then we . . .' Static sliced through her reply like an editor's red pen, only one word in God knows how many surviving, until a beep told him the call had been lost altogether. He picked the phone up, roaring in frustration. He hit redial but the call failed. A second time. A third. He jammed the phone roughly into the cup holder. Locke hoped she'd be ready when he got back. This wasn't the time to be dallying. For a man who had worked hard to project an image of strength for years, she was still a weak spot for him.

He glanced at the clock. Forty minutes and he'd be home. Just a little while longer and he could rest. Exhaustion washed over him, tugging at his eyelids. He couldn't remember ever being so tired. Feeling every year of his age, weary to the bone. One last call. A number he saved for special occasions.

'Two seconds.' Footsteps. A door closing. The voice came back on the line, a low hiss. 'We can't talk now. Later. Call me later.'

'Later's no good for me, George. It's time to call in one final favour.'

Styles yelped as his knee cracked against the passenger door with a heavy *thunk*. 'Easy there, Lewis Hamilton. You're not in your F1 car now, you know.'

Porter ignored him, eyes fixed on the road ahead. He was approaching the turn into Locke's street when he saw the dog patter off the pavement and onto the road. He slammed on the brakes, swerving away from the bemused animal. Its owner at the other end of the lead hit him with a glare that could shatter glass. With his cords and blazer, complete with handkerchief poking out of the top pocket, he could have been a distant cousin of Locke's, with that same air of entitlement. You knew when you were in an area out of your price range when folks dressed up like that to walk their dogs.

They drove through the already open gates of the Locke house, eyeing the Volvo parked outside with suspicion. The driver's door stood open, and . . . wait . . . was that somebody in the passenger seat? Porter gestured for Styles to go left, covering any escape if they bolted, while he circled around towards the open door. After what had happened down by the river, he wasn't taking any chances. He angled to get a clear line of sight into the car, and called out a warning.

'Armed police. Keep your hands where we can see them.' He wasn't a big fan of guns, but wished he had one now. He hoped whoever it was bought the lie, whether they were armed themselves or not. The figure inside the car didn't move. He called out a second time. 'Armed police.' He could see a pair of legs now, dark trousers disappearing into the footwell. Nothing. Not even a twitch.

Porter looked over the roof at Styles, raising a quizzical eyebrow. Styles peered down into the car, but stood back up a second later.

'Stenner,' he said. 'I think he's dead.'

Porter approached the car, stooping to peer inside. Stenner's head had rolled towards the driver's side, chin almost touching his chest, half-open eyes staring at nothing in particular. Porter saw the blood on Stenner's hand before he noticed the stain on the dark shirt. He leant into the car, touching two fingers to Stenner's neck. Nothing. Not even a flicker of a pulse.

He straightened up again, shaking his head at Styles, and looked towards the house. The front door stood open, only six inches or so, but open nonetheless.

'You call it in, then head down the side,' he said to Styles. 'I'll take the front.'

Styles nodded, putting his phone to his ear. Porter moved towards the house, feet crunching gravel like eggshells. He paused, peering into the half-light in the hallway. A sound came from somewhere inside the house. A chair leg scraping? Porter wasn't sure. He glanced across, seeing Styles disappearing around the corner, and pushed the door open gently with two fingers. Should he shout out another warning to whoever was inside, presumably Locke? He stayed silent for now, weight shifted forwards, light on his toes, and slid inside.

As with previous visits, the place was immaculate. Porter's eye was drawn to the post at the bottom of the staircase, a dark suit jacket crumpled over it like dirty laundry. Another noise, muted, but quite clearly a cough. Porter took a guess as to its source, poking his head around the kitchen door, seeing nothing. Slow, soft steps, as if walking a tightrope, he edged forward. Another door in the far corner of the kitchen stood open. A scuff of shoe on tile came from beyond it, and Porter was so fixated on the door that he nearly walked past the gun sitting in plain view on the counter. He assumed that Stenner had been hit by a bullet fired from a police gun, but he couldn't rule out the possibility that Locke had turned this one on his own man for some reason.

Porter reached down with two fingers and a thumb to pick it up, then thought better of it. If it had been used, he didn't want to contaminate any fingerprints. Besides, he should be able to handle an old man like Locke without a weapon, and it wasn't like Stenner was going to be sneaking up on him any time soon.

Muttering and the sound of running water came from the other room. Porter couldn't make out the words, or even confirm who it was, and made his way silently through the doorway. It was a utility room, washer and drier against the far wall, a window that looked out into the back garden. He wondered if Styles had made it that far yet. Locke stood with his back to Porter, bent over in front of an old-fashioned porcelain sink. A black canvas duffle sat on the bench next to him, zip open, but Porter couldn't see inside from this angle. Locke had the shirt sleeve rolled up high on his left arm, and had wrapped enough gauze around it to border on mummification.

'You'd be better off getting that seen to at a hospital, Mr Locke,' said Porter. He thought back to the pistol on the bench, wondering for a second time if he should have picked it up as insurance. Locke wound the bandage twice more around, reaching for a black-handled pair of scissors by his bag.

'I wouldn't do that if I were you. Might be seen as a weapon. We don't want anyone outside getting the wrong idea, now, do we?' The lie came easy to him.

Locke looked up, out of the window, searching for faces between the leaves outside. He drew his hand back away from the scissors, tucking the end of the bandage into the top for now. He turned around to face the doorway, and Porter swore he'd aged ten years since the river. *Could be blood loss, could be shock*, thought Porter.

'Is this where you tell me you've got armed officers with itchy trigger fingers?' he said, but there was little in the way of fight left in his voice.

'You know I wouldn't come here alone.'

'James?' Locke asked. There was something about the way he spoke; Porter couldn't decide which answer would satisfy him more, and just shook his head. Locke looked down at his feet, and when he looked up again, there was a little more determination in his face. 'Terrible thing if he hurt that poor girl,' said Locke. 'And those officers at the warehouse. Just doing their job.' He shook his head like a parent disapproving of their child's behaviour. 'I can't believe I didn't see this coming.'

Porter sneered. 'Save it, Locke. We both know you're not innocent in all this.'

'And just what have I done, Detective? Apart from get shot by a man I trusted for years? What exactly do you think I'm guilty of?'

'More than I'll ever be able to prove,' said Porter wistfully. 'But not even you can walk away from the mess you left back there at Atlas without mud sticking. And that's before we even get started on Natasha. I'll make damn sure you take your fair share of blame for what happened to those officers today.'

'We'll never get to the bottom of what happened to her now James is dead, will we? You lot have seen to that.'

'Jimmy seemed pretty adamant he had nothing to do with that. He seemed to think you might know more than he did. Now why would he think that?' Porter asked, leaning back against the counter, folding his arms.

'After what he did to those officers today, who knew what was going through his mind.'

'That's just it, though. If we'd taken him in for that he'd have gone down for life, no doubt about it. So why get on his high horse about Natasha? What's one more murder in the grand scheme of things?'

Locke shrugged, screwing his eyes shut as the pain lanced through his arm with the movement. 'No idea. Not my problem. So, you mentioned a hospital. Why don't we head there, and I can call Mr Jasper on the way?'

Porter ignored the request. 'See, that's where we disagree. I think it is your problem. There's something that's been bothering me about what we found at her flat. One thing that didn't make sense.'

'And what would that be?' said Locke, his voice weary now.

'We found blood on the carpet. Blood that didn't match Natasha, but more importantly, it didn't match James Bolton either.'

'So?'

'So what that tells us is that somebody else was in her apartment when her blood was spilt. Could be Olly Davies, could be someone else.' Porter paused. 'We haven't taken a sample from you, yet, Mr Locke. Bolton was adamant he had nothing to do with her death. Looked pretty pissed off that I'd even suggested it, to be honest. No, what I'm wondering is what would show up if we tested you?'

Locke coughed, wincing as a fresh jolt of pain washed over his face. 'Do what you like. No matter how much you want to believe I was there, I wasn't, and you can't prove otherwise.'

There was something in the way he said it, sounding so blasé that it made Porter pause. If not Locke, then who? Mary? No. What reason would she have had to lie about this? To hurt Natasha herself? He remembered what she had said about Ruislip Woods. The fourth man.

'Who else was there that night? There were four of you. Bolton and Davies I know about. Who's the mystery man?'

Locke's eyes widened, just for a second, but there it was. Porter knew he had hit the nail on the head, and went to push home the advantage while Locke was off balance, an idea landing front and centre in his mind. He went with it before he had a chance to think it through fully, but it felt right.

'Know what I think? I think you've had a police officer on your payroll for quite some time. I think there's no way you could have stayed one step ahead for as long as you have without a little birdie whispering in your ear every time we were looking in your direction.'

Locke's expression shifted, losing some of its defiance, and Porter finally started to feel pieces slotting into place.

'When did Anderson first start working for you? How did you twist his arm? Was he just after extra cash, or did you actually have something on him?'

Locke coughed again, but this one turned into a smile, despite the obvious pain. 'Why don't you ask him yourself, Detective? You might be meeting him again sooner than you think.'

Porter saw Locke looking past him, and turned a fraction too late. The blow caught him just behind the ear, and he crumpled to the floor, back rebounding off the nearest cupboard door. Black spots danced in front of him, and he managed to plant a palm to halt his fall. The left side of his head burnt like it had been rubbed raw with sandpaper. He pushed sideways with both feet, unsure if whoever had hit him was coming in with a follow-up shot. None came, though, and he looked up, blinking to clear his vision.

Superintendent George Campbell stood over him, staring at the gun in his own hand like he wasn't sure how it had gotten there. Porter stared into the barrel. Shit! It was the one from next door. Why had he not picked it up, moved it at the very least?

'Impeccable timing, George,' said Locke. 'Let's crack on, then, shall we? I've got a doctor waiting to patch me up.'

Campbell looked confused. 'Crack on? How the hell do we *crack on* from here? I need to think this through. Need to—'

'George!' Locke's voice was like a cracked whip. 'You need to step up. I need you to put a bullet in your man here, and get me the hell out of here.'

'That wasn't what we agreed. You said if I got you to whoever is going to stitch you up, then we're done: I'm free and clear.'

Locke nodded. 'I'm a man of my word, George, but how exactly do you propose we make good on our plans with him wandering round my house?' He pointed at Porter. 'He's not exactly going to sit here quietly and count to ten before he comes looking for us, is he?'

Porter pushed his back against the cupboard, IKEA's finest creaking as he did. Campbell extended the hand with the gun another few inches. 'Stay put, Porter.'

'Think about this, sir,' said Porter, formal address feeling somehow wrong tripping off his tongue as he looked at Campbell, seeing the barrel twitching but never leaving his centre mass. It reminded Campbell that he was an officer, or at least Porter hoped it did. He touched a hand to the back of his head as he spoke, pushing against the mini egg that had already risen. 'I called for backup before I came. None of us are walking out of here any time soon.'

Campbell gave a little smile, like a child who has just outwitted an adult. 'Nice try, Porter. I would have remembered something like that coming over the radio on the way here.' He pressed the heel of his free palm to his forehead, wincing as if with a headache. 'I just need to think.'

'If that's what you believe, sir.' Porter persevered with the weak bluff, but he knew it wasn't fooling anyone. 'Look, I don't know what he has on you that's put you here. That doesn't matter. All that matters is doing what's right. It's never too late to fix things.'

Campbell closed his eyes, shaking his head. Porter considered making a lunge for the gun, but his head hadn't fully cleared and he wasn't sure he could get the momentum from down on the floor.

'Of course it's too bloody late, you fool. It's thirty years too late,' Locke snapped. 'Now pull that fucking trigger or I'll come over there and do it myself, and you'll be the next one staring down that bloody barrel.'

Porter's dry mouth and spinning head made for something close to a hangover, but Locke's words worked like smelling salts. Thirty years too late? His eyes widened, hand coming away from his head, pointing at Campbell.

'You were . . . thirty years ago . . . You were there. You were the fourth man she saw. You were there the night Natasha died.' He realised his mistake as he said the words, even as he saw the truth of them in Campbell's face.

'She?' Locke spat out. 'She? That silly bitch put you up to this, didn't she?' He gritted his teeth, this time more in anger than pain. Porter hoped Mary Locke was anywhere other than in this house somewhere.

Campbell's arm sagged, gun bobbing gently until it pointed at his own feet. 'She just ran out,' he said, voice flat, eyes moistening. 'I couldn't stop in time . . . They just . . . She hit the other car so hard . . . I couldn't . . .'

'You?' Porter gasped. 'You killed her?'

'I was trying to help her. Trying to warn her. It was my fault they were going after her in the first place.' He looked over at Locke. 'His thugs were already there. If only I'd kept my mouth shut, none of this would have happened.' He was practically babbling now, getting it all out, relieving himself of the weight he'd carried for thirty years. 'She was only trying to protect her dad. His business.'

'Going after her? Who was going after her? Bolton?'

Campbell frowned. 'Bolton? No, not Bolton. Oliver Davies and some other bloke. Woodley, I think they called him. Big bloke, used to do security at the poker games. Bolton didn't turn up till later, at the woods. He sent Woodley off to sort my car out before we . . . before they . . . well . . . you know where they took her.'

Porter's head throbbed. The idea that Bolton might be innocent, of this at least, made his head spin faster.

'You stupid arse,' Locke shouted. 'He had nothing. Still has nothing! Nothing he can prove, anyway. We can both get clear of this, still, George. Just keep your fucking mouth shut and—'

He never finished the sentence. A shadow played on the door frame behind Campbell, a rustle of fabric. Porter instinctively angled his head a few degrees, trying to work out what it was. Styles was outside so surely it couldn't be him. Whether Campbell heard it too, or whether he reacted to Porter's movement, he half turned to look over his shoulder. Porter moved without thinking, pushing up, reaching for the hand that held the gun, grabbing his wrist, slamming it against the door frame.

The sound of the gunshot seemed to come at Porter from all sides, echoing in his ears even as he followed through with his charge. Campbell's fingers opened, and the gun fell, hitting the edge of the bench, spinning to the floor with a clatter that barely registered. Porter folded Campbell's wrist back on itself, one hand on his arm, forcing him down to the ground. Styles rushed in through the doorway. *He must have doubled back*, thought Porter. *Thank God he did.* Beneath him, Campbell had his eyes screwed tight, mouth opening and closing like a goldfish, but the sound that came out was barely above a whimper.

'Locke. Get Locke,' said Porter, looking over his shoulder, but his view was obscured by the corner of the bench.

Styles came to a halt by the sink, and Porter saw him look down at his feet. He adjusted his grip on Campbell, and leant backwards to get a better view. Locke sat upright, back against the cupboard door beneath the sink. His eyes were blank, mouth drooping at the corners as if he'd had a stroke. Porter saw the fresh splash of red on his shirt like a carnation in bloom, and knew instantly where the stray bullet had ended up.

He didn't know whether to laugh or cry, opting to just close his eyes for a second in relief that he hadn't been on the end of it. He looked down at Campbell again, no longer a threat. Just a pitiful man who had sold his soul years ago. Porter rolled off him and sat with his back to the wall, facing Locke.

'You OK, boss?' asked Styles.

Porter shook his head. 'I'm pretty fucking far from OK. I'm alive, though. That'll have to do for now.' He didn't trust himself to stand up straight away, feeling his hands trembling as the adrenaline rush of the last minute exited stage right. Instead he sat fixed in a staring contest with Alexander Locke, wondering how close Campbell had come to squeezing the last ounce of pressure. Too close.

MARY – APRIL 1983

She is careful. She waits until she hears the snick of the latch closing before she swings her legs out of bed. She hopes she's wrong, partly because she hasn't the faintest idea what she'll do if she's right. Confront him? What if he isn't alone? What if *she* is there, whoever *she* is? Mary hopes *she* doesn't exist. Hopes that it's just work. She doesn't ask too many questions about what he does. Learnt to take a healthy disinterest years ago, but the late-night calls set her insecurities scurrying in all directions like an Andrex puppy with loo roll in tow.

She grabs her silk robe from the back of the door. Alexander brought it back from a business trip to Hong Kong. Not one she would have picked for herself. It's too bright, too garish for her. Crimson, splashed with ash-white flowers she takes for azaleas. But she wears it for him. To keep him happy. Story of her life.

Mary is halfway downstairs when she sees the swoop of headlights arcing away from the house through the frosted glass of the front door. She picks up her pace. Pulls a jacket from the peg by the door, keys already strategically placed in the pocket. She's been doing this for two weeks now, ever since she decided that ignorance was no longer bliss. The coat slides over the silk robe with a whisper and she's in her Mini Cooper, engine running, before the twin ruby pinpricks of brake lights have turned the far corner. She keeps her headlights off until he's out of sight, then starts to mentally rehearse the excuse she has prepared in case she's rumbled. Splitting headache. No paracetamol in the house. Keep it simple.

She's relieved to see there's still enough traffic on the road that she doesn't stand out too easily. Mainly taxis, but at this time of night all Alexander will see in his rear-view are headlights either way. She mutters to herself as she drives. Tells herself again what a bad idea this is, but curiosity drives her on. She reminds herself it also killed the cat, but carries on undeterred. Mary sees him make a turn. At least she thinks it's him. She reaches the junction, sees that she was right, and panics because there's nobody else on the road now. Just him and her. She eases up on the accelerator, staying far enough back that she gets palpitations every time his lights disappear around a corner, not letting up until she rounds the bend.

She frowns as she sees the sign at his latest detour. Ruislip Lido. Her father used to bring her here as a child. At least once a month, weather permitting, she and her sister would squeeze into the back seat of her dad's pale cream Austin 7 and spend the day exploring the woods or splashing in the waters of the lido. It's seen better days, though. Not that Alexander would be heading there for a swim at this time of night, anyway.

She flicks off her headlights, coasting at little over ten miles per hour as she sees him pull into a car park ahead. Street lights hover overhead, casting an amber glow like giant fireflies, dim, but enough to make out three men waiting for Alexander as he gets out. She recognises two of them as men who work for her husband. One is the brute that Natasha had a thing with a few months back. The other has a mean face that only a mother could love. The third man is a mystery. He looks nervous, fidgeting, shifting from foot to foot. She doubts that she could hear what they are saying even if she got out of the car, and is deciding what to do next when she sees the big man pop the boot open, stoop down, straighten up with something over his shoulder.

It looks like a roll of carpet, kink in the middle, draped over front and back. Then she sees it. The hair. There's somebody in there. A woman. Not quite the rendezvous she thought she would be gatecrashing. There's something familiar about the hair, even in this pale yellow light. Long coils of it spill out like oil slicks, bouncing against his back as he turns towards the woods. It can't be, can it? Flashes of family photos in her mind. Hair, spread like raven's wings on her stepdaughter's shoulders. She curses her overactive imagination. Tells herself she needs to turn round and drive home the first opportunity she gets.

Up ahead, she sees her husband put an arm around the mystery man's shoulder, steering him towards the pub a little way back down the road. The other two men have faded into the treeline. She stares into the shadows, willing them to take form, to let her see where they're going. She has to know. Is it her? Was she hurt? A glance back to the pub confirms Alexander has disappeared inside, and before she can convince herself it's a stupid thing to do, she's out of the car and moving towards the trees. Every stone she kicks, every twig she steps on, seems to echo like a gunshot. The path ahead fades to black after a hundred yards, and the men ahead are shapeless lumps of black, just out of reach. *Just a little further*, she tells herself. Repeats it over and over like a mantra.

She steps carefully, lifting her feet now to avoid scuffing against anything. She has gotten her wish. There isn't anyone else. No matter who that is up ahead, she wishes now more than ever that life was simple, and that her husband was having an affair. That she could deal with. But this? This is something else entirely.

GEORGE – APRIL 1983

George sees the man walk through the door and realises why Locke has asked him here tonight. Nathan Barclay doesn't recognise him at first. Must be the lack of uniform, but by the time he gets within handshake distance, the confusion on his face tells George he's been made. Barclay stares at him for a few seconds, then looks to Locke. Realises he's standing beside the young sergeant, and tries to process what that might mean. Bolton and Rat Face, who George now knows is Oliver Davies, occupy the flanks.

The warehouse is empty at this time of night, and despite the cavernous open space, the five men gathering together so conspiratorially feels almost claustrophobic. George fights the urge to break ranks and head out, anywhere but here. He looks at Barclay's face, seeing it properly now that he's closer. Muscles in his jaw twitching back and forth, as if he's grinding his teeth. Plum-coloured shadows under his eyes. Barclay's whole body is rigid, and George struggles to read his expression.

'Nathan,' says Locke with what George guesses is meant to pass for warmth. 'Glad you could make it,' he says, holding out a hand.

'Where is she?' Barclay asks. It's barely above a whisper, and George stiffens. Just the mention of her, even unnamed, is enough to unnerve him.

'Have you brought it?' asks Locke.

Barclay doesn't break eye contact as he reaches into the pocket of his jacket, pulls out an envelope and gives it to Locke. George feels like an intruder. Like he has no part in whatever is going on here. Like it or not, though, he is involved. He is the reason this man's daughter isn't with him tonight. He isn't sure what haunts him more: the memory of Natasha splayed on the road, or what he saw in the flat in the hour that followed. What they did.

'Hope this is all in order, Nathan. We wouldn't want to have to send you another one.'

George tries not to react. Tries to pretend he doesn't know what Locke is talking about. Tries and fails to block out the memory of Oliver Davies coming back from what he now knows was the bathroom. Shirt speckled red like a butcher's apron. Feels light-headed as the image of a disembodied handshake swims before his eyes, her hand dangling from his, minus the one-fingered message intended for her father.

'It's done. Just tell me where she is.' Barclay's words are dripping with worry.

Locke opens the envelope, scans the contents, nodding in approval. Looks back up at Barclay with something of a twinkle in his eye.

'It's not that simple any more, Nathan.' He inclines his head towards George. 'You went to the police, after all. What's to say you won't try again? I can't very well have you talking to someone less . . .' He pauses, searching for the word. 'Less understanding than George, here.'

At the mention of George's name, Barclay eyes him with an *et tu, Brute?* look laced with contempt. George wants to apologise. To tell him he was trying to help the girl, but he knows how hollow that will sound. Barclay is breathing loudly through his nose, lips twitching as if he's swallowed something live and wriggling.

'This is all I have. What more could you possibly want?'

'I want you gone,' Locke says with as much emotion as if he were ordering a pint at the bar.

George watches as parallel troughs crease Barclay's forehead. *Leave the man be, for God's sake*, he thinks. He's already lost too much in the last twenty-four hours, more than he realises. He has no more to give. Then Locke explains. A gun beyond the door. Only one bullet in case he gets any ideas. Paper and pen to leave his daughter a note. The only way to secure her freedom.

George watches as Barclay goes from denial right through to acceptance It takes no more than two minutes. One hundred and twenty seconds to deconstruct a man, to break him down to his basest level, where all that matters is a father's love.

The door closes behind Nathan Barclay and, even before he hears the shot, George realises that his eyes have misted over. Sees for the first time that James Bolton is holding a camera, and wonders why. It seems so out of place here. He swallows hard, tensing himself for the sound. Praying it doesn't come. Knowing it'll take a lot more than a few prayers to make this right.

CHAPTER TWENTY-FOUR

Porter watched from the back of the room as Deputy Commissioner Adam Nesbitt scanned his notes. Wouldn't do for the star of the show to forget his lines at a press conference. Nesbitt looked up, caught his eye and beckoned him over. Porter weaved amongst the reporters looking for seats, and headed for where Nesbitt was tucked away in a corner, now studying his phone.

'Sir?' Porter said as he approached. 'You wanted to see me?'

'Ah yes, Porter.' Nesbitt looked over Porter's shoulder as he spoke, making sure the journalists were out of earshot. 'When's your appointment with the counsellor?'

'Three this afternoon, sir.' Porter wasn't a fan of the sessions, but they were mandatory for any officer involved in an incident like that.

Nesbitt nodded. 'Good, good. Might feel like a pain in the backside, but the sooner you get it done and get their thumbs up, the sooner you can get back to work properly. It'll be good to put this mess behind us.'

Was that it, Porter wondered? Was Nesbitt trying to show his softer, caring side? He doubted Nesbitt would be calling it a mess to the dozen microphones shoved under his nose in a few minutes. How would it go? Something along the lines of *best-in-class collaboration to bring down a nationwide criminal network.*

'Speaking of putting things behind us,' Nesbitt continued. *Here we go*, thought Porter. 'I was in a meeting with Superintendent Milburn this morning. He asked me to pass on his thanks for a job well done.'

Milburn had profited from Campbell's downfall, annexing his command in addition to his own, at least in the short term. Since the debacle at Atlas, he had ordered the place pulled apart by forensics. Every crate opened, every shipping container checked from top to bottom. Anderson's supposed protection had made them careless, and the quantity of drugs seized had astounded even Porter. Or was it Campbell giving them that feeling of smug security? How far the rot had set in with each of them was yet to be determined.

'Goes without saying, we won't be drawing anyone's attention to Mr Locke too much, or those pictures of him posing with me. Anyone mentions it, I can barely recall meeting him anyway. One face in a thousand, that type of thing. Anyway, the evidence doesn't support Locke being the one pulling the strings, so tomorrow's headlines will be about James Bolton.'

Porter was stunned. He might be dead, but that didn't mean Alexander Locke should keep his reputation. One he'd bought with drug money, at that. 'But sir,' Porter protested. 'What about the interview with George Evans? Locke's been at this for years. What about the fact he had some of ours on his payroll? Senior officers? He confessed to hiding Natasha's body, for God's sake!'

Nesbitt frowned, looking past Porter's shoulder. Porter looked to see what had distracted him, and saw a couple of the journalists in the front row trying their best not to look like they were eavesdropping. He was fairly sure his voice hadn't carried that far, but took a deep breath and lowered the volume.

'We can't just ignore that, sir,' he urged.

'And we haven't. We've considered that, along with the rest of the evidence, and there's nothing to tie Locke directly to any of it. The few employees we arrested all went through Bolton, or that other fellow we have in custody, Patchett. We have nothing usable to tie Doug Anderson or George Campbell directly to Locke, yet, either. Campbell's lawyers have worked out a deal with Superintendent Milburn. Can't go into all the detail, non-disclosure and all that. He's confirmed Bolton, Woodley and Davies being there the night that girl died, though, not that we can do much with Woodley. He had a heart attack a few years back. We do, however, know that Locke gave the order to have her picked up to blackmail the dad with. Campbell was there when her father topped himself as well. Nudged in the right direction by Locke, but he pulled the trigger himself, it seems.'

'You'll be telling me next we're not even charging Campbell with anything,' said Porter.

Nesbitt shrugged. 'There's nobody left to contradict him. No forensic evidence to use against him. And he's managed to give us enough of what he's picked up from Locke over the years that should help mop up what's left of the business. He'll be out of a job, that much is a given, but it does us more harm than good to crucify him in public with what we have.'

'Bullshit,' Porter hissed. 'I was there. He killed her. He nearly bloody killed me. He needs to answer for that. And what about Doug? He led us to Atlas for one thing. He led us to Bolton.' Porter could already feel himself swimming against the tide of a mind made up.

'Everything George has said in his statement will be fully investigated while he's on a leave of absence pending his enforced retirement. As for Doug, could have been there at the warehouse following up a line of enquiry as part—'

'He was there because of the fake line I fed him about Bolton.' Porter felt the warmth in his cheeks, fighting to keep his anger in check. 'The pair of them are a disgrace to the force.'

'And you think that's strong enough to justify the kicking this lot will give us?' Nesbitt said, nodding sharply towards the waiting journalists. 'You think if Doug was alive, that the CPS would prosecute with that evidence?' He shook his head. 'It doesn't matter what they did, Porter. It matters what we can prove. We can prove Bolton was a bad man. All we do by dragging Locke, Campbell and Anderson down with him is to hurt ourselves.'

'And if anyone gets wind of us covering this up, what do you think that'll do to us?'

'It would only get out if one of us puts it out there. And I don't know about you, but I'd say that anyone who wilfully did something like that to hurt our reputation, that took the shine off the good work we do, well, I'd say that they weren't cut out for a career in the police force. Wouldn't you?'

Had Nesbitt really just threatened him at a press conference? Of course not. In Nesbitt's own words, it would be what Porter could prove. This wasn't the time or place to say anything more, though. Porter saw the danger lurking in Nesbitt's eyes, almost willing him to keep going, to say enough to give him an excuse to make Porter's life hell at some point down the line.

'I suppose so, sir.' He tried to wrap as much disrespect around that last word as he could.

'Good. Glad we're in agreement. Now, if you'll excuse me . . .'

Nesbitt breezed past him and up onto the raised platform. The excited hum of the journalists behind ebbed and flowed as they jostled for pole position with their questions. Porter stayed with his back to them, composing himself, not turning around until Nesbitt spoke into the microphone. He strode down the side of the room without turning a single head.

The walls of the hallway felt like they were closing in as he headed for the front door. He needed to get away from here. From people. Get away to somewhere he could shout and swear with impunity. His hands unconsciously clenched and unclenched as he made it out into the fresh air, as if closing around Nesbitt's neck. He breathed in deeply, and out again, Twice more. Felt his head clearing. What made him even angrier was that part of what Nesbitt said kind of made sense. It would have been a hard conviction to secure if Locke had survived, but he would have given it a damn good go.

As far as the thing with Anderson and Campbell went, it stung him to admit it, but there was some truth to what Nesbitt was saying. There was nothing to be gained unless they could prove any of it, but it didn't stop Porter feeling betrayed. He and Anderson hadn't exactly been best pals, but Porter would put his life on the line for any one of his fellow officers, and he expected them to do the same for him. Not to stab him in the fucking back. As for Campbell, you took it for granted that even those who became pen-pushers and politicians were still on the right side. He cursed himself for not seeing it sooner, for not questioning why Campbell had been so obstructive when it came to Locke.

It was a fucked-up finale, that much was for sure. The fact that politics and perception were going to trump holding people to account for Natasha, and everything that had happened since, left him feeling hollow, like he'd been sucker-punched. If this was how policing worked now, he didn't know if he wanted any part of it, but that was a decision for another day.

Porter headed out into the car park. He needed to get away from here, just for an hour or two. He'd be back in time for his session. His mind wandered to Mary Locke. How could she have lived with that secret for over thirty years? Granted, she'd been working on the basis of a few assumptions: that it was definitely Natasha; that Locke and/or Bolton would have done something to her or Gavin if she'd spoken up. Porter shook his head at the thought. It spoke volumes as to just how complete Locke's influence over her was that she'd kept her mouth shut all these years.

There had been a moment last week, back at Locke's house. Only a fleeting one, but he couldn't get it out of his head. What if Styles hadn't doubled back around? What if Campbell had pulled the trigger? Would he have seen Holly again? He hadn't wanted to die, that wasn't it. He doubted he could explain it if anyone asked. Wasn't even sure he understood it himself, but there had been something so alluring about the possibility.

Should he mention it this afternoon to the counsellor? Probably not the kind of thing to bring up there. There was one place he could talk about that. One person he could tell. He checked his watch. He could make it to the cemetery and back in plenty of time. He couldn't hear Holly, or touch her, but just being close to her, talking to her, always levelled him out in a way nothing else could.

GEORGE – APRIL 1983

It's been three weeks since they ruled Nathan Barclay's death a suicide. Twenty-one days, and no knock on George's door to haul him into one of the boxy rooms for questioning. It's as if it all happened to someone else, like an out of body experience, or like he watched it on TV.

It feels all too real when he sleeps, though. The dreams are in technicolour with the volume cranked up to maximum. Tyres squealing. Acrid burning smell of rubber through his open window. The girl hitting the car like a bass drum. The taste of bile in his throat. He hasn't managed more than a few hours' sleep a night since it happened. Every time he sinks towards deep slumber, the dream slaps him awake. Maybe this is his penance? To be slowly chipped away at. To become so exhausted that he can't get out of bed or sleep. Stuck in his own version of purgatory.

He has vowed to never play another hand of cards again. Locke has promised his slate is wiped clean, but George was a fool to trust him. The envelope addressed to him that arrived today at the station is postmarked London. That tells him nothing. The list of names inside were already known to him; some of the most notorious drug dealers in the capital. Almost all of them. What wasn't known were the times and dates next to each. New shipments coming in. Addresses they'll be stored at.

Despite what happened three weeks ago, he's still a copper, and a good one at that. Knows what he should do with this information. Arrests like these would propel him up the ranks. They would also leave a gap in the market. A gap that a man like Alexander Locke would be well placed to exploit. Using this would make him Faust to Locke's Mephistopheles.

George weighs up the pros and cons. Decides that he needs some quick wins to atone for what he has done. He can deal with Locke later. He promises himself he'll get out from under this. That it was all a matter of circumstance and bad timing. Tells himself he's still a good person. That he hasn't sold out. He almost manages to convince himself that's true. Almost.

EPILOGUE

There was something infinitely sad about a badly attended funeral, one where you could count the mourners on one hand. Sadder still when that count included the priest. *Even a chapel full of snivelling relatives would be better than this*, Porter thought. It seemed almost cruel to bury Natasha a second time, so soon after she'd just been found, but at least this time was the real deal, not discarded in the woods like a piece of buried rubbish. A stiff breeze teased stray hairs from his forehead, sneaking its icy fingers down his shirt collar. He buttoned his coat right up to the neck and sunk his chin into the polo-neck-style ruff it made.

Gavin Barclay stood beside his mother, hands clasped in front, staring at the polished coffin. A single white rose covered the brass plaque bearing her name. Neither of them said much other than a mumbled 'thanks for coming' since Porter arrived. What else do you say under the circumstances?

The priest finished his eulogy, offering a few final words of comfort to Gavin before disappearing towards his own car. Gavin escorted Mary back to their car, then turned and came back towards Porter, holding out his hand. Porter gripped it, still trying to think of something worthy of the occasion to say, but Gavin saved him the trouble.

'Thank you, Detective. For everything.'

Porter shook his head. 'Sorry I couldn't have done more.'

Gavin gave a dismissive gesture with his free hand. 'Don't be daft. You found out what happened to my sister. That's what's important. That she's not left just lying there . . .' His voice trailed off.

Porter appreciated the sentiment but felt like a fraud accepting the thanks. Sure, they'd found her. Found those responsible for her death. But with Locke dead, and Campbell unlikely to see a courtroom any time soon, it left him feeling hollow. He left Gavin by the graveside and picked his way amongst the rows of headstones towards his car, some tilted like a game of Guess Who gone wrong. For all the visits he paid to Holly, cemeteries were still a series of contradictions he could never be comfortable around. Live mourners visiting long-dead relatives or friends. Slabs of cold marble and sombre granite contrasted with colourful splashes of flowers and even small toys.

He passed a row of children's graves, windmills turning lazy spirals in the breeze. Porter had only ever been to one child's funeral before. A cousin he usually only saw at weddings and funerals had lost a baby boy to cot death, and he'd gone along as much out of family obligation as anything. He shuddered as he remembered looking at the tiny coffin being laid on a table at the front of the chapel. The smallest coffins, it seemed, were the heaviest to carry.

He climbed into his car, glancing at the clock on the dashboard. Almost half past three. Shit! Could he still make it there by four? Probably not, but he had to try.

Porter scanned the entrance as he crossed the car park, but the only person he could see was a man leaning on a Zimmer frame, one hand pinching the folds of his dressing gown closed, the other holding a half-smoked cigarette. He checked his watch again. Two minutes past. Had he missed her? He cursed himself for not gambling on the two amber lights en-route.

The inner doors swished open, and the first thing Porter saw was the almost-white hair of the man pushing the wheelchair. Alan Simmons was looking down at his daughter, talking softly to her as he wheeled her through. Eve Simmons's head was bowed forward, hair in a loose ponytail, stray strands wafting either side of her face as she left the safety of the doorway. With her light grey cargo pants and navy blue hoodie, she could just have easily been off for a jog in the park, although Porter guessed it'd still be a while before she was up to anything like that.

They bore right, Alan Simmons positioning the chair next to a wooden bench, and started fishing in his pocket for car keys. Porter was practically next to her before she noticed him, squinting up as he approached. She still had a dressing over the wound on her face, but the swelling had all but subsided. The make-up she wore couldn't quite hide the dark circles under her eyes. She'd been unconscious for a big chunk of the several weeks she'd been in hospital, but it had been anything but restful. He guessed she was a good half a stone lighter. There hadn't been much on her to lose in the first place, and it made her look a little gaunt, but when she smiled in recognition, that didn't seem to matter.

'Fancy seeing you here,' he said, hands in pockets, making as if he just happened to be strolling past.

'Afternoon, guv.' A wisp of hair tickled her nose, and Simmons lifted a hand to tuck her it behind her ear.

'Mr Simmons.' Porter nodded a greeting to her dad.

'Ah, Detective Porter. Hello again. We were just about to head home.'

'Yes, sorry. I won't keep you. I just wanted to pop by and make sure you were OK.' He looked down at Simmons as he spoke.

'No, no. I didn't mean it like that,' said Alan Simmons. 'Actually, would you mind waiting with Evie while I grab the car?' He held up the keys to emphasise his point.

'Of course,' said Porter, and Alan Simmons nodded his thanks, hurrying off in search of his car.

Porter looked down at Simmons, feeling more than a little self-conscious towering over her, and took a seat on the bench next to her chair instead. 'So I'll see you back at work tomorrow, then?'

She touched a finger to the dressing on her face. 'Think I might wait till I don't scare the others, if that's alright.' She sounded so tired, and a little hoarse, but managed another smile.

'I'd say you don't look too bad, considering what you've gone through.'

'Not too bad, eh? That's the best compliment I've had in years.'

They both chuckled at that one, then fell into a comfortable silence, broken only by the smoker's cough of Mr Zimmer Frame as he made his way back inside.

'I heard about Bolton,' she said finally. 'Heard you were there when . . . well, when he died.' Porter nodded thoughtfully. 'I don't feel sorry for him. Not even a little bit. Weird thing is I'm pissed off at him for dying. For not being able to look him in the eye now I'm out, and tell him he didn't beat me. I'm still here, you know?'

Porter grunted in agreement. 'Yep. If anyone deserved to die, it was him, but yeah, I know what you mean. Feels like he cheated. Like he got away with everything. Same for Locke.' He felt himself tensing up. It still annoyed him how things had ended, but he'd have to come to terms with that. To stop taking it personally. He turned to face her.

'Seriously, though, Evie, it's good to see you up and about. You had me – ah, I mean us – worried for a bit there.' He reached out a hand, a gentle pat on the shoulder, almost without thinking. She turned her head to look over at him. Held his gaze. Silence again, but this one not so comfortable. Another few seconds and she looked down at her lap again, nodding, swallowing hard. Was she welling up?

Alan Simmons rolled to a stop in front of them, and Porter removed his hand, standing up in the same instant. Alan Simmons came around the front of the car, opened the passenger door and reached both hands down to his daughter.

'Would you mind, Detective?' He nodded towards the bag draped over the handles of the wheelchair, and Porter obliged. He popped the boot and placed the bag inside. Simmons lowered herself slowly into the seat, and swung her legs inside before her dad closed the door. As Porter came back round, her window slid down.

'Thanks for coming to see me off, guv.' If she had been getting upset seconds ago he couldn't tell now.

'No worries,' he said, taking a step back up onto the kerb. 'Coffee's on me when you get back.'

'I'll hold you to that,' she said, clicking her seatbelt into place.

Alan Simmons leant over from his side. 'Thanks again, Detective.' The window purred up as they pulled away, and Porter watched until they'd turned out of the car park and onto the main road. After all the shit that had happened in the last few weeks, it felt good to see her out of her hospital gown and on the road to recovery. It had been starting to feel like he'd playing against a stacked deck, but seeing her smiling, laughing, made today's glass half full.

His mind flicked back to the moment in the doorway, weeks ago. He instantly felt guilty. She'd almost died, and there he was wondering whether any of what she'd said or done smacked of ulterior motives. Last time he had visited Holly he'd talked to her about this. Not Evie in particular, but the notion of moving on enough so as to be open to possibilities. He was pretty sure that if she was able to, Holly would have laughed at him. Told him to man up and find someone. That everyone needs somebody. Somebody to care whether you came home at night. If only Natasha had been lucky enough to have a somebody like that, maybe none of this might have happened. Of course, Holly couldn't speak. He'd looked around, as if expecting some kind of sign or acknowledgement, but there had been nothing. Only the whisper of the breeze tickling its way past the wind chime hanging on a nearby headstone.

ACKNOWLEDGEMENTS

Some people say writing can be a lonely business, and there are times when that's true. But through it, I've met some awesome people, who've helped and encouraged me along the way, many of whom I'm now proud to call my friends. Whether you're reading this as a fan of crime fiction, as an aspiring author, or a bit of both, get yourself along to author events and festivals. We might kill people (disclaimer – only in books) for a living, but crime writers are as friendly a bunch as you'll find, and I always come away from them inspired to write. So, to the countless authors and fans I've met, spoken to, and had a drink with at these events, you've all played a small, if unwitting part, in pushing me forward to this point, and I thank you for it.

Mari Hannah – I still owe you a drink or three for persuading me to go to Creative Thursday workshop at the Theakston's Harrogate Crime Festival, not to mention all the advice since. Howard Linskey – thanks for the endless tips and encouragement over the last few years.

Jo, Amy, Olivia and the rest of the team at The Blair Partnership – thank you for taking a chance on my scribblings, helping to polish the rough edges off my words, and finding me such a great publisher.

Lesley and the team at Allison & Busby, thank you for believing in my books, and making the murky waters of getting published all the easier to navigate.

Thanks also to The Literary Consultancy, and in particular Sanjida Kay, my allocated reader, who was given my MS to edit, prior to me submitting to any agents. Without your input, it might never have turned into the half-presentable jumble of words it's become.

Shoutout to my regular Waterstones coffee crew, helping each other put the world to rights, one latte at a time. Wouldn't be right to mention them, and not do a plug for Newcastle Noir crime festival, where we all first met. It's the brainchild of Jacky Collins, held in May, and keeps getting bigger and better every year (http://newcastlenoir.blogspot.co.uk).

Mik Brown – my brother from another mother and regular partner in crime. If it wasn't for us being so competitive with each other, I might not have dusted off what I'd started years ago and gotten this far. Your turn next – get that book finished. Oh, and I nearly forgot, you lost the game.

Thanks also to my awesome in-laws, the Sages – Jude and Malc, plus brother-in-law Michael – for all the encouragement and support you give, and for putting up with a Geordie infiltrating your Spurs household. Hats off also to Tony Whaling, architect of my snazzy website, and photographer extraordinaire.

No round of thank yous would be complete without mentioning my mam and dad, who quite literally made me the man I am today. They've always supported and encouraged me, no matter what, and I owe them more than I can ever do justice to with these few simple words.

Last, but by no means least, a few words for Nic. My wife, best friend, soulmate, partner in crime and proofreader. You still married me in spite of my occasional untidiness, bouts of mischief, and my twisted sense of humour. Love you more than yesterday, but not half as much as I will tomorrow. To quote Edmund Blackadder, 'Life without you would be like a broken pencil – pointless.'

Robert Scragg had a random mix of jobs before taking the dive into crime writing; he's been a bookseller, pizza deliverer, Karate instructor and football coach. He lives in Tyne & Wear, is a founding member of the North East Noir crime writers group and is currently writing the second Porter and Styles novel.

robertscragg.com
@robert_scragg